... STORY-
... TION OF JOHN
BUCHAN, NEVIL SHUTE AND
A. J. CRONIN

The Douglas Affair is an adventure-
thriller with a difference—a story which
grips and excites from first page to last,
and a theme which is unusual, thought-
provoking and frightening in its sheer
possibility.

James Douglas is a militant Scot, a man
who smarts under English domination,
who is prepared to devote his wealth
and all his energies to the establishment
of independence for Scotland. He sets
in motion a fantastic sequence of events
which stirs the nation, and also brings
to the surface the hidden turbulence
in the lives of those around him.

His son, Archie, is now left to run the
giant family business, but is hampered
by a calculating, frigid wife, who drives
him to seek warmth and femininity
outside his marriage . . . His daughter
Anne suffers the torment and guilt of
her unconventional sexual
relationship . . .

And then inevitably the forces which
oppose Douglas take action, employing
undercover agents . . . sinister and
utterly ruthless . . .

The quotations on the back cover are taken from the following newspapers: *The Sunday Times*, *Good Housekeeping*, *Glasgow Sunday Mail*, *Manchester Evening News*, *Scottish Field*, *Glasgow Evening Times*, *Western Mail*, *The Daily Telegraph*

ALISTAIR MAIR

THE DOUGLAS AFFAIR

CORGI BOOKS
A DIVISION OF TRANSWORLD PUBLISHERS

THE DOUGLAS AFFAIR
A CORGI BOOK

Originally published in Great Britain
by William Heinemann Ltd.

PRINTING HISTORY
William Heinemann Edition published 1966
Corgi Edition published 1967

This book is set in
Plantin 10/10½ pt.

Corgi Books are published by Transworld Publishers, Ltd.,
Bashley Road, London, N.W.10

Made and printed in Great Britain by
Richard Clay (The Chaucer Press), Ltd., Bungay, Suffolk

FOR MY FATHER

CHAPTER ONE

IT was their last evening in Spain, an end and a beginning.

Margaret Douglas turned to her husband at the bottom of the stair.

'Don't be long,' she said. 'Remember you've a long drive tomorrow.'

'I'll not be long,' he said. 'I'll just have a smoke and stretch my legs. I'll be up before you're asleep.'

When she had gone, James Douglas stood alone in the big flagged hall of the country inn and looked at the dark heavy wood of the scanty furniture black-lined against the white walls, at the gleam of light on the copper pans, at the cold ash lying grey on the grey hearth of the stone fireplace, and for a moment he held his breath.

The air was thick with age and silence. Here in the north was no *flamenco* and bougainvillea. No sad guitar sounded through the soft scented night. This was the Spain that he remembered, austere and impoverished and proud, living with its guilty memories of dead brothers.

When he breathed again, he smelled the smell that he had first known as a young man, the smell that was inseparable from Spain, the smell of age and *anis* and garlic and Spanish tobacco and wine. The war hadn't changed it. But the war had changed little. And yet it had seemed such a hopeful war in that first six months, when the issues were still unclouded. Now, the only hope lay in waiting for the old man to die.

By God, thought Douglas, I'm glad I don't have to start here.

He crossed the hall and went out into the night.

The sky was clear. As his eyes grew used to the dark, the roofs of the village sharpened against it, and the stars came out, and there were lights here and there in the windows to light the unlit street; but the brightest light of all shone over the arched entrance to the headquarters of the *Guardia Civil*.

This, too, had not changed.

Within the shadow of the arch, two cigarettes glowed and died where the men on duty stood, shoulders to the wall, waiting. He scraped the bowl of his pipe with his knife and knocked it out and at the small sound the cigarettes vanished and he heard the faint metallic clink of arms. He filled his pipe by touch and watched and before he had done the guards had come out to stand silently and inconspicuously alert, one on each side of the arch.

He saw their faces. They were both quite young, conceived in the hungry bitterness of the unhappy peace after the war's end, when there was little comfort for a man in Spain outside the warmth of a woman's arms. He watched them till his pipe glowed red and wondered how deep the roots of loyalty went in men like that. Then he turned away, down the hill to the village.

But it was a poor village. Even by day, there was little to see there but a church, crumbling slowly into its own tombs, and dust deepening on the moth-holed slippers of a venerable bishop. At night, there were only shadows and the liquid chuckle of the Arga in its bed, the click of a tethered horse's hoof as it shifted sleeplessly and the wine-given possibility that you would hear the horn of Roland coming down at you from the pass with the wind.

Douglas heard only the Arga, running like a Highland burn.

It was fine for Roland, he thought. Then, courage was enough. Now, it's only a beginning.

He smoked his pipe and thought of the months that lay ahead until the night chill of the mountains made him shiver and turn back towards the inn. It was then, in a narrow place among the houses, that he saw the man. He was lithe and lean, moving fast and silently, slipping between him and the wall with the curving supple movement of a cat.

'*Buenas noches*,' said Douglas, as he passed.

'*Buenas——*'

It was little more than a murmur. When he looked round, the man had gone.

In the inn, he undressed quietly in the dark, for Margaret was already asleep.

*　　*　　*

The noise woke him just after two in the morning. He sat up at once. The window was bright with light from the road outside and there were men's voices and rapid shouted orders that he could not understand and running feet and the roar of engines.

'What is it?' whispered Margaret from her bed.

'I don't know,' he said, and swung out his legs.

From the window, he could see across the street, over the vehicles and men, to the house of the Civil Guard. A covered lorry stood before the arch, with a Land-Rover in front of it and two others behind, and seven or eight motor-cycle combinations were parked in irregular formation, their engines still running. Headlights shone on the black patent leather of the Guards' hats and glinted on the dull metal of the arms they carried and, in the brightest light, beneath the lamp, he saw their officers, three of them, one with a drawn revolver in his hand.

Margaret moved at his side.

'What is it?'

'God knows,' he said, and felt the beating of his heart, for there was a remembered order in the disorder below, a familiar forgotten pattern of movement, a sense of urgency and imminent action that he had never expected to feel again.

As he watched, the street cleared. The lorry filled with men carrying rifles and light automatic weapons, the tailboard clattered into place and the diesel engine churned into sluggish life. Two of the officers swung themselves into the back of the leading Land-Rover. The third moved down the hill to speak to the drivers of the other cars. The motor-cycle teams, two men in each, edged restlessly forward. Then, as the officer ran back, he waved his arm. The leading car was moving before he vaulted into it. It accelerated at once, leading the way up the long hill that led to the frontier. In less than a minute, they were out of sight.

Only two men were left. They stood in the middle of the street with their rifles slung on their shoulders until the engine noise had almost disappeared. Then they lit cigarettes and walked slowly into the shadow of their building.

When they had gone, Douglas looked the other way, down

11

the hill to where the people lived. No one moved there. No light shone. He turned back into the room.

Margaret was sitting on her bed with her dressing-gown wrapped round her.

'James,' she said, 'I'm frightened.'

'No need to be,' he said. 'It's nothing to do with us.'

He picked up his pipe, blew through it and put it down again.

'But what are they doing?'

'Some kind of manoeuvres. You see the same kind of thing at home.'

'Oh, James.'

He sat on the bed beside her and put his arm across her shoulder.

'Get back into your bed, Meg. You'll catch cold.' He took her dressing-gown and laid it on the chair and tucked the blankets close in round her. 'There,' he said gently. 'Go back to sleep.'

'But what about you? You've a long journey tomorrow.'

'I'm just going. Don't worry about me.'

She nodded and smiled.

'All right, James. Goodnight.'

He lay quietly, awake, until he heard her breathing change. Then he rose and filled his pipe and lit it and sat down on the chair by the open window from where he could see across the road to the silent house of the Civil Guard. And he thought for a long time about the man who had slipped past him among the houses. Here, close to the guarded frontier, it was not hard to imagine why he might have moved thus, furtively, under cover of the night. But when daylight came and the hard sun lit the high valleys, how would he fare then?

*   *   *

James Douglas polished the car windows in the sun of the morning. His mind was clear, but he was weary from the short night's sleep and the miles of driving that were behind him. A few years ago, he would have been unaffected. Now, at fifty-eight, the weariness was a straw in the wind. If the things he planned to do were to be done, the time had come.

'*Qué coche raro!*'

He looked up at the old man and smiled. Aye, man, he thought. You could live for five years on the cost of it.

'*Sí,*' he agreed. '*Es un buen coche.*'

'*Aiee!*' The man moved round it admiringly. '*Qué lindo! Estupendo! Es americano?*'

'*Inglés.*'

'*Dios! Cuántas pesetas vale?*'

'*Muchas,*' said Douglas. 'Many. A mountain of pesetas.' He straightened up. '*Hombre. Dígame.* What happened in the night?'

Expression vanished from the man's eyes.

'*No entiende.*'

'*No lo creo.*' He put the duster on the bonnet of the Jaguar. '*Lo he visto,*' he said gently. 'I saw it all. The men and the lorry and the *motocicletas* and the guns.'

The man shrugged his shoulders.

'*Contrabandistas,*' he said. 'Smugglers. There are many smugglers in the mountains. It is the nearness of the frontier.'

'*Sí,*' said Douglas. '*Claro.* But you do not use a large net to catch a small fish.'

'*No lo sé,*' said the man. 'This I do not know. There are no fishermen in the mountains.'

Douglas grinned.

'*Bueno,*' he said. 'A silent man lives long.'

'Evidently.'

He opened the door and put the duster in the glove pocket.

'*Dónde va?*' asked the man. '*En Francia?*'

'*En mi casa,*' said Douglas. 'I'm going home. I have problems of my own.'

'*Por supuesto que sí,*' said the man gravely.

He climbed in and pressed the starter.

'*Suerte,*' the old man said. '*Buen viaje.*'

'*Muchas gracias,*' said Douglas. 'That you may have a long life.'

He drove out of the courtyard and round to the door where Margaret waited with the luggage. She packed the boot while he paid the bill. When he came out, she was seated, ready to go. He looked at his watch. It was nine-thirty and no one

13

moved in the house of the Civil Guard.

He let the car find its own quiet speed on the climbing road.

'How far is it to the frontier?' Margaret asked.

'Not far,' he said. 'Ten or twelve miles.'

Not far for me, he thought. Far enough for a man on his own two legs in the dark of the night, counting the hours that were left till the sun came up, hearing the engines down on the road in the valley and seeing the lights, feeling the small jetting movement of fear in his bowels.

'It's a nice morning,' she said. There were wild roses by the side of the road and pine trees beyond and green bright fields with grazing cows. The sound of their bells came singing in at her through the open window. 'It's bonny,' she said.

'Aye,' said Douglas. 'It's all that.'

As they climbed, the valley narrowed, and the road twisted and turned on itself far above the stream, and the bare rocks of the high peaks came up against the blue sky. The land grew rough, strewn with great shining boulders, and the wind began to funnel in towards the pass, bending the grass at the verges. Douglas took it easily, driving carefully, letting his eyes stray up the sides of the hills ahead, but he saw no movement there above the leaning grass or among the stunted trees. And there was fine cover now for a hunted man.

He slowed down as the hillsides steepened and closed in and when he came on the road-block he was not surprised. The two guards stood in the middle of the road, their short automatic rifles crooked in their arms. Their motor-cycles were parked on the narrow verge and they were high-powered single machines that had not gone up with the column in the night. When he stopped, one moved to each side of the car. It was the one at Margaret's window who spoke.

'*Buen' días.*'

'Good morning,' said Douglas.

'*Son extranjeros?*'

'Yes.'

'*Habla Vd. español?*'

'*Un poquitín,*' said Douglas. 'A little.'

'*Los pasaportes, por favor.*'

14

He passed them over. The guard examined them. He was a Spaniard of the grave kind. He looked carefully at each page while his partner peered in at the empty back seat and moved round to join him. They murmured together and the grave one pointed.

'*Dónde está el equipaje?*' he enquired. 'If you are tourists, where is your luggage?'

'In the boot,' said Douglas.

The man extended his hand.

'*Pues, la llave.*'

Douglas pulled out the key and opened the door.

'I'll open it myself,' he said. 'You can do the looking.' The lid swung up from their bags and coats and parcels. 'Are you satisfied?' he asked. 'No poor bloody political fugitive tucked away in the corner?' They stepped back, their faces still impassive, and he slammed the boot lid shut. 'If that's the lot, I'll have our passports back,' he said, and held out his hand. The grave one handed them over slowly. Douglas put them in his pocket. '*Pues,*' he said, '*con su permisión.*'

He got into the car and started the engine.

'*Otra cosa más,*' said the grave one softly at the window. 'It is forbidden to stop between here and the frontier. *Entiende?*'

'Aye,' said Douglas. 'I understand all right.'

He accelerated fast until he had rounded the first corner. Then he eased his right foot on the pedal. Margaret sat forward in her seat.

'James what's wrong?'

'There's nothing wrong.'

'But . . . why have you slowed down?'

'No reason,' he said. 'No sensible reason. I've just got a feeling.'

He scanned the hillsides as he went, but nothing moved there, no sunlight glinted down at them from steel. They were alone, climbing slowly to the top of the pass, on the abandoned empty edge of the country. Then the road dipped and swung to the left into the beginning of the descent.

'It can't be far now,' he muttered.

But he could watch the hillsides no longer for the bends were tight and blind and he had to hold the car in close to the edge, conscious of its breadth on the narrow road. When the thing happened, it happened in the corner of his eye.

The man came from behind a bluff of rock barely fifty yards ahead and was on the road in two bounds, with a rush of movement that should have carried him over and down into the cover beyond if the burst of automatic fire had not caught him in the last six feet of exposure. He fell slowly, crumpling forward in the direction he had hoped to go, and he lay with his head on the short grass and his feet on the road metal. When Douglas reached him, he had already ceased to twitch.

Margaret saw the guard who had fired come running from the rocks which had concealed him and clamber down the slope to the road, but Douglas did not see him. He saw only the man who was dead. It was the lean man who had slid past him in the darkness among the houses of the village. All the time, he had felt that it would be him. Now, in the sun of the morning, he was dead.

He became aware of the guard at his side, still holding his automatic rifle in the firing position. The anger was rising in him slowly, coldly, as it rarely did nowadays.

'*Muerto*,' muttered the guard.

Douglas turned to him. He was a small man, with pale unhealthy skin and little septic spots where the patent leather strap of his hat chafed his jaw. His eyes were blank.

'*Muerto*,' he repeated, as though surprised.

A Land-Rover swung in and skidded to a stop in front of the Jaguar, blocking the road. Although it was only a few yards from the body and the two men who stood by it, Margaret saw that Douglas did not move. He was looking at the pale face with the short dark beard-growth of the night on it and the blank black eyes, seeing it grow closer, feeling the hate for it move into his fingers. She put her hand on the horn and let it blast.

Douglas turned in time to see the officer jump out. He was one of the three who had stood beneath the lamp, a handsome man, slim and elegantly uniformed. He glanced briefly and with distaste at the body. Then he saluted Douglas and smiled.

'Good morning,' he said. 'You must be Señor Douglas.' He indicated the Jaguar in which Margaret sat, holding in her

16

vomit. 'I have admired your car last night. We do not often see the Mark Ten in this part of Spain.'

He spoke in English. Douglas regarded him steadily while the moment of stupidity passed.

'Until there is a change in the régime and a return from barbarism, you won't see mine again,' he said.

The Spaniard changed his expression to one of polite enquiry, but he let the smile linger.

'Barbarism? I'm afraid I do not understand.'

'I'm sorry your English is so inadequate,' said Douglas. 'The word in Spanish is *barbarismo*, which is very similar. Or *barbaridad*. Or *inhumanidad*, if you'd prefer it. Who are you, anyway?'

While he spoke, the officer's smile slowly vanished. Now, he drew himself up.

'I am Captain Rafael Mondeño.'

'And where's your senior officer?'

'I am the senior officer here.'

'Are you? So you're the one responsible for this murder.'

Mondeño's eyes narrowed.

'I am responsible for this security operation.'

'Aye,' said Douglas. 'That sounds nicer. Especially in Spanish. *Operación de seguridad*. A lot better than *asesinato*.'

The skin tightened and whitened around the Spaniard's nostrils. Douglas saw it and remembered Margaret. But the smile came back, unexpectedly. Mondeño laughed.

'But of course!' he exclaimed. 'You do not know.'

'What do I not know?'

'You saw this happen, yes?'

'I did. And so did my wife.'

'Ah!' His hands spread in the intensity of his regret. 'I am distressed——'

'So is she.'

'Of course. Naturally. It is different for a woman——'

'So am I,' said Douglas. 'I don't like murder.'

'But this is what you do not know.' Mondeño grew persuasive. 'This man was a Basque, a Communist, an enemy of the State, a political agitator. For years, he was responsible for industrial unrest in the north. He was in communication

17

with Communists in France. He smuggled money. He brought illegal political literature into our country. We have known of him for a very long time, but we did not succeed in catching him until last year. Then, it was winter. We got information. He was taken in a cave in the hills near Pineda. He was tried by a court at Burgos and sentenced to death. But . . . unfortunately . . . he escaped. There was treachery. A foolish guard was bribed. He has been hunted ever since, and that was a year ago. Then two days ago, he was seen near Pamplona. Since then, we have been very close to him. He did not have a chance.'

Douglas looked at the body and the thickening blood.

'No,' he said softly.

'You did not know these things and it is natural that you should not understand,' said Mondeño. 'But it was not murder. The sentence of the court has been carried out.'

He looked at the old worn clothes and the thin soles of the shoes that had carried him so far.

'What was his name?' he asked suddenly.

'Matías Alfaro.'

What had seemed leanness and strength in the night was the thinness of starvation and the debility of poverty in the morning. The lines of his years were deep on his face.

'What age was he?'

'We have no record.' He looked at Matías Alfaro with indifference. 'It is said that he fought for the Reds in the war.'

Douglas raised his head.

'Thirty years,' he said. He looked into the officer's brown eyes. 'And what age are you?'

'I?'

'You.'

'I do not see that this has any——'

'What age are you?'

'I am twenty-eight.'

'So,' said Douglas. 'He was already in the mountains when your mother lay in your father's arms.' Mondeño was about to speak, but something behind the pale cold blue of the other's eyes stopped him. Douglas went on quietly. 'Do you believe in anything enough to fight for it for thirty years? Would you do

18

it for God? Or freedom? Or justice? Would you do it for your police state, Mondeño? Would you risk your life every waking day and live like a hunted beast and sleep the winter through in a cave for the men that condemned this man or the State that made you kill him?'

Mondeño, whose eyes had shifted in his uncertainty, pulled himself together.

'The State must be protected,' he said harshly. 'He was a Communist.'

'To hell with the State,' said Douglas. 'Men made it. Not God. If it's rotten, men'll tear it down. And by Christ it's rotten here.'

Mondeño's hand moved to the butt of his revolver.

'I cannot permit you to——'

'You cannot permit,' said Douglas contemptuously. 'You're right. You can do nothing. You're just a tailor's dummy.'

He turned away. Mondeño paused, then drew his gun.

'Stop!' he shouted.

Douglas stopped.

'Put it away and don't be daft,' he said. 'I'm no poor man that you can shoot down at the side of the road.' He saw Mondeño's hand slowly relax, saw his index finger shift from the trigger. 'Give him a decent burial,' he said. 'He was more of a man than you'll ever be.'

He got into the Jaguar and started the engine. Margaret moved at his side, her hand tight on his arm.

'James.'

'It's all right,' he said. 'It's all right.' He wound down the window. Mondeño had not moved. He pointed to the Land-Rover which blocked the way. 'Get your driver to pull into the side.'

Mondeño looked at Douglas for a long moment. Then he signed to the man who sat smoking disinterestedly at the wheel. When the way was clear, Douglas let the car coast down the hill. He looked in the mirror as they approached the first bend. No one had moved. Captain Rafael Mondeño still stood close to the stiffening body of the Basque, Matías Alfaro.

He'll never be far from him again, thought Douglas. Not till his dying day.

19

When they had disappeared from sight, he let in the gear and drove down to Valdecarlos, and France, and the long white roads that led northward to the Channel.

CHAPTER TWO

THREE days later, James Douglas let the Jaguar slip down the mile-long drive that led from his house of Gartland to the main road. In that time he had passed from early summer back to early spring. The lambs were crying and nudging their mothers in the fields around the home farm and Anne's ageing mare had a fine dark son running at her side in the long sheltered meadow by the Gart burn. The daffodils were out in wide golden drifts, nodding their dipped heads over the short grass between the raked gravel of the drive and the foreign unexpected glory of the early rhododendrons, and above them the first soft green of the beeches was breaking free into the new sun.

He saw it all, as he still saw each spring, with an enduring sense of wonder. The tyres hissed over the gravel on the slow hill and he smoked his morning pipe quietly, not hurrying, enjoying it, for it would be dark when he returned and the feeling of leisure would be gone, perhaps for ever.

Johnston, the shepherd, was far up on the hill close to the edge of the heather, his two dogs circling out from him to bring the wanderers down, and the clear shrill note of his whistle came in at the window over the hum of the car. He would be easy in his mind, now that the lambing was done. And MacCallum was working in the shelter belt of woodland that screened the Gartland fields from the main road and the south-west wind. The thin blue smoke of the brushwood he was burning rose straight up through the branches to the sky.

Douglas's nose caught the acrid clean smell of it as he passed through the trees, and he felt a twinge of jealousy that would have made both Johnston and MacCallum laugh if they had known. But he had no illusions about the true value of his success and the true importance of his money, whatever other folk might think. It was a thing he rarely spoke about. His enemies would simply have added hypocrite to the other names they called him. But he had learned the hard way that power and great wealth take more from their possessor than they give. This was a thing that Archie, his son, still had to learn.

He changed down to go through the gate, and turned south on to the road that led to Glasgow, the city that had been his life, the city that he both loved and hated.

There were some Americans taking photographs in the square at Drymen and a few tourist cars up on the Stockie Muir, but there was little other traffic until he reached Bearsden. Then the commuters began to dribble from the Drives and the Crescents. Up on the Switchback Road, the pattern developed. The young ones cut in and swung out and overtook, roaring past the older men whom they would call 'sir' later in the day, but Douglas stayed in the inner lane with those who had got wherever they were going and saw no point in hurrying any more.

He tailed a black Daimler through the complex intersections at Anniesland and on to the new ring road that circled the grey changing city, feeling his way through the thickening traffic towards the tall building which held the administrative brain of his small empire.

Its seventeen stories rose from the hill above Renfrew Street, the most beautiful, if not the tallest, building of the new phase. And it was beautiful because he insisted on beauty in every project for which he was responsible. Whether it was a dam or a hospital, a new road or a bridge or a college, he said much the same thing at the start of the planning stage.

'It's got to do its job. It's got to last. And it's got to be bonny.'

For this, among other reasons, his tenders were not always the lowest, but in recent years they had come to be the ones most often accepted.

When he saw the building on this morning, he was glad he had held firm to his demand for Aberdeen granite facing on the lower levels. There had been trouble about that at the time, especially from Archie and the accountants.

'Cost! You talk about cost!' He had hurled the words at them across the Board Room. 'You'll tell other folk to pay an extra point five per cent or so to get good design and you're not prepared to do it yourself! What kind of way is that to do business?'

'But we're not talking about design,' Archie had said. 'We're talking about materials.'

'Aye. A facing material. And what matters about that apart from durability? Texture. Texture and colour. Both part of design. As big a part as the fine lines you're so fond of. Just try and make the rest of the design and the rest of the materials live up to the granite. You'll have a hard job.'

But they had succeeded. Even James admitted it. It was the best advertisement the firm had ever had.

Now, the granite sparkled in the sun like a million diamond chips as he turned into the service lane at the back and nosed the car up to the lift entrance. The doors slid open and he smiled when he remembered that they had thought this another extravagance. But he had ruled that ramps to the basement car park dug out of the hill were absurd on a small and costly site. So he had nagged and coaxed the men in his research laboratories out at East Kilbride until they came up with a new type of electronically operated car lift. The research expenses and the initial cost had caused a furore when they appeared, but they had been covered a hundred times over by the profit his subsidiary had made on the ones manufactured and sold under licence since. And that, he had pointed out, was the way to do business.

When he had driven off at the bottom, the doors hummed as they closed behind him. He parked his car and took the staff lift to the top floor.

Here, he and Archie had their rooms, separated by the offices of their private secretaries and on the other side of the oval elegant hall from the opulent suite of lounges and conference rooms, dining-room and bar, which existed solely to make it clear to visiting tycoons that Glasgow could arrange such matters as competently as London or New York, in spite of its international reputation for dourness, drabness, drunkenness and dirt.

22

There was extravagance there all right, from the Iona marble ash-trays and the illuminated tanks of tropical fish that reached from floor to ceiling, to the lamps of hollow rose-pink quartz and the finest private collection of modern paintings north of the Channel.

It was partly revulsion from this display that had made him keep his own room simple, with beech-wood furniture and plain white walls and a few primary colours in the cushions to give it warmth on the short winter days when the city outside was dark and sombre. The only costly thing in it was the complex invisible system of communication that linked his desk with every department of his business, for, though he believed absolutely in devolution and the delegation of authority to carefully chosen men, he stayed in touch and in control.

Now, the room was bright with the morning light. He could have looked right over the maze of streets and the painted funnels of the ships in the river, through the haze that blurred Paisley, to the sun on the green Kilbirnie hills, but he had just reached the wide window when the communicating door to his secretary's office clicked.

'Good morning, Mr. Douglas,' said Miss Carmichael.

'Hello, Sally.'

She was thirty-five and unmarried and Douglas could never see why, for she was a bonny girl by any standards, with dark hair and a skin like cream and eyes that could be as still and black as a hill loch or dance with brightness like a burn. She had been with him for ten years now and they understood each other very well.

'And how are you?' he asked. 'Have you been behaving yourself? It's about time you didn't.'

'I'm fine,' she said. 'And what else could I do but behave myself, with you away? Did you have a good holiday?'

'Not bad.' He went to his coat pocket. 'I brought you a wee minding.'

'Och, you shouldn't have bothered.'

'Why not?' He gave her the parcel. 'You can open it later. It's a mantilla, but you can wear it as a stole. Is Archie in?'

She took it and thanked him without embarrassment and went straight on to business.

23

'He's through in Edinburgh. The Council are quibbling about the cost of the West End underpasses.'

'What about the cost?'

'They say if you make them three feet narrower on each side, they can save a hundred thousand pounds.'

Douglas snorted.

'Aye, and in five years, when the traffic chokes them, it'll cost them half a million to make them wider!'

Sally smiled.

'Anyway, that's where he is. He'll be back in the afternoon. I suggested you might see him at three. I've put a summary of what's been happening in that file on your desk, and that'll give you time to catch up.'

He sat down and pulled the folder towards him.

'No problems?'

'Nothing that matters. It's all there. If you want more detail or anything, you can give me a ring.'

She turned away.

'Before you go,' said Douglas, 'get me John Kinloch on the phone.'

Kinloch was the head of Information. He had a small office on the twelfth floor, next to the fifteen hundred square feet of floor space occupied by the files which extended the range of his own encyclopaedic memory. He was a quiet reserved man, with a more enquiring nose than a ferret.

'Hello, Mr. Douglas,' he said. 'Was there something you wanted to know?'

It was Kinloch's stock opening sentence.

'Before I went away, there was a printing press for sale,' said Douglas. 'I saw it in the *Herald*. It was somewhere in that warren between Argyle Street and the river, on the edge of the development area.'

'That would be the Rowan Press. A man Campbell had it.'

'Well, find out if it's still in the market. If it is, find out all you can about it, especially the capacity and age and condition of the presses. Let me have a report in writing by twelve o'clock. Oh . . . and John.'

'Aye?'

'Not a word about this enquiry to anybody, not even Archie. Right?'

'Right.'

He hung up the receiver and chuckled. That'll make him wonder, he thought. Then he opened the file and put the whole thing out of his mind. It was ten-thirty when he reached the note—

2nd April. Phone call received from Mr. MacDonald, B.B.C. Television, Queen Margaret Drive. Said to be a personal matter, unconnected with business. Request you phone back on return.

He read it twice and pressed the buzzer. Sally came in with her pencil and pad.

'What's this about the B.B.C.?' he asked.

'I don't know,' she said. 'When he heard you were away, he didn't seem to want to talk.'

'And who's MacDonald?'

'He was a bit vague, but I think he said Chief Programme Controller. I'm not sure.'

'He can't be that. That's a man Jackson. Anyway, get me him, Sally, and we'll find out.' He looked up at her. 'Maybe I'm at the start of a new career.'

She laughed.

'And why not? You'd do better than some of the people they've got.'

As he waited, he wondered. Then the phone rang at his elbow.

'Hello,' he said. 'James Douglas here.'

'Hello. Mr. Douglas? This is Bill MacDonald, B.B.C. Television.'

He sounded young and very eager.

'Good morning,' said Douglas. 'I hear you were phoning me.'

'Yes, I was. Did you have a good holiday?'

'Not bad.'

'Good weather?'

'On the whole,' said Douglas. He decided to hurry things on. 'If it's audience research you're doing, put me down for the

News, *Panorama* and Westerns. I haven't much time for anything else.'

MacDonald laughed nervously.

'Oh, nothing like that! I've got a programme ... I mean, I'm responsible for it. It's a fortnightly thing actually. You know ... a sort of series ... and ... well, I wondered if you would care to consider appearing?'

Douglas sighed. He was not at his best with inarticulate young men.

'What kind of programme?'

'Well, I'm going to be quite frank about this, Mr. Douglas, because I've been told you're the sort of man who likes frankness. I'm really quite junior here and this programme ... well, it's the first time I've ever been given any responsibility like this and ... well, frankly, if you would agree to appear, it would be a tremendous scoop for me.'

Douglas held on to his patience.

'What sort of programme?'

'Well, it would really be better if we could meet and sort of talk about it. You'd get a better idea——'

'I'm just back from holiday,' said Douglas shortly. 'I'm busy. Has your programme got a name?'

'Oh, yes! Yes. It's called *What I Believe In*.'

He paused.

'What I believe in,' he repeated softly.

'Yes, that's right. I know it's rather a corny title, but it's expressive, and——'

'Five o'clock,' said Douglas.

'What?'

'I'll see you at five o'clock.'

'Oh, that's marvellous! Now. Will I come to your office or would you rather we met here?'

'Neither,' said Douglas. 'I'll see you in the lounge bar of The Highland Tinker. You won't know it, but you'll find it. It's a pub in St. Vincent Street, out beyond the Argyle Street junction. And I wouldn't go talking about this yet, if I were you. I haven't committed myself.'

'No, no. Of course not. I mean, that's understood. But I'm tremendously grateful to you. I really am. I——'

But Douglas hung up on his rambling protestations of gratitude. While he filled his pipe, he allowed himself a few minutes to think about what this might mean. One thing was clear. If anything came of it, and if full use were to be made of the chance it gave, then there was a new need for speed. He lifted the phone.

'Get me Mr. Ewan Cameron, Sally,' he said. 'He'll probably be at Bardowie 0411. If he's not, his wife'll know where he is.'

He lit his pipe while he waited, but Cameron came on the line almost at once.

'Well, James. You've got back.'

Cameron was a lean dark man of great ability, who had married as a student and taught History in a city school because he had a family to feed.

'Back last night. How are things?'

'Oh, just the usual. I'm off the leash till next week. The Easter holidays.'

'Has anything been happening?'

'If you mean at Gordon Street, no. Does anything ever happen there? McKay had a letter in the *Herald* last week.'

'Any good?'

'Just McKay's usual. All words and figures. About as much appeal as a Biblical tract.'

'Aye,' said Douglas. 'Well, something's going to be happening.'

There was a pause. Then Cameron said—

'What?'

'I'll tell you,' said Douglas. 'But first of all, I want a full Committee meeting tomorrow night at seven-thirty. Can you fix it?'

'I can try. There'll be complaints that the warning's too short.'

'They can complain away,' said Douglas. 'Tell them I've certain plans I want to discuss. If anybody wants his views considered, he'd better be there. That'll fetch them.'

'Plans, James?' said Cameron softly. 'What are you up to?'

Douglas chuckled.

'Come over to Gartland tonight,' he said. 'About eight o'clock. I'll tell you then.'

He put down the phone, reopened Sally's file and went back to the problems of that already extensive and still growing enterprise, James Douglas Limited. It was five minutes to twelve and he had just finished reading, when the secretary's door opened.

'The report from Information that you asked for,' she said, and put the typed sheets on his desk.

He picked them up.

'Thanks, and if you'd wait a minute——' He read the report quickly. 'Right,' he said. 'Fine. Get me Alex McLintock of McLintock and Brown. We'll just catch him before he goes out to lunch.'

He waited. The phone rang.

'Hello, James!' McLintock sounded in good fettle. 'This is a hell of a time to phone. I was just on my way out.'

'Too bad,' said Douglas. 'I'll not keep you long enough to give you an ulcer. One small thing. There's a printing press for sale. The Rowan Press, Trinidad Lane. The owner is a man Campbell. The lawyers are Urie and Crichton. I want to buy it.'

'What the devil do you want with a printing press?'

'Never you mind, Alex. And a lot of people are going to ask the same question, so you'd better exercise your usual discretion. Now, the price. They want forty thousand. Offer twenty-five and go up to thirty if you have to. You'll get it for that.'

'Are you sure?'

'I'm sure,' said Douglas. 'It's all been checked.'

'Aye! I might have known. You're worse than M.I.5!'

'Better,' said Douglas. 'And I want it fixed up beyond possibility of error by five o'clock tomorrow. None of your unavoidable legal delays.'

'There never are,' said McLintock. 'Not with this firm.'

'True,' said Douglas. 'I grant you that. Anyway, phone me tomorrow at five.'

He hung up and sat back, feeling the beat of excitement in his middle. The first moves had been made. There was no way of predicting where they would lead, no way of knowing how events would move, how the ordinary folk down there in the shops and streets and offices would view what they would regard as Douglas's latest ploy when they came to hear of it. But they were the ones who were going to matter most at the end of the day, the city folk and the quiet canny men in the crofts and farms and villages beyond the Highland line, and their women-folk too, realists that they were, with their instinctive devotion to security, their ancestral memory of dead sons, their intuitive capacity to smell the lack of substance in a dream.

He thought about them, and the way they could sway the feelings of their men in the dark hours between dusk and dawn, and wondered.

*   *   *

He had lunch sent up from the staff dining-room and ate alone at his desk. During his meal and in the time that was left until three o'clock, he went over Sally's notes in greater detail, pursued a number of doubtful points and used his communications system to discuss progress with the men on the spot at sites as far apart as the Wash Reclamation Project, which was still in the investigation phase, and Loch Eriboll, where the new N.A.T.O. Northern Maintenance Depot was rapidly taking shape. By the time his son arrived, he was once more fully informed.

Archie entered the building on time and in confident good humour. The Council in Edinburgh had grudgingly accepted his arguments about the underpasses and his Lotus had covered the forty-four miles from city centre to city centre in thirty-five minutes, which he felt was very reasonable when one considered the archaic conditions persisting on certain stretches of the road. Moreover, Julia had been affectionate for two whole days and nights and that . . . so far as he could see . . . without strings.

As the lift bore him silently upward, he hoped very much that his father would do nothing to disturb the present smooth flow of events, but at the same time he felt that it was really too much to expect. His father's return from holiday usually meant a flood of new ideas, conceived as he lay shut-eyed in

29

the sun. They were generally good ideas, he admitted, but they still meant additional work, fresh complications and a new series of prolonged and wearing conferences which were not calculated to keep a man's blood-pressure low and his arteries soft.

He felt faintly apprehensive, therefore, as he entered his father's room.

Douglas looked up and smiled, for he was fond of his son.

'Hello, Archie,' he said. 'Come away in. How are you?'

He put his brief-case on a chair and relaxed a little. His father's desk was reassuringly clear.

'Hello, Dad. Had a good holiday?'

'Just the usual. Too much food and too much sitting around. But your mother enjoyed it.'

Archie grinned.

'It doesn't seem to have done you any harm. You look as fit as a flea.'

His father nodded.

'So I am.'

'And Mother?'

'Oh, she's all right. At least, she's all right now. She got a bit of a shake on the way home.'

'Why? What happened? You didn't crash the car, did you?'

Douglas looked at him and reminded himself that Archie was of the generation which had grown up since the war. All he knew of violent death had been learned from the newspapers and the history books. The murky canopy of the nuclear cloud had obscured the fact that men could die in many other, less expensive, ways.

'No,' he said. 'Nothing like that. She saw a man shot.'

'Good God! Where did that happen?'

'In Spain. Near the frontier. Some poor devil who couldn't accept that the Civil War was over. And he nearly made it. But the Civil Guards got him at the side of the road.'

'But that sort of thing doesn't still go on, does it? I mean, surely——?'

'Oh, it still goes on. Probably less than it did, but it still happens. They just don't talk about it. It doesn't sound too good, when American aid is helping to buy the guns.'

'But you'd think they'd have given up by now. I mean, old Franco's been in power for . . . well, as long as I remember.'

'There's always somebody who doesn't give up,' said Douglas. 'And if you shoot him, you'll find there's somebody else. It's the one thing that makes me hopeful.'

'Well, I don't know,' said Archie. He rose to get an ashtray. 'It seems pretty stupid to me. I suppose it makes you realise how lucky we are to live in a civilised country.'

'Aye,' said his father. 'In many ways, I suppose we are.' But there was no point in pursuing it. The gap between the thinking of their generations was too great. 'How's Anne?' he asked.

'All right, as far as I know. I haven't seen her for three weeks. She was still bashing away at her hunks of rock last time I looked in.'

'Still in Bath Street?'

'Yes, but God knows why. She doesn't have to work in a dump like that. I mean, she could move out to the country and keep her blasted rocks in the garden. It would be a damn sight cleaner.'

'But not so good when it rained.'

'Maybe, but really, the place she works in is a shambles. Ironmongery and lumps of stone and God knows what all over the floor and Anne in the middle of it, dust to the eyebrows and as happy as Larry.'

'Her flat's all right.'

'Sure, her flat's all right. But she's hardly ever there. She's always hammering away in her mason's yard. I don't know how she sticks it.'

'It's her job,' said Douglas. 'And she's done some good work.'

'Has she? I've never seen it.'

'Oh yes, you have. Some of it's down there, staring at you. And it doesn't mean any more to you than it does to me, because neither of us knows anything about it. But the experts on modern sculpture say it's good modern sculpture and you can't reject that if you're prepared to accept the opinion of experts in your own line of country. And I must say I don't know why you're being so critical. She doesn't have to con-

31

form to your standards, you know. Take her for what she is. I'm her father and I've no complaints.'

Archie looked at him curiously.

'You haven't?'

'None.'

'And you don't object to the kind of life she's living?'

'Why should I?' Douglas took the pipe out of his mouth. 'When people start objecting to the way somebody else is living, especially somebody as intelligent and as well educated as Anne, I begin to think they're either scared or jealous. Scared, in case this odd character produces something that's going to undermine all their values, or jealous, in case there's some spicy living going on here and they're missing out on it.'

Archie looked down at the tip of his cigarette and stroked it gently on the onyx ash-tray. It had never occurred to him before that his father did not know how Anne was living. For once, his spy machine had slipped up. No civilised person could call it spicy, but it was, by any of the family standards, irregular. However, it was clearly not his place to break the news.

'Well, anyway,' he said, 'I've got no reason to be either scared or jealous of her. I hardly ever see her.'

'Which is a pity, when there are just the two of you. But it's maybe just as well, if you're going to try to make her toe your line.'

'But I don't. I mean——'

Douglas interrupted.

'Let's leave it. You've both your own lives to lead. How's Julia?'

'Oh, she's fine. In her usual roaring form.'

'And Jamie?'

'All right. Growing out of all his school clothes. He's on holiday just now, though.'

'He will be. We haven't seen him for a while. What about coming over on Sunday, the three of you?'

'Well, I don't know about Sunday. Julia said she wanted to go skiing. There's still plenty snow at White Corries.'

'She could miss it for once,' said Douglas. 'In fact, it's the least she could do. Her time's her own, which is more than

32

mine is. And if she's that keen, she could go up on Monday. She's got a car of her own.'

'Oh, I know. It's just that all her crowd go at the weekend.'

His father cocked an eyebrow at him.

'Her crowd,' he said dryly. 'I thought you were married?'

Archie managed a rather strained grin.

'Well, of course we are! But . . . you know. I'm pretty busy. I can't go out with her all the time. She gets around on her own quite a bit.'

'And you don't object?'

'I don't see how I can. If I'm not available, she doesn't see why she should have to stay in and . . . neither do I, really. Why should she?'

'Within limits, there's no reason at all. It just depends on where you draw the limits.'

'Well, I go with her whenever I can, obviously. But quite a lot of the time I can't, and that's all there is to it.'

'Mmphm,' said Douglas. 'That wouldn't be a complaint, would it?'

Archie looked surprised.

'No, of course it's not a complaint. You shouldn't need to ask that question.'

Douglas raised his hand.

'All right, all right. I shouldn't need to, but I did.' He rose and walked across the room and back. 'I'll tell you why I did.'

Archie moved uneasily.

'I wish you would,' he said.

Douglas stopped and looked down at him.

'I asked you, because from now on you're going to have even less time . . . for Julia or anything else outside the business.' Archie raised his eyebrows, which were still elegant, but would one day be as bushy as his father's. 'Some day you're going to have to run this thing yourself,' said Douglas, 'so you might as well make a start by running most of it just now. No, just a minute. Let me go on. You've got your faults like the rest of us, Archie, and you look more like a male model than my idea of a working man, but you've never been afraid of hard work. I grant you that. If you want to go around with this great air of

33

leisure, that's up to you. As long as the work's done. Now, as you well know, this whole organisation is built on the principle of efficient administration under unified control, with good men all the way down from this room to the shop-floor and the site. As long as you hold to that system, and improve it where you can, and delegate work . . . and responsibility . . . to men you can trust, then you'll manage. But you're still going to have to do more work yourself and there's no good pretending you won't, so your share in the business and your income from it will go up in proportion. That'll maybe keep your Julia happy.'

My God, thought Archie, what's all this about? He watched his father trying to relight his pipe and suddenly he thought of illness. For an instant, it was inconceivable. Then it seemed so much the only possible explanation that he could hardly bear to ask.

But Douglas only laughed.

'No,' he said, 'I'm not ill. Far from it. And don't get the idea I'm retiring either. But you could call it a partial withdrawal.'

Archie sat forward. He was worried now.

'Look, Dad. You don't have to put on an act. I know you. You're not the sort of man who makes a partial withdrawal unless you're not feeling well enough to cope.'

His father looked at him sideways.

'Or unless I've something better to do.'

'Oh, come off it,' said Archie impatiently. 'You built this place out of practically nothing, this and all the God knows how many ramifications. . . . I never counted them——'

'You're going to have to.'

'All right . . . but you sit up here like a ruddy spider in its web, with strings that go out over half of Western Europe, not to mention America and Canada and what have you. And it's your life. The whole damn thing *is* you! You can't . . . partially withdraw!'

'No,' agreed Douglas, 'if you weren't here, I couldn't. But if you weren't here, I wouldn't run the thing the way I do. It would have been turned into a public company long ago. But you are here. And while I think you're a damn fool in many

34

ways, you've as good a business head on you as I have myself. The only thing you need is experience and that'll come.'

'So you're trying to tell me that you're partially withdrawing, as you call it, to give me more experience? Oh, no!' He screwed out his cigarette. 'I don't believe it.'

'I never said any such thing,' said Douglas equably. 'I said . . . or I hinted, anyway . . . that I'd something better to do.'

His son's face expressed his disbelief.

'At——' he began, and stopped himself.

Douglas chuckled.

'You were going to say . . . at your age. All right. Fifty-eight is my age. And you'll be surprised when you wake up on your fifty-eighth birthday and find you feel the same as you do today, at thirty-two. You'll still have dreams. You'll still have ambitions. You'll still have energy. And when you look at your wife, you'll wonder what's wrong with her that she's aged so much, when you're so young yourself.'

Archie reached for his cigarettes.

'All right,' he said. 'But don't tell me you're going to run away with Sally. I couldn't stand it.'

'No,' said Douglas. 'Though it's an idea with a lot to commend it.'

'Then what is it?'

His father looked at him, seeing a good deal of himself under the gloss that education and money had put on the top.

'No, Archie,' he said at last. 'I'm not going to tell you. You'll find out in good time. And I'd be grateful if you wouldn't mention any of this to your mother. The point is . . . you'll have to carry a bit more of the burden. I'll be here every day, and I'll still be in touch, but some of the work I'll be doing won't be business work. Let's leave it at that. If everything goes according to plan, your curiosity'll not have to wait long to be satisfied.'

Archie fingered his cigarette with his mother's nervous gesture, as uneasy as though the bed-rock of the world had moved beneath him.

'My curiosity'll kill me,' he muttered.

'I doubt it,' said Douglas. 'Now, let's hear what happened

35

in Edinburgh first. I've got to be out of this place by ten to five.'

*   *   *

He entered The Highland Tinker a few minutes after five o'clock.

It was an old Glasgow pub, all fly-stained mirrors and drab brown paint, full of the smell of stale beer and plug tobacco, one of the type whose numbers were mercifully becoming fewer each year. Yet, already the aura of false sentiment and spurious affection was gathering around it and its fellow survivors. The lucky few which the bull-dozers and the planners spared would be fashionable in a few more years, transmuted into quaint old-world howffs where a young man and his girl could sip their vodka and lemon in homely warmth, forgetting ... if they ever knew ... about the grandfather who had lived around the corner in a single-end and had lurched through that same door every Saturday night for forty years, blind drunk on beer and whisky chasers.

Now, when the old tenement population was dwindling away and the new society set had not yet spotted the Tinker's charms, Bill MacDonald arrived a little earlier and waited alone for the locked door to be opened at five o'clock.

As he entered on the heels of the incurious barman, he thought vaguely that there should be something here for the outside broadcast cameras. He ordered a lager and considered it. But it was the old problem. The best set in the world wasn't enough. You needed a good strong story-line. And where the hell was the story in a dying pub? There were dozens of them. Unless you made it representative. Did a series of flash-backs. A kind of social history, like a documentary ... oh hell, he thought, that's corny. It's out. That kind of documentary's dead. And the trouble was, everything was corny if you thought about it long enough. But this *I Believe* thing was the corniest yet. There had been an industrial chemist and a parson and a Trade Union leader and their TAM-rating was lower than the *Epilogue*. If Douglas didn't shoot it up, they'd take it off, for sure. And that would mean back to *Toddler's Teatime*, if it didn't mean out on your ear.

36

He had achieved a considerable depth of gloom by the time James Douglas came through the swing door, but he was a resilient young man and the very sight of that strong stocky figure restored his hope. He put down his glass and went to him with his hand outstretched.

'Mr. Douglas? Hello! I'm MacDonald.'

'Hello,' said Douglas, finding it hard to believe that this undergraduate figure held in his young grasp any part of the power of television, even a brief fortnightly spot.

'It was tremendously good of you to see me. But, look. Let me buy you a drink. What'll you have?'

'Whisky,' said Douglas. 'A small one.' He watched Mac-Donald fuss with the drink. He would fuss with everything. He would be conscientious, and limited in his talent, and would drive his seniors mad. 'Thanks,' he said.

'Anything in it?'

'The way God made it's good enough for me,' said Douglas.

'Fine. Well . . . cheers!'

'Here's to your programme,' said Douglas.

MacDonald grinned.

'Yes, indeed. Here's to that.' He drank some of his lager and crossed his fingers. 'Well, have you thought about it?' he asked.

'No,' said Douglas. 'There's no point, until I know what it's about.'

'No. Well, I suppose that's true. But the idea's in the title, really. You know . . . *What I Believe In*. The thing is, there's been an awful lot of talk about declining standards, morality, all that kind of thing. I mean, masses of people don't seem to believe in anything much any more. So we thought it would be an idea to put on a programme where somebody . . . well, somebody like yourself . . . talked to them about the things he believed in, his own sort of code of ethics, talked a bit about the things which he felt mattered . . . I mean, really mattered, as opposed to all the trivialities that people worry themselves sick about that don't really matter at all. Something like that.'

Douglas sipped at his whisky.

'It's a pretty wide brief,' he said.

'Yes, well, we felt it had to be pretty wide. You see, what

37

we hope is that the viewers will get something out of it that they can apply to themselves, perhaps something to aim at where before they felt they'd nothing. I mean, you know how easily the average person is influenced. What we feel is that it should be just as possible to influence them for good as for bad. And they're more likely to pay attention to the views of somebody like yourself who's tried out his beliefs and found that they work. You know . . . example is the best teacher and all that.'

Douglas regarded him sympathetically. If he truly believed these things, he was a very naïve young man.

'How long do you give your speakers?'

'Fifteen minutes. And it's on a Saturday night, at ten-forty-five usually. We've found that people are more receptive to ideas then. More relaxed, I suppose.'

'And what about subject? Can I talk about anything?'

'Well, more or less anything. If it's relevant, I mean. You want to keep things like sex out, of course. Religion's all right as long as it's non-denominational. And politics . . . well, that doesn't crop up much.' He laughed. 'Nobody believes in politics, anyway. Except the Communists, of course, and that's completely out, obviously. Otherwise pretty well anything. But I'll keep you right about that.'

Douglas looked at him quickly

'What do you mean?'

'Well, if there's anything in your script that——'

'Script?'

'Yes . . . you know. The sort of draft of what you are going to say.'

Douglas emptied his glass and put it down.

'Sorry,' he said. 'That can't be done. When I talk, I don't talk from notes. I think about it beforehand, but if I put it down on paper it's dead as far as I'm concerned. I can't stand read speeches.'

'But it's the usual thing,' said MacDonald unhappily. 'That's what's always done.'

'Not by me.'

'And you won't consider it?'

Douglas faced him.

'Not unless you give me complete freedom to say what I like, leaving out religion, Communism and sex.'

'But I can't do that. I told you. I'm pretty junior. I haven't got that kind of authority.'

Douglas laid a hand on his shoulder.

'Have another beer,' he said gently. 'And let's be a little more frank.' He signalled to the barman. 'Since I spoke to you this morning, I've been making a few enquiries. The general feeling seems to be that your programme's a flop. Oh, it's not your fault. Not entirely. It's the fault of your speakers. Although maybe if they'd been given a bit more freedom, they might have done better. But if another one flops, it's quite likely that they'll scrap the whole thing and pin the blame on you. And that wouldn't do your career any good at all. Right?'

'Right,' said MacDonald gloomily.

'Now, you want me because you think I might save the day. Is that correct?'

'Yes.'

'Very well,' said Douglas. 'The way I see it is this. If you don't get me, or somebody like me, you're liable to be finished as far as the B.B.C.'s concerned. They don't like young men with too many failures any more than I do. If you do get me, you might be all right. Now, you can take it from me that if you want success when you're older, you've got to take risks when you're young. And the risk for you is in letting me go on without having seen what I'm going to say. So let's put it bluntly. If I don't go on, you're finished. If I do go on, on my terms, you might be finished. But you might not.'

MacDonald nodded.

'That's about it.'

'Well, I know what I would do if I were in your shoes,' said Douglas. 'But since you're looking so damned miserable, I'll make you an offer. If I say anything that gets you into trouble, I'll give you a job.'

'What?'

'You heard me. We could use you either in publicity or public relations.'

'Do you mean that?'

'Do you want it in writing?'

'No, no! It's just . . . well, I mean, it's extraordinarily good of you——'

'It's not,' said Douglas shortly. 'But it lets you take out insurance on the risk. If you'll agree to these terms, I'll do it.'

MacDonald stared at him. The very idea of putting on an unscripted speaker made him squeamish; but so did the thought of yet another dud. He remembered the Trade Union leader, the clichés, the pedantry, the stilted stumbling delivery. At least, Douglas had a face like carved rock, and a voice, and a personality that would burst through the screen. He took a deep breath.

'Right,' he said. 'I'll agree.'

James Douglas let himself relax.

'Fine,' he said softly. 'When?'

'Well, we've got somebody for Saturday first. A University chap. He'll be dull as hell, but he'll be better than the ones we've had. It would be a fortnight after that.'

'All right. What time?'

'Well, it'll probably be the usual ten-forty-five, but we'd want you in a bit earlier to let you see the set-up, show you where the cameras are placed, all that stuff. You haven't been on television before, have you?'

Douglas laughed.

'No,' he said. 'Never. This will be my first and last time.'

MacDonald laughed too. He thought he was joking.

*   *   *

Ewan Cameron sat through the evening hours by the fire in the study of Gartland House. It was a big, perfectly proportioned room, almost unaltered since Robert Adam designed it in 1771, lit now only by the lamps on the twin tables which flanked the mantelpiece and by the flames which leapt in the deep dog-grate. The heavy embroidered curtains were drawn across the tall windows which opened on to the terrace, and he was enclosed by them and by the great cases of book-spines shining in the firelight, shut off from the world, shut in with the dreams of Douglas.

He had sat quietly for most of the time, listening to the

man, watching the shadows moving on his face, seeing the fire as a golden glow through the whisky that stood at his hand, and all the time reminding himself of the true nature of the land outside and the folk who lived in it.

For here, he knew, was seduction. And it was seduction of the kind most dangerous to him as a historian who loved the past and who despised so much of the present. But worst of all, it was seduction by an idea which he had accepted in principle already, years ago, when he had joined the Party of which he was now Secretary. Now, when the most significant stage in all seductions had been reached, when ideas and words threatened to turn to action, the ideas themselves suddenly seemed to need re-examination and reappraisal. So he held on to the clear part of his mind that remained and considered them and the arguments and tried to ignore the dangerous dreaming warmth of the fire and the whisky.

The moment came for him when Douglas leaned forward.

'And that brings me to you, Ewan,' he said.

'To me?'

'I'm going to need men with talent and training. Men with energy. Young men with ideas and old men with wisdom and experience. But I need you most of all.'

Cameron slid away from it, like a reluctant virgin.

'You'll not find many of them in the Party,' he said. 'You know that as well as I do.'

Douglas looked at the dark bony face, with the steady eyes astride the lean beak of a nose.

'No, Ewan,' he said softly. 'I'm not going to tell you everything tonight, so don't try and make me. But you're the only man to know anything at all and you'll be the first to hear the rest. As far as the Party's concerned, tomorrow night'll sift the wheat from the chaff and what wheat there is is good stuff, even if there's not much of it. But there's another Party, Ewan, or the skeleton of one, that I've built up over the years. The men I need are there already. All they want is a lead, from me . . . or you.'

Cameron stirred uneasily.

'Why me?'

'Because you've got something none of the rest of them

41

have. Oh, you've ability, too. And imagination, which is just as important. And you've a sense of history that lets you view the rights or the wrongs of the thing in a true perspective and not just in the twisting heat of a moment. But you've something else that's not so easy to name, some kind of inner strength of purpose and conviction that commands more respect than any amount of argument or fancy talk. If I'm spared, I'm prepared to lead, but I need a deputy leader at my back, a man who can step into my shoes if anything happens to me. And that's what I want you for. I want you for my shadow and my right hand at the beginning. And later, I want you to carry on when I leave off.'

Cameron looked at him thoughtfully.

'You're a fit man, James.'

'Aye,' said Douglas, 'but you're ten years younger. If I'm lucky, I might get fifteen years. If you carry on for another ten years after that, it's twenty-five. Long enough to set this country on the right road. What happens then will be for other folk to decide, men that are schoolboys today. We can't plan for them. But we can build them a good foundation.'

Something stirred in Cameron's mind, a foreboding as vague and fleeting as a bird's shadow. His gaze moved over Douglas, from the short broad hand that held the pipe to the strong wide-browed head set on the thick shoulders.

'If anything happens to you.' He lingered on it. 'What did you mean by that?'

Douglas looked into the fire. After a moment, he got up.

'I don't know,' he said. He walked over to the shelves and moved a book into line, not seeing what he did. 'You can plan till the cows come home, but the one thing you can't do more than guess at is the reaction of ... oh, the Establishment, the State, the Government, anything you like to call the authority that has the power in its hands.' He turned back to Cameron. 'In the past, we've been a joke, Ewan. Let's face it. Just a few eccentrics on what they used to call the lunatic fringe. And as such, we were maybe even useful to them. If anybody talked about loss of political freedom in Britain, they could point to us and say ... nonsense! Look at the Scottish nationalists. Look at the Welsh nationalists. They couldn't exist if Britain

42

wasn't free. And if ever some M.P. raised the subject ... not that many of them ever did, for they're tied like bairns to the Whips' apron-strings ... but if the subject came up they could say ... oh, but there's no real desire for independence in Scotland. Look at their Party! See how weak it is. And they'd pat us on the head and tell us to run away and play. But at the times when national feeling was rising, in the nineteen-thirties, or at the time of John McCormick's Covenant, or when the railway closures brought the Vigilantes to the fore, then they couldn't ignore it or jeer at it, so they went along with it. They made pre-election promises that they'd never any intention of fulfilling ... but they were enough to keep the votes with the big Parties. So the feeling died for want of purpose and direction and leadership, as they knew it would.'

He sat down, his hands on his thighs.

'But this is going to be different, Ewan. If I can rouse feeling as I think I can, the powers that be are going to know that this is no joke. They're going to know that I'll not be fobbed off with promises. And they know me well enough to realise that there will be plenty of purpose and direction if I'm involved. They're going to have to sit down and consider what they can do about it. The thing that matters is the decision they reach.'

'The decision they reach will depend on how seriously they take you, James,' said Cameron. 'But if they take you seriously enough, there'll be no holds barred.'

Douglas nodded.

'That's right. And that's why I said ... if anything happens to me. If they've any sense, it's me they'll strike at. Nobody else. It's a question of what they can do.'

'They can try to discredit you.'

'They can try, but they'll have a job, though I say it myself.'

'They can try to cripple you financially.'

Douglas smiled grimly.

'If they try that, they'll have an even bigger job, And I've got them tied to contracts for the next five years that they'll not wriggle out of in a hurry.'

Cameron leaned forward.

'James, don't underestimate them. There's nothing more ruthless than power trying to keep power. The power in this country is civilised and sophisticated, and they'll use civilised and sophisticated methods for as long as they can. But a hand in a velvet glove can strangle you just as surely as if it was naked.'

'I know that,' said Douglas quietly. 'I've no illusions.' He paused. 'I told you about the man I saw shot in Spain?'

'Yes, you did.'

'Well, you know, once I was away, thinking back on it, I couldn't help feeling that, bad and all as it was, there was a sense in which it was a more honest way to go about things. And I never thought I'd feel that about a police state, Ewan. But at least there's no hypocrisy about it, no pretence. Each side knows what to expect from the other. The only thing you know here is that you'll not get shot down at the side of the road. But they can kill you just as effectively in this country without a body left on their hands. If you're silenced and powerless ... and there's many a way of doing that ... you're as good as dead as far as they're concerned.'

Cameron watched him finish his whisky.

'I think you're wrong.'

His voice had changed. It was suddenly cold and objective, empty of expression. Douglas slowly lowered his glass.

'How?'

'I don't think political assassination is necessarily ruled out in a democracy like Britain. All you can say is that it hasn't been needed for a long time, because it's a long time since there has been an internal threat to the *status quo* of a magnitude or type that called for it. I'd like to think I was wrong, James, but if ever there was a threat of that order, one that could be dealt with by the killing of a single man, then in the name of State security and the welfare of the greatest number, I believe a democracy would kill.'

Douglas looked at him, his eyes narrowing.

'Man, man,' he said. 'Do you believe that?'

Ewan Cameron nodded.

'I'm afraid I do.'

'Well, now,' said Douglas, 'if you believe that, are you with

44

me, or are you going to go on dreaming and talking like the rest of them?'

Cameron grinned.

'You couldn't keep me out if you tried.'

Douglas grunted and sat back on the crumpled cushions.

'Man, you had me worried for a minute.'

'No,' said Cameron, 'if it's not now, it'll be never. And the talking and the dreaming have gone on for long enough . . . too long, in fact, for they've done more harm than good. They've sapped all the energy that could have been better used. But there is one favour I'd ask you, James.'

'What's that?'

'If it's accepted that there's a risk in this . . . and I believe there is . . . could you see your way to making some provision for Jean and the two boys? I've as much insurance as my income'll let me carry, but it's not much.'

Douglas nodded.

'I'll arrange it before the end of the week.'

'Thanks, James. And I'll need to go.' He stood up, straightening his long back, stiff after the hours of sitting. 'It's after twelve. She'll be thinking I'm lost. And there's tomorrow ahead.'

'Aye, there's tomorrow,' said Douglas. He grinned as he rose from his chair. 'Some of them'll not sleep much tomorrow night.'

Margaret, lying reading in her bed upstairs, heard the two men leave the study and cross the hall. She put down her book. For her, the loneliness had begun already. She heard the click of the outer door and the crunch of their feet on the broad gravel that lay between the house and the slope of the lawn, then the silence as they stood by Cameron's car.

Ewan paused to look at the glow of the sky over the city to the south, then westward, to the silver sliver of moon glinting on Loch Lomond, and round towards the north, where the mountains were black and quiet under a clear sky. He opened the car door.

'Well, I'll away, James.' He curled himself into the seat of the Austin. 'See you tomorrow.'

Douglas stood and watched until the red tail-lights had disappeared round the bend in the drive and the wind from the moor whispered through the trees above his head. The day was over.

When Margaret, listening, heard the stair creak under his foot, she turned on her side and pulled the bed-clothes up round her neck and closed her eyes, for she had always tried to hide it from him when she worried.

CHAPTER THREE

EWAN CAMERON, Party Secretary, looked at the men who sat round the old stained table, at the Chairman, and at Douglas, who had angled his chair and was impassively filling his pipe.

'Well, that's the minutes of the last meeting,' he said. 'Would somebody like to move that they're adopted?'

Willie Bain, a small, dark man who worked as a foreman welder in Fletcher's shipyard, raised his hand.

'Just a minute,' said the Chairman. 'It seems to me that these minutes don't give an adequate account of the last meeting we had. There were a lot of things said . . . I said a number of things myself . . . to which there's no reference made at all.'

Cameron raised his black eyebrows at him.

'They're minutes,' he said briefly. 'It's not a verbatim account.'

'I'm well aware of that, Mr. Cameron, but I still think they're inadequate. For example, you haven't even mentioned my suggestion that something more should be done to commemorate the anniversary of Wallace's death.'

Cameron shrugged his shoulders. In view of what lay ahead, there was little point in arguing.

'All right, then, I'll add it,' he said. 'With a rider to the effect that the suggestion did not find the necessary support.'

The Chairman moved uncomfortably. That fact still rankled.

'That's not the point,' he said irritably. 'The point is that

46

you left it out. I must say I think you're far too slap-dash in the way you deal with this sort of thing.' He threw down his pencil. 'You're not even paying attention. You might at least stop writing.' Cameron looked up enquiringly. 'It's your job to see that the proceedings of this Committee are properly reported. If you can't do that, then you'd better give some thought to whether or not——'

'Just a minute.'

The accent of the firm, intruding voice was broad and homely. The Chairman looked round in surprise.

'Yes, Mr. Bain?'

'I think the rest of us are well enough pleased with the job Mr. Cameron does. And he does it for nothing. I'd just like to move that the minutes are adopted.'

'Seconded,' said James Douglas.

The colour rose on the Chairman's face, racing like a dark tide over his brow and across his bald head. He spluttered.

'Well, James! I'm surprised that you as a business man should say that.'

'As a business man, my idea of what's important is maybe different from yours, Mr. Haig, since you're a school-teacher.'

'Headmaster.'

'Sorry,' said Douglas. 'But in my opinion, everything of any importance was in the minutes as they stood. If you don't agree, we'd better vote on it.'

Robert Haig, Chairman of the Party for the last three years and headmaster of a Junior Secondary School in a new housing area, glowered at him and tried to remember that Douglas was the wealthiest man he was ever likely to know. His wife would be none too pleased if he undid in the next few minutes the work he had put out over the years in cultivating what he liked to think was his friendship. He forced himself to speak reasonably.

'Yes,' he said, 'I think that's the proper step. Would all those in favour of adopting these minutes as they stand, please raise their right hand?'

Five hands went up quickly, followed, after a pause, by two more. Douglas's eyes flickered round the table. There were no surprises.

'Names,' said the Secretary. 'Gavin Hamilton, Norman Graham, James Douglas, William Bain, Liam Macquillan, Donald Gunn and Calum Macrae. Right. I've got that.'

'Those against,' said Haig tightly, and raised his hand.

Three other hands rose into the already smoky air.

'Hugh Ross,' said Cameron as he wrote. 'Peter McKay. Iain Campbell. And Mr. Haig, Chairman. Motion carried by seven votes to three, the Chairman voting against.'

Haig tried and failed to keep the tremor of anger out of his voice.

'Well,' he said, 'this seems to me a very significant motion.'

'Aye,' said Liam Macquillan briefly. 'It signifies that the minutes have been adopted.'

Two or three of those present tittered anonymously. Haig turned the full majesty of his headmaster's presence on Liam.

'That's not what I mean, Macquillan. Its implications are deeper than you seem to think. As far as I'm concerned, I must regard it as a vote of no confidence in myself as Chairman of the Party, but I feel obliged to add that it also makes me doubt my own confidence in you as a Committee. That being so, I must consider whether or not I should resign.'

'That would come under the heading of any other business,' said Gavin Hamilton with deceptive softness.

'At the end,' added Willie Bain succinctly.

Haig swept his quelling gaze from Macquillan to them, but they sat some distance apart and the need to move it from one to the other and back again diminished its effectiveness.

'It seems that, like Macquillan, you also fail to realise the significance of this,' he said. 'I've been Chairman now for three years, and in all that time I have never——'

'Mr. Haig,' said Norman Graham, 'I'm sorry to interrupt, but they're quite right. Anything concerning your resignation is any other business and comes at the end. And I think you're making a mountain out of a molehill anyway, but that's up to you. However ... what I wanted to say is this. I cancelled another appointment to come here tonight because a meeting was called to hear something Mr. Douglas had to say. That's the business of the meeting and that's what we're here for. I'd like to vote we get on with it.'

'Hear, hear,' said Willie Bain.

Haig pulled himself together.

'Very well,' he said. 'As far as I'm concerned, the matter isn't closed, but I'm prepared to sleep on it. And in any case it is, as you say, any other business. We're here, as Mr. Graham has pointed out, at the request of Mr. Douglas to hear something which he obviously regards as important. Otherwise he'd never have had a meeting called at such inconveniently short notice. However, Mr. Douglas is a distinguished Scot whom we are honoured to have in our Party and especially on our Committee, and I'd just like to say that, although we voted against each other just now, I bear him no ill will.'

He achieved a rather strained and chilly smile.

'Thank you,' said Douglas.

'But I won't keep you any longer, for I'm sure you're all as interested as I am to hear what he has to say. I'll just call on Mr. Douglas to . . . er, speak.'

Douglas looked round the table at the friends and the waverers and the potential foes.

'Well, I'll be as brief as I can,' he said, 'but I'm afraid that may not be as brief as some of you might like. In spite of that, I'm going to take ten minutes or so first to go over the history of this Party since it was founded, nearly fifty years ago.'

They listened with patience or interest or deference, according to their various attitudes, but as his survey approached the present time a mood of anticipation began to grow in all of them. Even Douglas couldn't expect them to endure this unless the titbit at the end was rather special.

'And now we're here tonight,' he said, and paused. They waited. 'Eleven men in an upstairs room, who start off by bickering about whether or not the Chairman should resign because the minutes of the last meeting aren't in order.'

Haig's head jerked up.

'But, Mr. Douglas,' he protested, 'I don't think it's right that——'

'Of course it's right!' cried Douglas. 'It's the right, logical and tragically inevitable end to half a century of petty-mindedness and failure and ineptitude, of schism and futility and sheer, airy-fairy beeheadedness that must be without equal

49

in the history of any so-called political party.'

'Oh, I say!' Iain Campbell still spoke with the bastard accent of the lesser English public school to which his ambitious parents had misguidedly sent him. 'I can't accept all that, you know. I think the Party has a very fine record. Not only politically, but as patrons of native literature and art, as custodians of a folk-heritage that——'

'Mr. Campbell, don't talk as if we were some Central African tribe and you were a member of UNESCO. Our art and literature aren't native. They're national. And they don't need patronage. What they need is free air to breathe and a reborn national consciousness to feed on. That, and the removal of the dead hand of class and kirk. It was a Scottish playwright . . . one of the few entitled to that description . . . who said a few years back that all art had to be national before it could be international. But it can't be national when you've no nationality. It can't have pride in its own national virility when folk like you refer to it as native and talk about patronage. And don't, Mr. Campbell, don't talk to me about folk-heritage——'

'You mean you're ashamed of it?' snapped Campbell.

'Yes,' said Douglas. 'Yes, by God, I am. There's not much to be proud of in the last two hundred and fifty years and plenty to be ashamed of before that too. But that's not the point. The rock on which this Party has perished from the beginning is its backward-looking, historically biased, Celtic twilight dreaming about a past that never had a fraction of the splendour and the glory that you and people like you seem determined to give it. But in spite of the worst efforts of forces outside and inside the country . . . and those inside have been as dangerous and silent as dry rot . . . the ones outside have been like honest wind and weather by comparison . . . in spite of them all, we remain a distinctive people, with our own peculiar national virtues and vices. That's perhaps the only point on which all eleven of us are agreed.'

'Thank God we're agreed on something,' said Willie Bain, and through the swelling murmur of other voices came the singsong whine of Hugh Ross, the draper, a little man with rimless glasses and an ingratiating manner.

50

'There's something else I think we're all agreed on, Mr. Douglas.'

Douglas looked at him coldly.

'And what's that?'

'We're wondering why you brought us here, if this is all you have to say.'

The Chairman beamed at him. Things were improving. With a bit of luck, Douglas might be about to learn that wealth could not always buy support. Give him a bit more rope and he'll hang himself, he thought grimly, and let his eyes twinkle with good-humoured tolerance.

'I think you can take it, Mr. Ross, that the speaker has got more to say. I imagine this is some sort of preamble.'

Iain Campbell tapped a cigarette sharply on the table and turned on his pseudo-military manner.

'Well, if you have more to say, may I ask you to make it brief and to leave out the insults, Mr. Douglas? I think all of us have had as much as we can stand.'

He flicked his lighter decisively and Liam Macquillan's grin widened.

'Man, you're thin-skinned,' he said.

The Chairman rapped the table.

'Please . . . gentlemen. Let the speaker get on.'

'Thank you,' said Douglas. 'And I'll be brief. I promise you that. But I can't promise to leave out the insults when I'm not sure what some of you may consider to be insulting. So, Mr. Chairman, I'd like to ask for no more interruptions.'

'Yes, of course.'

'Very well,' said Douglas. 'Anything I've said so far was to try and make it clear to you that the time has come to consider, coldly and without any false sentiment, the future of the Party and everything it stands for. If we intend to go on as we're doing, there is no justification for its continued existence, for it serves no useful purpose at all. If it is going to continue to exist, two things have to be decided. What are our aims and how can we achieve them?'

Ewan Cameron raised his eyes from his notes. Iain Campbell irritably flicked the ash from his cigarette.

'Mr. Douglas,' he said, 'I'd like to ask you what you think

51

we've been doing all these years if you——'

James Douglas turned to Haig.

'Mr. Chairman, I asked for no interruptions.'

Haig moved restlessly.

'Yes . . . well . . . er, later, Mr. Campbell, if you don't mind.'

'But I'll answer the question,' said Douglas. 'Nothing. We've been doing nothing of any practical value at all. What I'm saying is that the time has come for action . . . or extinction.'

He paused and let them wait for it. When they were motionless, he said—

'I am proposing that we should fight every local and parliamentary election from now on. I'm proposing that we should launch a publicity campaign to bring home to everybody in the country what it is we stand for, what it is we're aiming for, and how we propose to get it. And this time there won't be any emotion in the arguments, no harking back to the guid auld days and the Prince over the water. The arguments will be material. Factual. Hard, unanswerable economic arguments that affect every man, woman and child north of the Border. And arguments most of them can understand. But before we can do any of these things, we have to be clear ourselves on what it is we're aiming for and, for the time being, I want to define it as this . . . the setting up of a Scottish Parliament, loyal to the Crown and within the framework of the United Kingdom, with adequate legislative authority in, and complete and final responsibility for, all Scottish affairs.'

'Not enough,' snapped Campbell.

Peter McKay looked at him in disgust.

'Och, I've heard that one before. It's the same old mealy-mouthed compromise. What we're after is total separation . . . Government, Army, Exchequer, the lot. That, or nothing.'

'Then it'll be nothing,' said Douglas. 'A wise man aims for something he's a chance of getting, and you'll not get public support for anything more. That's fact, not a matter of opinion. And compromise is very often the same as common sense. If that definition is accepted as our general objective, and if we use every weapon that the big Parties use, I believe we can reach it within three years.'

'There's just one thing,' said Willie Bain.

Douglas smiled.

'I wish there was,' he said. 'But what's the one you've got in mind?'

'Funds.'

'And men,' said Norman Graham. 'Not to mention the kind of organisation you'd need for the like of that. We couldn't even get started.'

Douglas nodded agreement.

'Yes. As things are, we couldn't. But I think if you're honest you've all got to admit that I've some experience in building an organisation. And I'm going to build this one, with the help of those of you who are prepared to join me.'

Haig looked up quickly.

'What do you mean by that?'

Douglas turned to him.

'Just this, Mr. Haig. I've got certain plans which I'm proposing to put into action to achieve the objective I've defined. If this Committee, or a majority of it, accepts the objective and is prepared to back me, the whole thing can go ahead as a Party campaign. If not, then I'll form a new Party that will.'

'But that's absurd!' cried Campbell.

'It's a bit dictatorial, anyway,' said McKay. 'You're taking a lot on yourself.'

'Just a minute,' said Haig. 'Are you suggesting splitting the Party?'

'If necessary . . . yes.'

The Chairman rubbed his hand over his moist, pink head and looked at his Committee.

'Well, gentlemen . . . this is an astonishing thing.'

'It's a ridiculous thing,' said Campbell.

'We don't even know what your plans are.'

'No,' said Douglas slowly, 'and I'm sorry to have to say that I'm not going to tell you what they are until I've got your support in principle.'

'Why not?'

'Because discretion is not a quality possessed by everybody here. I don't want any long tongues wagging out of turn.'

The draper's words came singing through the protesting voices.

'What you're asking, Mr. Douglas, is that we should write you a blank cheque. I don't think you'd do it yourself.'

Douglas swung on him.

'What I'm asking is an expression of your confidence in my ability to carry this through. What I'm suggesting is that you get out of your comfy chair and into the streets and the public halls and do some work for a change. Man, you've had your day of dreaming . . . your years of it. If you don't see the need for action, you're a fool, and if you're not prepared to do some work you've no business being in the Party. You're just so much dead wood.'

Campbell sneered and crushed out his cigarette.

'Oh . . . fine words! And you expect us to support you, when you've made it clear you don't even trust us?'

'I do.'

'It's asking a lot,' said Donald Gunn.

'Far too bloody much,' said Campbell. 'I wouldn't touch it with a barge-pole.'

'Great God almighty!' cried Liam Macquillan. 'What did a man with the name of Campbell ever do to deserve to be trusted?'

'Gentlemen!'

'Och, gentlemen! There's none of us gentlemen! It's a damned English insult to be given the name.'

'Please . . . Macquillan. This is no——'

'All right. But I want to say this. You'll get nothing done as a yammering, useless Committee. What we've needed and never had is a leader. Now you've got one in front of you, you don't even recognise the fact. And there's no reason for him to tell us anything at all about his plans. Why should he? Get this into your heads, the lot of you. He doesn't need us . . . but, by God, we need him.'

'Have you finished?' demanded Haig icily.

Liam sat back in disgust.

'Yes, I'm finished . . . for the moment.'

Douglas stood up.

54

'There's been enough talk,' he said. 'I want to know just one thing. Who's with me?'

'Just a minute,' said Haig. 'You're infringing my function as Chairman.'

'Then I apologise. But, as Chairman, you'd better put it to the vote.'

Haig looked at him with frank dislike. He had ceased to care what his wife might think. The tenuous connection with wealth that was unlikely to rub off was less important than the reality of his present power. He would cling to that, such as it was, to the bitter end.

'I don't need to be told my job,' he said harshly. 'I'll put it to the vote and let you see how little support your ill-advised idea is likely to get from us.'

'Do that,' said Douglas.

'And I'll put it in the form of a motion. Are you ready, Secretary?'

Cameron nodded.

'Yes.'

Haig cleared his throat.

'Take it down, then. That this Committee is prepared to support the unspecified proposals of Mr. Douglas, with the aim of setting up a Scottish Parliament according to his broad definition. Have you got that?'

'I've got it.'

It's hopeless, thought Ewan. It always was. The Party's like a thrawn old man who won't die.

Haig looked confidently round the table.

'Right,' he said. 'Let's have it. Those in favour?'

He looked at the five raised hands and a pulse began to beat in his temples. It was narrower than he had expected. Too narrow.

'Record the names,' he said grimly. 'James Douglas, William Bain, Liam Macquillan, Gavin Hamilton and Calum Macrae.'

'I have them,' said Ewan.

'Those against?'

James Douglas looked at Norman Graham, but he avoided his eyes and raised his hand with the rest.

55

'And those names, too,' said Haig. 'You know them all. Five votes for and five against. The motion defeated by the Chairman's casting vote.'

Douglas pushed back his chair.

'Right,' he said. 'There's been enough time wasted. If the four of you are free, we'll go up to my office and get on with it.'

A slow smile crossed Willie Bain's face as he rose.

'Man, Liam,' he said, 'I never thought I'd live to see the day.'

Ewan Cameron quietly put his papers together and screwed the cap on his pen. He pushed the file across the table.

'You'll want to keep these, Mr. Haig, until you can appoint a new Secretary.'

'What do you mean?'

'I'm joining Mr. Douglas,' he said, and turned away.

Haig felt the blood surge through the swelling vessels of his brain, blurring his vision. He leaned forward, fighting to free his voice from the band that was tightening on his throat.

'If you do,' he hissed, through lips that scarcely parted, 'I'll break you, Cameron. You're a teacher. I'll see that the Education Authority deal with you in a way that——'

Douglas moved.

'You won't.' The words slashed through to Haig's diminished awareness. 'If there's any blackmail from you, it'll not be Cameron who's broken.'

Haig stared at him, held by the unfamiliar, cold, blue eyes. It was Liam Macquillan who ended the moment, and his grin had gone.

'Aye,' he said soberly. 'There'll be more than blackmail before this is done.'

*   *   *

The soft south-west wind came up the Firth from Ireland and the ocean, lifted over the green dome of Ailsa Craig, whistled through the broken teeth of the high rocks of Arran and funnelled into the river valley to sigh in the rigging of the empty, restless, freshly painted yachts, tugging them taut on their moorings, lingering there, sorrowing at the mid-week absence of white sails and blowing sadly on to the city to stir the hair of steel-erectors and young, spring-pretty girls and snatch the smoke from James Douglas's pipe as he stood in the wide-open window of his office, surveying the day.

'Good morning, sir,' said Sally happily as she entered. 'Isn't it lovely?'

'Perfect.' He turned and saw the brightness of the morning in her eyes and the bloom that the moist wind had put on her skin. 'You shouldn't be here on a day like this,' he said. 'You should be out in the country. Or lying on the deck of a boat with a man you love and the day ahead of you.'

She laughed.

'I'm a working girl. I've got to keep that for weekends.'

'It wouldn't be so bad if that was true,' he said, and watched her arrange the papers on his desk. 'Every decent man in the city must be blind.'

'Blind or married,' she said. 'Like yourself. Anyway, I hope you don't mind, but I opened the windows right up to clear the air. I don't know what you were doing last night, but I could hardly see across the room when I came in.' She wrinkled her nose. 'Thick! It was like an Argyle Street pub at closing time.'

He chuckled.

'A committee meeting,' he said. 'Half a committee, anyway.'

She picked up a flattened scarlet cushion and plumped it out.

'I thought it must have been a ceilidh ... by the smell of it.'

He grimaced.

'Oh, oh! Disapproval.'

'No! Not from me. You know that. But it must have gone on all night, judging from the ash-trays.'

'Five o'clock,' he said, 'and the dawn just breaking. It's the right time for a meeting to end.'

'Five o'clock!' She looked at him in horror. 'And it's just nine now. Och, you should have phoned me. You could have had a long lie. Your first appointment's not till eleven. You'll be worn out.'

57

'I'm not,' he said, 'and there's nobody more surprised than me. There must be life in the old dog yet.'

'Not so old.'

'Old enough, Sally. And getting older too fast. Anyway ... who's at eleven?'

'Mr. Anderson.'

'You found him?'

She nodded.

'After about an hour on the phone. When the *Glasgow Daily* folded, he got a job as a sub-editor on the *Citizen*——'

'A sub.?'

'So they said. Anyway, he was only there six months. He went as Features Editor to the *Manchester Weekly News*——'

'God help him.'

'—left them after another six months, got some sort of job with the Odhams group, stayed there for a year and then disappeared.'

'Disappeared?'

'Completely. I only found him because I thought he'd probably at least exchange Christmas cards with some of his old staff. So I started phoning other people who'd been on the *Daily* with him. I got his address from a compositor who's now with Outram's. He's running a hen-farm at Cottingham, not far from Hull.'

'Good God!' Douglas crossed to his desk and sat down. 'And that's another good example of how we treat our talent when it's over forty. What did he say?'

'Well, I said what you told me to say, and he didn't say anything. Just that he'd be up on the night train.'

'Good enough,' said Douglas appreciatively. 'That was a stout effort, Sally. You're sure you don't want the rest of the day off?'

She laughed and moved towards her door.

'Not me! I've got work to do.'

'Well, before you go ... two things. First, tell Roderick Grant in Publicity I'd like to see him at ten-thirty. Then bring me all the Scottish telephone directories ... and the London one. And there's a third thing. Give me an outside line that doesn't go through the switch-board downstairs. Right?'

'Right,' she said and left, wondering for the umpteenth time since his return from Spain what he was up to now. She felt reasonably sure that it had nothing to do with any of the firm's existing interests, varied as these were. And he would tell her in his own good time, for he always did. But it still was hell not to know.

Before Roderick Grant arrived, Douglas spent a busy and profitable hour or so on the telephone. He had just put the receiver down when Sally gave her soft double-knock.

'That's Mr. Grant,' she said. 'Will I tell him to wait or——'

'No, I'm finished. Just this minute. Let's have him in.' He grinned. 'Now, there's a man who's not married. And a good-looking chap, too.'

'Yes, I know,' she said frankly. 'I thought about him.'

'Well!'

He looked at her in surprise.

'I did. Really. But you know what it's like on this publicity-public relations business. You've got to be nice to people. The trouble is, he'd be too nice to too many too often.'

'Oh, surely not?'

'But he would. He couldn't help himself. It's the way he's made.'

'Well, I don't know. I think you're maligning him. I'd give him a chance, if I were you. He's good at his job.'

'Too good at the wrong job for a wife's peace of mind,' she said. 'Anyway . . . I'll send him in.'

As Douglas waited, he decided she was probably right. Grant was intelligent, able and shrewd, but he had a light easy charm that he could no more discard than his skin. He would give a wife many a restless wondering evening.

Now he was smiling, a twisted attractive smile that made his white teeth seem more even than ever.

'Good morning, sir.'

'Good morning, Grant.' He gestured to a chair. 'Have a seat.'

'Thank you.' He sat down, crossed his legs and slid out his cigarette case with the swift smooth elegance that characterised all his movements. 'Do you mind if I smoke?'

'Not me,' said Douglas. 'You can't compete with this infernal machine.' He tapped his pipe. 'One question to start with. What are your politics?'

Grant showed no surprise.

'None,' he said. 'That's not one of my vices.'

'You're thirty-eight,' said Douglas. 'You must have some ideas on the subject.'

'Only mistrust of all politicians, past, present and likely to be.'

'No exceptions?'

'One or two. Churchill, with one or two reservations. Gaitskell, probably. Tom Johnston, certainly.'

Douglas looked at him quickly.

'Tom Johnston?'

'Well, he was before my time, really. But from all I've heard, he was one of the few honest men with guts in politics this century.'

'Uh-huh. No party loyalties?'

'None.'

'Any loyalties at all?'

Grant grinned.

'Oh, yes.'

'What are they?'

'Myself, my job, my employer and money.'

'In that order?'

'More or less.'

'Mm.' Douglas grunted. 'Well, I've a proposition to put to you. But I want to make two points first. You're completely free to turn it down if you like and I won't hold it against you. Secondly, you must not, under any circumstances, breathe a word about this to anybody. If you do, you'll be fired on the spot.'

Grant looked politely offended.

'I told you I was loyal to my employer,' he said. 'You're my employer.'

'All right,' said Douglas, and swiftly outlined his plans. As he listened, Roderick Grant's controlled poise diminished as his interest grew. At the end, his long fingers carefully stubbed out his cigarette.

'Quite a job, sir.'

'Quite a job,' agreed Douglas.

'And where do I come into it?'

'If you want to, you come in to run publicity and take charge of all press and public relations. And that, I'm sure you realise, will be no small job. You'll be given accommodation and whatever staff you need. You'll be given a budget, and you'd better have good reasons for exceeding it. You'll be taken out of your present department for as long as is necessary, probably between one and three years, and you'll be paid by me, not by the firm, but I'll see that all your pension rights are unaffected. You'll be directly responsible to me alone, or, under certain circumstances, to my appointed deputy whom you'll hear about later. Now, the only other person who'll concern you closely is an appointment not yet confirmed, so we'll leave that for the moment. And the detail can wait too. But I want to know now . . . or by five o'clock today at the latest . . . are you interested?'

'Yes,' said Roderick Grant.

'Good.'

'There's just one thing. Forgive me for mentioning it——'

'Yes, I know. Salary.'

'It's . . . not unimportant.'

'No, I agree. You don't need to be bashful. You're on two thousand five hundred at the moment. You'll go up to three. And when you come back in here, you'll stay at that or higher. Acceptable?'

'Entirely.'

'All right, then. I'll let you know when you start, but it'll be within a fortnight. And I'll tell John Clark he'll have to move somebody up to your job. So . . . any questions?'

That, thought Grant, is the most damn silly question I've ever heard.

'Yes, sir,' he said. 'Plenty. But they'd better wait until I get my ideas sorted out.'

'Right,' said Douglas. 'You can get back to your gilded cage.'

He looked at the way the well-cut jacket sat on the broad shoulders and at the lithe movement of the slim hips and decided that Sally was probably being very wise. But it was a pity. Even an adventure would do her good, if it didn't break her heart. The trouble was, she had the kind of heart that a man like Grant could break and hardly know he'd done it. When the door shut, he pressed her buzzer. She came in at once, looking slightly flustered.

'What's wrong?' he asked quickly.

She pushed back a fallen wisp of hair.

'Nothing,' she said. 'Mr. Anderson's here . . . he's early . . . and there was a funny phone call.'

'What sort of phone call?'

'From the *Daily Express*. They wanted to speak to you, but I said you were busy and then they started asking me all sorts of questions.'

'What about?'

'Well, I don't know. It didn't make sense. It didn't have anything to do with the company, anyway, I'm sure of that. But there was something about a political meeting and had you really walked out and were you splitting the Party and . . . oh, a whole lot of things. So I said I knew nothing about it . . . well, I don't . . . but they didn't believe me and——'

'They tried to pump you?'

'Well, yes . . . they did a bit.'

Somebody's talked, thought Douglas grimly. Haig, Campbell or Ross. Probably Campbell. But they're quick off the mark, just the same. And it means Grant will have to start sooner. Monday, at the latest.

'All right,' he said. 'If any other newspapers call, put them through to me.' He smiled at her expression and spoke gently. 'Yes, there's something going on, Sally. I'll tell you about it one of these days, but you're not involved. If anything out of the ordinary comes your way, pass the buck right up to the top. You're not being paid to fight off this particular lot of wolves. Will you do that?'

'Yes, sir,' said Sally, feeling, for some unimaginable reason, distinctly relieved.

'Fine. Off you go, then, and ask Mr. Anderson to come in. And bring in some tea whenever you like.'

He met Anderson half-way to the door and gripped his

hand. The palm was rough, as it had not been before.

'Jock,' he said. 'Man, it's good to see you. It's been a long time.'

'Four years,' said Anderson, 'and you haven't changed a bit.'

And I can't say the same for you, thought Douglas. The long, intelligent face was leaner and more craggy than ever, the hair more grey, the skin looser between his neck and chin. And the suit he wore was clean and well-cut, but no amount of care could have hidden the age of it. He felt sudden anger at the men who had taken over the old *Daily* and then killed it with such little thought for those whose life and livelihood it was.

'Sit down, Jock,' he said. 'You'll be tired. And Sally'll bring in a cup of tea.' He pressed the buzzer. 'You met Sally?'

'I met her just now, but I remember her. She was here . . . in the old days.'

'She's been here for ten years. And she's first class. I couldn't get better.'

'She must be first class or she'd never have found me,' said Anderson, almost regretfully. 'I thought I'd covered my tracks pretty well.'

'So you did,' said Douglas, and looked round as the door clicked. 'You gave her a difficult time of it. Didn't he, Sally?'

She glanced at the older man with the smile she kept for those she liked, and put the tray on the desk.

'Och, well,' she said, 'I found him. That's the main thing. And I brought some sandwiches in case you'd come hungry off the train. Is that all right?'

'It's fine,' said Anderson appreciatively and smiled back at her, but stiffly, tightly, as though the movement was only half-remembered.

'See what I mean?' said Douglas, when she had gone.

'Aye. I see what you mean.'

He poured the tea for them both, pushed Anderson's cup across and set the plate of sandwiches near to him. There was no need to ask if the man wanted food, for the true hunger-gleam was there in his eye. He looked away.

'And why did you bother to cover your tracks, Jock?'

Anderson looked at him over the rim of the cup.

'Where are the bodies of all the dead birds?' he asked, and drank till Douglas thought he could see the warmth of it reaching right through to his pale skin. Then he said—'I'm like them, James. I didn't fancy dying in public.'

Douglas looked up with quick concern.

'But you're not ill, are you?'

'No, I'm not ill. Not ill, not well. Not dead, not alive. I'm surviving, though. And I suppose I should be grateful, but I'm not even that.'

'A bad time, Jock?' said Douglas softly.

'Bad enough,' said Anderson. 'But it's my own fault, so I'm not going to girn about it.'

'How is it your own fault?'

'Pride, I suppose.' He took another sandwich. 'If I could have contented myself as a sub., or writing trash for the pulp magazines, I'd have managed all right. But I couldn't go back, James. I couldn't take orders from men who haven't even begun to learn their job. And I couldn't stand all the kowtowing that goes on, all the yes sir, no sir, three bags full sir. It made me want to puke. In my day, it was ability that mattered, not your accent or who you knew. Och, it might have been different if I'd been younger. But you can't have your career and get to the top, James, and then go back to the bottom and start all over again. It's not humanly possible.'

'So what did you do?'

Douglas filled his cup.

'Quit,' said Anderson bitterly. 'Ran away. And that was pride too, I suppose. I covered my tracks and went where nobody knew me. I started a hen farm . . . in a small way, but it was all I could afford . . . and hens are maybe stupid birds, but they're a joy to work with compared to some folk I could name. And they've a better idea of an honest day's work. Anyway, there it is. A potted version of the decline and fall of Jock Anderson. If you're interested.'

Douglas felt thankful that he had got him in time. A little later would have been too late.

'I'm interested,' he said. 'And you might as well finish the sandwiches. There's no good leaving one.'

Anderson took it without arguing and looked at him curiously.

'And why would you be interested?'

Douglas smiled.

'Well, that's not quite true. I'm not so much interested in your past as I am in your future.'

Anderson was suspicious at once.

'I'm not needing any help, if that's what you mean. Just because we're old friends doesn't mean that——'

'Come off it, Jock,' said Douglas. 'Your pride'll choke you one of these days. You got my message, didn't you?'

'I got your message all right, but what brought me up was sheer curiosity to know what it meant. "I need your help." What kind of message is that to get from James Douglas, who doesn't need anybody's help and never did?'

'But that's where you're wrong,' said Douglas bluntly. 'I've needed help all my life. I wouldn't be where I am without it. And the fact that I've paid for it doesn't alter anything. This time it's your help I need and I'm prepared to pay for that too. So don't get the idea I'm handing out any favours. I'm asking them.'

'Oh, aye,' said Anderson tolerantly. 'You're a great talker, James. Always were. But you'll need to surpass yourself to convince me there's anything I can do for you.'

'All right,' said Douglas. 'I need an editor——'

'An editor!'

'Just a minute . . . I need a top-class, experienced man to take complete charge of a newspaper. Starting salary, three thousand five hundred. The job's vacant. Make me out a short leet.'

Anderson hesitated, then laughed.

'Och, you're an awful man! What paper have you gone and bought?'

'None. I'm starting one.'

The laugh died quickly and he sat up straight.

'Then you're senile,' he said. 'You're crazy. With newsprint the price it is? And wages? And the competition from the big groups? No, no, James. If you want to lose every penny you've ever made, you're going the right way about it. It's a psychiatrist you need. Not me.'

Douglas suppressed a grin as he watched the man come back to life.

'All right, Jock,' he said. 'If you're not interested, we'll just leave it.'

'Well, I mean, have you gone into it at all? Have you any idea what you're taking on?'

'Oh, I think so.'

'Och, you can't have! Look.' He leaned forward. 'Take staff. What staff have you got?'

'None,' said Douglas simply.

'None! Holy Mary! When is this . . . this broad-sheet supposed to start?'

'A fortnight next Monday. The twenty-sixth.'

'Great God above! And it's the seventh today. Two and a half weeks!' He sat back. 'You're out of your mind.'

'Well, it's a bit neat for time,' said Douglas.

'Neat! Look. Staff. Do you imagine for a moment you can just go down to the Labour Exchange and say . . . please, I want the complete personnel for a newspaper . . . just like that? Do you?'

'No,' admitted Douglas. 'But a good twenty or thirty from the *Daily* never found a job. They were a bit like yourself, I suppose. Just a wee bit too old. I thought if you could get hold of them, it would be a good nucleus of trained men for you to build on.'

Anderson's eyes narrowed.

'By God, I was right when I said you hadn't changed,' he said slowly. 'You're still an old bastard.'

'Of course, it's a big job,' said Douglas. 'I know that. And you're maybe not up to it. I mean, physically. And if you say it can't be done in the time . . . well, that's that. You're the expert. Anyway, there's not much point in pursuing it, if you're not interested.'

'You're not only an old bastard,' said Anderson. 'You're an old twister. I didn't say it couldn't be done and I didn't say I wasn't interested. I said you were out of your mind and I still

66

say it. But I've always been interested in insanity. So what's the big idea?'

Douglas grinned and settled himself in his chair.

'I'll tell you,' he said.

CHAPTER FOUR

ANNE DOUGLAS lay in her bed and stretched her contented naked body and listened to the bells that rang over the Sabbath-sleepy city.

'Wet or dry?' she murmured drowsily.

'Neither.' Peter Colquhoun turned back from the window. 'Damn, dreich and dismal.' He yawned. 'Oh, well. We should worry.'

Through half-closed eyes, she watched him stretch, rising on his toes, extending his long lean legs, his abdomen held indrawn and rigid beneath the strong expanding muscles of his chest, his head thrown back under his ruffled soft black hair, his arm upraised, his only arm, straight and strong and slender to the tips of his five feeling fingers.

'Peter,' she said gently.

He came to her on quietly padding feet. He bent over her, smiling.

'Oh, to be in Glasgow, now that spring is here. Damp and dreich and dismal, full of Sabbath cheer. City, once with promise, promise unfulfilled, where has all the life gone? Has laughter, too, been killed?'

'Darling.'

She slid the sheet down over the creamy skin of her firm breasts until the white edge of it bisected the rose-pink aureolas of her nipples and held out her arms to him. He sat beside her, his fingers cool and moving, and, though he had just left her, she shivered again at the nearness of him, shivered as if with cold under the whorls of transient bliss that his fingers drew on her expectant body.

'There's more,' he said. 'Better than that. Do you want to hear it?'

'Of course I do!'

'All right.' His fingers found her hand on the hem of the sheet and gently freed it. 'In this little flatlet, all that matters lies. Hope and youth and beauty, in you survives. Though the sun has vanished and the mist has come, warmth and sunshine linger ... on your flat tum.' He whipped the sheet from the bed to the other side of the room and laughed aloud. 'Tum of the morning! Beautiful tum!'

'Peter!' she cried in protest. 'Peter, you horror! I'll get cold!'

'You won't.' And he was beside her, all the six warm and wanting feet of him, enfolding her. 'You won't, will you?'

'No! No, I won't.'

'And you have a marvellous tum. I've told you——'

'Yes, you've told me.'

'And I love you.'

'I know. Oh, Peter, please——'

'Anne.'

She lay in the grey Sunday morning light and the church bells were still. Her arms lifted and fell with his quiet breathing. Beyond his head, she could see the silver-framed photograph of her father on the walnut escritoire which was the one piece of furniture she had brought from home and she thought ... I should get up.

From home. How long did it have to be, what did you have to do, before it ceased to be home? What did this place lack, when you had planned and furnished every corner of it, lived in it, slept in it, loved in it? If you could buy an aerosol of home and spray the rooms with roots and memories and deep, warm, inexpressible sensations of unfocussed yearning ... would that do? Or would you want to run away again? From what, to what?

She stroked her finger-tips over the fine down of his back and thought ... this is home. A man. Not place, not time. This man in any place or time.

She looked where there was no arm and the scar tissue was still pink and shiny, like a new-born child. And puckered round the edges, like an old man's mouth. And from that pink and puckered place had sprung the mate of the arm which bore

68

the hand which held her breast. She saw it now, lying where it would lie for ever, fleshless, skeletal palm upturned to the sun which could never reach it through the high jungle roof, white bones shining in the deep leaf-shadow, and, lost and invisible beside them, the missing part of Peter.

Involuntarily, her muscles tensed and he stirred.

'I'm not asleep,' he said.

She smiled at the ceiling.

'I know. You never sleep.'

'I do ... sometimes. But I'd rather be awake.' His lips moved into the hollow of her neck. 'Asleep, there's nothing. Awake, there's everything.'

'Everything?'

'Everything.'

If that were true, she thought. If only that were true.

'No. That's not true.'

'What isn't?'

'Asleep, there's nothing. Asleep, there are dreams.'

'Still?'

'Still.'

'And awake?'

'Awake, it's all right.'

'Honestly?'

'Honestly.' She felt him withdraw and turned her head and he was smiling at her from the white pillow. 'Especially awake, and here, and now.'

'I know,' she said. 'For me, too.'

His hand moved from her breast and curved to the curve of her cheek. His eyes had the dark, far look which came sometimes, which she half-loved, half-dreaded, wondering what lay hidden in the hurt, healing places of his mind. His lips moved.

'Dónde está mi corazón? Entre los brazos de tuyo. Dónde está mi vida? Entre los muslos de tuyo. Dónde están las palabras ... que cantaban ... en mi alma? Entre los labios de tuyo.'

She laid her brow on his.

'Peter.'

'Bad poetry,' he said. 'Bad Spanish.'

'I like it.'

69

'You don't speak Spanish.'

'The sound of it.'

'Yes.' He rolled on to his back, wide-eyed. 'The sound of it, the look of it, the feel of it. For you, the feel of it. For me, the look of it. I'm a better poet in paint. The only trouble is, it's a minority opinion. A minority of one.'

'Two.'

'Yes. Two.'

They lay silent.

'I should get up,' said Anne.

'It's Sunday.'

'But I'm going to Gartland for lunch.'

'Oh, hell! Are you? And I brought a bottle of wine.'

'It'll keep. And I have to go. I haven't seen them since they came back from Spain.'

'Which was it? Costa Brava or Costa del Sol?'

'Neither,' she said. 'And that's not fair. You don't know Daddy.'

'No. I don't, do I?'

She looked at him.

'You can if you want to,' she said.

'I know.' She watched his face harden. 'But I don't want to. The one-armed bandit. Your money or your daughter. Or both. Preferably both.'

The sick feeling came back.

'It wouldn't be like that.'

'It would look like that.'

'Not to Daddy.'

'It did to your brother.'

'But he's different.'

'Yes.' He swung his legs from the bed and stood up. 'And I really mean, no. He's not different. We are. You said so yourself. They put him in the mould when they took him out of the womb and eighteen or twenty years later ... hey presto! Ready for public exhibition, a flawless production, straight out the sausage machine, programmed to think, act and talk according to the punch-holes on the in-put tape. For example. Exhibit ... one crippled artist, poised before canvas, brush in his solitary hand. Reaction ... good God! What an odd-

70

looking, anti-social type. Speech ... glad to meet you. Thoughts ... what the hell do you think you're doing, hanging around my sister? The whole thing automatic. Like that.' He clicked his fingers and flicked his string vest from the chair. 'Oh, believe me. Our system had conditioning taped generations before Pavlov or Marx were born.'

She leapt from the bed and ran to him.

'But he's not like that! Not really. All that's just on the surface. I know him. Underneath, he's just——'

She stopped. He tilted her face up to his own and smiled.

'Like you and me?' he asked gently. 'No, darling. That I don't believe.'

She clung to him until the mesh of the string vest began to hurt her skin. Then she drew back.

'No,' she said. 'He's not like us. I admit that. But he's not like what you said either. And Daddy really is different.'

'Yes,' he said, and started the slow, still difficult process of buttoning his shirt. 'Daddy's different. I know. All God's children are different. Only some are more different than others. Us, for example.'

She turned away.

'I wish you wouldn't——'

'I said us. Not just me.' She stopped. 'It's a step forward, isn't it?' His arm circled her waist from behind, his chin sank to her shoulder. 'Isn't it?'

She held her cheek to his.

'Yes, Peter. It's a step forward.' Gently, she released herself. 'I've got to go.'

'I know.'

'And I won't be late.'

'Which means?'

'Nine o'clock? All right?'

'All right.'

She kissed him quickly.

'I'll have an in-and-out bath, and I'll wear ... what'll I wear? Oh ... I know! I'll wear my silk tweed thing. You know. The suit with the skirt that you thought was marvellous. That'll really shake Julia.' He smiled. 'What are you smiling at? You did think it was marvellous, didn't you?'

71

'Yes, I did,' he said. 'I wasn't smiling at that. I was just thinking ... when you're different, you can get such a terrific kick out of pretending you're not.'

*   *   *

Julia opened her jewel case.

'Will Anne be there?'

'As far as I know.' Archie adjusted his breast-pocket hand-kerchief before the mirror. 'Why?'

'It has a bearing.'

'On what?'

'On what I wear.'

He turned to her.

'But I thought you said ... oh, you mean jewellery. But what the devil does it matter whether Anne's there or not? Wear whatever you like.'

'No, dear.' She lifted the trays out one by one. 'That's the sad part about being a woman. You're very rarely able to wear what you like. Or do what you like, for that matter. Today, for instance.'

Archie paused, then lifted his wallet and checked its contents. This was it. The end of yet another little honeymoon was now in sight. But it had lasted almost a week. One mustn't complain. That was at least three days longer than usual. And now, for two or three months, things would return to normal. They would be very correct to each other, exceedingly polite, considerate in the presence of witnesses, avoiding mutual abuse or cloaking it in smooth words even in private, eating at opposite ends of the long table and sleeping apart, living the normal life that became more and more intolerable each year. He thrust the wallet savagely into his pocket and smothered what felt dangerously like the onset of anger, for there was no point in getting angry with Julia. Anything so uncontrollable had no chance against her diamond-hard defences.

'It's a filthy day,' he said. 'I shouldn't think the tow will be working.'

She held a necklace round her rather-too-long, rather-too-slim throat, considered it, rejected it.

'That isn't really the point, dear, is it?'

72

'What is the point?'

'Just that I have to trot along and be nice to your family, whether I want to or not.'

'Is that so hard?'

She turned to him, smiling.

'But of course not, dear! They're charming.' She held a piece of carved, polished wood, pendant on its thin, gold chain, so that it hung above the cleft of her small breasts. 'And I shall wear this.'

He looked at it.

'Well ... please yourself. But I still don't see why you should worry about——'

'Worry?' She raised her dark, symmetrical eyebrows in pseudo-surprise. 'I'm not worried, darling. Just getting a little tired of your sister criticising my jewellery.'

'Anne? Surely she doesn't——?'

'Not in words, I quite agree. But she seems to think that being vaguely connected with art gives her some sort of right to express her criticism with her very expressive eyes. So ... I shall wear this, because it's the sort of thing she might have worn herself.' She turned, posing her head. 'You like it?'

He shrugged his shoulders.

'It's ... all right.'

'It's ghastly, actually, but Anne will love it and be madly jealous and that's the main thing. Well ... let's see if that girl's got Jamie ready. And could you bring the car round?'

He watched her long, provoking legs carry her across the wide, close-carpeted landing towards the nursery and sighed. Damn, he thought. Damn, damn, damn.

In the garage, which had once been the stables, he patted the Lotus lovingly.

'Not today,' he said. 'Tomorrow. If I can't find a good reason for a nice long trip to somewhere far away, I'm losing my touch.'

He drove the bottle-green Mercedes round to the front door and sat smoking at the wheel with the window open on the mild moist morning. The sea was flat and grey where it lapped the shingle, the mist low on the water, almost hiding the motionless abandoned boats.

And this is one summer when there will be mighty little sailing, he thought. Mighty little anything, except work. Which is maybe just as well. And if she still insists on going to Rome . . . all right. She can go alone. I'd rather have a wet summer in Helensburgh than a month of riotous living in Rome, with Julia in a bitchy mood. And it couldn't be a month, anyway, in Rome or anywhere else, if the old man meant what he said. More like a weekend at Turnberry.

He rubbed a yellow duster over the instrument panel and felt better, just thinking about the implications of what his father had said. If it meant more work, it also meant more independence of action, more opportunity to implement his own ideas, a chance to show certain top-line executives that when the time came he would run the show by reason of his own ability and not just because he happened to be his father's son.

And more work would mean less time to worry about Julia, less time to feel the emptiness that her attitude left in his life.

He heard the front-door click and looked round. Oonagh, the Irish nanny, was making last-minute adjustments to Jamie's sporran. He watched her feminine unfussy movements with a kind of sadness.

She had been with them for a year, yet her presence was as disturbing now as it had been in the beginning. When he had heard that the new nanny was Irish, he had half-expected some thick-ankled peasant girl, potato-fat and freckled. Instead, he had found Oonagh, darkly elegant, light-hearted, with a muted Dublin accent and a flair for clothes. And more than that. Much more. She had all the warmth and femininity and gentleness that Julia lacked. Even he, clinging to his illusions, could not fail to see it. And Jamie adored her.

Had that not been so, Julia would have found some good reason for getting rid of her long before now. She was not normally tolerant of rival suns. But she remained, to diminish the inconvenience of the boy's presence during his holidays from prep. school and to remind Archie of the emptiness.

'There you are then, Jamie,' he heard her say. 'On you go to your Dad. And be a good boy at your Grandpa's.'

74

Archie smiled at her and opened the rear door.

'Where's Mummy?' he asked.

'Talking to cook,' said Jamie. 'And she's wearing a funny bit of wood round her neck.'

'I know,' said Archie. 'I saw it.'

'Why is she wearing it?'

'Well ... because it looks nice, I suppose. You know. Like your sporran.'

'My sporran's for keeping pennies in,' said Jamie. 'I've got threepence in it already.' He shook it happily. 'Do you think Grandpa Douglas'll give me half a crown! He did last time.'

'I don't know,' said Archie, 'but if you ask him for one, you'll catch it. You don't ask people for money.'

'Oh, I hope he does,' said Jamie. 'Grandpa Fletcher never gives me more than sixpence.'

'And quite enough too,' said Archie dishonestly.

Grandpa Fletcher, Sir Charles Fletcher, shipbuilder and mean, old skinflint, was a widower whose one extravagance in the old days had been the adornment of his daughter. And even that had not been so much an extravagance as an investment, a question of aiming for a higher price by offering the goods in an attractive wrapping. When her engagement to the Douglas heir had been announced, his friends had grudgingly conceded that the policy had paid off. Prices didn't go any higher.

Archie, knowing now where the gingerbread stopped and the gilt began, saw her appear in the doorway and switched on the ignition.

'All right?' he asked, when she was seated.

'Yes, of course.'

He let the Mercedes coast down the curving drive to the road.

'Daddy, let's go by the shore road,' said Jamie. 'I want to see the ships at the Tail of the Bank.'

'We're going by the glen,' said Julia. 'Balloch's bad enough, without having to drive through all these sordid places in the Vale of Leven.'

'But I want to see the ships.'

'Don't argue, Jamie, or you'll go straight back home.'

'The shore road's a bit longer and we're late as it is,' said Archie. 'We haven't really got time.'

'But I want to see the——'

'Now——' She swung round. 'Not another word.'

Archie met his son's eyes in the driving mirror and watched his face crumple. The delimiting sign flicked by. He shifted down a gear and accelerated and held the drift of the car on the first bend of the hill. Julia snapped her lighter.

'We may be late,' she said, 'but this isn't Silverstone.'

'No,' said Archie, and watched the speedometer needle climb round the dial.

*   *   *

'Well, I must say you're both looking marvellously well,' said Julia. 'Don't you think so?'

'Yes, I do,' said Anne, and turned from watching the dove-grey mist rising from the dripping hill. 'Can I put this somewhere?'

'Anywhere, dear,' said her mother. 'Are you sure you don't want some more?'

'No, thank you, Mummy.'

She put her empty coffee cup beside the photograph of Archie at the age of four and thought . . . I wasn't born then. Neither was Peter. Peter was a foetus, with two foetal arms growing into an unequal future. And Archie was a little boy in a kilt, stopping to look at a box Brownie and running on, towards wealth and Julia and God knows what. She sat down by the window and smoothed the silk tweed over her crossed thighs. When she looked up, she caught the flicker of irritation on Julia's face before it vanished.

'Are you going away?' asked Julia.

'I don't know,' said Anne. 'I may do.'

'But surely? I mean, you can't possibly not go.' She laughed. 'Heavens! I couldn't bear it. The very idea of spending the whole spring and summer in Glasgow!'

'I don't mind it.'

'Don't you?'

'No,' said Anne. 'I rather like it. And anyway, my work is here.'

76

And other things, thought Archie. He cursed himself again for ever telling Julia about his meeting with Peter. She would be discreet, maybe, but only as long as it suited her. When she needed the weapon of her knowledge, she would use it. And she could be very patient when she wished. Now, she was looking politely puzzled.

'Your work? Oh yes, of course. I keep forgetting.'

'All the same, dear, you should have a holiday,' said Margaret. She felt vaguely worried, wondering why her daughter was so quiet and withdrawn. For she seemed well enough. And contented, too, in a funny sort of way. Perhaps there was a boy. It would be nice if there was, nice if she would get married, and settle down, and have children soon, before Jamie was too old to play with his cousins. 'You really need a holiday,' she said.

'She does not.' James Douglas emerged from a fantasy in which he had treated his daughter-in-law as she deserved, as old Fletcher should have treated her years ago when her bare bott had no sexual connotation. 'No healthy person does. I've enjoyed many a holiday in my time, but I've never needed one. I just went to please you.'

'Oh, James! You did not.'

'Well ... maybe not entirely. But all the same, if you enjoy your work, you don't want to go away and leave it just to sit in the sun and get bored. Isn't that right?'

'That's right,' said Anne.

'Any word from that chap in Holland? What's his name? Blumen-something.'

She looked at him quickly. The capacity of his memory still kept surprising her.

'Hans Bloemendael,' she said. 'No, Daddy. Not really.'

'It's about time there was, isn't it? I mean, this is April.'

'Yes, I know. But I think it'll be all right. It's just ... there's nothing definite.'

'But you think they're going ahead?'

'I think so, yes.'

'Fair enough,' said Douglas.

'Hey, listen,' said Archie. 'What's all this about? Have you been holding out on me?'

77

'And who is Hans Bloemendael?' murmured Julia, thinking how satisfactory it would be if Anne married some dull, industrious Dutchman and vanished to live in one of those busy little towns with utterly unpronounceable names.

'I haven't been holding out on you,' said Anne. 'I just haven't seen you. And Hans . . . well, I don't know what you'd call him. He's a kind of art dealer, I suppose. But he writes books and criticism and things about sculpture.'

'Really?' said Julia, and lost interest. He didn't sound like a serious rival for the armless, absurdly romantic character whom Archie had met. For he really was absurd. Long hair and one arm and paint stains on his trousers. Just too fictional for words. And so like Anne to get her sex and her maternal instincts confused.

She looked speculatively at her sister-in-law and wondered if she paid him an allowance, or subsidised his keep, or what? And did she do his washing? She probably did. It was all rather sordid, and laughable, and tremendously good luck that Archie had come out with it. It made putting up with his clumsy attentions for a day or two well worth while. She smiled comfortably to herself and felt that everything was really very satisfactory. She would move back to her other room tonight and that would be that, at least until Rome. Or longer, if she felt like being difficult. Sooner or later, he would have to learn that, although he would one day rule the Douglas empire, at home he would have no power at all. And really, now that Jamie was away at school, it would be a kindness to make that clear quite soon. But he was still prattling on about this Dutch thing.

'I'm still none the wiser,' he said. 'What's the tie-up between you and this chap, and you think what'll be all right? Come on, Anne. Give.'

Douglas chuckled.

'You should keep in better touch with what goes on,' he said. 'You don't seem to realise you've got celebrities in the family.'

'Oh, sure,' said Archie. 'We're all very talented. But who and what in particular?'

'This man Bloemendael wants to put on an exhibition of

Anne's work in one of the Rotterdam parks right through the summer.'

'No!'

'Oh, yes.'

'But that's big stuff.'

'I know it is.'

'But in a park? You mean, outside? Lawns and flower-beds and things, with Anne's hunks of rock dotted tastefully here and there, complete with price tabs on the bottom right-hand corners?'

'More or less.' He grinned. 'I thought you'd get interested when you heard there was money in it.'

'Yes,' said Archie. 'Yes, indeed.' He looked at her reflectively. 'You're really a dark horse, aren't you?'

'But I'm not,' she protested. 'I haven't seen you since ... well, not for ages.'

'No,' said Archie, remembering when he had last seen her. 'It's some time.'

'Well, I hope it comes off,' said Margaret. 'It would be very nice for you.'

'Nice!' said Archie. 'It would be fantastic.'

'It certainly would,' said Julia.

'Nothing fantastic about it.' Douglas spoke as amiably as he could, but Julia was irritating him even more than usual. 'If you want to establish a reputation in sculpture, or painting, or anything like that, get the hell out of Scotland. We're a nation of Philistines. We'd rather have our tongues cut out than use them to praise that kind of thing. Oh, it's all right at school. Wee Johnnie's good at art. See the nice picture of a house with smoke coming out the lum. But when you've left school ... forget it. Suddenly, it's suspect, sinful, subversive, anything you like. And if you're unlucky enough to have an artist in the family ... well, it's like insanity. The last thing you do is talk about it.'

Anne laughed.

'Daddy!'

'Well, it's true. Can you see Julia admiring something you've made, going all lyrical about the form and texture and proportions, telling you how clever you are? Not in a million years.'

'That's being rather unkind,' said Julia, in a cool, level voice. Archie glanced at her apprehensively. 'I don't think you know enough about my attitude to art to comment.'

Douglas almost guffawed.

'Och away!' he said. 'You haven't got an attitude to art. Or if you have, you got it out the Sunday papers since the last time I saw you.'

'Now you're being unjust as well as unkind.'

'I'm not. It's perfectly true. And the same applies to the rest of us . . . except for Anne. We may know nothing about it, but that doesn't stop us condemning and criticising and generally crying down anybody who's mad enough to think they can earn a living by it. And as if that wasn't enough, we take it a stage further. We make damn sure they can't earn a living by it. We ignore them. We don't regard them as really socially acceptable. And we don't buy their stuff so that they can earn enough to become socially acceptable. And then we say . . . oh, what a scruffy lot! . . . and go home to our desirable, detached residence with its fitted carpets and its three-piece suite and look at the thirty-bob van Gogh print above the fireplace and think . . . how nice! Cypresses. But the last thing we think about is the poor, tormented, one-eared madman who painted it.'

Anne looked at her two hands, quiet and resting in her lap, and wondered how much he knew.

'Well, of course,' said Julia, 'I know nothing about that.'

'No, that's true enough,' said Douglas. 'The criteria for judging a picture that's to go on your walls are different. The artist has to be non-British, preferably dead, and his work should be likely to show a reasonable capital gain . . . say, five hundred per cent . . . in the next twenty years or so. And if it also happens to go with the curtains, you're in clover.'

Archie watched his wife's expression change from veiled hostility to stony hate and wondered if his father knew just what kind of fire he was lighting.

'I don't know what I've done to be attacked like this,' she said coldly, 'but I'm not going to——'

'Nothing.' Douglas interrupted her quickly. 'And you're not

being attacked. You're not even being criticised. It's the way you were brought up, just as I was brought up not to take sugar on my porridge. But the outlook for art is pretty grim in any country where the two social groups who should be interested . . . and can afford to be interested . . . have such little conception of what the word means.'

Julia looked at him down her long, straight nose.

'As far as I'm concerned, the outlook for art is utterly unimportant,' she said.

'Exactly.'

'And I think we ought to change the subject, don't you?'

Douglas paused, then shrugged his shoulders. There was enough trouble brewing without stirring up Julia. And it was Archie's problem, anyway. Or should be. But the silly ass didn't seem to realise that sooner or later she would have to be taught which side her bread was buttered on. A controlled leak of information about the state of shipbuilding in general and her father's shipyard in particular would be no bad thing.

'If you like,' he said, and picked up his pipe.

'I've been trying to for the last ten minutes,' said Anne, 'but I couldn't get a word in edgeways. It was when you said something about celebrities in the family. I mean . . . plural.'

'Ah,' said Douglas.

'Well, I know you think I am . . . and I'm not really . . . but who else?'

She saw his eyes lift to her own with a twinkle which went far back in her memory.

'Me,' he said.

Archie laughed and reached for his cigarettes, grateful that the heat was off. Julia would sit and simmer for the rest of the afternoon, but there was no need to worry about that until they got back home. Then, with luck, he could plead paper-work and dodge her till bedtime. And he suspected that there would be little, if any, contact even then, if her conduct followed the pattern which had gradually developed over the last two or three years. She would plead insomnia or some such thing and move out, to stay out until the unpredictable time when her fickle libido brought her back. The thought, which would once have been depressing, even humiliating, was now almost welcome. So he laughed and said—

'That's not news. You were a celebrity when I was in short pants.'

'When you were in short pants, I was anything but,' said Douglas. 'I was a struggling builder who hadn't even made his first hundred thousand.'

'You poor thing,' said Anne.

'I don't know how he ever survived,' said Archie sarcastically. 'Sweating over a hot cement mix day after day.'

'The younger generation won't do it,' said Anne.

'They won't,' agreed Archie. 'They're not the men their fathers were.'

'They've broken the mould,' said Anne.

'All right,' said Douglas. 'That'll do. And anyway, this is different.'

'Oh no!' cried Archie. 'Don't tell me you've gone and taken over Unilever!'

'Now you're being silly,' said his father. 'Even you and I couldn't run Unilever as a family business. And it's nothing like that. When I said celebrity, I meant celebrity. Like the ones on television.'

Archie and his sister stared at each other in disbelief.

'No!'

'Seriously?'

He nodded.

'Seriously.'

'Oh, James,' said Margaret reproachfully. 'You never told me.'

'I was saving it up as a surprise. But you don't need to look so damned astonished, the whole lot of you. It's not all that surprising.'

'A man in your position,' said Archie. 'Quite. Not really surprising at all. And when is this unique occasion?'

'A fortnight last night. Saturday, the twenty-fourth.'

'Saturday night.' Archie grinned happily. 'I can see it now. The star of our Saturday Variety, James Douglas! Assisted by ... Sally! The sleekest secretarial stripper who ever rolled a carbon between sheets!'

'Archie!' His mother looked shocked. 'That's not very nice.'

'I don't know about nice,' said Douglas, 'but it's certainly not accurate. It's a serious programme.'

'Of course,' said Archie gravely. 'It was bound to be. Which one is it? *Pulpit* or *What I Believe In*?'

'*What I Believe In*.'

Anne, who did not have a television set, saw the corners of Julia's ungenerous lips move in a brief, humourless smile and heard Archie groan.

'Oh, no! It can't be.'

Even her mother seemed disturbed.

'Why not?' asked Douglas.

'Because it's the lousiest programme they've ever put on. Production, content, speakers, the lot. It's so bad, it's a joke.'

His father puffed comfortably at his pipe.

'I know,' he said.

'But you can't know, or you'd never have agreed to appear. It's as much as your reputation's worth.' He sat forward. 'Look, Dad. For God's sake, don't, repeat don't, do it. Wait till the last minute and say you've a sore throat or any damn thing, but don't do it.'

'But I've committed myself,' said Douglas. 'I can't get out of it just like that.'

'Oh, for Pete's sake!' said Archie impatiently. 'You can get out of it if you want to. Don't tell me that goggle-box glamour has got you too.'

'I won't, because it hasn't,' said his father. 'And I'm not as daft as you seem to think. I know all about how bad it is. And so do they. That's why I've been asked to do it. They think I can turn a bad programme into a good programme and fair enough. They're probably right.'

'Like hell they are.' Archie crushed out his cigarette. 'There's no fool like an old fool just about covers it.'

'Now, Archie,' protested his mother.

'And not so old,' said his father. 'Anyway, they're happy enough and so am I. I've got a few things I've been wanting to say to the viewer audience for some time.'

'About what?'

'Wait and see. Ten-forty-five on the twenty-fourth ... if you think you can bear it.'

83

'With bag ready packed for a quick getaway,' said Archie. 'That's one Monday I won't be in the office, anyway. I wouldn't dare.'

'You'll be in the office, son,' said Douglas grimly. 'That Monday and all subsequent days thereafter. Including the month of June, when you meant to go to Rome . . . just in case you'd forgotten to mention it to Julia.'

'Oh, God, yes, I had, too.' He turned to her. 'Look, dear, I'm sorry. I completely forgot.'

It had become surprisingly easy to lie to Julia. But on this issue he had stalled since his father spoke of it, for the request for secrecy had made it rather hard to produce good reasons. Now, with a little luck, the cover story would come from Douglas himself. That hopeful thought enabled him to face his wife's coldly probing eyes with composure.

'What did you completely forget?' she asked politely.

'Just that the Rome thing was off, that's all. I can't get away.'

'Why not?'

'There's a new project,' said Douglas, who had been watching his daughter-in-law's face and thinking what a cold fish of a woman she was. But if she was going to be difficult about Rome, now was the time to straighten the matter out. Now, and in public. Judging from her expression, an explanatory session for two in the privacy of their own home would be a lacerating experience for Archie. He went on quietly. 'It's going to mean a lot of extra work for a lot of people, Archie included.'

'That's right,' said Archie gratefully. 'There's not a hope in hell of getting away this side of Christmas. But we might be able to fiddle a fortnight's skiing after the New Year.' He turned to his father. 'Don't you think so?'

'Maybe.' Douglas looked non-committal. 'It depends.'

'I had assumed that we would be doing that in any case,' said Julia. 'We always do. And I still don't see why the Rome trip should be cancelled. I thought one of the advantages of being at the top was that one could plan to go where one wished, when one wished, without having to stick to the

Glasgow Fair like a junior clerk. And if what you say is true——'

'It's true,' said Douglas, and held on to his temper.

'All right. If it is, then surely there's been bad planning somewhere?'

'Look, dear——' began Archie, but he was too hesitant. She swung on him.

'I'm speaking to your father.'

And more fool you, thought Douglas. He took a crumpled cleaner from his pocket, straightened it and began carefully to clean the stem of his pipe, a pursuit that he had always found soothing to himself, but frequently provoking to others.

'Well?' demanded Julia. 'Don't you agree?'

He eyed her reflectively.

'I was just making up my mind whether to give you an answer or a skelp,' he said.

'James,' said Margaret quietly.

'A skelp would be foolish,' said Julia.

'It would be pointless,' said Douglas. 'It's too late for that. So I will give you an answer. First, there are far more snags than advantages to being at the top, and if you haven't learned that by this time, then your father didn't get much value for his money when he paid your school fees. Second——'

'Second,' interrupted Archie, in a clear level voice which his father had occasionally heard in the office, but which was strange to everyone else in the room, including his wife. 'Second, from now on you will not comment on or criticise any aspect of the business, or generally stick your nose into it at all. Is that clear?'

Her nostrils narrowed and whitened for a moment before she laughed.

'But that's absurd! After all, I am your wife. Surely I have the right to——'

'In the business, you haven't got any rights. None. And I can't think of anyone less fit to criticise someone else's planning than you, when you know perfectly well you couldn't plan a Sunday School trip. You pay other people to plan for you. And fair enough. Why not, if you can afford it? But at least have the honesty to admit your own limitations.'

Douglas adjusted the fit of the stem to the bowl with as much concentration as if it had been a micrometer screw. The Sunday was jiggered now, all right, jiggered beyond redemption, but a sticky few hours was a small price to pay for seeing Archie don the trousers in his own home. After nine or so years, he had begun to think it would never happen. And it was just as well that Kirstie had whipped young Jamie off to the kindlier atmosphere of the kitchen, for his mother without her mask was an instructive, but unattractive sight.

'I don't care to pursue this conversation in public,' she said icily.

'You started it by criticising the planning efficiency of the business which Dad and I run. It's a family business, the family's here and you're part of the family. It can't be considered public.'

'I still don't care to pursue it.'

'I'm sure you don't, but we will, just the same. As far as the third point which calls for an answer, and that's Rome. The question of my going to Rome doesn't arise. There's nothing to discuss. But there's no reason at all why you shouldn't go alone if you want to.'

Anne saw fear and uncertainty flicker for a moment in Julia's eyes.

'Alone?'

Archie nodded. He was a little pale, and he was having some difficulty in keeping the tremor out of his voice, but he was resolved.

'Why not? You go skiing without me. You go to parties without me. I can't see any basic difference, except the length of time.'

'I see,' said Julia. She took a cigarette from the slim, gold case he had given her before they were married and held it between steady fingers. She was suddenly thoughtful, almost subdued. 'And you've quite made up your mind that you're not going?'

'I've no option. That's what you don't seem to grasp. You may think it sounds corny, but the business does come first. Without it, there wouldn't be any trip to Rome, or Davos in January, or anywhere else.'

She snapped her lighter and laughed into the smoke.

'Oh, really! Everybody goes to Rome nowadays, or Greece, or somewhere like that. Don't try to make out that this is some tremendous privilege. And anyway . . . you seem to forget that I do have money of my own.'

Douglas did not care for the change in Julia. The mask was on again, but it was a new mask, and he liked it even less than her naked anger.

'That's the trouble,' he said quietly. 'You've always had money of your own. So has Archie. So has Anne, except that she doesn't seem to want it. But even she will, some day. And none of you has ever known what it's like to be without it. But your father knows, Julia, just as I know, and it's something you never forget. So Archie's quite right when he says that the business comes first. Without it, and your father's, the whole world as you know it would disappear.'

She smiled tolerantly.

'But isn't this rather an unnecessary sermon? It's not going to disappear.'

'It could,' said Douglas grimly. 'That's what all three of you are liable to forget, because you've never known anything else and you can't imagine life without it. But it could vanish like snow off a dyke. A few months' neglect can destroy a lifetime's work . . . and going to Rome when you're needed here is neglect.'

'Oh? Do you really think? I find it hard to believe that James Douglas Limited is liable to go bankrupt just because Archie takes a month off.'

'Hard to believe or not, in principle it's a fact.'

'And you've just done what I told you not to do,' said Archie. 'You'd be safer not to refer to the business at all.'

Anne stood up quickly and cut off Julia's reply.

'Let's have tea early, Mummy. I'll go and ask Kirstie.'

'What a good idea!' Margaret did not try to hide her relief. She got up at once and started bustling around, moving little tables. 'It's such a grey, miserable day. Really, you'd never think it was April. But a cup of tea'll cheer us up and . . . oh, James. Could you put some wood on the fire, please. It's nearly out. And I was just thinking. Why don't you all come over here to watch the television thing? Anne hasn't got a set yet, have you, dear?'

'Not yet.'

'And you two could leave Jamie with Oonagh and come over for dinner.'

'Anne, too,' said Douglas.

'Yes, I mean that. All three of you.'

'It may not be possible,' said Julia.

'It will be,' said Archie. 'It's just a question of keeping that evening free.'

He rose and crossed to the misty windows and looked at the rain-broken daffodils lying on the sodden grass and nothing had changed in the garden. The tree-house still showed through the green, defending leaves of the holly tree, the knotted rope still hung from the great side limb of the tallest oak. There, on the lawn, where the cricket stumps would go, the grass was cut and rolled already, as it always was when you came home for Easter. He closed his eyes. The logs thudded into the fire from his father's hands and the flames began to roar in the throat of the chimney. Cups rattled and spoons clinked and it was as it had always been. Sunday tea. Unchanged through peace and war and peace.

'Come on, Archie,' said his mother, as she always did. 'Your tea's poured.'

'All right,' he said, and turned to face Julia.

Later, Jamie returned from the kitchen and played with his grandfather, who gave him half a crown; and Anne talked to her brother more than she had done for years; and Julia watched her, and wrapped her little bit of secret knowledge up with her resentment and her hostility and put them all away, to be kept safely until the time when they could be used to best advantage; and, in spite of tea and hot buttered scones and Kirstie's best shortbread, it remained a grey, miserable day until the end.

Archie drove home through the wet, dark tail of it, with Julia brooding in silence by his side and Jamie drowsing on the back seat. He felt no apprehension in being alone with her, no sense of dreading an onslaught to come. He merely wondered what had changed his attitude. The answer came as they were leaving the harsh orange lights of Balloch, when she said, apparently as a simple statement, without comment or feeling—

'You've never spoken to me like that before.'

'I know,' he said. It was suddenly clear and simple. 'I probably never would have, if you hadn't tried to interfere in the business. From your point of view, it was a bad mistake.'

'A mistake?'

He felt her eyes on him and nodded.

'That's right. That's something I had to take a stand on. I'd no alternative. But taking a stand on something is rather like getting a divorce. The first time is the most difficult.'

She lit a cigarette and looked out at the night and wondered if he could really believe that it would be as easy as that.

CHAPTER FIVE

DOUGLAS'S tweed hat left his hand a fraction of a second after Sally opened her door. She paused to let it spin smoothly past her, but the brim tipped the peg and it fell to the floor. She picked it up and hung it in its place.

'Thanks,' he said. 'But I'd have done it that time if you hadn't come in.'

A part of her mind noted that he was wearing a tweed suit and a wool shirt with a check as bold as a horse-blanket and that this, on a Monday morning, was unusual even for Douglas, but too many things were happening to leave time for curiosity.

'Torquil Jackson's just off the phone from Loch Eriboll,' she said. 'There's trouble.'

'What kind of trouble?'

'Something to do with the foundations for the lead shields. They can't find rock. I said you'd phone back.'

'Right,' said Douglas, and crossed swiftly to his desk. 'Is Archie in?'

'Ten minutes ago.'

He picked up the direct line to his son's office.

'While I'm on to him, get hold of Roderick Grant and tell

him I want him here at nine-thirty. Then get Mr. Smith in the Transport Division on the line and put him through whenever I'm finished with this.'

'Yes, sir,' said Sally and departed, prepared to cope with a bad day. All the storm signals were flying.

'Hello!' Archie sounded surprised. 'You're in bright and early.'

'Not early enough,' said Douglas. 'Jackson's been on the phone from Loch Eriboll. According to Sally, they can't find rock for the lead shield foundations.'

'But that's impossible! They got rock with every test bore except one.'

'Except one,' said Douglas. 'Exactly.'

'Oh, God!'

'And it's your baby. Get on to them now. Find out what's happened and who's mucked it up. Then get the original of the site survey out of Records ... the whole thing, test borings, samples, the lot ... and go up there fast. Take Chambers with you.'

'Chambers?'

'If my guess is right, you'll be glad of him. And get this clear, Archie. I don't want any slip-up with this or any other Government contract. They've got to go absolutely according to the book. And don't ask why. Just see that it happens.'

'Right,' said Archie. Trouble at a distant site had never come at a more suitable time. He glanced at his watch. 'It's just on nine-fifteen. It's going to be near enough ten before I get away. And you know what the roads are like. Even pushing it in the Lotus, I can't be there much before three-thirty.'

'That's all right. Don't kill yourself. You'll still have a good six or seven hours of daylight up there.'

'And when will I phone you?'

'You don't have to phone me,' said Douglas. 'You're in charge. Phone when you've something to say.'

He hung up and grunted. That was throwing him to the wolves with a vengeance. But it would do him no harm. And he would have enough on his plate for the next few days to put the problem of Julia into perspective. After straightening this lot out, Julia wouldn't seem like a problem at all. Just so long as he does straighten it out, he thought grimly. Trouble with a Government contract at this point in time didn't bear thinking about.

The buzzer rang and he flicked the switch.

'Mr. Smith's on the line,' said Sally.

'Fine,' said Douglas. 'Put him through.'

He lifted one of the internal phones.

'Good morning, sir,' said Smith.

'I've known better,' said Douglas. 'How are we off for private cars?'

Smith paused. His years in the Army, protecting his precious vehicles against smooth-talking predators of all ranks, had left him permanently suspicious of all such enquiries.

'Not bad,' he said cautiously.

'Relax,' said Douglas. 'I'm not going to take any away. I just want to know. What have we got?'

'Two Bentleys and one Rolls,' said Smith. 'One Rover functioning and one being serviced. Three Minis, all roadworthy.'

'What colour are the Minis?'

'Red.'

'All right. Have one of them at the main door by nine-thirty, with a driver in plain clothes.'

'You did say plain clothes?' asked Smith.

'I did,' said Douglas. 'MacAdam, if he's available. And keep him on call for me from now on, with Kirk covering his off-duty.'

'Very well, sir.' Smith noted it and decided that the old man must be feeling his age. 'Anything else, sir?'

'Yes,' said Douglas. 'Get hold of a couple of second-hand cars with regional registration numbers. Dumfries or Nairn or somewhere like that. Any make and colour you like, as long as it's common. Have them checked over whenever you get them and keep them both serviceable. I'll use a red Mini until they're ready.'

'Very well, sir.'

It's not age, thought Smith. He's up to something. And the best of British luck. Another half million or so at the far end and five years off his life. He's round the bend.

His own ambition was to run his department as smoothly as

91

a perverse world would allow and to produce bigger and better perpetual flowering carnations. All other forms of ambition were akin to madness. He felt vaguely sorry for his employer.

'I'll let you know,' he said.

'Do that,' said Douglas.

He hung up and pressed the intercom switch.

'Is Grant there?' he asked.

'Just arrived,' said Sally. 'Will I send him in?'

'Not yet. Tell him to wait and come in yourself.'

She appeared almost at once, looking cool and slightly formal as she always did on the bad days. He smiled at her.

'You've got your crisis manner on,' he said. 'We're not that busy.'

She relaxed a little.

'It's not half-past nine,' she said. 'When it starts like this, anything can happen.'

'Forget it,' he said. 'Take things as they come.' He pushed a key across the desk to her. 'That's a duplicate key for this drawer.' He tapped it. 'If I'm not in the office by nine-thirty on any morning, open it. You'll find two things. First, a sheet of paper with my movements for the day ... where I'm going to be at any given time, with telephone numbers, and the ones I don't want you to use except in an emergency will be bracketed. Like this.' He slid the drawer out and handed her a foolscap sheet. 'Now, in general, I don't want to be contacted at all, but today, for example, or any other time that Archie's away, you may have no option. The principle that one or other of us can always be got still holds. But if he's here, pass all business problems over to him. Anything else, especially anything like the press enquiries last week, put through to that extension ... three, one, six.'

'A new one,' commented Sally.

'That's right. And from today on, Roderick Grant will be at it. There's no point in trying to tell you briefly what to push through to him, but you'll soon find out. Now. The second thing will be this ... tape of any letters I want you to do and any instructions for the day. Do an original of each letter ... no carbons ... and post them yourself. When you've finished, wipe it all off. And at the end of each day, destroy the foolscap. Burn it, chew it up and swallow it if you like, but don't use the waste-paper basket. And when you're not actually using the tapes or the movements sheet, keep them in there, locked up, with the key stuck in the top of your stocking or wherever else you think might be safe. Right?'

'Yes, sir,' said Sally, and looked more formal than ever.

Douglas laughed as he put the things back in the drawer.

'Away you go and don't look so serious,' he said. 'Pretend you've transferred to Intelligence. Enjoy yourself. Sally Carmichael, the beautiful spy.'

She gave a rather strained smile.

'I was just thinking that's what it sounded like,' she said. 'You're not planning a revolution or anything, are you?'

He looked at her quickly.

'No,' he said. 'Not exactly. Anyway, on you go and send in Grant.'

Roderick Grant came in, hoping fervently that he did not look as tired as he felt. Douglas was lighting his pipe, apparently as relaxed and fit as though he were about to settle down with a Glenlivet after a good day's fishing. The sight produced a sensation which was a curious blend of anger, respect and envy.

'Have a seat,' said Douglas through the smoke.

'Thank you, sir,' said Grant, and sank gratefully into a chair.

'You got my memorandum?'

'Yes, sir.'

It had arrived on his desk late on Friday afternoon, sixty pages of foolscap, with single spacing and no padding. It had taken him two fourteen-hour days to digest properly. Altogether, memorandum seemed something of a misnomer.

'Any questions?'

'Well, yes. I'm afraid there are a number——'

'Let me have them in writing by tonight.'

'I've got them here,' said Grant wearily, and drew a file from his brief-case. He had finished drafting them at two o'clock in the morning, just when the coffee ran out.

'Good,' said Douglas, and stretched out his hand. 'Let's have a look.'

93

He leafed through them quickly and smiled to himself. This time, Sally would be wrong. The shadows around Grant's eyes had not been caused by dissipation. It was all sound, relevant stuff.

'Fine,' he said. 'I'll give you replies tomorrow. Now, one or two points. Then I've got to go. Your accommodation's ready, so you can move in now. You know where it is?'

'Yes, sir.'

The accommodation was the only happy thought on this grey Monday morning. It was first class, better, even, than that of his former chief.

'All right. Get yourself a secretary out of the pool. Select for efficiency, obviously, but forgive me if I remind you that in this instance discretion is more important than bedworthiness.'

'Yes, sir,' said Grant formally, and thought of Paula.

'And you'd better contact Anderson. I'm going down there now and I'll tell him. Fix a meeting for this afternoon or tomorrow morning. And for God's sake, work with him. You don't have a thing in common, so you'd better remember that he's just as good at his job as you are at yours. And finally, the first joint meeting of the Committee and its advisers will be at seven-thirty on Friday. That's the sixteenth. I want you there, because these are people you've got to sell. You've got their names——' He paused. 'I imagine some of them surprised you.'

'Nearly all of them surprised me. It's quite a list.'

Douglas chuckled.

'It's all that. And you'd better get yourself briefed on every one. Background, careers, publications, achievements, everything relevant. But if you're going to sell them, you've still got to meet them, talk to them, assess what aspects of their personalities you want to put over. That's why I want you there and I shouldn't need to tell you that this is vital. Politics and policies are nothing without the men to inspire belief in them. We've got the men. It's up to you to see that every person of voting age gets to know it.'

Grant nodded.

'Yes, sir.'

Douglas stood up and went for his hat.

94

'If you've absolutely got to contact me during the day, Sally can arrange it, but you'd better have a good reason. You aren't being paid to pass the buck.'

'I realise that,' said Grant.

'Oh, and one more thing.' He turned at the door. 'If by any chance Sally should attract you, you might remember . . . she's more breakable than most.'

The heavy door shut almost silently behind him and Roderick Grant let his shoulders sag a little now that the need to compete with his employer's vitality had gone. He would collect Paula and move into his quiet corner on the floor below, where the files and the ash-trays were empty and the phones silent, and he would take it easy for the day, arrange a few meetings, fix a few contacts, start the slow build-up that would lead to . . . what?

He shook his head and wandered over to the window. On Friday, he would have laid a hundred to one on the thing being hopeless, crazy, doomed to fail before it even got moving. Now he was by no means so sure. If other aspects of the campaign had been worked out as carefully as that memorandum . . . and it seemed certain that they had . . . then the people of this big, sprawling city and of all the lesser places from Berwick to Yell were going to wonder what had hit them.

The only mildly eccentric thing was this planned attempt to hijack fifteen minutes of television time. That was a straight gamble on the responsible man not pulling out the plug. But if it came off, the sheer piratical impertinence of it would win supporters. And if it didn't, what the hell? No skin off anybody's nose. Fault in transmission. Pity old Douglas was cut off last night. Should have been interesting. Astonishing chap. And from Douglas's point of view, nothing would have been lost. There were other methods of communication. The new paper might be still unborn, but Jock Anderson had been around for a long time. It would be born, on time, a professional job from the first issue. And the modified hydrofoil from the Dutch yard was due in Cork in a week for installation of the radio transmitters which would be powerful enough to cover half the country. Once she was operational, with her radio crew on board, she would be his very own baby. He

95

sweated slightly at the thought.

And the men. Since he had first read their names, his thoughts kept coming back to the men. There were economists and barristers, professors and Trade Unionists, scientists and planners, men who were experts in every aspect of the running of a country, men who could move in when the time came and have the thing ticking like a clock within a month, young, brilliant men with advanced ideas and older men with established reputations, a perfectly conceived balance between stability and tradition on the one hand and economic and social revolution on the other. The thing was fantastic. He must have been at it for years, choosing men, persuading them, holding their loyalty and discretion, building the skeleton that was now about to be clothed in flesh.

He looked out at the wet roofs of the city and for the first time in years he wondered if he had bitten off more than he could chew.

A door clicked and he turned.

'Oh,' said Sally. 'I thought you'd gone.'

She looked at him curiously. It was unusual to see Grant with the charm and the smile switched off, Grant tired, less assured, lonely in an empty room.

'I'm just going,' he said. 'I was day-dreaming.'

'I thought you'd got a brand new office,' she said. 'Extension three, one, six.'

'That's where I'm going.'

'You don't have to.' On an impulse, she smiled at him. 'There should be some coffee in a few minutes.'

He watched her soft black hair brush forward on her cheek as she stooped over the desk and felt suddenly irritable.

'If you're all that breakable,' he said suddenly, 'you've no right to look so damned attractive.'

She straightened quickly, but was too late to see more than the flick of his jacket round the edge of the quivering door.

*　　　*　　　*

Douglas picked his way through the puddles of Trinidad Lane towards the pseudo-Corinthian half-columns flanking the main door of the building which housed the Rowan Press.

It was a gaunt, soot-blackened relic of Victorian barbarity, hardly a century old, yet already dying without dignity between the charred skeleton of a bonded warehouse and a scrap-merchant's graveyard of corroded lamp-posts and contorted beds. It took all his faith to believe that it could still have any part to play in life, for to enter it was to step back almost fifty years into the world of frosted glass and cast iron and sad brown-painted wood which he had known as a boy. Even the smell was unchanged, the smell of age, faintly musty, faintly sour, as if the breath of the pale fourteen-hours-a-day dead men still lingered.

He stood in the echoing shell, listening to the distant sounds of unseen men at work, and the impulse to destroy rose up in him like anger, to smash the glass and burn the wood and flatten the walls as he had flattened others like them by the score. That he came this time with the reprieve instead of the execution order, gave him no satisfaction at all.

Light it, he thought grimly. Light it and let the sun shine in through clear panes studded with extractor fans. Heat it. Paint it with white paint until it shines like a young girl's bedroom. But leave the outside alone to crumble and rot away, in case some penny-wise mean-minded fool is ever tempted to let it live too long. Let it live just long enough for the presses to labour and bring *The New Scot* into viable existence.

He looked at them, squatting like silent monsters under the yellow light of weak dust-darkened bulbs, and wondered if they could indeed spew out the fifty thousand folded copies he demanded as a minimum starting figure. They were past their first youth, but at least they were reel-fed rotary machines, lacking some of the refinements of their successors, but looking impressively functional to his uninformed eye. He was leaning over one, peering at the plate cylinder bearings, when Anderson's dry voice drew him back.

'Well, James? Are you impressed?'

He turned quickly, smiling, uncertain of the reception he would get, for Anderson had written him a letter in which he stated bluntly the problems involved, the difficulties in solving them and his reasons for believing that Douglas was beyond question certifiably mad, but all was well. The shadows were deep in the laughter lines around his eyes and he was dressed as he had been in the old days, in a soft shirt, with a tweed tie and a knitted cardigan, flannel trousers and suède soft-soled shoes. Douglas let the smile remain.

'Impressed by the sheer size of the thing,' he said. 'But I'll be more impressed if you tell me that it works.'

'Oh, it works,' said Anderson. 'They all do, even if the engineers say they should have been scrapped years ago.'

'I've heard much the same thing said about people,' said Douglas, and Anderson grinned.

He gave the big machine an affectionate kick.

'Aye, they're like me in more ways than one. We'll do our turn yet.' He moved away. 'Have you had a look round?'

Douglas followed him past the presses to the passage from which he had entered.

'Most of it,' he said. 'It takes you back.'

'It takes you back all right. It's put me off talking about the good old days, anyway, I can tell you that.'

Douglas looked around him curiously.

'Yes. It's funny. You remember it, and yet you forget all the drabness of it. It's the men you remember. And the things that happened.'

'I don't have to remember the men,' said Anderson over his shoulder. 'I've got them here. There's not a man in the place so far under fifty-five.'

'Men from the *Daily*?'

'Most of them.'

'And what have they got to say about it?'

'About what? The place, or the whole idea?'

'Both.'

'Oh, they think you're daft. So do I, for that matter. But you're paying them, so it's a useful kind of insanity.'

'And the place?'

Anderson stopped with his hand on the handle of his office door.

'They don't like it, James,' he said seriously. 'If it wasn't better than hanging round the house, having the wife jump down your throat for getting in the way of the housework, there's not one of them would stay. Not one of them. And I

98

can't say I blame them.' He entered the room and stood still. 'Right enough, it's not very cheery.'

Douglas looked at the battered swivel chair, the old desk scarred by innumerable cigarette burns, the chipped filing cabinets.

'We can do something about that,' he said.

'Oh aye. When we're organised. Maybe in about six months. But there's only twenty-four hours in the day and damned few days left before that ironmongery you were looking at is supposed to start rolling. First things first.'

Douglas stared out at the scrap-merchant's yard. If it could be bought, and despatch organised with a drive-in door through the end wall on to it, that would get the traffic off the narrow lane. The lane had been worrying him.

'We'll get something done before then,' he said. 'I'll get electricians in this afternoon and painters in tomorrow. By the time the first issue comes out on Saturday week, you'll not know the place.'

He turned round slowly. Anderson's eyes were narrowed.

'It was to be Monday,' he said accusingly. 'A fortnight today.'

'I know it was,' said Douglas. 'Now it's to be Saturday week.'

'God in heaven,' said Anderson weakly.

Douglas went to him.

'Come on and sit down,' he said gently. 'There's a lot to talk about between now and dinner-time.'

'Sit down yourself,' said Anderson. 'I'm an old man, and it's just the back of ten o'clock, but before there's any talk I'm away to the bathroom. You can while away the time reading all about yourself on page three of the *Glasgow Tribune*.'

The paper was lying on the desk. Douglas folded the first page back and smiled. His picture headed the gossip column, and that alone was enough to produce derisory chuckles from Jock. He spread it out on the flat top and sat down to read it.

'Stocky Scottish industrialist, James Douglas, who recently returned with an expensive tan from a holiday with his wife on Spain's millionaire coast, had a family gathering yesterday at his country home near Loch Lomond. His handsome playboy son and partner was there with his beautiful wife, Julia, daughter of Sir Charles Fletcher, the wealthy shipbuilder, and sister Anne, the pretty young sculptress, came along to add an artistic touch.

'A family gathering for members of a family business, you may say. But was it? We wonder. James Douglas has been doing strange things since he returned from Spain. Last week we reported that he was said to have been involved in a rumoured split in the Home Rule Party—in itself, an odd interest for a busy business man—and this week we would like to state that we believe another Douglas plot is hatching.

'Some people may feel that this is none of our business. We disagree. We think it is. Throughout Scottish history, when a Douglas has plotted, things have happened.

'With this particular Douglas, these things have always been agreeable. Fine buildings have risen from the rubble of slums. Elegant bridges have spanned rivers. Unemployment figures have fallen. And more money has flowed into the coffers of those five pleasant people who met yesterday for Sunday lunch.

'We believe this to be wrong.

'No one has done more than James Douglas to improve the working conditions of the Scottish labour force, to raise wages, to improve the relationship between man and management. We admit it. And we honour him for it.

'But surely the time has come to let the thousands of small investors in this country join the Sunday lunch, share in the family prosperity, feel that they have a cosy dividend-producing egg in the huge expanding Douglas nest?

'We believe it has. And it will be our policy to discover what is now being planned and to attempt to persuade this great man to become even greater by sharing his good fortune with others.'

He leaned over it, brooding, until Anderson's voice brought him back to the bare brown room.

'Well, great man? A penny for them.'

He straightened.

'No man's great to his editor,' he said amiably, and pushed the paper across the desk. 'What do you make of it?'

Anderson picked it up, crumpled it and tossed it contemptuously aside.

'The usual *Tribune* trash.'

'Just that?'

'Aye, just that. What else can you expect from that lot?'

Douglas suppressed his smile.

'You know, Jock,' he said, 'your face is the best testimonial you've got. You're a bad liar.'

'At the salary you're paying me, you can call me names if you like,' said Anderson tolerantly. 'I still say it's trash.'

'You're being paid to edit and organise and all the rest of it,' said Douglas. 'You're not being paid to act the mother hen. You know damn well there's some meat in that trash.'

'How do you make that out?'

'Because a journalist uses words the way a bricklayer uses bricks. He doesn't say plotting, when he means planning.'

Anderson folded his long length on to a rickety upright chair.

'Uh-huh. I thought you might say that.'

'Well, isn't it true?'

'Up to a point, James. Only up to a point.' He tilted his chair back on two tottering legs. 'They don't say plotting when they mean planning, but when they say plotting they don't necessarily know what they mean.'

Douglas stared at him.

'Look, Jock,' he said. 'I'm a simple man. Keep it lucid. Save the subtlety for your editorials.'

Anderson grinned.

'Well, let's say they're curious. They're maybe even suspicious. But that doesn't mean they've actually got any facts. Far from it.'

'But you know what reporters are like. They've got noses on them like ferrets.'

'Some of them.'

'Och, some of them! Any I've ever known. They'll find out

101

anything there is to find out. It's just a question of how long it takes them.'

'Unless they happen to be content with what you want them to find out,' said Anderson cannily.

Douglas paused.

'Go on,' he said.

'You don't want anybody to know anything about the political implications of this thing until after Saturday week. Right?'

'Right.'

'So you let them find out about something else, something that could account for most of your movements and justify a bit of secrecy.'

'Such as what?'

'The paper. Give them a couple of days on the scent and then let the news about that leak. Say, on Friday. On Saturday, get this fellow Grant to issue a statement reluctantly admitting it. With a bit of luck, that'll keep them happy for the week that's left. And anyway, James, we're going to need a bit of advance publicity. Otherwise, it'll be more like five thousand copies you'll sell. Not fifty.'

Douglas considered it.

'Fair enough,' he said finally. 'That makes sense. You'll be seeing Grant today or tomorrow. I told him to contact you. Talk about it with him, arrange how you're going to handle it, and I'll get him to organise a publicity build-up for the whole of next week.'

Anderson nodded.

'That's the idea.'

'And in the first issue . . . and that's the Saturday, mind?'

'Aye,' said Anderson glumly. 'That's the Saturday.'

'Well, you can feature a biographical block about me right on the front page, and put in a plug for the television thing at night, but keep anything political out of that too.'

'Aye,' said the Editor derisively. 'We'll stick to the usual image-building guff.'

Douglas laughed happily.

'I should resent that,' he said, 'but I don't. There's going to have to be a hell of a lot of image-building from now on. And not only mine. Anyway. Come on, Jock.' He pulled in his chair. 'Let's get on with it. How far have you got?'

*   *   *

On the evening of the following day, Jock Anderson succeeded in contacting Sam Gold. He was a swarthy, mercurial Jew whose parents had left Poland after the First World War and settled finally in Glasgow, in a tall, friendly tenement not far from the old Gorbals Cross. There, the family lived a life of secure, calculated routine. His father walked each day in his dark clothes through the dark streets to the dark back-shop where he worked as a watch and clock repairer, returning always at precisely the same time to his wife's *borsch* and *bigos* and to the son who became each year more and more of a cuckoo in the nest. For Sam hated routine and despised security.

He left school at the age of fourteen, got himself a job in the *Glasgow Herald* office and so launched himself on a newspaper career which had taken him successively to Dundee, London, Toronto, Detroit and New York. Now, some thirty-five years later, he was a highly experienced journalist who had come to accept as a curious weakness the fact that he still regarded Glasgow as home.

His parents were dead and the tenement block had vanished, but he owned a white villa on the Broom Estate where his wife lived with their three children during his variable absences on Agency assignments and to which he returned from covering incomprehensible frontier disputes in South-East Asia or vaguely ideological revolutions in the Arab states, to cut the grass and prune the roses and wonder why he was ever fool enough to go away.

It had taken Anderson six days to track him down at home. It took four hours more to persuade him to accept the job of news editor. Sam began by laughing till his gold fillings shone.

'Boy, can you see it! Me in a desk job. Feet up. Phones ringing like mad. The old teleprinter clicking away. Things happening out there and me chair-bound, getting boils on my fat ass!'

'Not on this paper,' said Anderson grimly. 'You'll be damn lucky if you get a chair.'

'Yeah? Well, anyway. Some other guy, Mac. Not me.'

So Jock told him the story. Then he faced an interrogation that dragged out of him every detail that he knew. It was after eleven o'clock when Sam picked up the glass with the tail end of his whisky in it and wandered round the room. Jock watched him and waited. He lifted a piece of stone that sat on a velvet mat on a bookcase top and tilted it so that the pale silhouette of a leaf showed on its darkened surface.

'Nagasaki,' he said. 'I picked it up a couple of months later. Every time I look at it, I think . . . you know, I ought to care about that.'

'Do you mean you don't?'

Sam stared at the stone in his hand.

'No,' he said. 'I guess I care a lot. Sunrise and singing birds. Then . . . pfft.' He put it down. 'For me, that's thermonuclear warfare.'

'That's any kind of warfare.'

'Maybe.' He dropped into an armchair, one leg slung over the side. 'But it's too big, Jock. The whole damn thing's too big. You're outside looking at it, thinking . . . that's a hell of a thing. But it's too big to hit you. Whether it's nuclear stuff on Nagasaki or Hiroshima, or high explosive on Warsaw and Berlin, or fire bombs on Dresden, the same applies. If I want to get dragged by the emotional short hairs into a sense of man's inhumanity to man, I don't think about Nagasaki. I think about Guernica. I don't think about Auschwitz. I think about Lidice. And I think about that leaf, even though I've never seen anything but its shadow. For you can narrow it right down to that. Right down. The world's got small, Jock, but people seem to forget we've stayed more or less the same. If we want to get out some kind of anchor . . . and everybody does . . . we've got to get hold of something we can comprehend, something that gets under our skin and hurts . . . like a leaf, if you like. It's got all the slushy emotional associations . . . spring and youth and hope and peace and all the other corny, beaten-up words that we've sucked dry of any meaning they ever had.' He stopped, and let his mouth smile. 'Oh, to

104

hell with it!' He stood up. 'Have another drink.'

Jock covered his glass.

'Not for me, Sam.'

'Well, I'm going to have one.' He poured himself a double from the decanter. 'Another bob for the defence budget.' He squirted in some soda, and added ice. 'And if you think I've turned into an alcoholic, Jock ... relax. I'm not even a regular.' He lifted the lid of a record-player, switched it on and waited for it to warm up. 'But when I'm trying to figure out what I'm doing on the face of this crazy globe, what I'm trying to get out of it, that's when I need two things.' He tapped the decanter. 'This ... and Bach.' He adjusted the volume till the music from the hidden stereo-speakers flowed round them like the waters of a quiet river. Then he raised his glass. 'Prosit!'

'Slàinte,' said Anderson, and waited.

Sam Gold sat down and stared at the glowing bars of the heater.

'I don't know,' he said at last. 'I've been around as much as anybody, I guess. I've seen just about the lot. And out of everything I've seen on five tormented continents, there are only two places and maybe a dozen people that matter a damn to me.' He took a cheroot from a wooden box and lit it carefully, then held the match vertically so that it burned like a candle flame until it died on the edge of his thumb. 'There was once a village in Poland,' he said. 'When the family left it, I was three. I've never been back. But I could see it in that flame as clearly as if I was there. And that's the only place I ever will see it. The Panzers and a handful of Stukas wiped it off in 1939.' He looked up with an odd, half-apologetic smile. 'But that village matters, Jock. Even the ghost of it. And the other place that matters is this.' He slapped the arm of his chair. 'This.' The smile grew to a grin. 'And you're supposed to be surprised.'

Anderson drew thoughtfully on his cigarette.

'Why?'

'Because it doesn't make sense. A poor dung-stinking slum of a village that I left when I was too young to remember. And a country that's never been more than a base to get out of.'

'And what's supposed to be surprising? Since when did the

slushy emotional associations you were talking about have anything to do with reason?'

Sam stared at him.

'Yeah. I guess so. But I like reason. That's why I like Bach. He doesn't twist your guts with a longing for something you can't even define. But I grant you there's no reason in this.' He rolled the cheroot slowly between his fingers. 'This country. This city. A tenement block that your friend probably pulled down when he was making his first million. This one-third of a suburban acre and everything in it. They matter. That's what the whole bloody business of ideologies and power and first-strike capacity comes right down to in the end for me. And if it's like that for me, it's like that for most people. It's got to come down to something a man can comprehend.' He looked up. 'That's why I think your friend's got the right idea.'

Anderson spoke softly.

'Does that mean you'll take it?'

He did not wait only for Gold's reply. He waited for the reply of a thinking man in that year of grace to the appeal of Douglas's dream.

'That's right.'

He breathed deeply and lifted his empty glass.

'If that offer still stands,' he said, 'I'll join you in a wee one.'

*   *   *

On the following Friday morning, Sam Gold dropped in for coffee at a place near Albion Street which was much frequented by newspapermen.

Later that same day, James Douglas was in his office finalising arrangements for the evening meeting between his Committee and its advisers. The buzzer at his side purred softly, twice. He flicked the switch.

'Yes?'

'Mr. MacDonald, B.B.C. Television, on the line,' said Sally. 'Shall I put him through?'

'Yes,' he said, and lifted the phone. 'Hello. James Douglas here.'

'Hello? Mr. Douglas? This is Bill MacDonald, B.B.C. Television. Look, I'm sorry to bother you——'

'That's all right.'

'Well, I don't know how to put this, but . . . well, the thing is, I've just heard a rumour that you're starting a new daily newspaper and——'

'Where did you hear that?' asked Douglas sharply.

'Well, it was in a pub in Byres Road, actually. I was talking to this chap and he asked me if I'd heard and I said no I hadn't and . . . well, I thought I'd better ring you and find out.'

He sounded a very worried young man.

'I see,' said Douglas gravely. 'Why do you want to know?'

'Why? Well . . . I mean, there's the programme next week.'

'What's that got to do with it?'

'Well . . . I mean . . . oh, hell, I'm making a mess of this.'

'You are, aren't you?' said Douglas gently. 'I'll give you a hand. First, I'm not prepared to comment at all on a rumour. Secondly, if there's nothing in it, then obviously nothing has changed. And thirdly, you should know my reputation well enough to realise that if I wanted publicity for a commercial interest, I'd buy advertising time on the commercial channel like other people. Right?'

'Yes. Yes, of course. I do realise that.'

'I'm glad.'

'It's just . . . well, it's just that I had to check.'

'All right. You've checked. Now tell me this. Was the chap in the pub a reporter?'

'No, he's not, actually. He works in a bookshop down near Charing Cross.'

'Fine,' said Douglas softly. 'Let's hear from you next week.'

He hung up and chuckled. The story was out. He buzzed Sally.

'There's a rumour I'm starting a newspaper,' he told her. 'If there are any enquiries, put them through to Mr. Grant.'

'Very good, sir.'

She switched off at once. He hesitated for a moment, then called her back.

'Sally?'

'Yes, sir?'

'I am starting a paper. I thought you might like to know.'

107

'Thank you, sir. I thought you might be.'

He stared at the neat impersonal grille from which her voice came and was suddenly angry. Something had to be done to strip off the armour of politeness that she'd been hiding behind for a week. There was little satisfaction in maintaining good labour relations with thousands of men, when you failed with your own secretary.

'Damn it,' he said. 'Come in.'

She appeared almost at once, cool and composed, her pad and pencil in her hand.

'You wanted me, sir?'

He looked at her briefly.

'Yes,' he said. 'Sit down.'

She sat down as she always did, the edge of her skirt demurely bisecting her knee-cap, her notebook on her thigh, waiting. He avoided her eyes.

'Is everything ready for tonight?'

'Yes, sir.'

'The rooms?'

'Everything but the flowers. The girl's coming at five.'

'Catering?'

'It's arranged.'

'Hm.' He grunted. 'And you're wondering what it's all about?' She did not answer. 'You're wondering why I haven't told you.' She looked down at her lap. 'You are, aren't you?'

'Yes, sir,' she said unhappily.

'It never struck you that life might be a lot easier for you if you didn't know?'

She looked up then.

'Yes, it did. You said something about that once before. The day the *Express* phoned.'

'All right, then. I meant it. It's not that I don't trust you. You should know that by this time. I trust you the way I trust my own right hand. But I don't want you involved. I don't want you hurt——'

'Hurt?'

Her eyes widened.

'Well, intimidated,' said Douglas irritably. 'Bothered by people trying to pump you. That sort of thing.'

108

When she did not answer, he looked up. Her eyes were scanning his face. They were very honest eyes.

'I don't care,' she said slowly. 'I'd rather know.' A faint flush rose on her face and slowly deepened. 'I think . . . after ten years . . . I've got a right to know.'

He stared at her, wondering. Yes, he thought suddenly. Yes, by God, you have.

He unlocked a drawer by his knee, drew out a spring-back folder and slid it across the desk.

'All right,' he said. 'It's all there. And it'll not be confidential in another week or two, but just now it's the most confidential document in the place, so don't leave it lying around.'

She smiled.

'I won't.'

'And I'd like it back by five o'clock. You'll get through it by then, if you start now.'

She pushed back her chair.

'Thank you, sir.'

He watched her rise, her black hair swinging forward over the still heightened colour of her cheek, watched her hold the folder to her breasts as she crossed the room. At the door, she turned.

'If I'm here by a quarter past seven tonight, will that be soon enough?'

'Tonight?'

'You'll need a secretary,' she said composedly. 'I kept the evening free.'

'You what!'

'Well, I know Mr. Cameron is really Secretary, but somebody with shorthand could give you a fuller account, a proper record of everything said, and you might want that . . . later, I mean. It's hard to remember . . . everything . . . at a big meeting like this.'

She wound down, a little afraid, and waited. When Douglas grinned, she let herself relax.

'Sally, Sally,' he said gently, 'if you come tonight, you'll be in up to the neck.'

'I hope so.'

'And it's not business. It's politics.'

'I don't care,' she said. 'I'd rather be in it up to the neck, than left high and dry.'

* * *

Wee Willie Smith, the baby of the *Tribune* reporters, squeezed himself further into the shelter of a doorway down the service lane from the Douglas building and wished to heaven it were the dark, concealing heart of winter instead of seven-twenty on a bright spring evening. Since late forenoon, when he had first picked up the story of the new paper, he had been tailing Sam Gold. He had had neither lunch nor tea, and his pale face was even more pinched than usual, but for ten minutes, he had been receiving his reward.

Gold had arrived on foot at seven-ten, to be followed within a minute by old Jock Anderson, former editor of the dead, now almost legendary, *Glasgow Daily*. That, in itself, was hardly surprising, for an unemployed, experienced, top-level news-paperman was a comparatively rare creature and Anderson would be an obvious possibility for a job on any aspiring, staff-seeking new paper. But it was a useful piece of hard information to stiffen the rumour.

He wrote it down and looked up in time to see a man and a girl meet at the lane's mouth and go in together. A secretary, he guessed, and some kind of P.R.O., if the good looks, the well-cut suit and the confident manner meant anything. It was unexciting, but he noted it.

Then came the first surprise. A long, black, chauffeur-driven car slid to a stop outside the main entrance and Lord Kilconner, Chancellor of the University of Dunblane, hurried up the granite steps, swinging a slim brief-case in his hand. As his car moved away, a mud-spattered Land-Rover driven by a tall, bony, brown man in tweeds turned into the lane and parked near to the private entrance.

Willie Smith stared. The man was Brigadier Sir Jack Armstrong, former Chairman of the Highland Redevelopment Commission, who was said to have resigned in disgust after the biggest row even that disputatious body had ever known.

It was hard for Willie to see the connection between the

110

pale academic peer and the weathered soldier knight, but when Will Strachan, the boss of the Amalgamated Scottish Trade Unions, followed them into the building with Sir Robert McColl, Chairman of Scottish Chemical Industries, hard on his heels, he stopped trying to interpret. He dutifully recorded the names of those he recognised and the car registration numbers of those he did not, and every nerve fibre of his thin body tingled with the certainty that, whatever they made of it in the office, it added up to a scoop.

At seven-thirty, when five whole minutes had passed without another car, he slipped the notebook in his pocket and hurried away, down the quiet back lanes of the city, towards the river and the *Tribune* office.

At seven-thirty, Roderick Grant glanced at his watch, Sam Gold lit a cheroot and settled himself in his seat, Sally Carmichael nervously thumbed the edge of her shorthand pad and James Douglas rose to his feet.

Silence spread swiftly from him down the long length of the table.

'Gentlemen,' he said, 'let me welcome you. You all know me, as I know you, but not all of you know each other, and one of the three main objects of this meeting is to put that right. In the coming months, you'll get to know each other very well, but to make recognition easier you'll find a lapel badge with your name on the table before you. If you'd be good enough to wear these tonight, it will make things easier for all of you later on, when we're through in the lounges.

'Now, these badges bear only your name, and this alone is not enough, so I propose to introduce you . . . very briefly . . . to each other.

'On my left is Mr. Ewan Cameron, formerly Secretary of the Home Rule Party, who is my own deputy and who'll have complete authority to act on my behalf in my absence. Next to him is Lord Kilconner, whom most of you will know, Chancellor of the University of Dunblane. Then Mr. Will Strachan, equally well known, who is Chairman of the Amalgamated Scottish Trade Unions. Mr. Paul Lindsay comes next, Principal of the Scottish College of Accountancy, and Dr. Duncan Ross, Professor of Civil Law at the University of Inverness.

Sir John Cumming, Professor of Government and Administration at the University of Dumfries, sits next to him, then Dr. Charles Craig, Professor of Sociology at the University of Dunblane. Sir Robert McColl, Chairman of Scottish Chemical Industries, whom many of you know, is next, followed by four faces likely to be unknown to anyone else but themselves. They were formerly Committee members with me in the Home Rule Party and they share my views on that organisation. They are ... in order ... Mr. William Bain, Mr. Gavin Hamilton, Mr. Liam Macquillan and Mr. Calum Macrae. When you get to know them, you'll realise their qualities and understand why they are with us.

'Beyond them, are three other strangers to you. Mr. John Anderson, formerly Editor of the *Glasgow Daily* is now Editor of the *New Scot*, which starts publication a week tomorrow. Next to him is Mr. Sam Gold, whose reputation is international. He will be News Editor on the paper. Then comes Mr. Roderick Grant, one of my own men, who will handle all our Press and Public Relations.

'Now, coming further up this side, we have Dr. John Carrick, of the Department of Scientific and Industrial Research and Dr. Tom Wright, of the Agricultural Research Council. Then Mr. David Armstrong, Senior Lecturer in Town and Regional Planning at the University of Dumfries, and Dr. Donald Fraser, Professor of Political and Social Philosophy at the University of Inverness. Next to him is Sir William Robertson, Professor of Public Law at the University of Dunblane, and lastly, Brigadier Sir Jack Armstrong, formerly Chairman of the Highland Redevelopment Commission.

'But not lastly. Last is my secretary, Miss Sally Carmichael, whose discretion is as great as your own.

'Now——'

Sam Gold nudged Jock Anderson.

'How the hell did he do it?' he breathed.

'God knows,' whispered Jock. 'The good Lord only knows. But I'll tell you this. If he doesn't pull it off with a team like this, no man born of woman ever will.'

Roderick Grant sat very still, memorising the faces to go with the names and appointments he already knew. All thoughts of his own possible inadequacy had been driven out by the atmosphere of the meeting. His eyes slid over the faces round the table. Few were old. Most were men of middle age, in the prime of their ability. A few, especially the scientists and technologists, were young. Some looked distinguished, others were sandy, featureless, nondescript. Some, like Jack Armstrong, were brown, relaxed and at ease. Others, like Willie Bain and Calum Macrae, were pale and tense with the importance of the occasion.

All evening, Grant listened and watched. A Steering Committee was appointed to decide priorities and immediate matters of policy and, as discussion dragged out on the question of the extent of its mandate, he let his thoughts wander in uneasy speculation on where, at the end of the day, all this would take him and the other men around the table. But the raising of the third major issue of the evening brought him back to the present.

Local elections would be held in May. The last day for the lodging of nominations was April twenty-second. He glanced quickly at the calendar in his diary. There were six days left.

'It isn't long,' said Douglas, 'but at least we've a month until the elections themselves, a month to convince the electorate that we mean business. We're not likely to have any great success in that time, but it doesn't matter. We'll have got the thing off the ground. And next year, not just in the local elections, but in the General Election which is almost certain to be held, it'll be a very different story.'

Yes, thought Grant. Maybe. But it's a hell of a long time till next year. Let's concentrate on May.

Douglas paused and glanced at his watch.

'Well,' he said, 'I think you'll agree it's time we had a break. You'll find a buffet in the lounge beyond these doors. The bar is beyond the lounge on the left. We'll meet again here in half an hour.'

The silent men around the table stirred, easing their chairs back on the thick carpet.

'Christ,' said Willie Bain quietly.

'Come on,' said Liam Macquillan. 'I need a drink like I never needed one before.'

113

But Roderick Grant sat on, watching the ghost of an unborn Government pass by and vanish through the double doors.

'Come on,' said Sally softly. He looked up. 'You need something after that.'

'Yes,' he said. 'Yes. Sure.'

And he followed her thoughtfully towards the rising hum of voices.

CHAPTER SIX

ARCHIE closed his eyes and thought how the warmth of the sun shining on skin was as selfishly and sensually perfect as any gratification of the senses could possibly ever be. Behind and above him, the cluster of three jet engines on the tail assembly of the VC19 thrust him forward at a little less than the speed of sound, leaving their roar behind them so that the cabin was quiet, full of a murmur like that of bees on a summer day. At twenty-thousand feet, the sun slanted through the glass at him from the deep blue empty sky, warm and sleep-making and relaxing, and he lay, still as a lizard, soaking it up, full of the agreeable knowledge that he had earned every minute of this sybaritic bliss.

For things had gone well at Loch Eriboll. It had taken two days to verify that the man responsible for the error in the siting of the lead shield foundations was an Admiralty representative, since departed to another project. Then it had been necessary to fly from Wick to London to convince their Lordships that only the incompetence of their own employee could have led to such gross misinterpretation of the plans accurately drawn up by James Douglas Limited. Ultimately, they had agreed, had apologised and had promised to confirm in writing that any resultant delays would in no way be regarded as the fault or responsibility of the contractors.

Altogether, things could have been a lot worse. James's precious reputation with the Government was unimpaired. Chambers had driven the Lotus down from Wick without incident and a driver would have it waiting for him at the airport. And Julia had had almost a week to cool off and reconsider the wisdom of her various attitudes. It seemed unlikely, after such a lapse of time, that she would want to resume hostilities where they had been broken off. Certainly, he was not prepared to let that possibility diminish his present contentment.

He lay and drowsed in the Saturday morning warmth and thought of nothing in particular until a change in the engine note and a tilting of his seat brought his eyes lazily open. He looked out. Far below, the shallow waters of the Solway Firth glittered in the spring sunshine. Ahead were the Galloway hills and the green fertile ribbon of the Nith valley and, beyond them, on the hazy rim of the world, the pale yellow effluvia of Scotland's industrial centre hung in the sky. Already, the aircraft had begun the long downhill slide from the English border.

He eased his legs. There was barely time for a cigarette. He fastened his safety belt, rested his head on the seat back and let his eyes close again. As he sank slowly down over the low, spring-green, sheep-dotted hills of the southern uplands, he slept.

Macpherson, one of the drivers from the pool, was waiting at Abbotsinch with the Lotus. Archie allowed himself to be driven into the city, for the sense of leisure which the early flight had induced was rare enough to be worth prolonging. And the day was young. Saturday or not, many things might still happen before nightfall. And Julia had to be met, and lived with. For the time being, he preferred not to think about Julia.

He left Macpherson to park the car and made his way to his father's office, already aware, as the lift bore him upwards to the seventeenth floor, that his mind and body were tautening in readiness for whatever might be awaiting his return.

But the first glimpse of James Douglas was reassuring. He was reading the *Tribune* and smoking his pipe, looking quietly pleased with himself.

'Hello,' said Archie tentatively.

Douglas glanced up and lowered the paper.

'Ah!' he exclaimed. 'There you are. When did you get back?'

115

'This morning,' said Archie, and put his brief-case and coat on a chair. 'Half an hour ago. I came straight in from the airport. Did you get my tele-message from London?'

His father nodded.

'Yes. I got it last night. And all's well?'

'All's well. We're in the clear.'

'I never doubted we would be. How did their Lordships take it?'

'Pretty well. We parted the best of friends.' Archie stretched himself and sat down. 'I'll write a full report for the file, but I'd just as soon leave that over till Monday. It's been quite a week.'

'I'm sure it has.'

'And how are things at this end?'

'Oh . . . fine.'

'Good.'

Douglas fiddled unnecessarily with the ash in his pipe.

'Seen the paper?'

'Which? The *Tribune*? No, I never see it. It's not worth reading.'

'Ah, but that's where you're wrong.' Douglas pushed it across the desk. 'Every now and then, it gets a scoop. Have a read at that.'

Archie stared at the column headline—

JAMES DOUGLAS'S FOLLY?

'What the devil!' he exclaimed.

'Read it,' advised his father.

Archie glanced at him suspiciously, uneasy at something vague but unfamiliar in his expression. Then he read it.

'Recently [the paper said] we told you in this column that we had reason to believe that millionaire industrialist, James Douglas, was planning some new move to add to his already immense fortune. And we indicated that in our opinion the time had come for him to turn his vast private empire into a public concern, permitting the small investor to share his good fortune.

'On both these issues, we have to admit today that we were wrong.

'He is planning a new move, yes. But it is more likely to lose him millions than to add one penny to his bank balance. In our opinion, the private investor is well out of it.

'For all our information leads to one conclusion.

'James Douglas is proposing to start a new daily newspaper.

'This, at a time when papers are dying and have been dying by the dozen for a decade, can be regarded as nothing else but the sheerest folly.

'The *Tribune* believes that competition is a good thing and fears no rival, but we have to say, in sorrow, that we lament the appearance of such an ill-judged enterprise as this appears to be.

'The Editor-elect is a man well known in the journalistic world of this city, a man of experience and integrity. The intended News Editor has a name known to reporters on every continent. And if one may judge the constitution of the Board of Directors by the distinguished men who visited the Douglas building last night, then there will be no lack of competent advisory talent. But such talent has to be paid. And highly. These people are unlikely to accept peanuts.

'And where is the money going to come from?

'We fear that it will come from Douglas's other undoubtedly lucrative interests. If it does, they will soon cease to be lucrative. For there are few ways of losing a fortune so quickly as attempting to run an uneconomic newspaper.

'And it will be uneconomic. Make no mistake about it. The tragic ghosts of those which have died line the road that James Douglas is choosing to travel.

'Well, it is his own money. To that extent, it is his own affair. But if James Douglas falls, tens of thousands of men and women in his employment will fall with him. And this is a risk he has no right to take.

'He has no right to gamble the security and the happiness of these people to gratify what must be no more than the whim of an ageing man.

'So we would say to him—think again.

'Now.

'Before it is too late.'

117

'Good God!' said Archie.

His father grinned.

'What's wrong?'

'What's wrong!' He threw the paper down. 'Is this drivel supposed to be true?'

Douglas shrugged his shoulders.

'Up to a point.' He pushed a sheet of paper across the desk. 'I had that statement released this morning.'

Archie read it quickly.

'Mr. James Douglas wishes it to be known that he has formed a new company to be known as "New Scot Publications Ltd". This company will commence publication of a new daily newspaper, *The New Scot*, and the first copies will be on sale on the morning of Saturday, April 24th.

'Mr. Douglas, who is the only shareholder, will form a Board of Directors to assist him in the administration of the company and will be Chairman of that Board.

'Mr. John Anderson, former Editor of the *Glasgow Daily*, will be Editor of the newspaper, assisted by Mr. Sam Gold, who will be News Editor.

'No financial or other link exists between this new company and the other companies with which Mr. Douglas is concerned.

'Further information will be made available to the Press and the public during the coming week, but, in view of the inaccurate rumours believed to be circulating in the city, it has been thought advisable to issue this statement now.'

He put it down slowly.

'So,' he said, 'now we know the reason for your partial withdrawal.' He pushed the statement away in disgust. 'For heaven's sake!'

Douglas lifted a grizzled eyebrow in surprise.

'It's not in fact the reason. Only part of it. And there's nothing indecent about starting a newspaper.'

'There's always something indecent about wilful stupidity. Or don't you realise that this is liable to lose you a couple of million?' He ground out his cigarette. 'Don't expect me to think that's a good idea.'

Douglas placidly blew out a plume of smoke and looked thoughtfully at his son. The concern that showed through his hostility was rather touching.

'When did you ever know me start something that didn't pay?' he asked mildly.

'Oh, you're not in the habit of it. I quite agree.'

'Then why should I suddenly start? And what makes you so sure it won't pay?'

'God knows why you should start, but the economic facts of newspaper business are clear enough. It can't pay. Look at the history of the last ten or fifteen years ... the *Glasgow Daily* and all the rest. Take a look at the simple basic statistics that Kinloch could give you in ten minutes if you lift the phone.'

'Aye,' said Douglas. 'It's not just the loss of the money that's bothering you? The possibility that you might inherit a bit less?'

'No! What bothers me is the idea of putting good money into bad business. Otherwise, I don't give a damn. The money you made, you can spend. On anything you like. When I want money, I'll make it myself.'

Douglas nodded and hid his satisfaction.

'Fair enough,' he said. 'Since you're not personally involved, you can simmer down and listen. This paper'll lose money hand over fist for one year and possibly two. By the third year, it should break even. After that, it'll pay ... and pay as well as any paper in the country. And if you think this is just ... what was it? ... the whim of an ageing man, you can think again. I worked for my money and I'm not going to throw it away, except ... *except* ... on something that I think is important.' He pointed his pipe stem at the *Tribune*. 'What they say or think doesn't matter. They called you a handsome playboy last Monday and that doesn't matter. You know you're not. I know you're not. But they know nothing except the scraps of information that some reporter doing his job can pick up. They don't know that this paper's a means to an end for me. They'll find out what the end is soon enough. And so will you. But I'd ask you to be a little less quick to condemn

119

something you know nothing about.'

Archie looked away.

'Sorry,' he muttered.

'It's all right,' said Douglas, and smiled as he got to his feet. 'Just watch it the next time.'

He pressed the buzzer and Sally appeared as he was taking his coat from the peg.

'Hello, Sally,' said Archie.

'I'm away,' said Douglas. 'If you want me, the sheet'll tell you where to find me. And there's a tape there with letters on it. Try and get them off this morning.' He turned in the doorway. 'And 'bye, 'bye, Archie. Give my love to Julia.'

Archie thought hard as he watched him go. Something was strange, indefinable but strange, not only in his expression, but in his whole attitude. He turned to Sally.

'Where's he off to?' he demanded.

'I don't know,' she said.

'And what's this about a sheet?'

She gathered together the papers on the desk.

'Och, it's just a note he's left of where he's going. But I haven't seen it yet.'

There was something odd about Sally too, something secret hidden in her eyes.

'Listen,' he said. 'What's going on?'

'Nothing,' she said innocently. 'Just the usual.'

'There's something,' said Archie. Her face was turned from him. She did not answer. 'There's something,' he repeated. 'It's not like him to tear around on a Saturday morning.'

Sally straightened from the tidied desk.

'Och, he's a busy man,' she said.

'Sure,' said Archie ironically. 'Sure. He's a busy man.'

*   *   *

During the next five days, he was an exceedingly busy man.

He regarded the forthcoming local elections as little more than a trial run, but some sixty potential candidates, selected months before, had to be contacted again and given a fresh briefing. They were scattered throughout the country, but with concentrations in the counties and burghs where national or

Liberal feeling ran highest. Many of them were destined to stand for Parliament itself eventually, but first they had to show their quality in this preliminary canter.

It was up to them to make the power, purpose and vitality of the new Party felt throughout the land, to create a new political feeling which was at once personal, national and classless. They had to restore national pride after two hundred and fifty years of erosion and yet avoid any flavour of chauvinism, parochialism or insularity. The picture of a nation controlling its own destiny, reconstructing its society, revivifying its deserts, restoring the imbalances of its economy, rediscovering the uniqueness of its culture, must be made to seem no dream, but rather something which the Party under Douglas's leadership could make an attainable reality.

During these five days, all sixty of these men were seen by either Douglas or Ewan Cameron. In the lounges of small town hotels, in the sitting-rooms of anonymous suburban houses, in the saloon bars of country inns and the cocktail bars of city restaurants, the spark was kindled.

On Thursday, the twenty-second, nominations were lodged. That evening, shortly after five o'clock, Douglas returned to his office. He was tired. After five nights of talking into the small hours, he could have been nothing else. Yet weariness was eased by a sense of achievement.

Sally had already gone, so he lifted the phone and rang Roderick Grant. It was Paula who answered.

'Hello. Mr. Grant's office.'

Her voice was husky and low-pitched, making even that sound like seduction.

'Douglas here,' he said. 'Is Mr. Grant with you?'

'Oh yes, sir. One moment, sir.'

The soft, bedroom note had gone. Grant was on the line almost at once.

'Yes, sir?'

'Just to let you know I'm back. Any problems?'

'None.' Grant sounded enviably fresh. 'I've spent this week concentrating on plugging the paper. I thought we could start the local election campaign next week, once the paper's launched. Is that all right?'

'Yes, fine. I'll give you biographies of the candidates by . . . well, it'll be Saturday. Enough to start on and you can work them up yourself. And co-operate to the full with local papers.'

'Absolutely. Now, there's just one thing. You'd better give a Press conference, sir. The question is . . . when? Saturday morning?'

'No,' said Douglas. 'Monday morning. Eleven o'clock. Then they'll really have something to ask questions about. Until Saturday night's over, there's only the paper to talk about. And after Saturday night, we want as much publicity as we can get.'

'Sure. And what about B.B.C. Television? If they take the pet about Saturday, they'll not come on Monday.'

'Ask them, anyway. And the Independent lot as well. Then we're sure of at least one.'

'Right. Now, one more thing, sir. Sir Jack Armstrong's got a lot of ideas on the Highlands and since he quit the Highland Redevelopment Commission he's anxious to air them. What about giving him a centre page leader or some such thing next week?'

'That's Anderson,' said Douglas. 'Just watch the overlap. But I quite agree. It's a good idea. I'll put it up to him. Nothing else?'

'Not at the moment, sir.'

'Right. You'll get me here all day tomorrow if you want me.'

He hung up and rang Jock Anderson.

'Hello, Jock,' he said. 'How are things?'

The Editor did not sound pleased to be disturbed.

'Hellish,' he said. 'Bloody awful. And I've no time to talk.'

Douglas paused.

'You'll make it for Saturday?' he asked quietly.

'If we work right through, we will, God help us. But it's the biggest guddle I've ever seen in a lifetime of journalism.'

'And you'll manage fifty thousand?'

'We'll print fifty thousand, but how the hell we're going to distribute them, God alone knows. There's no despatch worth speaking about. We've only six vans——'

'How many do you need?'

122

'About another ten, and even——'

'Buy them,' said Douglas.

'Buy them, for God's sake! What about drivers? They don't drive themselves.'

'Hire them. And hire more staff for despatch if you need it, but get them out, Jock. And now get me whoever's handling Features.'

'There's nobody. Not yet. Sam Gold's doubling up.'

'All right, then. Get me Sam Gold. And cheer up, for heaven's sake. It's better than raising chickens.'

Douglas held the ear piece away and grinned. If only half of that was acting, things were happening in Trinidad Lane. In contrast, Sam's voice sounded relaxed and easy.

'Gold here.'

'Hello,' said Douglas. 'How's it going?'

'Oh . . . you know. Soldiering on. Another thirty hours and we'll be running them off.'

'And you're doing Features?'

'Temporarily. I hope, temporarily.'

'Well, Grant's come up with the suggestion that we give Jack Armstrong a chance to spread himself on Highland development. Talk to Jock about it. If he agrees, give him a leader next week some time, but let me see it before you print it.'

'A straight article or an interview?'

'Any way you like.'

'Well, if it's all right with you, I'd handle that as an interview. Print question and answer. I did a series in the States way back on the Tennessee Valley Authority and it's a subject I've got views on myself. I could feed him the right questions and see what comes out of it.'

'All right,' said Douglas. 'Do it that way. But you're not the only one with views. I still want to see it. We've got a policy on this.'

He hung up and sat on, his elbows on the desk, his head resting in his hands. It was now that fatigue came, sleep-lack lying heavy behind the eyes, stifling thought. But there was little more to do. Tomorrow, he thought. Anything else can wait. Tonight, a good meal, a whisky by the fire with Margaret and an early bed. And tomorrow, the television thing. Look out the draft. Build it up. Build it up early, so that if a cut comes something at least will be said. But that can lie. Thank God for something that can lie.

The great tower of granite and glass and concrete and steel was quiet now, the typewriters silent, the offices still, the rest rooms emptied of the chatter of secretaries and clerks, quiet but for the rattle of a distant cleaner's pail and the hum of the city beyond the window, a somnolent sound that pressed on the eyelids and lowered them gently and slowly withdrew to the threshold of audibility, letting sleep come near, waiting to comfort and ease the ache of weariness.

His head was nodding when the door opened, but he was awake at once.

'I was on my way out, when I saw the car,' said Archie. 'I didn't know you were in.'

'Just ten minutes ago,' said Douglas. He felt for his pipe. 'Have a seat.'

'I'd be glad to,' said Archie wearily. 'It's been quite a week. Where have you been?'

'Oh . . . here and there.'

'Getting the paper organised?'

'More or less.'

He looked at his father curiously. His tan was fading and some of the glow of well-being had gone from his skin. In his eyes, the brightness was diminished. If this is the paper, thought Archie, it's knocking him more than the business ever did.

'And how's it going?' he asked.

'Fine,' said Douglas. 'What about your end? That's the bread and butter.'

Archie grinned.

'And the jam,' he said. 'With more jam yesterday. We landed the Loch Ryan N.A.T.O. contract.'

'Did we, indeed?' Some of Douglas's weariness departed. 'On the basis of the tender?'

'Just about. One or two minor changes that don't make any difference to us.'

124

'Good.' He felt himself waking up. 'And anything doing at the Wash?'

'Nothing new. Still surveying, boring, arguing . . . you know.'

Douglas nodded.

'I know. I've had two years of it.' He glanced up at his son. 'And how are things at home?'

'Oh . . . all right.'

'Julia?'

'She's fine.'

He met his father's eyes briefly, and looked away. He had never been very good at lying to him. Though it was not exactly lying to say that. She was fine, as she was always fine, with a fine, firm, disease-resistant body which he had not seen since his return from London.

She had been out that day, with friends, she said, and had returned in the Mercedes just in time for dinner. Throughout the meal they had talked of trivialities, but in a manner near enough to normal to encourage in him the belief that the incident at Gartland the previous Sunday had been forgotten. Not until they had taken their coffee into the lounge did she refer to it. Then she said—

'I confirmed the Rome bookings this afternoon.'

He looked at her in surprise.

'But I told you. I can't go.'

She lit a cigarette with the silver table lighter and held it, irritatingly, to the centre of her lips.

'You told me . . . yes . . . something about the business and being unable to get away, but of course that's nonsense. I said so.'

'I know you said so. You said so very rudely. But both my father and I made it clear that——'

'Oh yes, you tried to. But really . . . it's too absurd. You didn't think you'd convinced me, did you? I mean, that you're utterly indispensable?'

He did not answer her. He went to the drinks cupboard, took out a bottle of Remy Martin and poured himself a brandy. With the glass cupped in his hands, he returned to the fire.

'I told you not to interfere in the business,' he said quietly.

125

'Is our holiday business? I wouldn't have thought so. I wouldn't have thought it unreasonable for a wife to feel a holiday should be shared. And your father's in no position to tell you that you can't go, when he's been away himself.'

'My father isn't telling me. The facts are telling me. It's impossible.'

He sipped the brandy, rolled it on his tongue and let it go over.

'The facts?' She gave a little laugh, false and unmusical. 'I suppose you mean this absurd newspaper? Oh yes, I've seen the evening papers. He's released a statement. And really . . . I don't know which is worse . . . the rumours or the facts. I suppose it's senility, really. A sort of exhibitionism.'

'It's his affair,' said Archie shortly.

'But it's not. Not if it's going to mean you have to do his work. Which is what it does mean, doesn't it? This talk of a new project! Did you think it would deceive me?'

'There is a new project. One of the biggest we've ever had. And I never have deceived you. Not in all these years. But there's not much point in being so frank in the future, if you're going to disbelieve me.'

The eyebrows lifted above her steady, arrogant eyes.

'What do you mean by that?'

'I dislike being called a liar.'

'Then don't lie, darling,' she said. 'It's perfectly obvious. Your father's got a new toy. He wants time to play with it. So you have to do his work. And we have to suffer. I have to suffer. Well, I don't see why I should. I don't see why I should give up my holiday to pander to his whim. And I'm not going to. There's nothing more to be said.'

He drank the rest of the brandy quickly. It stretched in a burning cord from his throat to his stomach. He put down his glass and held on to his anger.

'Do you realise how much you owe to my father?' he asked quietly.

Her surprise was not feigned.

'That I owe to your father? Oh, my dear man! Don't be absurd. I'm not entirely without means of my own, you know.'

126

He nodded.

'I know that. But don't imagine for a minute that your means would allow you to live as you do.'

'What do you mean by that?'

'Just that you haven't the slightest idea how much it costs us to live. Your own resources would let you live like this for about three months in the twelve.'

'Oh, really!'

'The other nine months you owe to my father.'

She laughed.

'Does your father pay the bills?'

'I pay the bills, thanks to my father. I own this house, thanks to my father. Every penny of capital I possess, I owe to him. And I work for my income, a substantial income that you would go through like a dose of salts if I didn't control it. And if I have to do more work this summer, I'll be paid more for doing it. Nothing could be fairer.'

She sat up straight.

'Nothing could be fairer! We lose our holiday and you say that nothing could be fairer! Really! How pathetic to see a man of your age so much under his father's thumb!"

'Leave my father out of it.'

'How can one, when he's entirely responsible.'

'I am responsible.'

'Are you?' She rose and stood in front of the fire, her elbow on the mantelpiece, looking down at him with a half-smile. 'You poor deluded boy!'

Her eyes were steady. The flames, bilaterally reflected, burned in her pupils like twin fires. Above them, her eyebrows ran upwards and outwards to the drawn-back hair at her temples. Once, they had seemed elegant. Now, they were slim slanted artefacts above her unfeeling immobile features. She was pale. Her lips were thin, and lifted over her even white cat's teeth. He looked at her as if he had never seen her before and did not hear the knock at the door.

'Come in,' said Julia.

Archie turned his head. Oonagh stood there, with Jamie in his pyjamas hanging back, staying in the comforting protection of her nearness.

'I brought him down to say goodnight,' said Oonagh. 'When you didn't come up, I thought——'

'We were busy,' said Julia shortly. 'All right, then, Jamie. Come on. It's time you were in bed.'

He moved, hesitantly.

'Go on, Jamie,' said Oonagh softly. 'Say goodnight to your Mum and Dad.'

Archie watched the boy turn his face to take his mother's kiss on the cheek.

'Goodnight, sonny,' he said, and held out his arms. The young animal body was firm and pliant, the ruffled hair springy beneath his fingers. He whispered in his ear.

'Have you had a good day?'

'No.'

The reply was clipped, heartfelt. He held him away and looked at him.

'Why?' he asked. 'Why not?'

'I'd nobody to play with. I'd rather be at school.'

'But you can't be at school all the time.'

'Why not? It's more fun at school.'

'But if you were at school all the time, we would never see you.'

Jamie looked at him and did not reply and Archie's anger died away entirely into sorrow.

'We'll tow the dinghy up to Rhu tomorrow,' he said softly. 'And we'll go out and row round the boats and have a good look at them. All right?'

Jamie nodded just once, but his eyes brightened.

'On you go, then. Sleep tight.'

He looked at Oonagh and she smiled her thanks as clearly as she dared. When the door had closed behind them, he took out a cigarette and lit it, and watched the dead match burn quickly away in the fire's heart.

'We leave on Friday, the fourth,' said Julia.

'You may if you wish,' said Archie wearily. 'I certainly don't.' In the hot caverns of the fire, under the arching flames, he saw the quiet eyes of Oonagh. He looked away from them, up at his wife. 'I thought I'd made that clear. I've promised my father——'

'Your father!' Her upper lip rolled back. 'If I hear that word again tonight, I'll scream! There are times when I hate your father.'

'So I gather,' he said dryly.

'All his smug pomposity! And daring to talk to me the way he did last Sunday, with Anne there, your slut of a sister!'

'Be careful,' said Archie, and felt the rising thud of the pulse in his ears. 'You'll go too far.'

'Yes, I will.' She was suddenly calm. 'I think I will. We're going there on Saturday, aren't we? You insisted.'

'My mother asked us,' he said carefully. 'I accepted.'

'All right, then. He'll be there at dinner, before his silly television thing. It'll be a good chance to tell him how his darling Anne is living, keeping this poor wretch of a so-called artist, sharing that filthy slum of a studio with him, sleeping with him in her flat——'

'You wouldn't dare.'

He rose slowly to his feet.

'But I would. If you didn't want me to, you shouldn't have told me.'

He moved away from her.

'I told you,' he said with difficulty, 'because . . . at that time . . . I thought you were trying . . . to be a good wife. Something like that. I thought . . . if I gave you trust . . . you might give me loyalty. I didn't realise that you were . . . seducing me. I should have known. You'd done it before. For money or information. One or other.'

'I'm a woman,' said Julia. 'I have to use a woman's weapons.'

'Some women don't feel they have to,' he said bitterly.

'Some women?'

She watched him take the Remy Martin bottle to the coffee-table and pour himself another brandy. He glanced at her.

'Don't worry,' he said. 'There isn't another woman. You put me off the whole sex.' He let the brandy linger on his tongue and put down the glass. 'Are you serious?'

'Of course I'm serious.' She let her features soften. 'Unless, of course, you agree to go to Rome with me and end this silly nonsense.'

He looked at her then, levelly, with eyes as cold as her own.

'You blackmailing bitch,' he said softly. 'I should divorce you.'

She smiled.

'But you won't, darling. You're not the type.'

'You could be wrong,' he said. 'And you're certainly wrong if you believe that blackmail will work. I'm still not going to Rome.'

Julia shrugged her shoulders.

'As you wish. But I thought you cared more for your sister.'

He stopped, looking down at her.

'I care for my sister. We're about as different as we could be, but I still care. It's something I don't expect you to understand. You never cared for anything except yourself ... and money. So I'm going to hurt you a little.'

She stared.

'What do you mean?'

'You have an allowance from me of two thousand a year. Net. That is, you may remember, additional to housekeeping expenses. You agree it is additional?'

She nodded slowly.

'Of course.'

'Well, if you do this, it stops at the end of this month.'

She wrinkled her nose.

'How childish!'

'It's not a very childish sum of money.'

'And do you imagine I care?'

'I think you will, when the time comes. Rather more than you expect. And now, if you'll excuse me, I'm going out.'

'Where to?'

'Does it matter?'

She looked quickly away.

'No.'

'Very well, then.'

He took out the Lotus and drove carefully out of Helensburgh towards the city. At the first public call box inside the city limits, he stopped. As he waited for Anne's number to ring, he seemed to have stopped thinking, seemed to have lost all capacity to feel anything but the cold nip in the air of the spring night. When she answered, he said—

'Anne? I want to see you.'

Her voice changed.

'Is something wrong?'

'In a way. Anyway, I want to see you. Is . . . is Peter there?'

There was a pause before she said—

'Yes.'

'Could he go away? I'd like to see you . . . alone.'

Again she paused. He shivered a little.

'Where are you?'

'In a call box out on the Boulevard.'

'How long will you be?'

'A quarter of an hour. Or a little less.'

'All right.'

'And you'll be alone?'

'I'll be alone.'

Her voice was low. He heard the click of her phone going down and hung up. Back in the Lotus, he shivered again and turned on the heater. Above him, the orange overhead lights fled by as the car slid through the endless, weaving traffic of the new approaches.

The stairway to her flat still seemed to hold the cold of winter, but the place itself was warm. Twin bars glowed on the wall-mounted heater in the sitting-room. He moved near to them, rubbing his hands. Behind him, Anne said—

'You'd better have a drink.'

He turned and looked at her. She wore black tapered slacks and a black jumper with a wide, loose, ribbed collar, and he realised with a start that she was beautiful, more beautiful by far than Julia, and with a soft inviting warmth that reminded him, far back in his memory, of his mother, and childhood, and the lawns at Gartland on a summer day.

'I . . . I had a brandy before I left,' he said.

'I'd never have known,' she said. 'You look as if you need one. I've never seen you so pale.'

'All right. I'll have a whisky. With a lot of water.'

As he waited, he looked round the room. It was modern, simply furnished, but with elegance and taste. And it was warm. It was welcoming. This above all. It had some quality which no room in his own house had ever had, something that made you feel it had been waiting, ready and inviting, to take you and keep you against the onslaught of the world. He looked at his sister curiously when she came back, for this was her environment, something she had made.

'Thank you,' he said, and took the glass from her. 'What about you?'

'I won't.'

'I think you should,' he said gently.

Alarm flickered momentarily in her eyes. She did not argue.

'All right. I won't be a minute.'

He took his drink to an armchair and sat down, suddenly feeling the tiredness from the week that had gone. He put his glass on the little table and tried to make himself relax, letting his left arm hang, stroking the pile of the carpet idly with his fingers, touching an object, playing with it, holding it, rolling it. Then, incuriously, he picked it up. When Anne returned, he was looking at it.

'It's Peter's cigarette-holder,' she said. 'He thought he'd lost it.'

He gave it to her and she put it on the bookcase top, close to a framed photograph which he had not noticed. He pointed to it awkwardly.

'Is that . . . him?'

It was a quarter plate study of a young man in the uniform of an army officer, a handsome, alert young man with good-humoured eyes and lips whose lines still carried traces of a recent smile. On each of his two equal shoulders he bore a solitary pip and his two arms were folded across his chest.

'Yes,' she said. 'That's him . . . a year or two ago.'

She sat down on the other side of the electric fire and tucked her slim legs up on the cushion beneath her. She raised her glass.

'Cheers,' she said.

'Cheers.'

He sipped his whisky and felt the dead weight of their blood relationship lying between them. She looked at him levelly.

'It's Peter you've come about, isn't it?'

132

'Yes,' he said.

'Has Daddy found out?'

He moved uneasily.

'Not yet. But he's going to. On Saturday night.'

She was very still.

'How?'

And he told her. He told her what Julia had said, what Julia was, what Julia had been throughout the years of their marriage. He began hesitantly, stumbling over words, seeking through the barrier for the kind of contact that had existed between them in the old days when there was no Julia, no Peter, then finding fluency and letting it tumble out in a great unburdening of all the things he had told no one, partly through misplaced loyalty, partly through shame, partly because, as long as it was known by no one else, a part of him could pretend to believe that none of it existed. Now, to talk of it was a liberation that left him drained, and clear-headed, and with an empty glass in his hand.

'So there it is,' he said at last. 'I've made a hell of a mess of it and now you're being dragged in. I'm sorry.'

'Don't be sorry.' Her voice was flat. 'It's not your fault.'

'But it is my fault. I should never have told her. But I thought all this ... tenderness, all this loving, was real. I should have known. But you always hope that ... this time it's real. This time it's going to be different. This time it'll last. But of course it never does. I should have known that.'

'I knew that,' said Anne quietly.

He looked at her in surprise.

'You did?'

'I've known for a long time.'

He looked away.

'I didn't know it showed,' he said bitterly. 'I tried to hide it. In public, I tried to hide it and pretend that everything was all right. And I must say I thought I'd succeeded ... in that, at least. But if you knew, everybody will know.'

'Why should they?' she asked. 'I'm your sister. And I'm more like you than you think. I'm another woman, and that makes it easier. And I'm not in love with her.'

'Nor am I.'

'But you were.'

'Yes,' he said. 'I suppose I was.'

'So, if you can remember what it was like,' said his sister quietly, 'you'll know how I feel about Peter.'

He looked at her. Her features were soft, her grey eyes warm.

'Yes,' he said. 'Yes. I had forgotten.' Suddenly the whole thing was important to him too. 'Anne,' he asked urgently, 'what are you going to do about Peter?'

She gave a little shrug.

'Nothing.'

'Nothing?'

'There's nothing I can do. Daddy was bound to find out, sooner or later. We were never very ... secretive. I'm surprised he hasn't found out before now.'

He put his glass down on the floor.

'It'll shake him.'

'Will it? I don't know. I think he's quite a lot like us. It might not. I think it'll hurt Mummy more.'

He met her eyes and said—

'Why don't you marry him?'

She smiled ruefully.

'There's nothing I'd like better. But he won't agree. Not yet.'

'*He* won't agree?'

'I'm afraid not.'

There was so much that Archie did not know, so much he might not understand. After the months of worrying and hoping and loving and loneliness, it was hard to think of talking about it.

'And why——?' He stopped. 'No, never mind.'

'Why won't he?'

'It's none of my business,' he said, 'but ... well, I thought you might be glad of the chance. I mean, to talk about it. If I can help, I will.'

'Do you mean that?'

He looked up at her and nodded.

'Yes.'

Her eyes searched his face. Then she slid her legs down and got to her feet.

'I'll make a cup of tea,' she said. 'Come on through to the kitchen.'

And in the kitchen, while they waited for the kettle to boil, she began to tell him about Peter.

He scarcely remembered his father, she said. He had been a Regular Army officer with limited private means who had been killed during the withdrawal to the French coast in the summer of 1940. His mother had been sensible enough to realise that the boy, who had now no male relatives, was going to come too much under her influence and so she had sent him to a public school in the north of Scotland where male influence was strong and emphasis was placed on masculine pursuits.

But this had only been a partial success. He had turned out to be artistic, with a passion for painting which the school tolerated but did little to encourage. And the long years of paying heavy fees sadly depleted the modest estate that his mother had inherited. But he had gone from there to Sandhurst and so, eventually, to a commission in his father's old regiment.

And always, he had painted.

'I met him about then,' said Anne. 'Not long after he joined the regiment. He was up in Edinburgh on leave. There was some exhibition on he wanted to see. And he was staying with a friend of mine. I met him there.'

She sipped her tea and remembered how he had been that night. It seemed very long ago.

'I thought he was . . . well, just wonderful. I still do. But he was full of fun then. And so fit it made the rest of us feel ashamed. I suppose I was in love with him from the beginning. But nothing happened. He went away and I thought . . . that's that. But we met again, quite by chance. Then he wrote to me and we met . . . oh, several times that year. Then just after Christmas, the Christmas before last, he went away . . . for good.'

Her voice quivered and Archie looked at her quickly, but she was composed, for she had learned to live with this thing.

'For good?' he asked quietly.

135

'For good,' she repeated. 'You see, when he did come back, he wasn't quite the same.'

'Where did it happen?'

'Sarawak. Just a month after he landed. He was out with a patrol in the frontier area and they got caught in an ambush. A mortar bomb blew off his arm. His sergeant got him back. Then they patched him up and sent him home. But he was never going to be much good to them again, so when his wound had healed they discharged him. That was almost a year ago.'

'And since then?'

'Well, I knew nothing about this for . . . oh, it seemed like years. He didn't answer my letters. So eventually I wrote the War Office and they told me. They were very good, really. I got his address from them. And I went straight down. That was last autumn. He was living alone in a tiny cottage in Suffolk, in one of those flat, horrible places by the sea, miles from anywhere. And he was painting, grey pictures of the sea and the flat shore, full of pale, watery light and pearl-grey mists and opalescent, hopeless clouds. And he was like that himself, all grey and hopeless.'

'But he came away with you?'

'Not at first. He wouldn't. You see——' She broke off. 'Oh, Archie, I don't know if you can understand.'

'I can try.'

'Well, it wasn't just his arm. It was far more than that. He'd always believed in the old Greek idea that intelligence and wisdom and artistic sensibility should live in a perfect body, that a man is mind *and* body linked harmoniously to live a life which is a balanced combination of the physical and the intellectual. Now, suddenly, he was shattered. He'd rather have died. He was a cripple in his own eyes. He didn't want to live at all if it meant inhabiting what he thought of as a deformed shell.' She looked away. 'I had to teach him to love and respect his body again by showing him that I loved and respected it.'

'And you have?'

She shook her head slowly.

'Not quite. I almost have. But he still feels that he's gro-

136

tesque ... deformed. He still feels that people's eyes are on him as if he were some sort of exhibit at a freak show. But he's better than he was. Now, his world contains us both. He's not alone any more. But he's frightened to go outside it. He's frightened to meet people. And when he does, he isn't very charitable. He sees them in black and white ... he saw you that way the day you looked in. He saw you as the public school product ... the bad kind ... snobbish, conventional, smug, intolerant, critical, suspicious ... oh, I don't know.'

'He was right,' said Archie. 'I was all these things.'

Anne smiled.

'Yes ... I suppose you were ... that day. But you're not really. I tried to tell him that.'

'You did?'

She nodded.

'Yes.'

'I didn't deserve that much consideration.'

'Well ... I think you do.'

He looked at her, and despised himself, and hated Julia for what she was and for what she planned to do.

'And what happened? After you went to Suffolk?'

'I stayed with him for ... oh, six weeks. Something like that. Then I found a little flat for him in town. Not far away. It's tiny, but ... he couldn't afford anything more. And it's near. He paints there. Sometimes he comes down and paints with me when I'm working, but usually there's too much dust. And he's using colour again, just in the past month. That's one thing that makes me hopeful.'

'And money?'

'He has a pension. That's all.'

'But you have money?'

She smiled.

'Yes, I suppose I have. And most of the time I wish I hadn't.'

He stared at her.

'Why, for heaven's sake?'

'Because it's another barrier, Archie. That's all. If I were poor, I think he'd marry me. As it is ... well, he thinks it would look as if he were marrying me for my money. And of course it would, to some people. To people like Julia.'

He thought of Julia and realised how utterly unimportant she was beside this man, how her only importance lay in the trouble she could cause him and in the scars she could leave on the developing personality of young Jamie. Outside these things, she was irrelevant, with the nuisance value of a gnat on a summer night. Suddenly, he was awake.

'Bring him on Saturday,' he said.

Anne's eyes widened.

'On Saturday?'

'By bringing him, you can spike her guns. Completely.' He leaned forward. 'Anne, there isn't any scandal to tell if they've met him, if you let just a little of the story leak. And Mum and Dad aren't fools. They know you're not sixteen. They'll guess at the relationship. Mum will, anyway. And they'll be gentle with him. I know they will. And Julia will be left with nothing to say.'

His sister's grey eyes were thoughtful.

'I don't think he'll come,' she said.

'If you try, you can make him come.'

'I've asked him before and he wouldn't.'

'But he's better. You said he was better than he was. And they'll have to meet him sooner or later. It's better that they should meet him before they get some filthy, distorted, second-hand story.'

'Yes,' she said. 'I don't want that. If he ever got to hear of it, it would finish him.'

'All right, then.'

She made up her mind suddenly.

'I'll try.'

He smiled.

'Fine. If you try, you'll do it.' He rose to his feet. 'And now I really must go. It's after eleven.'

She reached out her hand for his.

'Thanks, Archie,' she said. 'And I'm sorry I can't help you with Julia.'

'I don't need any help,' he said. 'Not now.'

She slid to her feet and faced him.

'What are you going to do?'

138

'I don't know,' he said. 'I haven't the slightest idea.'

Now, five days later, as he left the office with his father, he still had not the slightest idea. And he still had not heard from Anne. That worried him as much as anything. If Peter continued to be difficult and refused to come, Julia would be triumphant, his mother would be deeply hurt in the core of her kind, conventional heart, Anne's position in the family would be made intolerable, Peter would be barred for ever from full acceptance by the others, and his father—— He glanced at that strange man and surprised a sideways glance at himself.

Douglas looked away. The boy had problems. No doubt about it. That shrew of a wife was problem enough for any man. And he had to work it out alone. It was just to be hoped that it didn't affect his efficiency in the business, for the week or two of increased responsibility that he had had was a mere taste of what was to come.

They emerged from the lift together.

'My car's over there,' said Douglas. 'See you the day after tomorrow.'

'Sure,' said Archie. 'Saturday night's the night. What time will we come?'

'Oh ... six-thirty. Seven. Round about then. Time for a sherry before dinner. And I don't have to be at the B.B.C. until ten o'clock, so there's plenty time.'

Too much time, thought Archie. Too much time for the kind of evening it's likely to be.

'Fine,' he said. 'I'll see you then.'

*   *   *

They were five anxious days for Anne, but she could not stop work, for the exhibition in Rotterdam was now definitely on, all the exhibits had to be crated and despatched by the end of the month, and she still had to finish the head of a child on which she was working. It was Peter's head, based on an old snapshot she had stolen from his room, and it was somehow terribly important that it should be there. But it would not be for sale.

And he did not come to her studio on any of these days. He

was working on a picture, he said. It was going well. And he could not risk the dust.

So they were together only in the evenings in her flat and not once did she have the chance to raise the question of Saturday.

She watched him and waited, worried and wondering, for there was something strange about him. There was a new tension in him which diminished the attacks of apathy to which he was subject, an undercurrent of excitement which she sensed rather than saw, lighting his face sometimes without any clear cause, making him laugh too much at little things, then leaving him for short periods when he would lapse into strained, thoughtful silence. She watched, and did not know whether this was good or bad.

Then, on the Friday afternoon of that week, he arrived unexpectedly at her studio, holding a picture wrapped in brown paper beneath his arm. The excitement had bubbled over.

'It's finished!' he cried. 'You've got to see it.'

He held it between his knees and tugged at the string.

'But, Peter! Is it dry? The air's dusty. I've been working——'

'Dry enough,' he said, and pulled off the paper. 'No, don't look. Go over there. That's right. And wait.'

He walked quickly round the room, looking at the way the light was falling. Then he placed it carefully against a bust which faced the north window and stepped back.

'All right,' he said. 'You can look.'

She approached slowly, afraid that it would not be good, then stopped, and her fears vanished. It was good. It was as good as anything he had ever done and it was of another human being.

In all the months since his injury, there had been no people in his pictures. Only empty estuaries. Vast, empty moors. Empty, hollow streets. He had painted a world empty of people who might stare at his empty sleeve. Now he had painted the blind fiddler who played at the Sauchiehall Street corner and the opaque, sightless eyes had been unable to see that there was no hand to hold the palette. He had painted him

140

with honesty and skill, but also with new understanding and compassion.

She turned to him.

'It's . . . it's good,' she said, almost unable to speak.

He stumbled to her over the rubble on the floor.

'Do you really think so? You know him, of course. Do you think I've got him? Not just the look . . . the feel of him?'

'Oh yes, you have!'

'Honestly? You're not just——'

She smiled.

'You don't need me to tell you,' she said. 'You know you have.'

He grinned and circled her body with his arm.

'Yes, I know.' His strength drew her to him. 'I knew while I was doing it. And the old rascal cost me five bob a session. But it was worth it.'

'Every penny.' She stood on tiptoe and kissed him. 'Let's celebrate.'

'How?'

'Tonight. Come to dinner. I'll cook a special meal and we'll have some wine and celebrate. Just the two of us.'

He laughed.

'I will if you kiss me again.'

'Oh, Peter,' she breathed. 'Peter.'

When she slipped from his embrace, she was trembling.

'Yours is finished,' she said. 'I've still got work to do.'

He looked at the child's head emerging from the stone.

'This?'

'Yes, I want to finish it by the end of next week.'

'Who is it?'

'Just . . . a child.'

He stared at it.

'It looks vaguely familiar,' he said.

'Perhaps it reminds you of someone.'

'Yes . . . maybe. Anyway.' He picked up the brown paper and string from the floor. 'I'd better wrap this up before you start.'

'You'd better take it out,' said Anne. 'This dust gets into everything.'

She watched him wrap it up with one hand, watched him tie the string, holding an end with his teeth, and the need to help was like a pain that had to be borne silently. That, and the pain of his departure. She went with him to the door.

'Seven o'clock,' she said. 'Can you make it?'

He looked at her with a shadow in his eyes.

'There's nothing to stop me making it,' he said. 'Nothing and no one.'

*   *   *

That night, in the earliest hours of the new day, when the life of the city was running down like a tired clock, she lay on her back and looked at the white light of the full-grown moon on the turned-back sheet. It seemed to cradle her, this soft, pale, diffused radiance that left the shadows so deeply dark, touched the black mass of Peter's hair with silver, glinted on the silver frame of her father's photograph as though it were a bright sword blade poised above the looming bulk of the walnut escritoire. She lay in it, warm with loving and soothed by wine, and the night-muffled sounds of the still wakeful city did not reach to her above the quiet regular breathing of Peter, who did not sleep.

She knew he did not sleep, though his eyes were closed, black lashes still above moon-bright cheeks. She turned her head to him, her pillowed face in shadow, watching him, wondering what thoughts stirred in the wounded, thinking part of his quiet body, wondering what sort of life the future held for them both when Julia had done, for, in all the evening of their modest celebration, there had been no chance for her to ask him to come with her to Gartland.

He had been unusually quiet all evening, his tension gone, the excitement drained from him now that his picture was done. And he had loved her with a passion which seemed more a driving search for reassurance than the climactic expression of his love, an urgent thrusting coupling in which he sought to rediscover, briefly, the physical power he had had when he was whole, a union in which her only part was to be devoured, consumed to feed the diminished fire of his hidden self. It was unlike him. Yet, if it had been as he wished it, she did not care.

142

She lay and watched him in the moonlight and, when he moved, she let her eyelids fall until he lay between them, in a tremulous slit.

Then, restless as he always was in the hour after love, he rose and stood in the window like a statue, marbled by moonlight, gazing at the light-flecked spread of the city. She heard him sigh. A match flared and, when the flame died, he was dark as Pan behind the red burning spot of his cigarette. His shadow masked her father's photograph. He lifted it and looked at it for what seemed like many minutes. Then he put it down. When he spoke, he was near to the window again, as though the city had drawn him to look down on it, to stand like a maimed white god above its living and its dying, saying to him—this is the world of men. Without darkness. Without silence. Without peace.

'What will become of us?'

He spoke quietly, knowing that she was awake.

'I don't know.'

She let her eyes open wide.

'Will we marry and have children and live tiny lives, passing the buck, hoping our children will do the things we did not do, live the kind of lives we did not live? Is that the aim and object of each generation?' She did not answer. 'It seems . . . like a betrayal.'

'It needn't be like that,' she said softly.

He came and sat on the edge of the bed, his body dark and lined by moonlight, his face shadowed.

'What do you want for us?' he asked gently.

She searched his face, probing the darkness that hid his eyes.

'Happiness,' she said.

The shadows moved in a smile.

'We have that,' he said. 'What else?'

'Marriage. A commitment to each other.'

'And we have that.'

'But it should be like justice,' she said. 'Not only done, but seen to be done. That's why I said marriage.'

'You mean seen by the world? The stifling, strangling, bloody world.'

143

'Yes. We're part of it, Peter, part of the stifling, strangling, bloody world of others, part of the kindness and cruelty and goodness and greed, whether you like it or not. And marriage is only the formalising of our commitment in the eyes of the world.'

'Is it? Or is it something the world contaminates by witnessing it, turning it into something drab and loveless, killing beauty as the years go by, bringing illness and pain and the slow death of conformity, bricking love up in a little square house and heaping debt and hopelessness on top? Doesn't it do that?'

She turned her head away.

'Sometimes it does that,' she said. 'But it wouldn't do that to us.'

'Why not? Are we so different, so resilient, so indestructible?'

'No!' She almost shouted her conviction. 'No! You're missing the point. We're vulnerable. Separately, we're both vulnerable. You know that. But together we're whole, without any seed of self-destruction in us. And these things only happen when the seed is there. Oh, Peter!' She put out her hand and touched his thigh. 'Don't you see it wouldn't be like that for us? Even my parents . . . it wasn't like that for them.'

'Your parents?'

'Yes. Both of them. They've been happy.'

'Your father's been happy?'

He sounded puzzled.

'Yes.'

He paused, then went and brought the photograph, tilting it to the moon.

'Is he really like this?' he asked.

'Like what?'

'Strong, and thrusting, with a sense of humour, the kind of humour that likes slapstick comedy, likes seeing a custard pie thrown in someone else's face.'

'No, he's not!' She reached out her hand. 'Peter, let me see.' He gave her the photograph. The features were vague, blurry in the dim light. 'You don't really see that there.' She looked up anxiously. 'Do you?'

144

He laughed.

'No, not really.' He watched her. 'What do you see?'

'I don't know,' she said slowly. 'He's too near for me to see him clearly. He's kind and gentle——'

'He's a millionaire,' said Peter. 'That makes it hard to be those things.'

'But he is. And he doesn't care about being a millionaire. Really.'

'Then why is he one?'

'I don't know,' she said hopelessly. 'It just happened that way. But I still say he doesn't care. Not about money.'

'Power?'

'I don't know.'

'But he may care about power?'

'Maybe. I don't know. But he's happy. I'm sure of that. Happily married. Happy in his work. Everything.'

'A stable, well-integrated personality.'

She did not notice the bitterness in his voice.

'Yes, I think so.'

'Stable, meaning he's well set in his rut, making money, wielding power, living the nice, conventional, top-income-bracket existence. Well-integrated, meaning his conscience has come to terms with his way of life.'

She sat up quickly and threw her arms around him, choking.

'Peter! Peter darling! He's not like that. Believe me. He's not!'

She buried her face in his breast and his hand came up to hold her there, gently.

'Anne,' he whispered. 'Anne. I didn't mean to hurt you.' She bit back her tears. 'He's your father. You're bound to feel as you do. But to me he's everything I'm not. He's strong. Successful. Able to give you all the things that I can never give you. Able to take the world . . . which is like a wild animal growling at the door to me . . . able to take it in his hand and make it do what he wants. And now you tell me that he's happy too.' His hand tightened. 'It's too much.'

She lay still, her cheek on his beating heart.

'If only he'd been unhappy,' he muttered. 'Then it would seem like retribution. Then I could endure it.'

145

She drew slowly back, her head strangely light, her face as pale as the moon itself. The words came to her from far away, as though spoken by somebody else.

'You're like the God of the Old Testament. You want vengeance and retribution. An eye for an eye and a tooth for a tooth. My father's unhappiness for the loss of your arm.' She felt him wince and his hand moved from her. 'You want the meek to inherit the earth. You want a world of blind fiddlers and poor artists, where the weeds can grow equally with the flowers.'

'Anne——'

'That's what part of you wants. And the other part of you wants the kind of world they had on Olympus, a perfect world peopled by gods and goddesses, where everything physical is the perfection of the physical and a man can write an ode in the morning and die cleanly in battle in the afternoon, where all women who are not mothers are virgins and youths play naked in the sun and no one talks of homosexuality.'

She slipped from him and stood up. His eyes were hurt and bewildered, his lips protesting.

'Anne——'

She ran to the window and threw it open.

'But what you've got is this! Dirt and riches and squalor and fine buildings and people who are neither blind fiddlers nor gods but just people. People like you and me, all saying—what will become of us? All worried sick about tomorrow. Then forgetting for a time and being happy and loving . . . and enjoying it. Enjoying being alive! Enjoying it in spite of everything. That's what you've got. That's what you've got in me. That's what you've got to live with if you live with me.'

'Anne——'

His voice besought her. His arm stretched out to her. She went to him, wondering what she had done. She sank on to him, sobbing, feeling the new chill on his skin.

'You've got to know that, Peter. You've got to know that.'

His arm gathered her to him.

'I know that,' he said deeply.

Her head lifted with his breathing, lifting higher, faster. Then it checked.

146

'Do you really want to marry me?' he whispered.

'More than anything in this world.' The words were little more than a breath on his skin. She tilted her face to his. 'But you mustn't ask me, Peter. Not just now. It's not fair.'

'Not fair?'

'Not fair to you. Not after what we've been saying. I don't want you to ask me when I feel that I've persuaded you.'

'Persuaded! Oh, Anne!' He sank his lips into her hair. 'Anne. Anne. Don't you realise that I want to marry you more than I want to live? But I can't ask you. Not yet. There are too many things not clear to me. And I've no money——'

'But——'

He crushed her mouth to his chest.

'No, don't say it. I know you have. But I've still some pride. If I can sell my pictures——'

'You will.'

'Maybe. But if I can, if I can make enough to let us live simply, like we do now, then I might feel I could ask you.'

'And I have to wait?'

'We have to wait,' he corrected gently.

She lifted her lips to his and closed her eyes against the moonlight.

'Peter.'

When at last his cheek lay against hers, his lips close to her ear, she heard his breathing and the soft night sounds of the city as though they were one sound and the words, when they came, whispered through it.

'But there's one thing I'd like to ask you now.'

'Anything.'

'Let me meet your father.'

She lay still, wide-eyed in his shadow.

'Are you sure you want to?'

'Yes,' he said. 'I'm sure. I'm sure now.'

CHAPTER SEVEN

ON the following morning, James Douglas rose somewhat earlier than usual and shaved standing by his bedroom window, letting the cutting head of the razor purr over the skin of his face as he looked down at the garden.

There, the stubby pruned roses in the neat turned beds were scarcely more than dormant, but beyond them, across the lawn, the sweet-scented azaleas were already alive with bees, the great flower heads of the rhododendrons nodded and dipped in the light wind of the morning, and the great rock wall above the turn of the drive was already aglow with colour, warm purple where the early heaths clung precariously to narrow peat-filled ledges, golden where the alyssum grew from splits and crevices in the rock, pink, mauve, and violet in a hundred shades where the trailing aubretias hung downwards over the sheer faces of the grey lichen-encrusted stone.

He could see the wall from where he breakfasted in the little Victorian conservatory which stood at one end of the terrace. He ate unhurriedly, enjoying it all, letting the warmth of the sun soak into his body through the glass. For this, he believed, could shape his day, could build a mood which could influence his attitude to events and so, indirectly, would influence events themselves. And this day, which would mark the end of the beginning, would be a day of events.

He let the Jaguar take him at its own speed through the awakening countryside and stopped it when the traffic began to thicken, at a little newsagent's shop near to Bearsden Cross.

The man behind the counter was elderly, with traces of his porridge still clinging to the sad yellowing edge of his moustache.

'An ounce of Balkan Sobranie,' said Douglas. 'And I'll take a copy of the *New Scot*.'

He lifted one from the small pile that lay on the counter among the great stacks of the big national dailies. The man handed him the tin of tobacco and nodded his head lugubriously at the paper.

'I'll no' sell mony o' these.'

Douglas tucked it under his arm.

'Why not?' he asked.

'Och, there's enough papers.'

'There's always room for a new one if it's good.'

'Aye. If.'

'Have you seen it?'

'No, I've mair to do. And that's eight and four. Seven and eleven for the tobacco and fivepence for the paper.'

It was an inauspicious start.

The *New Scot* remained folded until Douglas reached his office. Then he spread it out on the desk and lit his pipe, eager to see what use Jock Anderson had made of his editorial freedom. When he turned over the last page, he was well enough pleased. It was a competently produced first issue, light on features, carrying rather too much agency news and distinctly too little advertising, and with a dignified editorial stating the paper's aims, standards and intentions as far as these could be stated at this point in time.

There was also a first-class unsigned leader, behind which Douglas thought he detected the polished hand of Sam Gold. In it, the basic causes of Scotland's current economic problems were brilliantly summarised and placed in a historical and an international context and perspective, and it concluded by making it clear that this was to be regarded as a kind of prologue to a series of articles which would be of great national importance. These would permit the various points raised to be dealt with by acknowledged experts who would analyse them at length and would discuss the lines of action most likely to produce lasting solutions. In parallel with these articles, the paper would provide a platform where anyone qualified to comment would be invited to do so and where discussion could take place on these and any other matters relevant to the well-being of the nation.

It was a useful beginning.

He had just finished reading when Archie rang through.

'I didn't know if you'd be in or not,' he said. 'I thought you might be down at the birth of the new baby. Congratulations.'

'Have you seen it?'

'Only to glance through. But it looked all right to me. Are you busy?'

'Not bad,' said Douglas. 'Come through for coffee.'

Coffee was, by tradition, at ten-thirty. In the time left to him, Douglas dictated half a dozen letters on to tape and brought his movements sheet up to date. Then he rang for Sally.

'Nothing much,' he said. 'A few letters I'd like to go out this morning. When they're done, you can go away home. And Archie's coming in for coffee, so maybe you could bring two cups.'

'Yes, sir.' She picked up the tape and the mail for filing. 'I'll be watching tonight,' she said.

He laughed.

'Och, Sally! You'd be better away out a walk with some nice boy or other. It's a full moon, very nearly.'

She smiled at him and shook her head.

'Not me. I wouldn't miss it for anything.'

'Or anyone?'

She blushed.

'Or anyone.'

'Well,' he said, 'more fool you. When you're old and grey, you'll think back to the night the moon was full and you didn't go out and you'll think . . . that might have been the night.'

'Och, away you go!'

'I'm serious.'

She laughed to him over her shoulder.

'Anyway . . . good luck!'

'Thanks, Sally.'

Archie, when he came, seemed more than usually preoccupied. Douglas, sure that he would find out why eventually, let the conversation meander round the byways of the paper and the business until the coffee had been brought and Sally had gone. Then he said—

'Well, what's on your mind?'

Archie looked up in apparent surprise.

'How do you mean?'

'Well, you must have something on your mind. You wanted to see me.'

'Oh, yes, I wanted to see you, but I've nothing on my mind. It was just that Anne phoned.'

Douglas felt that that was rather less than the whole truth.

'Isn't she coming tonight?' he asked.

'Oh, yes, she's coming. But the thing is, she's got some boy friend she'd like to bring with her.'

Archie, watching his father closely, saw his eyebrows lift a little in what appeared to be mild approval.

'Fine,' said Douglas. 'She'd better let her mother know, though. It'll mean another one for dinner.'

'Yes,' said Archie. 'She . . . she said she'd phone her.'

Douglas looked up at him briefly.

'Do you know this chap?'

'No, I don't. Not really. I met him once, just for a few minutes. I happened to look into the studio and he was there. That was two or three months ago. And I didn't have much time. But he seemed a decent enough fellow.'

'He is,' said Douglas.

When his father glanced across at him, Archie found himself staring and Douglas laughed.

'You needn't look so surprised,' he said. 'Glasgow's far too wee a place for a bit of news like that not to leak out.'

'You mean you . . . you know?'

'If you mean, do I know about Anne and Peter Colquhoun, then of course I know. I've known for six months.'

'But you never said anything.'

'No, I never said anything. What good would there be in saying anything? She's twenty-five. She's a big girl. There was no call for me to interfere. The only way to run a happy family, Archie, is to let them get on with it, leave them to live their own lives. Time enough to interfere when it looks as if they're heading for disaster. And from what I've been able to find out about this man Colquhoun, there was never likely to be anything very disastrous about this affair. Unless, of course, it fell through. For a girl like Anne, that could be disastrous.'

'Well, I'm damned,' said Archie slowly.

His father chuckled.

'I must say I thought you knew I knew. You said something to me . . . oh, I was just back from holiday . . . something about—did I not object to the kind of life she was living? And I said I didn't.'

'But I never guessed——'

'No, I know you didn't. But at the time I thought it was this you were objecting to. The kind of life she's living! Man, you sounded like a Free Kirk minister!'

'There's just one thing,' said Archie soberly.

'What's that?'

'He's an artist, and he's only got one arm.'

Douglas nodded.

'I know that.'

'And he's hardly any money.'

'I didn't know that,' said Douglas, 'but I guessed it. Do you think it matters?'

'It matters to him,' said Archie.

His father stared at him.

'Oh,' he said thoughtfully. 'Is that the way of it?'

'That's the way of it,' said Archie. 'He's so damned in-dependent that up till now he'd have nothing to do with us in case it looked as if it was money he was after.'

'So. And what's made him change his mind?'

Archie looked away.

'I've no idea.'

His father considered that.

'Can he paint?' he asked.

'Anne thinks he can. I wouldn't know.'

'Well, I'll take her word for it.' He looked directly at his son. 'And let's be frank about this, Archie. You've been a bit critical of Anne in the past, critical of things that were no concern of yours. I hope you're not going to be raising any damn fool objections to this.'

'Not me,' said Archie. 'I'm only realising now what a com-plete balls-up I've made of my own marriage. I'm in no posi-tion to go around handing out advice.'

'All right,' said Douglas. 'But what about Julia? She's not going to like it.'

'I'll handle Julia.'

'Well,' said his father, 'I hope you can. But if this Peter is the kind of man I think he may be, Julia could take him apart between the soup and the fish. She'll need watching.'

'I'll watch her all right,' said Archie grimly. 'I'm not going to stand any more trouble from Julia.'

*　　　*　　　*

When Archie went to his wife's room early that evening, he was aware that, for once, his position was strong. Even she could hardly produce her sensational revelation in Peter's presence. But what she might do was unpredictable. Long experience had taught him that. As he knocked on her door, he made up his mind to play his cards as they came.

'Come in.'

She was seated at her dressing-table, just finishing the careful preparation of her face. Her eyes turned to meet his briefly in the mirror.

'You know I don't like being disturbed while I'm dressing,' she said.

He closed the door behind him.

'I know.'

As he watched her draw the new outline of her mouth, watched her roll her lips together, spreading the lipstick, he wondered at his own calmness.

'Well?' she demanded irritably. 'What do you want?'

'I'd like to save you from making a damn fool of yourself.'

'Oh?' She reached for her jewel case. 'How very considerate of you. And how unnecessary.'

'I don't think so,' he said. 'You see, your little bombshell about Anne won't be news after all. My father knows.'

Her hands checked briefly in lifting a tray.

'Do you expect me to believe that?'

'Please yourself. But he's known for six months. Longer than I have.'

'And did nothing about it?'

'Like a sensible man, yes.'

She turned her head and shoulders to look at him.

'You're lying,' she said at last. 'You're lying to try and stop me talking. How very naïve of you.'

Archie rose to his feet. There was no point in prolonging it.

'I told you last Saturday that I didn't like being called a

153

liar,' he said quietly. 'Tell your story if you like. But even you may find it a bit embarrassing. You see . . . Peter's going to be there.'

Her eyes flickered, then hardened.

'I don't believe you!'

He shrugged his shoulders.

'All right. Wait and see. Presumably you'll believe me when you meet him.'

Her lips grew thin.

'Get out! Get out of this room!'

'I'll be glad to,' he said. 'I'll see you downstairs when you're ready.'

He crossed the wide landing and paused at the head of the stair, listening to the silence. The whole house was silent now that Jamie had gone back to school, silent and empty and lifeless. He stood in the big bay window of the drawing-room which looked over the garden and the sheltering trees to the sea beyond, and the emptiness seemed to be within himself. There was a certain sadness even in the sight of the sailing dinghies leaning before the light wind, in the tall white sails of the graceful Dragons, in the cabin cruisers rocking at their moorings while their owners pottered happily around on deck, busy with the innumerable tasks of preparation for the summer season ahead. Sadness, mingled with envy, and self-pity, and nostalgia for something familiar and well-loved that had some-how become unattainable, part of a way of life that had slipped into the past, a past which, in retrospect, seemed to have been so simple and carefree and utterly desirable. His own boat still lay in the yard at Dumbarton, painted and fitted out, ready for the water. Now, it hardly seemed worthwhile putting her in. He had almost decided to sell her when Oonagh came.

'Your wife asked me to tell you that she's not feeling very well. She thought you might be as well to go on without her, seeing it's nearly half-past six already.'

She stood in the shadows by the doorway. For a moment, their eyes met. Then his pulse fluttered and he looked away.

'Is there anything she wants?'

His own voice seemed distant, unfamiliar.

154

'From what she said, I don't think so.'

He forced himself to move towards her, avoiding her quiet disturbing eyes.

'All right,' he said. 'Tell her I won't be late. I'll leave just after the broadcast.'

The Mercedes was ready, waiting at the door, but he paused with his hand on the ignition. It was the family car, with too many associations. He drove it back to the garage and took out the Lotus. Swiftly, he lowered the soft top, flicked the engine into life and drove off, feeling the wind cold on his brow.

Oonagh watched him go, coasting down the drive to the gate, the engine idling, then saw his hair lift and flatten as he turned on to the main road and accelerated towards Balloch and his father's house.

Later that evening, she sat with a book unopened on her lap and watched the gloaming thicken, watched the boats return one by one, ghosting over a calm dark sea to their moorings. The house was quiet and Julia had vanished after dinner. There was nothing for her to do but watch, with Jamie back at school. Watch the boats and watch the family. That, or return to Dublin. She smiled to herself. She would not do that. Not yet. But it was a long time waiting for Archie to see what surely should be clear before his nose.

*   *   *

At that same quiet evening hour, which is neither night nor day in Scotland but something much better than either, the Douglas family and Peter Colquhoun rose from the dinner table at Gartland.

'We'll have coffee in the drawing-room,' said Margaret Douglas.

'I wanted to show Peter the garden,' said Anne. 'It isn't dark yet.'

'All right, dear. Just for five minutes. Then the coffee will be ready.' She turned to Peter. 'Do you take black?'

'Yes,' he said. 'Black or white, I don't mind.'

Margaret smiled at him. He was really very easy. It was such a relief. And it wasn't really so difficult to avoid looking at that empty sleeve.

155

'Then we'll all have black,' she said. 'I'll tell Kirstie.'

James Douglas stood in the wide window. Outside, the light had already begun to fade and the wind had died. The garden was changing into a place of mystery where the shadows massed and merged and deepened and the flowers grew grey and luminous and Anne walked hand in hand with Peter on the edge of the pale lawn.

A carriage clock behind him struck quietly nine times, an antique tinkling sound, and a blackbird near to the window threw a flurry of notes to the sky and fled from the coming night. In half an hour, he would have to leave. In two hours, it would be over, for good or ill.

When Margaret came to his side, he nodded his head towards the two figures strolling in the early dusk.

'Well?' he said. 'That's what you've wanted, isn't it?'

She sighed.

'Yes,' she said. 'It's what I've wanted. And he's a nice boy. It's just—— Och, I don't know. It seems such a shame.'

'Do you mean his arm?' asked Douglas. 'Or the fact that that's what she's chosen?'

'Both,' said Margaret honestly. 'She could have anyone.'

'Aye,' said her husband. 'So she could. That's what makes me glad she's chosen him.'

She watched them, remembering, and slid her arm through his.

'Did you see his suit?' she asked.

'I did.'

'It's old.'

'It's clean.'

'Oh, I know, but it's old. We'll need to help them.'

'He'll not accept it,' said Douglas. 'I can tell you that now.'

'But we'll need to, James.'

'Don't worry,' he said. 'I will. But it'll be in my own time. And only when I can be sure he'll never know.'

Her hand tightened on his arm.

'Go carefully with him,' she said. 'She needs him.'

'They need each other,' said Douglas. 'I never saw two people that needed each other more.'

'Ah,' said Archie from the doorway. 'There you are. Loving

156

couples inside and out. I'm way out on a limb. Is the coffee there?'

'I'll ask Kirstie to bring it in,' said his mother. 'And you'll need to watch your time, James.'

'Och, there's plenty of time,' said Douglas. 'Nearly half an hour.'

He threw a log on the fire and began to sweep the ash from the hearth.

'Well,' said Archie, 'what's the verdict?'

'All right,' said Douglas. 'Just don't go waving your bank statements around in front of his eyes. But time'll fix that.'

'He's quiet,' said Archie. 'He's hardly said a word.'

His father glanced at him.

'If you were broke, and the daughter of the house brought you out here to meet the family with a big question-mark hanging over your head, you'd be quiet too. I don't blame him. And while your mother's out the room ... what's this about Julia?'

Archie shrugged his shoulders.

'A diplomatic illness.'

'To avoid meeting who? Peter or me?'

'Both. All of us, I suppose.'

'Had you a row?'

'We've had several.'

Douglas eyed his son shrewdly.

'Did you know that the shipyard's heading for disaster?'

'No,' said Archie. 'I didn't. Why? What's happening?'

'Just the usual creeping death. Orders drying up and over-heads going on. Foreign competition. Failure to keep up with modern techniques. The old story.'

'I see.'

Archie thought carefully. That could change a lot of things. He tried to remember if all her money was in the yard.

'You're better to know,' said Douglas. 'If she changes her tune, you'll know why.'

'But she doesn't know about it.'

'She will,' said Douglas. 'The whole city will before another year's out. However, we'd better leave it. The others will be back any minute.' He crossed the room to the Georgian corner

157

cupboard. 'Let's give Peter a brandy and see if it loosens his tongue.'

But it did not. He sat on the edge of the conversation and wondered at how easy it all was. The wine had helped, of course, as the brandy was helping, but there was more than that. Anne had been right. Money didn't seem to matter to them. The possession or the lack of it. But then, you probably couldn't feel like that unless you had it, unless you had so much of it that you could forget about it entirely. Yet it didn't seem like that either. There was no vulgar ostentation, no obvious extravagance, and he had seen no servant but old Kirstie. The house, for all its size, was essentially homely, comfortable, livable-in. And the people, even Archie, were the same. So easy to like. So easy to join.

He caught himself quickly. It was a form of seduction, he reminded himself. That they were kind, generous and under-standing meant nothing. He still had to be able to pay his wife's bills.

'Watch your time,' said Margaret.

'A quarter of an hour,' said Douglas. 'There's no hurry. I've been meaning to ask you,' he said to Anne, 'what about that thing in Holland?'

'It's fixed,' she said. 'I've got to get the stuff away by the end of next week and it opens a fortnight after that.'

'Are you going over?'

'I suppose I'll need to. At least for the opening. But it'll only be for a couple of days.'

'I might go over myself,' said her father thoughtfully. 'Either then or later. How long is it on for?'

'Nearly four months. Till the middle of September.'

'Oh well, there's no hurry.' He turned to Peter. 'And what about you? No exhibition coming off?'

'I'm afraid not,' Peter said.

'There should be,' said Anne. 'He's got a roomful of stuff. The trouble is, he's too modest.'

Peter smiled.

'I'm not really. They're just not good enough.'

'But they are,' protested Anne. 'Everything you've done in the last six months is good, some better than others . . . like the fiddler . . . but they're all good enough to sell.'

'He's not being modest,' said Douglas suddenly. 'He's being shrewd.'

They both looked at him.

'What do you mean?'

Her father laughed.

'I would have thought it was obvious. He's going to wait till he paints something he thinks is really good. Then he'll sell it for, let's say, two hundred guineas. Maybe more. After that, all he needs is publicity. A write-up in two or three papers. Approving comment from one of the well-known critics. And right away you've inflated the value of all his earlier work. It's as easy as that.'

Peter looked at him curiously. This was precisely what had struck him earlier in the day, when he had been thinking seriously about ways and means to earn enough to marry. Indeed, he had thought of little else since his talk with Anne the night before.

'But that isn't so easy,' he said slowly. 'It's damn difficult for an unknown name to sell anything for a high price, whether it's good or not.'

'But you admit that's how it would work?'

'If you got that one sale, it probably would.'

'And from the look on your face, I'd guess you'd thought of that yourself.'

'Yes,' admitted Peter. 'I did.'

Anne looked incredulous.

'You didn't!'

'I did,' said Peter.

'There you are,' said Douglas. 'He's a business man at heart.'

'He's not,' said Anne firmly.

'He must be.'

'No, I'm not,' said Peter quietly. 'But I admit I've got to start thinking about selling.'

'All right,' said Douglas. 'And if you're going to sell, there's no point in putting a ten guinea label on a thing that might go for a hundred.'

'It's not so easy,' muttered Peter.

'No,' said Douglas. 'It's not so easy. And one of the reasons why it's not so easy is that you've got to overcome what's practically a national characteristic nowadays. Some damned cancer has eaten away our pride. We undervalue ourselves, underestimate our potential. Oh, not just you. Industry's just as bad as art. But you can't give of your best when you persist in thinking that your best isn't very good.'

'He's off,' said Archie.

'Oh, Daddy,' said Anne. 'Save it for the telly.'

'I've enough material for the telly,' said Douglas equably. 'You're welcome to the overflow.'

'But it's time you were away,' said Margaret. 'It's nearly half-past.'

Her husband laughed and knocked his pipe out in the ash-tray.

'You just want to get rid of me,' he said. 'That's all. Anyway. If you're feeling like it, we can carry on when I come back.'

Anne and Peter glanced at each other.

'We'll probably be away,' said Peter hesitantly. 'I'd better say goodbye.'

'So had I,' said Archie. 'I said I wouldn't be late.'

'Did you?' said his father. He looked at the three of them and chuckled. 'Well . . . please yourselves. But it wouldn't surprise me if I came back and found you all still here.'

*   *   *

Sam Gold looked at his watch and stood up.

'Well,' he said, 'three minutes to go. I'll switch the thing on.'

'And when you're on your feet,' said Jock Anderson, 'have you such a thing in the house as a wee drop whisky?'

Gold laughed.

'You're the man who was refusing it the last night you were here.'

'It's medicinal,' said Jock. 'Just to see me through the next quarter of an hour.' He watched the drinks being poured as the television set warmed up. 'I don't mind telling you, I'll be glad when it's over.'

160

'It'll maybe be over sooner than you think,' said Gold. 'If one of the top boys is watching, he'll get somebody to pull the plug whenever he goes off the straight and narrow. Anyway, try some of that and you'll feel a lot better.'

'Thanks,' said Jock, and raised his glass. 'Slàinte.'

'Salud!'

He smacked his lips.

'Man,' he said, 'there's nothing like a good malt.'

'Smith's Glenlivet,' said Gold. 'The finest whisky in the world.'

Jock grimaced at the screen. The credits for the Saturday night play were rolling.

'What do you think his chances are?'

'God knows,' said Gold, and turned his chair round to face the picture. 'Fifty-fifty. Maybe better. They'll not be looking for trouble on a programme like this. If this fellow MacDonald plays along, he might get away with it.'

'*The next programme follows in just under a minute,*' said the lady announcer, '*when Mr. James Douglas, the well-known millionaire industrialist, will be the speaker in tonight's edition of What I Believe In. But first, a word about the programmes for tomorrow evening——*'

'Come on,' said Jock softly.

'I don't know what you're worried about,' said Gold. 'I thought the Scots were a phlegmatic people.'

'Aye,' said Jock. 'That'll be right.'

The lady announcer vanished. The programme announcement came up on a blank screen, then, behind it, James Douglas was suddenly there, comfortably seated in an armchair by a coffee table bearing a water carafe and a glass. The words faded and the camera moved in.

'*Good evening,*' said Douglas.

His face filled the screen, a kindly, rugged, ugly, attractive face.

'*Let me say right away that I'm not going to talk about Christianity, or integrity, or doing to others as you would be done by, or any of the other standards of morality and conduct that I do believe in most strongly. I'm going to talk about you, the people of Scotland, and about this country of Scotland in*

161

which we live, because these are two things about which I hold passionate beliefs.'

The camera tracked back for a medium-shot, showing his crossed legs and the pipe held easily in his hand.

'Now, I'm not going to talk about your faults and your virtues ... though heaven knows you've got plenty of both ... but I am going to say this. With all your good points and your bad, you make up a nation which has given as much to humanity and the progress of civilisation as any other nation on the face of the earth. For five hundred years, this country has been the source of a stream of talent which has found its way into the far corners of every continent and has made a greater contribution to the progress of the human race than any other country of comparable size.

'It's something to be proud of. But there's little cause to be proud of the other side of the penny. The world's gain has been Scotland's loss. Now, in this day and age, we're a backward, poor, underdeveloped country with a standard of living that's far from being as high as it ought to be.'

'Here we go,' muttered Jock Anderson.

What the hell, thought Archie.

'Countries smaller than we are, far newer than we are, with fewer natural resources and far less native talent, have gone away ahead of us in the race. Now, this is a tragic state of affairs and one which surely, surely, we can't allow to go on.

'All right, you may say. Fair enough. But what can we do about it? Successive governments, Tory and Labour both, have tried and failed. We've had committees and commissions and development schemes and heaven knows what and they've made next to no impression on the root causes of the problem. We've still got an unemployment rate that's twice the national average. Depopulation of the Highlands still goes on. And the able young men still take the road south to London, or the boat over the sea to join the millions of people of Scots descent who are there already.

'Well, I'm going to tell you what I believe should be done. I believe the time has come to end the Union of the Parliaments. Until we have a Parliament of our own in Edinburgh, with full responsibility for the control of all our domestic affairs,

162

we'll get nowhere. Only then can we set about building a nation, creating a country that able men won't want to leave because it will present opportunities equal to anything London or the Commonwealth countries can offer.

'Now, I want to make one thing clear. This isn't just talk. The rest of my life ... and I'm by no means an old man ... will be devoted to achieving this objective.'

'Good God!' Archie swung on his mother. 'Did you know anything about this?'

'Yes,' she said unhappily. 'I knew.'

'But he never said! He never told me!'

'Sssh!' said Anne. 'For heaven's sake! Let's hear what he's saying.'

'... a new political party has been created. All my own financial resources are at its disposal. But the support that matters must come in the form of votes from you, the people of Scotland.'

'They'll cut him for sure,' said Gold.

'Shut up,' said Jock Anderson tersely.

'... naturally want to know what you're voting for. Well, you'll be told in various ways during the coming months. You'll be told everything you want to know, not only about our plans and intended policies, but about the men who will put them into practice. For this will be no government by faceless men. It will be government by Scotsmen who were born and bred here and know you and the problems of the nation by first-hand experience.'

'Oh, Christ,' said Bill MacDonald softly, and bit his thumbnail to the edge of the quick. The cameraman was glancing round at him. He looked away.

'Now, some of you may feel,' went on Douglas, *'well, this is all very interesting. But we've been united with England for too long. It's not practicable. Not after more than two hundred and fifty years. If so, let me remind you of Norway. Norway became independent in 1905, after five hundred and eight years of union with Sweden or Denmark or both. Today, Norway is a free, proud and prosperous nation. Her geographical and economic problems are very like ours. Her population is even smaller. But in terms of progress and material*

163

prosperity she is far ahead of us. Surely if Norway could do it, we can do it?'

'This is not going to win us any Government contracts,' said Archie tightly.

'Or friends in high places,' murmured Peter.

'*. . . if the will is there, it can be done. Within five years. Even within three. And my job is going to be to initiate and maintain a campaign which will shake the apathetic, disinterested Government at Westminster into realising that here in Scotland a new nation is rising out of the dust of history, with a new vitality and a new sense of purpose added to all the old traditional qualities of our race, a nation that will not be fobbed off with another industrial estate or an order for a new ocean liner to be built on the Clyde.*

'*No, friends. The day for that is past. Let me tell you something of my plans for the new days that lie ahead.*'

Bill MacDonald had vanished. The cameraman glanced at the clock, shrugged his shoulders and tracked his camera in for a close-up. There might be a hell of a row to come, but it was good television while it lasted.

Archie lit a cigarette from the stub of his last. Anne's hand crept on to Peter's lap and he took it and held it. Jock Anderson drained his glass and did not notice the fine quality of the malt. Sam Gold's teeth bit on the end of his cheroot.

'*. . . but these local elections are only a beginning. Next year it is more than likely that there will be a General Election. When that time comes, we shall be ready. Indeed, we are ready now. Every single one of the seventy-one Parliamentary seats in this country will be contested. Every voter in this country will have the opportunity to vote for the policies which will be presented to you in detail before that time.*

'*Nothing will be rushed into. And there will be no attempt to rush you, the people of Scotland, into premature judgements. You will be given the facts and time to consider them. If, as I believe——*'

'That's it,' said Sam Gold.

The picture had vanished.

'They've cut him off,' said Archie. 'They must have.'

164

Jock Anderson glanced at his watch.

'Seven minutes,' he said. 'I didn't think he'd get as much.'

'No,' said Margaret. 'Look.'

'There is a fault. Do not adjust your set.'

'Fault my foot,' said Archie. 'They've cut him.'

'Now the lady,' said Sam. 'Any minute.'

She appeared, looking cool and unruffled.

'We apologise for that break in transmission from our Glasgow studios,' she said. *'Our engineers are trying to put this right. Meanwhile you might like to see some film taken when our outside broadcast cameras were in the Hebrides last summer.'*

'And so endeth the first lesson,' said Sam Gold softly as he switched the set off. 'It'll be interesting to see what comes out of that.'

'The Hebrides last summer!' Archie crossed the room swiftly and switched off the set. 'What the hell's he thinking about?'

'Archie, please!' said Margaret.

'I don't know what's biting you,' said Anne. 'It sounds to me like a good idea.'

'You're mad!'

'I agree with her,' said Peter. 'It's high time something like that happened in this country. I must say I hand it to him.'

'Then you're both mad! How do you think I'm going to run the business against the kind of Government opposition we're going to have from now on?'

'I wouldn't know about the business,' said Anne. 'I still think it sounds like a good idea.'

'Your father had thought about all that,' said Margaret quietly. 'I think you should talk to him about it.'

'Don't worry! I will.'

His mother sighed and rose from her chair.

'I'll make a cup of tea,' she said. 'I think we could all do with it.'

'I need more than a cup of tea,' said Archie and turned to the corner cupboard where the drinks were kept. But the telephone rang and he snatched the receiver from the rest.

'Hello!'

'Hello. Mr. Douglas?'

'Yes! Who is it?'

'The *Tribune* here, Mr. Douglas. We'd just like a few comments from you on your father's television broadcast.'

'You'll get no comment from me,' said Archie harshly and hung up.

'That won't help,' said Anne evenly. 'I think you should talk to Daddy before you start throwing your weight about.'

He turned and stared at her for a moment, then went on to the cupboard.

'Yes,' he said heavily. 'I suppose so. I just hope he knows what he's doing.'

Jock Anderson stretched himself.

'Well,' he said, 'I'd better away home.'

'I'll come with you,' said Sam Gold, and grinned. 'If home means where I think it means. I'll grab a coat.' He was back in a moment, carrying it folded on his arm. 'Come on,' he said. 'This is no time to be out of the office.'

Anderson was very silent as they drove through the thin traffic into town. Gold glanced at him and nodded his head at the late night pavement strollers.

'Wondering how they'll take it?' he asked.

'Yes. Wondering how a lot of folk will take it.' He paused. 'You know,' he said slowly, 'when you think about it, it's damn near treason.'

'Not quite.'

'Maybe not quite. But the powers that be aren't going to like it. The question I keep asking myself is . . . what can they do about it?'

'Nothing,' said Gold. 'Not at this stage. Except to use every dirty political trick in the book the nearer it gets to election time. And that's normal. No. I don't know, but I think the dangerous time will come for friend Douglas when it seems like he might win.'

Anderson looked at him.

'Dangerous?'

Gold nodded.

'That's what I think. And if it was any other country but this, I'd say I was sure. I'd bet my shirt on it. Hell, what do

166

you do with somebody who's trying to overthrow a government? You get rid of him. That's what you do. And wrap it up any way you like, that's what he's trying to do, aided and abetted by us.'

'But, man, you can't get rid of him.'

'No?' Gold shrugged his shoulders. 'I wouldn't know.'

'Well, you can't, Sam. You're not in Malawi or South Vietnam, you know. That kind of thing doesn't happen here.'

'Maybe so. I still say I wouldn't know. The whole affair is the kind of thing that hasn't happened here for one hell of a long time. The only thing I do know is that for Monday we've got a story.'

Anderson looked out at the shop-fronts sliding by, shuttered and empty now at the end of the day.

'Aye,' he said. 'And for a good few Mondays to come.'

CHAPTER EIGHT

ON a fine Saturday evening in June, all the routes that lead from the city to Loch Lomond and the Trossachs are thronged with people. All over the great complex of mountains and glens and lochs and streams that forms Glasgow's back garden, the massed cars move slowly, bumper to bumper, in no hurry to get home, edging out into the centre of the narrow roads only to overtake the cyclists and the strollers and the bands of red-faced, bare-kneed hikers. Grannies watch indulgently as children drink lemonade and eat potato crisps and litter the grass verges with empty paper bags and cartons, banana skins and orange peel, their progress across the land marked by refuse, as though an army of barbarians had passed that way. Smoke curls reluctantly upward from fires coaxed into life by perspiring fathers and in the shade of trees by the water's edge young lovers sit in the strange silence of young love and wait for the long northern evening to end, for even the gregarious people of the city like darkness and the illusion of solitude for their love-making.

But there is no silence even when the sun goes down. The

last cars and touring buses still grind homeward along the inadequate roads. Voices, and giggles, and the clunk of oars on rowlocks sound across the dark, moving water of the loch. Lights flicker mysteriously on the coloured canvas walls of tents and from the shadows around the camp-fires comes singing, and the sound of guitars, and laughter. It is the people of the city at play and there can be no silence.

James Douglas sat in his garden and heard the sound only as a distant, unending hum. The seat was placed in the shelter of a curving bank of azaleas and rhododendrons whose flowers were faded now, looking across a lily pond to the lawn rising gently to the terrace and the house beyond. It faced the evening sun and, though the shadows of the trees were lengthening, it would be another half-hour or more before the distant hills cut off the last of the light. He smoked his pipe and watched the insects darting over the water and the slow, sleepy rise and fall-away of the feeding goldfish. The hum did not bother him. He scarcely noticed it until a noise detached itself and grew slowly louder, becoming identifiable as a car climbing the long drive to the house.

He waited. The little blue Austin appeared on the brow of the hill and swung round to the front door. He knew it was Ewan Cameron before that tall, lean man emerged. But he did not move. It was too far to shout. And Margaret was there, somewhere. He waited until Cameron was half-way across the wide lawn. Then he stood up and waved to him. They met on the far side of the lily pond and he led him back to the seat.

'I thought you'd have had Jean and the boys out for a run,' he said.

'Not me,' said Ewan. 'There's no pleasure in it any weekend from now till September. No, I was over at my brother's.'

'I thought he was in England.'

'So he was. But he came back up just before Easter. He's got a new job.'

'Still in hospital?'

Cameron nodded.

'Yes. In the Western, which is where he's always wanted to be. When old Harrison died, they advertised the consultant vacancy and he got it.'

'Good,' said Douglas. 'That's his troubles over.'

'That's not what you'd think if you heard him. However, that by the way. You knew Tom Bruce, the Member for Stirlingshire North, was ill?'

'I heard that. I didn't hear how seriously.'

'Seriously enough now,' said Cameron. 'He died this afternoon.'

Douglas looked at him quickly.

'How did you hear that?'

'He was in Iain's ward. The House Physician phoned while I was there. He was admitted last week with a coronary. And he wasn't too bad. But this afternoon he had another one. And that was that.'

'A by-election,' said Douglas softly. 'And if I remember rightly, a Government majority of about two thousand.'

'One thousand, nine hundred and ten,' said Cameron, 'with a Liberal standing and getting about six thousand votes.'

Douglas stared at the lily pond.

'Henderson,' he said. 'Henderson got in there at the local election.' Suddenly, he smiled. 'Man, Ewan, we've a good chance!'

'Fair,' said Ewan cautiously. 'Dunblane University's just over the border, so Kilconner, Robertson and Craig might be a help.'

'And there's an area of hill-farming and marginal land that stands to benefit from Tom Wright's ideas for the Highlands, not to mention Jack Armstrong's scheme for land reclamation.'

'And there's a good bit of Forth valley industry that'll still go solid Labour,' said Ewan bluntly. 'It's not ideal.'

'Heavens, you want it on a plate,' said Douglas. 'The chances of getting one that's ideal are about nil. We're damn lucky to get a by-election at all.'

'If we win it,' agreed Cameron. 'Nothing succeeds like success. It's infectious. But so is failure. I'd rather have none at all, than fight this and lose it. It wouldn't do morale any good.'

'Morale could stand it,' said Douglas. 'Nineteen men were defeated last month. But forty-one got in. And all the prophets said we hadn't a hope in hell of getting any in at all. This time

169

they'll maybe not be so cocky.' He stooped to knock out his pipe on the paving stones. 'No, no, Ewan. We'll fight it and we'll have as good a chance in Stirlingshire North as we'd have anywhere else. The thing is . . . when will it be?'

'Not before the end of July,' said Cameron. 'All the Stirlingshire holidays come in that month. It's more likely to be early in August.'

'So we've six weeks?'

'I would think so. Fully that. But the sooner we get things going the better. Do you want me to phone Henderson?'

Douglas considered. 'You know,' he said, 'I don't think we will. Except as a matter of courtesy.'

'But he was the man we had in mind for there.'

'I know he was. But he got in at the local election and fair enough. Let's leave him where he is meantime. It's always a toe in the County Council door. Let's give John Gibson a chance. He was defeated at Falkirk in May, but he did well and he's dying for another crack at it. He's a good man.'

'And he's a local man,' said Cameron. 'He was born in Bridge of Allan. His parents are there yet.'

'All right,' said Douglas. 'Gibson it is. Phone him tonight and check that he'll stand. Get an answer before this time tomorrow night and we'll release the news on Monday. Tell him to hold himself ready to co-operate with Grant on all the publicity stuff. And tell him to keep next Saturday evening free. If it's all right with Margaret, we'll get him out here for a meal.' He stood up. 'In fact, we'll just go in and ask her. And you might like to come over yourself.'

Cameron smiled wryly.

'I'd like to,' he said. 'But my conscience is bothering me. I've been leaving Jean alone enough as it is.'

Douglas glanced at him as they walked together over the sprawling shadows on the lawn.

'Is she complaining?'

'No,' said Cameron. 'She's not complaining yet.'

'Well, I think you should be there,' said Douglas. 'Tell her I'd like you to come. And I'm sorry if she's annoyed, Ewan, but if you're in this thing you're in it up to the neck. Family and everything else has to take second place. You know that.'

'I know that,' said Cameron evenly. 'If you want me to come, I'll come.'

*　　*　　*

James Douglas reached his office just after nine o'clock that Monday morning. It had been a good weekend, during which he had achieved a nice balance between intellectual activity, gentle exercise in the form of gardening and total relaxation under the warm mid-summer sun. He felt fit and ready for what promised to be a good week. Sally straightened up from the cluttered desk and welcomed him with a smile.

'Good God!' he said. 'Is all that stuff for me?'

She laughed.

'Yes! Fan mail, mostly.'

'I'm sure it's not.'

'Well, I don't know. I was just sorting it out.'

He waved his hand at the mess.

'Look, Sally, be a good girl and take them all away. I'll be bogged down here all day if I begin. Sort them out a bit. Answer the ones you can cope with, tear up the ones from the nuts and bring me the rest. All right?'

'Yes,' she said. 'Of course. And there's a bit in the *Tribune* you might like to see.'

She handed him the paper, open and folded at the usual *Tribune* gossip column and began to gather the mail into manageable bundles. He quickly read the paragraph she had marked.

'Mr. Tom Bruce, the well-liked Member of Parliament for Stirlingshire North, has died. The king is dead, long live the king! But who will the new king be? Or rather, the new Member for Stirlingshire North? Mr. Bruce held the seat for the Government last time with a comfortable majority of almost two thousand. Will his successor hold it for the Government again?

'We would dare to prophesy, without even knowing the name of the new candidate, that he will.

'For the people of Stirlingshire North are shrewd and sensible. They will not be led up airy-fairy garden paths to the cloud-cuckoo-land of a separate Scotland by the

171

blandishments of Mr. Douglas's so-called National Party.

'If he is rash enough to contest it ... and we have reason to believe that his organisation is far from ready, so that, in spite of his promises, he very well may not ... but if he does, he will learn this sharp lesson.

'Money can buy many things, but in this country it cannot buy votes.'

'Well,' said Douglas. 'They've certainly got their knife in me.'

'They have,' agreed Sally. 'And they're getting worse.'

'Yes, they are,' said Douglas thoughtfully. 'I wonder who is at the back of it.' He paused. 'Sally, put me through to Kinloch in Information.'

He picked up the *New Scot*. On page two, there was a generous obituary of the deceased M.P. The paragraph he expected to find was below it.

'Mr. John Gibson has been adopted by the National Party as their candidate in the by-election which will be held in the constituency of Stirlingshire North later this year.

'Mr. Gibson, who is married with two children, is a lecturer at the Institute of Business Management in Edinburgh.'

'Mr. Kinloch's on the line,' said Sally.

'Right.' He took the phone from her and handed her the paper. 'That's the answer to the last bit,' he said. 'You're as well to keep abreast.'

'Hello,' said John Kinloch. 'Was there something you wanted to know?'

'Yes,' said Douglas. 'One small thing. And nothing to do with the business. Who's responsible for the gossip column in the *Tribune* and why have they got their knife in me?'

Kinloch laughed.

'I can tell you that now,' he said. 'I was wondering myself, so I made a few enquiries. It's written by a man Colin Campbell——'

'Campbell?'

172

'Aye, but you don't know him any more than he knows you. The man you know is his brother Iain.'

Douglas grinned.

'Iain Campbell! Lately a fellow committee member?'

'The very same.'

'Well . . . now I understand.'

'I thought you would,' said Kinloch. 'Was that all?'

'That was all,' said Douglas. 'And thank you.' He turned to Sally. 'It's entirely personal,' he told her. 'It doesn't mean a thing.'

'I still don't like it,' she said.

He shrugged his shoulders.

'Sticks and stones may break my bones. I'll not lose any sleep over it. Anyway, before you go. Two things. Tell Roderick Grant I'd like to see him at ten o'clock. And give Archie a ring. If he's in, ask him round for coffee. I haven't seen him for over a week.'

By ten o'clock, when Sally returned with the letters for his personal attention, he had read all that interested him in the day's newspapers.

'Mr. Grant's here,' she said. 'Do you want to look through these first, or will I show him in?'

He returned to his desk.

'Show him in,' he said.

Grant entered with a new spring in his step. He had spent the last two days helping to crew a friend's twenty-foot yacht down to Campbeltown and for once he felt fit. The fact that Paula had been difficult last week no longer mattered. A few hours of lying out on the weather side of a heeling sloop, in the sun and flying spray, had been enough to put her in perspective. Recently, she had become possessive. And she always had been just too easily available. The combination repelled rather than appealed. Sally, on the other hand, seemed more desirable each time they met. When she smiled and said— 'Would you go in now?', he decided that the time for action had come. He was still speculating on the approach most likely to succeed, when he sat down opposite Douglas.

'Have you seen the papers?'

173

'The papers?' He pulled himself together quickly. 'Yes. Yes, I have.'

'So you know there's going to be a by-election in Stirlingshire North?'

'So I gather.'

'And that we're putting Gibson up as candidate?'

'Yes, I saw that.'

'Right. Well, you'll have a file on Gibson already, but you'd better see him and fill any gaps that may exist. Now, we don't know when the by-election's going to be, but we think early in August. That gives you six weeks' minimum to put him across. And make no mistake about it. The local elections were a good enough trial run, but this time you've really got to sell him. Go out to the constituency, see anybody you like, but find out the angles most likely to appeal. Any special local problems. Any grumbles. Get right down to the roots of it.'

'Yes, sir.'

'And contact some of the Dunblane University people. They may be able to help you.'

'But that's Perthshire.'

'Just over the border,' agreed Douglas. 'But its links are more with Stirling. See Charles Craig. He's likely to be the most useful man there. I wouldn't bother Lord Kilconner and Sir William Robertson, except to get them in as speakers at one or two meetings each. But I'll have a word with them about that. And bring Tom Wright and Jack Armstrong into as many of the meetings in the rural areas as they're prepared to face. And remember. The public meetings are vitally important. There has to be as much personal contact as we can manage.'

'What about booking halls?'

'We can't till we know the date. And that's the agent's job. But work closely with him in getting as much publicity as possible for everything we do.'

'Literature?'

'You write it, let me see it and Jock'll get it printed. The new machine is in. And the same goes for photographs. Arrange them with Gibson. They can be taken any time and the sooner the better. It's one less thing to be done later. The

174

other thing Jock will be doing is a series of leaders on the area and the problems it presents, plus a splash on Gibson himself nearer the time. Now, there's one other thing.'

'Yes, sir?'

Douglas grinned.

'The good ship *Navarra*. How's the work going?'

Grant moved uneasily. Thoughts of the *Navarra* had disturbed his sleep more than once.

'Well, she's still in Cork. But according to the last I heard, the transmitters should be installed and operational by the end of this month.'

'Fine,' said Douglas. 'Just nice time. We'll need to talk about it with the Master and the radio people, but I would think she'd be as well lying off the Firth of Forth, maybe four miles out. There are an awful lot of hills between Stirlingshire North and the west coast. They'd be bound to affect reception.'

'I suppose they would,' said Grant without enthusiasm.

'And I've been thinking a bit about her. I don't see why we shouldn't follow the example of others and use her as a commercial pirate radio for the hours when we don't want her ourselves. We could sell time in the usual way. It would always bring in a bit of money towards running costs. What do you think?'

'I don't see why not,' said Grant. 'Might as well be hung for a sheep as a lamb.'

Douglas laughed.

'Is that how you feel?'

'As far as the boat's concerned, yes. It seems to me a doubtful proposition.'

'Doubtful, yes. But anything that gives you radio coverage of half the country any time you want it seems to me worth a try. Anyway, you might look into the commercial side. See what the chances are of getting buyers. And you'd better find out what kind of arrangement is usual with the gramophone record people when you're at it. There's bound to be some fairly standard way of going about it.'

'Yes, sir,' said Grant resignedly, and added to his notes.

It promised to be one hell of a six weeks.

The buzzer beside Douglas sounded softly, twice, and he depressed the switch.

'Yes?'

'Sorry to disturb you,' said Sally, 'but Mr. Buchanan's on an outside line. Will you take the call?'

'Buchanan?'

'Yes, sir. The Secretary of State for Scotland.'

'That Buchanan,' said Douglas softly. 'Yes, indeed. I'll take it.'

Grant rose quickly and Douglas nodded.

'If you don't mind. But keep in touch.'

He picked up the white external telephone as the door shut.

'Good morning,' he said. 'James Douglas here.'

'Good morning, James. Getting through your morning's paper work, eh?'

'Slowly,' said Douglas. 'I don't have a retinue of under-secretaries to do it for me.'

The Minister chuckled. He appeared to be in a good humour.

'But you should, James. You should. With the Government contracts you've got just now, I should think you could afford it.'

'I manage,' said Douglas. 'Private enterprise isn't as in-efficient as some of you chaps seem to think. And how are things in the big world of bureaucracy, Alex? I haven't seen you for months.'

'Not since the Trades House dinner.'

'January,' said Douglas. 'There's been a lot of water under the bridge since then.'

'Some of it put there by you,' said the Minister more coolly. 'I was thinking it was about time we had a little chat together, you and I.'

'Well, now,' said Douglas cautiously, 'I would have thought that might have been rather indiscreet.'

'Indiscreet?' Buchanan laughed. 'You mean, now that you've started dabbling in politics? No, I wouldn't think so, James. We're old friends.'

'That's true,' Douglas admitted. 'And I hope we'll be friends again some day, Alex. But just now I'm not going to risk any accusations of running with the hare and hunting with the hounds.'

There was a significant pause.

'Am I to take it,' asked the Secretary of State, 'that you're not prepared to meet me?'

'Let's say that I think a meeting would be unwise for both of us,' said Douglas.

'I see.' The Minister's voice lost what little warmth it had had. 'I see from your newspaper this morning that you propose fighting Stirlingshire North.'

'That's right,' said Douglas. 'I'm glad to hear you read it.'

'My dear man, you've succeeded in making it obligatory reading for every thinking person in the country. I don't read it because I like it. Still less, because I agree with it. But that by the way. You realise that, under by-election conditions, the intervention of a fourth candidate might reduce the Government majority to something very marginal indeed?'

'I certainly do,' said Douglas. 'I'd go further. I think my own man has as good a chance as yours, or better.'

'Well, of course, that's simply wishful thinking on your part. But I admit there is a danger of us losing this seat if you insist on contesting it. You'll split the vote even further. In fact, I must tell you that we feel that this intervention, with the state of the Parties as it is, is both frivolous and irresponsible.'

'We,' said Douglas softly. 'Who's we?'

'My colleagues and myself. And I must also tell you that certain Government departments with which you have been associated will be asked to re-examine their connection with you if you don't withdraw.'

'Not with me,' said Douglas quickly. 'With the companies now almost wholly controlled by my son.'

'I would doubt if that distinction will be thought important,' said the Minister.

'Well, Alex,' said Douglas, 'you might tell them to make that re-examination thorough, because if there's any breach of existing contractual obligations, you'll spend more time in the Law Courts than you'll spend in St. Andrew's House for the next twelve months.'

He heard the intake of Buchanan's breath.

'Is that a threat, James?'

'No more than your own earlier remark was,' said Douglas. 'And we might as well stop beating about the bush. We know each other well enough to have a fair idea of what the other fellow will do. And certainly you should know me well enough to realise that I'm not likely to be influenced by threats.'

'So you insist on contesting it?'

'I do,' said Douglas. 'I stand by everything I've said in public. We'll fight this and every other constituency in the country as and when it becomes possible to do so.'

Buchanan sighed.

'I wish you wouldn't, James.'

His voice was suddenly unexpectedly human. Douglas chuckled.

'Well,' he said, 'you know what to do, Alex. If you can't beat us, join us.'

'That remark was not really in very good taste,' said the Minister wearily.

'Neither is politics,' said Douglas. 'It's a dirty business.'

'And you're not prepared even to reconsider this decision?'

'I'm afraid not,' said Douglas quietly. 'Not even for a knighthood or a life peerage.'

'Then there's nothing more to be said.'

'Nothing,' agreed Douglas. 'We'll meet one of these days, Alex. And thanks for phoning.'

He put down the phone. Authority had spoken at last. And the fact that its mouth-piece was that reasonable man, Alex Buchanan, made no difference. He would be given no quarter. He had known that all along. But now that the time had come the knowledge produced a strange fatalistic calm. There was no excitement now. It was simply a question of soldiering quietly on, being true to one's principles and beliefs until——

Until what? Until the day when he walked in procession down the grey High Street of Edinburgh to the opening of a Scottish Parliament? But that day was too far ahead to see. Until tomorrow. It had to be only until tomorrow. Let that part of the mind that plans coldly think far ahead over the broad pattern of the whole campaign, but let imagination stop with to-

178

morrow. That, it can always accept. But don't let it go probing on into the shadowy possibilities of distant weeks and months. There is no consolation there. Only uncertainty, and wondering.

The buzzer drew his thoughts back.

'Yes?'

'Your son is here,' said Sally. 'Are you free?'

'Yes,' said Douglas. 'Send him in. And let's have the coffee any time you like.'

*　　　*　　　*

Unlike his father and Roderick Grant, Archie felt neither fit nor contented on that Monday morning.

He had spent the previous evening with an old acquaintance called Gilchrist whom he had met by chance a couple of days earlier in the bar at his club. He had dined there regularly since Julia left for Rome, returning to the office afterwards to work on until perhaps ten o'clock, for the increased pressure caused by his father's withdrawal was now making itself felt. Yet he did not really mind. It gave him a good excuse for not going back to the Helensburgh house. With Julia away, Jamie at school and Oonagh despatched to Dublin for her annual holiday, it had become intolerable. Indeed, outside his work, living had become a dull, lonely and unrewarding business. He had been sitting with a sherry, considering his bleak domestic future, when Gilchrist appeared.

'My dear Archie, how are you? I haven't seen you for months.'

He was smiling blandly, immaculately dressed as he always was, a tall, rather distinguished figure with greying hair at the temples of his brachycephalic skull.

'Fairly well,' said Archie, 'considering I'm trapped in this bloody city. And I needn't ask how you are. You're looking disgustingly fit.'

'Tolerably fit,' said Gilchrist. 'I just came back last week from an idyllic month in the Lebanon, so I should be.' He tentatively moved a chair. 'May I, or are you expecting someone?'

'No, please do. And what about a sherry? Have you time?'

'Oh yes, I've time. But please. Let me. Finish that and have another. I hardly ever see you here.'

He signalled to the barman.

'I hardly ever am here,' said Archie. 'But I'm being forced into bachelor habits. Julia's away till the end of the month.'

'My dear chap! How absolutely dreadful. Mary went off last year for a long weekend with some girl friend or other and I found it quite unendurable. You must come and have a meal with us one evening.'

'I'm working most evenings,' said Archie.

Gilchrist's eyebrows rose fractionally.

'Really? Is running the Douglas empire such a full-time occupation?'

'It is at the moment.'

'But of course. Father being rather involved with other things. I'd forgotten about that. Well, look. What about Sunday? Could you manage?'

At any other time, he would probably have refused this invitation, for he did not know George Gilchrist well. Indeed, he had always regarded him with some mistrust. His manner was a little too easy, his charm a little too cloying. And his position in the city was difficult to determine. He was a director of a number of companies, but those fees were known. His wealth clearly came from somewhere else. Moreover, he was always singularly well-informed about matters which one would not have expected to concern him. He successfully gave the impression of a man who always stood on the edge of great events, involved, yet aloof, a vaguely god-like figure whose worldly manner just failed to conceal his mystery. But it was hard to discover what substance, if any, lay behind this public image.

Now, he was at his most charming.

'Do come,' he said. 'Mary would love to have you, I know.'

Archie had accepted gratefully. He had even looked forward to the evening as a break in what had become a tedious routine of work and sleep. But it had not been entirely successful.

The half-hour or so with drinks before dinner had been most agreeable. The meal itself had been excellent. It was a little later that the conversation took a turn which Archie

180

found disturbing. They were sitting in the library over brandies and coffee when Gilchrist said—

'And tell me, Archie. How is your dear father?'

'Fine, as far as I know,' said Archie. 'I don't see much of him these days.'

'He must be busy, of course.'

'Yes, I think he is.'

'And ... if I may ask you ... do you support this new party of his which has come along to confuse our lives?'

Archie laughed.

'No, I certainly don't.'

'Meaning by that that you oppose it? Or am I wrong?'

'I neither support it nor oppose it. I've nothing to do with it. I'm not a political animal.'

'You are, you know,' murmured Gilchrist. 'Forgive me for contradicting you so flatly. By reason of your companies and your status in society, you can't avoid the issue. You're already committed.'

'To what?'

'To supporting what used to be called the Establishment. Such a horrible word, I always thought. No, you're one of the more massive pillars of what is and must remain a capitalist society, regardless of the political colour of the Government of the day. Not a truly right-wing capitalist society, naturally, but capitalist undoubtedly. As a nation, we have remarkable skill in bringing a Government back to the centre. Whether it starts off on the left or the right is really immaterial. And this, of course, is an excellent thing. And what I'm trying to say is this. You are committed politically as one of those stabilising forces which makes certain that this happens. As such, you have an invaluable part to play.'

'But I don't play any part.'

'But ... forgive me ... you certainly do. By being what you are, by running the remarkable private industrial empire which you run, you play it every day.'

'No more than my father did.'

'Than your father did, yes. But now, I'm afraid, your father politically is in outer darkness. He has been, in his day, an extremely powerful figure. What I'm rather afraid he doesn't

181

realise is that by his actions of the last few months he has stripped himself of that very power which made these actions possible.'

Archie stirred uneasily.

'I'm sorry,' he said. 'I don't know what you mean. I don't see how his position has changed at all, except that he no longer plays such an active part in the business.'

Gilchrist looked amused.

'You know,' he said, 'you're even more politically naïve than I imagined.'

'I'm not politically anything,' said Archie. 'I told you that.'

Gilchrist raised his hand in a quietening gesture.

'No . . . please. Let me explain. Those stabilising forces that I referred to, which are committed to maintaining the *status quo* in this country, are interdependent. Each is enormously reinforced by the power of the others. The power of any one is comparatively small. The power of the whole is incalculable, as some of our more potentially radical Governments of the past discovered very quickly. Before these recent events, your father's powerful position was in part due to the reinforcing presence of all the other comparable forces, in commerce and industry and outside it. But right at the beginning, on the night of that unfortunate television broadcast of his, he overstepped the bounds of permissible conduct. He isolated himself. And in doing so he reduced his power to a fraction of what it formerly was.'

Archie tried again.

'Look,' he said, 'if I'm being dumb, I'm sorry, but I still don't get it. He starts a new political party. All right. What difference does——'

'Just a minute,' said Gilchrist. 'Let's get the nature of this party clear. Its stated objective is the setting up of a separate Scottish Parliament to deal with Scottish affairs. Am I right?'

'As far as I know, yes.'

'All right. Such a party must, by its very nature, be revolutionary, because its objective is the destruction of an existing institution. Furthermore, because of Scotland's political tendencies, it must become a party of the Left. Probably, ultimately, of the extreme Left. Now that, quite clearly, is something which cannot be allowed to happen. In other words, these Establishment forces, of which he was formerly one, are going to become united in their opposition to him.'

'But just a minute, George,' said Archie. 'You talk as if this party of my father's presented some sort of serious threat. But it doesn't, surely? It isn't a threat to anybody. It's just a bee in his bonnet. There have been movements like this before in Scotland. None of them ever came to anything.'

'My dear man!' Gilchrist was regarding him with amused tolerance. 'You really are quite astonishingly ill-informed.'

'About what?'

'About the significance of what's happening. I think you'd better have another brandy.'

'I'd be glad of another brandy,' said Archie. 'But for God's sake, stop being so bloody mysterious. I know as much about it as anybody else.'

He had begun to find Gilchrist's condescension irritating.

'Well, let's say you know as much about it as the average person. Possibly a little more. But it's quite clear that you've no knowledge of the overall picture.' Gilchrist placed the replenished glass on a little table by his side and smiled. 'And you are certainly wrong in one particular.'

'Which?'

'Nothing quite like this has ever happened before.' Gilchrist sat down and carefully fitted a cigarette to his holder. 'There have been movements in a similar direction before, I quite agree. But they have always lacked two things. Money, and a leader. Now, the leader aspect is important. He has to be a powerful figure, a man of character, capable of inspiring confidence and even affection. But in this hypocritical bourgeois society of ours, he has also to be respectable. This is terribly important. And your father satisfies all these requirements. In addition, he has money. Immediately, you have a new and unprecedented situation.'

'All right,' said Archie. 'So that's new. I quite agree. But where does it take you?'

'It takes you farther than you seem to think,' said Gilchrist. 'You also happen to have a tolerably favourable climate of opinion.'

'Do you? I wasn't aware of it.'

'Few people are. I'm not even sure if your father is. I rather suspect he's not, since he's putting so much effort into the creation of one. But in fact he'll find less difficulty than he seems to anticipate. You have a country which is disenchanted with both of the big parties. And the Liberal Party is not sufficiently positively anything to command popular support. So here you have something of a vacuum, a mood receptive to new and appealing ideas. Then, internationally, the trend is towards nationalism, towards an acceptance of the rights of minorities. This, in a country like Scotland, where nationalism has never been entirely dead, has an effect on the nation's subconscious. And you have the Scottish inferiority complex. Douglas himself is the answer to this. He's the self-made man, the local boy made good. So people will say ... all right. If he's got the secret of success, let's cash in on it. If he can do as well for the country as he has done for himself, then we all stand to profit. Let's give him a chance. It's a very human and understandable attitude.'

'But all that's theoretical,' protested Archie. 'I can't see evidence for any of it.'

'Then you haven't got your ear to the ground,' said Gilchrist. 'Believe me, there are movements of opinion in the country that provide plenty of evidence. You're making a big mistake if you dismiss this as merely a bee in your father's bonnet.'

'But look,' said Archie stubbornly, 'at the beginning you seemed to indicate that by getting involved in this thing at all he had lost the power he formerly had. Now you're suggesting, if I understand you correctly, that his power is growing.'

'His new power is growing,' said Gilchrist. 'His former power was founded on his wealth and his place in the Establishment. His new power is beginning to be founded in what I suppose one must call the will of the people. And I don't use the word people in any Marxist sense, for his appeal, at this stage in the thing, is classless. There's no doubt at all that he'll have an appeal for the working classes ... for what he is as a man, for his reputation with the Unions as an employer, for his audacity in challenging authority. His piece of television

184

piracy had its greatest impact on them. But he's a reassuring figure to the middle classes, too. He's respectable, responsible, successful, with the good taste not to flaunt his riches too openly in their faces. That adds up to the best image of all for them . . . to look like one of themselves. To the so-called upper classes, of course, he means nothing at all, except to a minority of upper-class intellectuals linked to one or other of the universities. But make no mistake about it. There is a potential supporting body of opinion which could count for a great deal.'

'Are you trying to tell me,' asked Archie carefully, 'that he might be successful?'

Gilchrist smiled.

'No,' he said. 'I'm not. I don't believe that there's the slightest chance that he will be successful.'

Archie stared at him.

'Then what are you trying to say?'

'I'm trying to tell you,' said Gilchrist, 'that I believe your father is heading for some sort of disaster. And I'm trying to explain to you why I believe this is so.'

'Well, you haven't been very lucid,' said Archie. 'In all you've said I can't see anything likely to lead to disaster. Failure, maybe, but that's a very different thing.'

Gilchrist sighed.

'You know, one would almost think you were being wilfully blind.'

'I assure you I'm not.'

'Oh, perhaps you are, subconsciously. Some sort of Freudian repression. In any case, let me explain where I believe the danger for him lies. It lies in the very fact that it looks as if he might be successful. If this movement of his had the smell of failure, the Establishment, the Government, the stabilising forces of law and order, this *thing* in Britain which ensures the continuity of the nation as we know it, could afford to ignore him. But there is no smell of failure. Far from it. Even in these early days, there is a distinct odour of success. So it cannot be ignored. It must be dealt with. Indeed, it must be eliminated.'

'How?'

'Ah,' said Gilchrist, 'that I can't tell you. Nevertheless, I'm sure that it will be eliminated.'

Archie considered Gilchrist's handsome, rather complacent features and decided finally that he did not like the man at all.

'Is this intended to be a warning?' he asked bluntly.

'Frankly, yes,' said Gilchrist. 'A warning to yourself. In spite of your father's withdrawal from the business, it might prove difficult to isolate the Douglas companies from whatever disaster threatens Douglas the man. That would depend on the nature of the measures finally taken.'

'I see,' said Archie.

'You understand, I'm sure?'

'Yes,' he said. 'I think I do.'

He was suddenly certain that the less he said the better.

Gilchrist stood up, smiling his charming superficial smile.

'And now let's join poor Mary. She must be wondering what on earth we've found to talk about all this time.'

Two hours later, he drove slowly home.

That night he slept fitfully and at breakfast his uneasiness remained. It took his father's reassuring presence to diminish it.

Then, as they talked over coffee of the business and the pleasantly safe routine things arising from it, Gilchrist's almost sinister analysis of the situation became less credible. He had wondered earlier if he should tell his father what had been said. Now, he decided he could not. But when business topics had been exhausted, his curiosity made him say—

'And what about your own affairs? How are things going?'

Douglas sucked contentedly at his pipe.

'Pretty well. You probably saw that we've got a by-election coming up.'

'Yes, I did. And are you going to fight it?'

'Of course we are. What's more, I think we stand a chance of winning it.'

'And after that, what?'

His father shrugged his shoulders.

'After that, we plod on. Publicity and propaganda. The slow business of putting our ideas across. And all leading up to

186

the General Election, of course.'

'What about your chances then?'

'Too soon to say. Good, I hope. But I don't know.'

Archie stroked the tip of his cigarette on the edge of the deep glass ash-tray.

'There's one thing I've been meaning to ask you,' he said. 'What effect do you think all this will have on the business?'

Douglas smiled.

'I've been wondering when you'd ask me that. It's been on your mind for a while.'

'Yes,' admitted Archie. 'It has.'

'Well, one immediate effect is obvious. There won't be any new Government contracts. This is something you just have to face.'

'I realise that.'

'On the other hand, it will be almost five years before all existing contracts are completed. And that's a long time. Quite frankly, when that time comes I hope you'll find yourself dealing with a Scottish Government. If so, there won't be any problem. If not, well, Government work accounts for only some twenty-two per cent of our total. Other work will have to be expanded to take its place. In any case, I think you should aim at this sort of expansion. We've been a growing company for thirty years. You want to try and keep it that way.'

'But you don't expect any other adverse effects?'

'No, I don't,' said Douglas. 'Why should there be?'

'No reason that I know of,' said Archie. 'But I'd been wondering. And in the immediate future? I mean, the next few months. What are you going to be doing?'

'Nothing very exciting. Preparing for the by-election. Building up the regional organisation. There's just one thing.' He grinned. 'And it's still strictly confidential. But we've got a pirate radio ship due to start operating by the end of the month.'

'For God's sake! That'll cost you a packet.'

'Not necessarily,' said Douglas. 'We'll get some revenue by running it commercially, using a base outside the pact countries. But of course its main function is propaganda. Then we'll have our first public meeting at Bannockburn on Thurs-

187

day week. That's the anniversary of the battle. And I'm not expecting very much. It's more of a trial run.'

Archie looked at him curiously.

'Is that a good idea? I mean, I thought you wanted to get away from all that historical stuff. Didn't you complain that there had been far too much of it in the past, far too much slushy nostalgic nonsense and not enough looking ahead?'

His father nodded.

'So I did. And I still do. But you can't dissociate yourself from it entirely. And it would be wrong to do so. The mistake in the past was in placing far too much emphasis on it. But the historical stuff, as you call it, is there. It did happen. And it has a certain romantic appeal which is worth exploiting as long as you don't overdo it. But taking specifically Bannockburn, that happens to be in the constituency of Stirlingshire North. It's too good a chance to miss.'

'Yes,' said Archie. 'I suppose it is.'

But when he left his father's office, some of his apprehension remained. One phrase of Gilchrist's lingered. 'It will be eliminated.' It was difficult to imagine how. Yet he considered it unhappily at intervals for several days until the mounting volume of his work drove out these and all other extraneous thoughts.

*   *   *

A week later, James Douglas had just begun to deal with the morning's mail when Roderick Grant called him.

'Good morning, sir,' he said. 'One piece of news you'll want to know about. There's a letter in from the Chief Constable refusing permission to hold the meeting on Thursday.'

'The devil there is!' exclaimed Douglas. 'What does he say?'

'Just that sufficient notice had not been given and that existing arrangements for that day do not allow permission to be granted.'

'Well, I'm not entirely surprised that it wasn't sufficient notice,' said Douglas slowly, 'but it couldn't have been any longer. Only the by-election made me decide to hold it at all. But I'm damned if I know what other arrangements he's talking about. Anyway, thanks for letting me know. I'll phone him and ring you back.'

He called Sally.

'Get me the Chief Constable for the area,' he said. 'I'm not sure if it's Burgh or County.'

He commenced the soothing occupation of filling his pipe, but the phone rang before he had finished.

'Good morning, Mr. Douglas,' said the Chief Constable. 'I gather you got my letter.'

'Yes,' said Douglas, 'I've just heard about it. I'm sorry you can't see your way to giving permission.'

'Well, you know, sir, you didn't give us much notice.'

'I realise that,' said Douglas, 'but I gave you as much as I could. And I thought I'd have a word with you in case we hadn't made it clear that our intention was to hold this meeting right at the Borestone, beside the statue and the rotunda. It's well off the main road.'

'No, sir, you made that quite clear. But there's an agricultural show on that day, you know. We're expecting fairly heavy traffic. And your meeting could conceivably cause congestion on the approach roads from the A80 to the Borestone. If that was sufficient to build back on to the main road itself, we'd be in trouble.'

'An agricultural show?' said Douglas curiously. 'I didn't know there was one in Stirling on Thursday.'

'Well, it's not actually in Stirling. It's in Perth.'

'But if it's in Perth, you're not going to get heavy traffic south of Stirling, surely?'

'I'm afraid we have to go on the assumption that we may.'

'I see,' said Douglas slowly. 'And I gather from the way you're speaking that you're not likely to reconsider your decision.'

'We're not in a position to reconsider it. All the arrangements for that day are complete.'

There was a note of finality in the official voice.

'Well, I don't suppose there's any more to be said,' said Douglas thoughtfully. 'Except perhaps one thing.'

'Yes, sir?'

'As you probably know, it's the anniversary of Bannock-

189

burn. Would you have any objection to myself and a number of friends simply laying a wreath at the foot of the statue?'

'No,' said the Chief Constable. 'That would be in order. Provided you don't make any speeches, of course. No public address system or pipe bands or anything like that.'

'No, no,' said Douglas. 'Nothing like that. Just a simple ceremony of laying the wreath.'

'All right, then. You can go ahead with that.'

'Thank you,' said Douglas. 'And next time we'll try to give you longer warning.'

He hung up and thought for a moment before phoning Roderick Grant.

'Hello, sir,' said Grant. 'Any joy?'

'None,' said Douglas. 'And I'm sure this thing's a put-up job. There's an agricultural show in Perth. To talk of that causing heavy traffic south of Stirling is nonsense.'

'I would have thought so,' said Grant. 'Any idea why?'

'None at all, except that if authority is beginning to be obstructive, we must have started making some impression. Anyway, he did give permission for me to lay a wreath at the statue. No speeches. No loud-speakers. No pipe bands. But I must admit I'm tempted to be naughty.'

'In what way?'

'Well, he didn't say anything about a single piper. I think I'll get Calum to bring along his pipes. And we'll make up a party of about ten. I'll give you the names later today. But we want John Gibson, obviously. It'll be his first public appearance in his future constituency. And contact Jock Anderson. Get him to put advance notice of this in the paper on Wednesday morning and again on Thursday. Not a big splash. Just a discreet wee paragraph in a prominent place. Then we'll wait and see what happens.'

'That's unpredictable.'

'I know it,' said Douglas. 'That's our trouble at the moment. We've no way of finding out what impression we're making. And that's one of the reasons I wanted this meeting. We might have got some idea of public reaction. Anyway, we'll have to make do with what we've got.'

'Just one thing,' said Grant cautiously.

190

'What's that?'

'We could start a crowd. Twenty or thirty chosen people in the right place at the right time. With that kind of thing, all you need is a beginning.'

Douglas considered it.

'No,' he decided. 'We'll leave it. We'll wait and see what happens.'

*　　*　　*

On Thursday, June the 24th, Archie spent a tedious but profitable morning in consultation with the Port Authorities in Dundee and left after lunch in a good humour. The contract for work on the proposed extensions to the now inadequate dock facilities was not yet in the bag, but it had come very near. He made good time on the new road south from Perth until he reached the approaches to the town of Stirling. Then the traffic began to thicken.

Even on the dual carriageway ring road, designed to avoid the town centre, the streams were dense in both directions, that on the north-bound track evidently beginning to increase speed away from the source of trouble while the line in which he moved closed up and slowed down steadily as they approached the southern fringe of the town. When at last he drew abreast of the sweating constable on point duty at the St. Ninian's intersection, he rolled down the window and called to him.

'What the devil's going on?'

'Keep in line, sir. Don't try to overtake.'

'I'm not trying to overtake. I'm not mad. But what's going on?'

The line of traffic juddered to a halt and the policeman abandoned the struggle.

'Something going on up the road, sir. They say it's that fellow Douglas.'

'Douglas?'

He remembered. It was the twenty-fourth. The anniversary of Bannockburn.

'He's been laying a wreath up at the statue. Anyway, so they say. But to look at that lot you'd think it was a ruddy Cup Final.' The car ahead crept away and the policeman stepped back. 'Come on, sir. Keep moving.'

He slipped the Lotus into low gear and crawled on with the stream up the long slow hill that cut across the old battlefield until he was able to swing out of the traffic into a cul-de-sac between two old buildings on the left. Then he got out quickly, locked the car and ran back to the kerb of the main road.

As the policeman had said, it looked more like the crowd leaving a Cup Final than anything else, but there was much less evidence of police control. Both traffic lanes on both carriageways were solid with cars and buses and heavy goods lorries, but this seemed to be simply a build-up of normal traffic. The block was farther up the hill, where the access road to the Borestone turned off. He ducked and sprinted across the road between the vehicles to the other side, then carried on through the thickening press of people to the side-road opening. From there on, movement was almost impossible. The narrow road up to the statue and the rotunda was jammed with cars and walkers who were trying to squeeze past each other along the hedges. The car park, which he could just see in the distance, was full and over the whole area between it and the memorial a mass of people swirled and eddied under the direction of the few police whose chequered caps showed up here and there above the throng.

There was not the slightest chance of getting through that way. He looked round quickly, then slipped through a break in the hedge into the field. As he ran on over the coarse grass, he heard a piper playing above the noise of engines and the murmur of the crowd, and somewhere a police car was forcing its way through, its blue light flashing, its horn sounding, and then he was within fifty yards of the rotunda, separated from it by the hedge and several hundred people. But here there was no gap. He forced himself through the thorns to emerge, breathless, beside the legs of a police constable who stared disapprovingly down at him.

'Here! You're going the wrong way, aren't you? You want to get out of this.'

'Press,' said Archie quickly. 'Where's Douglas?'

'Never you mind where he is. Come on. Get out of it.'

Then he saw him, one of a small group forced back against the plinth of the statue.

He dived into the crowd, forcing and pushing his way through, aware that the police car was nearer now, that the pipes were louder, playing a fine ranting tune that rose clear above all the noise of the afternoon. Then, suddenly, he was there, beside a somewhat shaken John Gibson, prospective Member for the district, with only Sir Jack Armstrong between himself and his father. He stretched out his hand and grabbed his sleeve. Douglas turned quickly.

'Archie! What are you doing here?'

'I might ask you the same,' shouted Archie. 'What the devil's going on?'

'We were going to lay a wreath,' called Douglas. 'Then this mob appeared. God knows where they came from.'

Archie heard not a word that came from that grinning, jubilant face. He spread his hands hopelessly.

'Come on,' said Jack Armstrong. 'Change places. You can't hear yourself think in this racket.'

Quickly, they squeezed past each other. He clutched his father's shoulder.

'There's going to be a hell of a row about this,' he bellowed. 'I ran into it coming back from Dundee. There's a jam about a mile long each way from the road end.'

'There's going to be a hell of a row, all right. And it's going to start in a minute. The police car's nearly through.'

His father pointed and Archie swung round. The blue flashing light was only a few yards away. Then the car had stopped, the doors were opening and the crowd parted before the tall figures of the police officers.

'The best defence is attack,' muttered Douglas, and stepped forward. 'Which of you is Chief Constable Smart?' he demanded.

One of the officers detached himself. He was white with anger.

'I am,' he said. 'Are you Douglas?'

'That's right, and I'd be glad of an explanation——'

'You'll get no explanations,' snapped Smart. 'You'll give them. And get that piper to shut up. You'd no permission to have a piper.'

'I'd no permission to have a pipe band,' said Douglas

evenly. 'You said nothing about a piper.'

He nodded to Calum Macrae, who grinned and folded his pipes under his arm.

'You'd no permission to hold a meeting at all,' said Smart. 'I could get you on half a dozen charges.'

'I think you'd better be careful,' said Douglas. 'I held no meeting. I came to do what you gave me permission to do. And I've got a taped recording of the conversation when that permission was given. If there's been confusion, it's your responsibility. You didn't have a single constable on duty here when I arrived.'

'I wasn't aware that your presence called for special police action,' said Smart sarcastically.

'Well, you'll be aware of it next time, won't you?'

'Listen, you held a political meeting——'

'I did not,' snapped Douglas. 'And I don't intend to say that again. I apologise for the fact that my presence attracted so many people. I didn't think it would attract quite as many as this. But your job is to anticipate this sort of thing and take the necessary precautions. And now, instead of standing arguing you might clear a way to let us out of here.'

'That'll be a pleasure,' said Smart tightly. 'Where's your car?'

'In the car park.'

'Right. Give me your keys and I'll get a police driver to bring it over.' Douglas handed them to him. 'Then you'll follow us down to the station.'

'I think not,' said Douglas quietly. 'You know who I am. And if you decide to bring any charges you'll deal with my legal advisers. But I'd think very carefully before you do. And when I do hold meetings in this area, as I'll be doing soon, I don't want a repetition of this afternoon.'

He looked into Smart's cold, angry eyes.

'Don't worry,' said the Chief Constable as he turned away. 'I'm not likely to forget you.'

'Damned insolence,' muttered Jack Armstrong. 'And damned incompetence.'

Archie drew out a crumpled packet of cigarettes.

'Well, I don't know,' he said. 'It seems to me he can surely

194

get you for something. You didn't see the jam down on the main road.'

'But that's nothing to do with us.'

'Except that you caused it.'

'Not knowingly,' said Douglas. 'It just happened. And nobody's more surprised than I am.'

'Surprised and delighted is what he means,' Armstrong said. 'It looks pretty hopeful for Gibson here.'

'If they didn't just come out of curiosity,' said the prospective Member.

'Which they probably did,' said Douglas. 'Anyway, let's get away. Here's the car.' He turned to his son. 'What about you?'

'I'm all right,' said Archie. 'My car's in a lane off the main road. I'll find my own way back.'

He watched the Jaguar and Armstrong's Land-Rover move slowly off through the thinning crowd, then began to walk back down the road towards the Lotus. Everyone was going now, drifting away from the great statue of the mounted Bruce, talkative good-humoured groups moving more quickly since the police had cleared the jam at the main road junction. He found himself beside a man in his working clothes who turned to him, laughing.

'By here, he's a helluva man, that!'

'Who is?'

'That fella Douglas. He's a great wee chap, right enough.'

Archie glanced at him.

'Would you vote for him?'

'Aye! Christ, aye, I'd vote for him. Might as well give him a bash at it. He couldnae do ony worse than the rest o' them.'

'Do you think he'd do better?'

'Aye, by here, I think he would. Did ye no' see him talking to the polis? He didnae give a damn for them. Not a damn!'

Archie left him laughing happily at the memory and turned the Lotus in the cul-de-sac before edging out into the southbound stream of cars. For a mile or two, he took it easy, until the traffic had sorted itself out. Then he cut out into the fast lane and accelerated hard towards Glasgow.

195

CHAPTER NINE

JULY of that year was a month of sunshine, a rare month when summer day succeeded summer day, transforming the city, flushing the pale faces of its people with new colour, bringing them a new vitality, a new lightheartedness, filling the grey sun-drenched dusty streets with the swirling patterns of summer frocks and gay shirts, tempting James Douglas from his desk to look from his office window over the changing rooftops to where the great white buildings of the redeveloped areas glittered against the even hazy blue of the sky.

He thought of Gartland then, where the roses were blooming on the green edge of the hills, but that was now something only to be savoured in memory, or briefly in the last hour of the long evening, when the air was full of perfume and the cool of coming night. But he had no regrets for what he no longer had time to enjoy.

Slowly, painstakingly, the web of his organisation was being woven across the country from the Borders to the Pentland Firth. There was no drama in this, only routine administrative work, broken by meetings with his new executive committee and his panel of advisers, made bearable by journeys to the outlying districts when the laden cars and caravans and heavy touring buses seemed part of another world. But he returned refreshed from these journeys. There was a movement of opinion in his favour which it was easier to feel in the towns and villages of the periphery than in the heart of the city itself. There, one was less aware of the silent impersonal power of the State. There, in the company of men who talked of human problems, it was possible to realise the weakness of the great remote administrative machine which could neither know their needs nor formulate solutions from which humanity was not excluded.

It was during that month of July that Douglas first began to feel an optimism which had some foundation in concrete reality.

Meanwhile, the election campaign in Stirlingshire North went ahead smoothly. The polling date had been announced as

August 12th and in mid-July the first public opinion polls were held. On the morning of the publication of the results, Douglas was sitting considering them when Archie came.

'Have you seen them?' he asked.

'Not really,' said Archie. 'They don't really mean much, do they?'

'Not all that much, when there's still nearly a month to go,' agreed Douglas. 'But it's more than a straw in the wind. Have a look at them.'

He passed the paper over and Archie scanned the table quickly.

'In reply to the question, "How do you intend to vote in the coming by-election?", answers were obtained, in percentages, as follows:—

Socialist	29
Conservative	27
National	23
Liberal	9
Don't know	12

He whistled.

'You agree that's more than a straw in the wind?' said his father.

'I certainly do.'

'If you look at the figures last time, you'll see that we're taking votes from the Socialists and the Tories almost equally. And we've clipped a couple of per cent off the Liberals. In fact, if they weren't standing, we'd be in.'

'By the look of this, you might be in anyway,' said Archie. 'Given a decent share of the "Don't knows".'

His father nodded.

'That's right. They hold the key. And we've less than a month to win them. So things are going to move in Stirlingshire North. We've sixty meetings booked so far and more to come if we can get the halls.'

'And no trouble from the police?'

His father laughed.

'Not a word. I didn't think there would be. We were both in

197

the wrong that day. The best thing to do was let it slide.'

'Well, I didn't think they would,' said Archie. 'You didn't see the mess-up on the main road.'

'But it didn't last long. And the press didn't get hold of it, which was just as well. But nevertheless, that turn-out backs up the figures on this poll.'

'Well, it impressed me,' said Archie. 'That's when I began to realise this wasn't just a joke.'

Douglas glanced at him quickly.

'It's no joke,' he said. 'Far from it. And when they see these results this morning, a lot of other people are going to realise the same thing. Anyway.' He folded the paper and put it in a drawer. 'How are things with you?'

'All right. Nothing much to report.'

'No confirmation from Dundee?'

'Not yet.'

'And what about Julia? Any more word from her?'

'A postcard today,' said Archie. 'She'll be home next Wednesday.'

'Three weeks late?'

'That's right.'

'And no explanation?'

'None,' said Archie. 'Just the letter I told you about.'

That letter had arrived almost at the end of June, after a silence of two weeks. It told him that she had decided to stay on longer in Italy. She had met some charming people who had asked her to stay with them. They had a villa near Fiesole, not far from Florence. It would be less hot there, in the Tuscan hills. And Rome in these last days had become insufferable. She had decided to go.

He had acknowledged her letter without making any pretence of regret at her prolonged absence, but he had reminded her of the date when Jamie was due back from school. Now, the postcard indicated her intention to return the day before. The implication could hardly have been more obvious.

'It's a funny thing,' said Douglas thoughtfully. 'She's never done anything like this before, has she?'

'Not like this. She's been away for a weekend. Never longer.'

'And you've no idea why?'

Archie moved uncomfortably. It still embarrassed him to talk of anything personal with either of his parents.

'No,' he said. 'Except that just before she went away things were worse than they'd ever been before.'

'Because of what?'

He shrugged his shoulders.

'I don't know. Everything, I suppose. The fact that I wouldn't go with her to Rome. You, that night at Gartland. This business with Anne and Peter. And me.'

'What in particular about you?'

'Well, I think . . . everything. But especially that I spend too much time working.'

His father snorted.

'She doesn't know what side her bread's buttered on. How does she think you can afford to keep her living the way she does?'

'She doesn't. She doesn't think at all. She's no idea how much it costs to live the way we do. And then, she's got money of her own, as she keeps reminding me.'

'Not as much as she thinks. All her capital's in the shipyard, isn't it?'

'As far as I know.'

'Well, she doesn't bother to read her balance sheet or she wouldn't be so cocky. That shipyard's on the way down the hill. I told you that before.'

'Yes, you told me. But I didn't tell her. There didn't seem to be any point. She wouldn't believe me.'

'She'll believe it when they go into liquidation. Which they'll have to do within a couple of years. Old Fletcher's past it. There's nobody to take his place. Their equipment's out of date. They can't face foreign competition. It's just a matter of time.'

'I didn't know it was as bad.'

'It's bad, all right. And it might be no bad thing if she knew. It might bring her to heel. Assuming that's what you want.'

'What do you mean?'

'Just that if a marriage isn't a success after ten years, it

199

never will be. If she did come to heel, would it make any difference?'

'I don't know.'

'It's none of my business,' said his father. 'But you should know. And you do know, if you would only admit it. The answer is, it wouldn't.'

'So what can I do?'

The question came out, almost against his wishes. It was the question he had asked of himself so often during the past months.

'One of three things. Carry on the way you've been doing, making the best of a bad job. Separate. Or get a divorce.'

'On what grounds?'

'That I wouldn't know,' said Douglas. 'But it seems to me as a cynical old man that her holiday might be worth looking into.'

Archie's cigarette halted on its way to his lips.

'I never thought of that,' he breathed.

Douglas smiled.

'You know,' he said, 'outside the business, you're like your mother. You think the world's full of nice, decent folk like yourself. The only way you'll ever learn otherwise is to come up against what it's really like. And your mother never did. She never will, now. But there's hope for you yet.'

'Yes,' said Archie thoughtfully. 'Yes. Maybe there is.'

*   *   *

But when Julia returned, the edge had gone off her hostility. She was once more friendly and considerate in public, polite and coldly correct in private, but without the displays of venom which had made her conduct in the month or so before her holiday unusual. And there was nothing in the story of her Italian holiday as she told it to arouse a breath of suspicion. Photographs were produced of the villa in the Tuscan hills, of the Italian couple in their garden, on a balcony at Positano, on the terrace of a Roman restaurant. The husband looked like a stockbroker in early middle age, though he was, in fact, an engineer. And his wife, some ten years younger, had a dark beauty which did not conceal a hardness of the kind possessed

200

by Julia herself. It did not seem an improbable friendship. Certainly, short of employing a private investigator, there was nothing Archie could do but await developments.

This, for a few days, he consciously did. But within a week he had learned that it was easier to try to forget, for the routine to which life returned was more pleasant than the lonely emptiness he had endured in Julia's absence. Jamie was home, and the gentle Oonagh had returned from Dublin, and it was possible to pretend that a home existed. This, he knew, was weakness. But it was a weakness that made life infinitely more tolerable.

He said so to Anne one evening when he called on her at her flat. He had visited her several times since that night at Gartland when Peter was introduced to the family. And sometimes Peter was there. Sometimes she was alone. It no longer mattered. He realised too clearly how much he had missed by allowing the years to carry them apart. Nothing had replaced the old warm relationship of their youth. In it, had been none of the barriers which separated him from his parents and from his wife. It had meant understanding, consolation, a refuge. This he set out to re-create before it was too late. Now she said—

'I don't blame you. And yet in a way I do. It means living a lie.'

'But the alternatives are just as bad. Whether it's separation or divorce. For Jamie, they're both worse.'

'Are they? I don't know. I'd just hate to think of it happening to Peter and me.'

'But it won't,' he said. 'With Julia, the writing's been on the wall since the beginning. There was some sort of seed of destruction there before we even got married. With you two, there's nothing like that.'

She looked at him curiously.

'You know, I said that once. To Peter. He'd been worried about . . . well, this sort of thing happening to us if we did get married. And I said the same as you did. The seed of destruction's there from the start.'

'And did he agree?'

'I don't know.'

201

'But you're still not married.'

'No,' she said. 'We're still not married.'

'Still for the same reason?'

She nodded.

'Yes.'

'In spite of the fact that you've enough money for both?'

'That's not the point,' she said. 'He's lost so much pride already. I mustn't hurt what he's got left.'

'So you're like me,' he said. 'There's nothing much you can do but wait.'

But in waiting there was now hopefulness for Anne. Peter had agreed to hold an exhibition in the winter. He was now painting with that end in view. And with the creation of an immediate objective, with the rediscovery of method directed towards it, had come a gradual restoration of his personality.

As a result, Anne had spent a happy summer. She worked steadily each day, as Peter did, but often in the evenings or at weekends they went together in her car to the sea or into the hills, seeking out quiet back roads undiscovered by the tourists, picnicking on the empty shore or on short, sheep-cropped grass beside a burn, lying outspread, almost naked, in the sun, talking through the gloaming into the dusk, lying in each other's arms under the strangely luminous night sky of the northern summer.

It was after such a mid-August evening that her father phoned. She had returned to the flat late, close to midnight, after taking Peter back to his rooms. The place felt empty, abandoned, as it always did at night now when Peter was not there, and she was humming to herself, trying to ignore the silence, when the strident bell jabbed her nerves. She ran to the receiver.

'Anne?'

'Daddy! What on earth are you doing, phoning at this time!'

'To tell you the news. We've won!'

His voice was jubilant. And she remembered. All day she had been thinking of him while she worked, imagining those anonymous voters filing into the booths to make the mark that this time was so important, but Peter had made her forget. She felt almost guilty.

'Gibson's in with a majority of six hundred and ten. And the Socialists demanded a recount. But that's been done and he's still in. The Liberal lost his deposit.'

'Oh, Daddy! How marvellous for you!'

'Marvellous for more than me,' said Douglas. 'From now on, we mean something. We can't be ignored. It's marvellous for the whole organisation.'

'Oh, I know! It's tremendous. And it's the very first one you've fought.'

'That's right.' Her father chuckled. 'A case of starting the way you mean to continue. But listen. That's not the only reason I phoned. I'm going to Holland tomorrow——'

'Tomorrow!'

'Well, I couldn't go till this was over. And your thing closes in a month. I want to go now, before something else boils up. So what's the address of this man Bloemendael?'

'Heemraadsingel 241. But Daddy, I wish you'd let me know. I could have told him you were coming.'

'It doesn't matter,' said Douglas. 'I'll find him. And now I've got to go. There's some sort of celebration brewing. But I'll ring you when I come back. I'll only be away a couple of days. And you'd better spell that address out while I write it down.'

He folded the piece of paper and put it in his wallet as he stepped out of the phone booth on to the pavement. The crowd was dispersing now. The newspapermen had long since gone. But here and there little groups of people still chatted about the political sensation, about how, from being two points behind on the last public opinion poll, the new party had surged ahead to gain a three per cent majority. He looked around for some of his friends, then spotted Gibson in the doorway of the hall with the agent and Sir William Robertson. He was crossing to them when the defeated Tory candidate stopped him.

'Just a minute,' he said. 'I ought to congratulate you.'

'Thank you,' said Douglas.

'But I'm not going to. You're the power behind this National farce. I just want to say that I think it's disgraceful.'

'That what's disgraceful?'

'The whole thing. Your whole campaign. The fact that you're able to use your influence to whip up feeling in the way you did. This doesn't reflect public opinion at all. It reflects the artificial feeling that you've created. And I can tell you this. I'll be making a few enquiries into the question of your election expenses.'

'You do that,' said Douglas. 'You'll find everything legal.'

'Will I? What about this newspaper of yours?'

'If *The Times* makes comments favourable to the Tories, is that to be criticised? If the *Daily Worker* backs a Communist candidate, does anybody complain?' Douglas smiled and turned away. 'You're just a bad loser, that's all.'

'Just a minute,' said the man harshly. 'If you think either my Party or the Government of this country is going to let you carry on with this, you're very much mistaken.'

'That's a different question,' said Douglas gravely. 'It remains to be seen what they can do about it. And now, if you'll excuse me——'

Along with the new Member, the Party workers and some of his more influential supporters, he went to the impromptu celebration at the home of Lord Kilconner in Dunblane. At two o'clock in the morning, he set off for home. Less than eight hours later, he took off on a K.L.M. flight bound for Amsterdam.

* * *

On the day of his arrival, he did not attempt to contact Hans Bloemendael immediately. He lunched in Rotterdam alone and spent the afternoon wandering in the park where Anne's sculpture was displayed. But it was warm there, in the sheltered gardens, and the park was large. When he came to a little rose-garden tucked behind clipped hedges in the light shade of a grove of tall, slender trees, he sank gratefully on to a seat, feeling at last the impact of the final, hectic, pre-election days.

As he sat in the dappled sunshine he looked around him at the beds of Frensham and Korona and Sarabande, confined by edges of diminutive box, separated by the narrow paths of raked pea gravel which converged on the plinth from which

Anne's 'Head of a Child' gazed tranquilly across the raised trusses of soft, rich colour.

It was a charming head. Of all the things he had seen that afternoon, he liked it best. It had an unusual delicacy, a strangely moving quality, some extra thing which he could not define. Her technique with it had been traditional, rather than boldly imaginative as with her other work. But it was more than that.

As he considered it, it occurred to him that the sensitivity of feeling with which she had handled it could only have been founded in deep feeling for the flesh and blood original. It was as though a mother had lovingly created with her hands an enduring replica of her own son. Yet Anne had no son. He chewed thoughtfully at the stem of his pipe. There was something familiar there, in those sightless eyes, in the childish curve of those cold lips. Bloemendael might know. Or if a catalogue existed, it might contain explanatory notes. He would ask him.

But that night, after he had telephoned the Dutchman and arranged to meet him for lunch on the following day, the answer came to him. It must be Peter. Taken from a photograph, perhaps. But Peter, when he was a child, and whole. The child-image to be loved all the more for what was later to happen.

It was then a certain scheme suggested itself to him.

On the next afternoon, he asked Bloemendael when they stood together in the rose garden.

'But I have no idea who this is,' he said regretfully. 'For this, there are no notes. But I agree. It is probably the best thing here. But not typical of her style. Not contemporary in mood. Although this is not to criticise. It is outside time. There is no need for justification.'

'And she said nothing that gave you a hint? She didn't say that it was a friend, or a relative?'

'Nothing. Although clearly she values it herself, since it is not for sale.'

'It is not for sale?'

'Not this. Everything else is for sale. And many have been sold. The exhibition has been a success. But this I could have

205

sold twenty times. It is small, you see. And, of course, it has an appeal which is universal. Many people have come to me and asked, but'—he spread his hands—'I have had to say ... sorry. She was very firm on this.'

Douglas looked at the head. Now, behind the eyes, he saw the eyes of Peter. Through the soft contours of the face, the features of Peter were drawn by his mind's eye. He was now sure.

'I'm sorry that it's not for sale,' he said slowly. 'I would have liked to buy it myself.'

'Yes,' said Bloemendael, 'this I understand, but——'

'I thought perhaps two thousand guineas.'

The Dutchman stared at him in amazement.

'Two thousand guineas!'

'That's ... what? Roughly twenty thousand gulden.'

'But this is a fantastic price! The value of her work will grow, of course. But just now she is comparatively unknown. She cannot command such a figure!'

'I'm offering it,' said Douglas gently. 'Let's sit down and talk about it.' He led the way to the seat under the trees where he had sat on the previous day. 'Now,' he said, 'I must put my cards on the table. I believe this to be the head of someone who is now a young artist of great promise. I think you know that in Britain to show great promise is not enough. You will still be allowed to starve. To get financial recognition, you must have a name, a fashionable reputation. I'm offering to buy this head for two thousand guineas on two conditions. One, that under no circumstances do you reveal the name of the buyer. And two, that the sale gets maximum publicity. In other words, both here and in Britain it becomes widely known in the circles that matter that the head of a child, now the brilliant young artist Peter Colquhoun, the work of Anne Douglas, has been sold for this large figure. People will then say ... who is Peter Colquhoun? And at least one of the leading critics is certain to tell them. And that is how reputations begin. It's entirely wrong, of course, but I think you'll agree that's what happens.'

'Yes,' said Bloemendael. 'That is what happens. Here in Holland too.'

206

'All right, then. That's why I want it. And I need hardly tell you that Anne mustn't know anything about it. You wait till the exhibition is almost over. Then you write and tell her that you've had this offer from a wealthy customer who doesn't wish his name to be known.'

'But she still may not agree,' protested Bloemendael. 'She is a determined girl.'

Douglas chuckled.

'I know,' he said. 'I'm her father. And if she doesn't agree, you increase the offer until she does. Four thousand. Even five thousand. I don't care. The money stays in the family in any case. But she'll agree below five thousand. She pretends to despise money, but she's not a fool.'

'And this young man,' said Bloemendael. 'You know him?'

'I know him slightly. Let's say I have his interests at heart.'

'And he is truly brilliant?'

'From what I've heard, he may well earn that reputation.'

'But you are guarded.'

'I'm not an expert. But if you like, I'll tell you when he has an exhibition. Then you can come and see for yourself.' He smiled. 'It may be that you can do for him what you've already done for Anne. I'm told that your special skill is in finding new talent.'

'That is my chief interest, certainly.'

'All right, then. Will you do it?'

'How can I refuse?' He grinned. 'You seem to have forgotten that you will also be increasing the value of the work of Anne Douglas. This, I'm sure you know, is in my interests too.'

'I rather thought it might be,' said Douglas.

When he left Bloemendael, all arrangements had been made. The news would be cabled when the sale had been authorised. Then Bloemendael would release the information to the Dutch press and Douglas would arrange that it be duly noticed in the correct British publications. Thereafter, the pattern of events was unpredictable, but it seemed likely that Colquhoun's winter exhibition would arouse considerably more interest than he expected.

* * *

On the evening of that same day, Douglas flew back to London. He was sitting in the departure lounge at London Airport, drinking coffee and waiting for the Glasgow flight to be announced, when a voice beside him made him look up from his evening paper. He looked at the tired, elderly man in the raincoat without recognition and the man smiled, a worn, humourless smile.

'It's been a long time,' he said, 'but I didn't think I'd changed as much as that.'

But the voice had not changed. Douglas sprang to his feet, appalled at his failure to know him at once.

'Jimmie,' he said. 'I must have been day-dreaming.'

'I doubt it,' said the Member for the West Central division of Glasgow. 'When I look in the mirror, I hardly know myself these days.' He put his brief-case on the table and sat down with a sigh of relief. 'Man, it's great to get off your feet.'

As Douglas looked at him, he had to hide his feelings. Jimmie Marshall. Almost a legendary figure in the political history of the city. The sole survivor of that early band of rebels who had fought bitterly through the twenties and the thirties for the rights of the workers whom they represented. And now this old man, old and ill, the skin of his face sallow and drawn, only his clear blue eyes left to recall the man he once had been.

'Have some coffee,' said Douglas. 'There's still time.'

'No, I'll not bother. The stuff they serve in here's like dish-water anyway. It's my bed I'm needing. My bed and a good dram and a night's rest.' He pulled out a packet of cigarettes. 'Are you still on the pipe, James, or will you have one of these damned coffin nails?'

'No, I'll stick to the pipe,' said Douglas. He held out his lighter. 'You know, Jimmie, I don't think I've seen you in three years.'

'It'll be that,' agreed Marshall. 'And we're both three years older.' The smoke caught his breath and he started coughing, a harsh staccato cough that racked his body and filled his eyes with tears. When the bout ended, he wiped them with the handkerchief from his breast pocket, a white handkerchief where before he had proudly worn one the colour of blood.

208

'Och, James, I'm done,' he said at last. 'I've got to give in.'

'You've had a long time of it,' said Douglas gently.

'Thirty years a Member,' said Marshall. 'Forty-two years last backend since the day I first walked into the House, and twelve of them in the wilderness like many another good man. It's long enough. I'm due a rest and I don't mind telling you I feel I need it.'

'You've earned it,' said Douglas. 'And you've lived to see everything done that you set out to do. I'd like to think I'd be as lucky.'

Marshall's old eyes twinkled.

'Well,' he said, 'you're off to a flying start. I wish you'd seen the Scottish Members yesterday morning when they got the news about Stirlingshire North. It would have done your heart good. They were clucking about the place like hens on a hot girdle.'

Douglas grinned.

'It would be good for them.'

'Oh aye, it would be good for them. They've had it too easy, the most of them. They've never had the fight that I had, up against public opinion, employers, the Government, the police. Talk about every man's hand being raised against you. By God, every man's hand was raised against us at yon time. That lot could never have done it. Can you see any of them standing firm in George Square with the police charging the crowd on their horses, with the women screaming and that roar beginning to come from the men that tells you hell's going to break loose any minute? Can you see it? Man, they would have been away like snow off a dyke!'

'It's changed days,' said Douglas.

'Aye, it's changed days. There's none of the old lot left, bar me.'

'And none of the old causes.'

Marshall looked at him.

'No,' he said, 'but yours is one of the new causes that's likely to run into about as much trouble as I ever did. You're not exactly well liked in official quarters these days. You'll know that.'

'I know that,' said Douglas. 'I'm not surprised.'

'Maybe not,' said Marshall, 'but you might be surprised at how high the feeling's running. And not just among the Scottish Members. They're out to get you, James, I don't mind telling you. And some of them'll be none too fussy about their methods. You're a threat to Parliament as we've known it for two hundred and something odd years and they'll not take that lightly.'

'I never expected they would,' said Douglas. 'But given public support, I don't see how they can stop us.'

'Given public support, they'll have a job, I agree. But I've been at this game a long time and I wouldn't put anything past them.' He grinned. 'Man, to tell you the truth, if I was a few years younger I'd join you myself. It's about the only cause bar Socialism as I used to know it that would be worth the fight.'

Douglas laughed.

'But you're not too old yet, Jimmie. Your name would be worth a good few votes in West Central.'

Marshall's eyes clouded.

'Aye, James,' he said. 'But I've fought my last election, in West Central or anywhere else.' He held up the end of his cigarette, then crushed it out in the ash-tray. 'And these are the bloody things that have killed me.'

Douglas stared.

'What do you mean?'

'Just what I say,' said Marshall evenly. 'I've been to the doctor. They've taken X-rays and stuck a tube down my throat for a bit look at it and they're all agreed. It's cancer.'

'No!'

The conventional protestation came out. But he knew that it was true. The man's death was written on his face.

'Aye, but it's true. There's no doubt about it. It's cancer of the lung. And the chances are, when the General Election comes, I'll not be here.'

The loudspeaker wheezed and came alive.

'Will passengers on Flight Number 253 to Glasgow, please go to Gate Number 4. Passengers for Glasgow to Gate Number 4, please. Thank you.'

'I'm sorry,' said Douglas quietly.

Jimmie Marshall smiled wryly.

'There's no need to be sorry,' he said. 'They're all away but me anyway. I've had a good enough run for my money.' He rose stiffly from his seat. 'And anyway, James, it's an ill wind. You'll maybe fight another by-election yet before the spring.'

Douglas sat beside him on the flight north, but Marshall slept, a deep, calm sleep that was like a rehearsal for the death that awaited him. All the years of hunger and hope and endeavour were past. He was flying back to people who were prosperous by all the standards of his youth, well fed and for the most part well housed, with the rights that he had fought for now secured.

Yet it was not enough.

During this quiet revolution, something had been lost. A pride in workmanship. The kind of honesty that gave a fair day's work for a fair day's wage. The sense of unity that had held men together during the years of struggle. Intangible things, whose loss was a wasting sickness in the industrial body of the country.

Was Jimmie Marshall, at the end of the day, satisfied with the fruit of his life's work?

That was the question he would have dearly liked to ask. But he could not ask it. He let the old man sleep on until the aircraft was dropping over the Kilbirnie Hills on its swinging approach to the runway at Abbotsinch. Then he nudged him.

'Just about there.'

They parted at the main entrance of the terminal buildings, where Douglas's driver stood waiting with the car door held open.

'I'll run you home,' Douglas said.

'Och, I'll get a bus,' said Marshall. 'It drops me off at the door.'

He had never changed his ways, not even when the salary of Members was raised to a level that would have seemed fabulous in his youth.

They shook hands briefly. Douglas sank into the soft cushions of the car and looked back at him once, a drab, tired figure carrying a worn brief-case standing alone at the kerb of the road. Then he turned away, saddened.

In two months Jimmie Marshall was dead.

CHAPTER TEN

AUTUMN came early that year, and with it, now that the care-free days of summer were over, the first renewed rumblings of the nation's discontent. The lives of Archie and his executives began to be harassed by a new round of wage demands, by interminable negotiations with Union leaders who claimed that the rising cost of living had altered the basis on which previous agreement had been reached.

And they were right, of course. Now, on the edge of winter, increases in the cost of coal had been announced. Electricity, the principal source of all heat in the new housing areas, was to be more expensive. Milk was up in price. And meat. Bread had risen by another penny on the ordinary loaf. And within the city rents were to be raised to a more realistic level, since the ratepayers could shoulder no more of the massive burden of housing subsidies.

The validity of their arguments could not be disputed. But theirs was only one aspect of the national problem for which it seemed no solution could ever be found.

'If your lot can produce an answer out of the hat for this,' said Archie wearily, 'I'll be converted.'

'I think they can,' said Douglas. 'They think they can. But only when the Scottish economy is separated from that of England.'

'If it ever is.'

His father smiled to himself and said nothing. There was no point in saying anything to Archie. He knew nothing of the accumulating evidence of increasing support. He hadn't attended any of the crowded meetings, where speaker after speaker rose from the floor and expressed the new optimism which the National Party had roused by its dynamic approach. He didn't know that the daily circulation figures of the *New Scot* had passed the quarter of a million mark or that the audience figures for the evening Party broadcasts from the pirate radio ship were nearly one and a half million.

But these things did nothing to alter the fact that at present the country as a whole was in trouble. The gold reserves continued to fall. The monthly export-import figures showed all too clearly the knife edge on which the economy was still balanced. Industrial output per man was the lowest in industrial Europe, while work-hours per man lost through strike action, official or otherwise, were the highest. The nation was sick. But it was a sickness that made the people of Scotland all the more ready to listen with an open mind to what the National Party had to offer. And this was a mood which Douglas was prepared ruthlessly to exploit to the full.

He showed the same ruthlessness in commencing the preparation for a by-election in Glasgow West Central while Jimmie Marshall was still alive. This, he realised, was a vital constituency. The problems it presented were in all respects different from those in Stirlingshire North. And if it could be won, other similar industrial constituencies throughout the country could well be swayed when spring came and the General Election followed. All the more reason, then, to plan carefully and in time.

He called a meeting of the small executive committee and presented them with the facts. A candidate was chosen, a man of thirty-five called Bill Macfarlane, who had been born and brought up in a single-end a stone's throw from Anderston Cross and who was now, as a result of his own effort and ability, a lecturer in the Glasgow Institute of Technology. He was the perfect candidate, linking a brilliant mind to a deep personal knowledge of the people of the district and to a tongue that could, on occasion, speak their own harsh, expressive language. Around him, as summer gave way to autumn, a campaign was quietly planned.

These September days in the city had a beauty of their own. The hard contours of the buildings were softened by the hazy golden sunlight. The skyline had a new delicacy, melting and merging even the stark masses of the new towers into the pale blue wash of the sky. And in the park, at lunch time, when Anne walked there with Peter, the air was acrid with the smoke of the first burning leaves.

'It's sad,' he said. 'I can't stand this bloody season. Let's go back.'

She squeezed his hand.

213

'All right.'

They walked together to the gate and she said—

'Can't you come to the studio? I want to show you something.'

'I ought to work.'

'You've been working seven days a week for a month. You need a break.'

'It was you who nagged me about an exhibition,' he said. 'And you can't have an exhibition without pictures. That's the point of it.'

She laughed.

'And now I'm nagging you to come to the studio. Just this once. There's something I've done in clay and I don't know whether it's right or not. I don't want to take it any further till I'm sure. And I'd like you to see it. Please, Peter.'

He walked with her through the last of the lunch-hour traffic and held open the old, heavy door, relic of the days when the building had been a fine town house. It was when he closed it that he saw the letter lying in the letter-box. He pulled it out and handed it to her.

'From Holland,' he said.

'It'll be from Bloemendael. The thing ends sometime soon. I think the end of this week.'

She opened it and read it. As she read, her expression changed. He looked at her curiously.

'What is it?'

'It's . . . it's nothing.'

She thrust it quickly back into the envelope and turned away from him.

'I don't believe you,' he said gently. He followed her into the work room. 'It's a good thing I'm not jealous. You must admit it looks bad.'

She was standing gazing out of the window at the autumn sunshine in the grimy yard.

'It's nothing like that,' she said.

'Then what is it?'

'I did a head of you.' Her voice was flat. 'I mean, a head when you were a child. I pinched a photograph. Oh, months ago. I put it in the exhibition.'

214

He stared at her.

'All right. So what? You can give me the photo back.'

'But I've just been offered two thousand guineas for the head.'

He threw back his head and laughed.

'But that's marvellous! I don't know who would be mad enough to pay that for it, but it's still marvellous.'

She swung round. Her eyes were full of tears.

'But it's not,' she cried. 'I don't want to sell it!'

He went to her quickly.

'Then you don't have to.'

'But it's crazy not to! And I don't want to. Oh, damn!' She twisted away from him. 'No, Peter. Not just now. I don't know what to do.'

'You could make another.'

'But it wouldn't be the same!'

'It might be better.'

She looked at him uncertainly.

'Do you think it might?'

'I don't see why not.'

She paused, thinking.

'Give me a cigarette, Peter, please. I don't know where mine are.' He lit one and gave it to her. 'Thanks.' She moved away from him. 'Peter, what would you do?'

'I'd take it. I'd take it like a shot. Then I'd make another.'

'Yes,' she said, almost to herself. 'That is what you'd do.' She sat on the edge of the bench and looked at him. 'Peter, I'll sell it on one condition.'

'What's that?'

'That you let me put the money somewhere so that it's there for buying a house. This, and any other money I make from selling things. I mean, it's never been Daddy's, so you needn't feel anything about it. I earned it, so it's mine and that means it's ours. Will you let me do that?'

His eyes clouded and shifted.

'Well . . . what can I say to that? You'd be mad not to take it.'

'But it will be our money. It's not like getting help from Daddy.'

'No, it's not, I must admit. But it's still a kind of one-sided arrangement. I haven't sold a thing.'

'But you will. You haven't really tried to. When your exhibition's on, you will.'

'Will I?' He shrugged his shoulders. 'I don't know. I'd like to think you were right.'

'You will!' She ran to him and let his arm encircle her, drawing her near. 'Darling, I know you will.'

He sank his lips into her hair.

'Let's hope,' he whispered. 'Let's just hope.'

* * *

After the frosts and the golden sunshine of September came the autumn gales, wild October days when the winds howled out of the cold north-east over the grey sea and threw themselves upon the shores of Scotland, sweeping inland over the bare stubble fields to strip the last tattered leaves from the dark, dripping trees and whistle impotently down glistening city streets, snatching at the skirts of the leaning, laughing typists and crying like a banshee round the austere mass of St. Andrew's House.

The Secretary of State for Scotland moved away from the window.

'I detest wind,' he said. 'It's too primitive, too barbaric.' He put his coffee cup and saucer on his desk. 'And it's too damned destructive. That's the trouble about the new-fangled industrialised building techniques. The buildings aren't strong until they've been completed. If a gale like this hits them in the construction phase, they fall down like a house of cards. If this doesn't set the factory building programme six weeks behind, I'm much mistaken. It's been blowing like this since Tuesday night.'

'It's six weeks behind already,' said the Permanent Undersecretary. 'And that's on average. The Lanarkshire project is ten weeks behind if it's a day.'

'I'm well aware of it,' said the Minister. 'And that project means ten thousand jobs. Ten thousand jobs that aren't going to be there in April, which is when the General Election's likely to be. And that leaves you with a five and a half per cent

216

unemployment rate in an area with two nearly marginal constituencies. It doesn't bear thinking about.'

'London's not going to like it,' said the Parliamentary Undersecretary.

The Minister snorted.

'I don't give a damn whether London likes it or not. I don't like it. But there's nothing I can do about it. And there's nothing London can do about it either. Because things are booming in the south-east, they think they ought to be booming up here. They still don't seem to have got it into their thick heads that it's a different problem. It's one point where I'm inclined to think James Douglas is right.'

The Permanent Undersecretary contemplated the burning end of his cigarette.

'There would seem to be a widespread feeling that James Douglas is right in more things than that.'

'Widespread?' enquired the Minister. 'How widespread?'

'Sufficiently widespread to alter the meaning of the word marginal.'

'How do you know?'

'Oh, one hears things,' said the Undersecretary vaguely. 'One tries to keep in touch with trends of opinion. He appears to have built up a fine organisation.'

'So I believe,' said Buchanan.

'And I gather he's got a good man for Glasgow West Central. Had you heard?'

'Yes,' said Buchanan briefly. There were times when the Permanent Undersecretary had an infinite capacity to irritate.

'A man Macfarlane, it seems. A local chap, but he seems to be all right, apart from a tendency to produce the glottal stop from time to time. But a brilliant brain, I'm told.'

'But surely that's a safe seat?' said the Parliamentary Undersecretary. 'Marshall's been there for years.'

'Ever since the war,' said the Minister. 'And off and on before that. But I must admit I don't know whether it's safe or not. It's one of those seats where they vote for the man and not the Party.'

'How is he, by the way? Marshall, I mean. I haven't heard for a week or two.'

217

'Dying,' said Buchanan.

'And likely to die soon?'

'Any day.'

'So we have a by-election before Christmas.'

'Very probably.'

'And in a constituency,' said the Permanent Undersecretary, 'which is an example of what I was saying about "marginal". I'd rate his chances high.'

'Oh, surely?' The Parliamentary Undersecretary protested. 'Even allowing for the personal vote, I would have thought that seat as safe as any in the country.'

'And how safe is that?' The Minister drew his pipe from his pocket and regarded it thoughtfully. 'What we've got to realise is this, no seat in Scotland can now be considered safe. And that's not a matter of opinion. It's fact.' He pointed the stem at the Permanent Undersecretary. 'I asked you a minute ago why you thought there was widespread feeling in Douglas's favour, but I'd no need to ask. I have my own sources of information. And I believe that every seat in the country is threatened. I know the man. I know the power of his personal appeal. I know his ability. And I know enough about the organisation he's built up and the men in it to have an unqualified respect for its strength. And that, let me remind you, has been built up in six months. They still have another six months before the Election, there or thereabouts. I don't believe you can overrate the threat they'll present by that time.'

'And London knows this?' asked the Parliamentary Undersecretary.

The Minister nodded.

'Of course. They've been kept informed from the start.'

'And what do they propose to do about it?'

'I've no idea. One might ask, what can they do? There are various obstructive tactics open to us, of course. We can block hall bookings. We can use the police to limit or prevent open-air meetings on one pretext or another. That sort of thing. But it's only playing with the problem. None of these things is likely to stop Douglas. I know him too well.'

'Douglas,' said the Permanent Undersecretary softly. 'In the end, we always come back to the man. One has to ask, would

218

his organisation continue to exist without him? And the answer, one feels, is that it probably would not. Would it be correct to say that there lies his greatest weakness?'

'I think it would,' said the Minister.

'Well then. Isn't it simply a case of dealing with this one man?'

Buchanan looked at him sharply. It was the second time in just over a week that he had heard this point of view expressed. The first time had been when he had been instructed to place all the information he possessed about the Douglas organisation in the hands of the security services.

'But this is not a security matter,' he had protested. 'It's purely political.'

The reply had been chilly.

'We regard it as being a security matter. We are not concerned with this organisation as a whole or with other individual members of it. Information we already possess limits our interest to James Douglas. In our opinion, he presents a risk to the internal security of this country. You will please co-operate fully with the security services in dealing with the problem in the manner they may deem most expedient.'

He had not cared for either the tone or the content of that reply. Nor did he like its implications. He had been a politician long enough to dislike and mistrust the secret, hidden aspect of the State machine, which did not find it necessary to let humanitarian principles modify its actions. And James Douglas had, at one time, been something of a friend.

'And how do you suggest we do that?' he demanded. 'How do you deal with a man who is breaking no law, an honest reputable man who is campaigning for something in which he believes, a man who is the leader of a perfectly legal political party which threatens to command a majority opinion in the country? How do you do it? You tell me. Because I don't know.'

'I haven't the slightest idea,' said the Permanent Under-secretary.

'Exactly,' said Buchanan shortly. He pulled some papers towards him in a gesture of dismissal. 'And now, if you gentlemen will excuse me, I've got work to do.'

When they had left the room, he remembered again the meeting in London with the security chief. He did not like these men who stood on the edge of the political world, who probed and investigated the lives of their fellows, trusting no one, spying here, suspecting there, dealing in lies and subversion and intrigue ostensibly in the cause of the welfare of the State and the integrity of the realm. He remembered the pale blue expressionless eyes, the flat, rather high-pitched voice.

'He represents a risk to the internal security of this country.'

He could warn him. He had thought of that. But against what? Against that lean blond man who now sat in his London office with all known information about the Douglas affair? Against the Government in which he was a Minister? His lips tightened. It was ridiculous. He could tell him nothing that he would not already know or guess. And there was nothing to warn against. There would be no midnight knock at the door, no silent faceless men in raincoats standing in the dark, no fast car stationed by the gate, its engine running. This was Britain. Not Stalinist Russia or Hitler's Germany.

And yet. And yet.

How different was it? The question nagged at him. Different certainly, within the framework of the law. But without the law, in the murky world of the security men, how different was it?

He, a Minister in Her Majesty's Government, had to admit that he did not know the answer to that question.

He sighed and turned away from the window. Douglas would have to work out his own salvation, continue along his chosen road to whatever lay at the end of it. There could be no turning back for either of them. But he earnestly hoped that the security forces would not call on him for assistance when the time came.

As he reached his desk, the internal telephone rang. He picked it up.

'Hello?'

'Hello, sir. I thought you'd like to know. The Member for Glasgow West Central died at breakfast time this morning. That was Marshall, you may remember.'

'Yes,' said the Minister heavily. 'I remember. Thank you.'

He replaced the receiver and sat still. There was so much to remember. He was the last of the old brigade. His death marked the end of a political era, as Douglas, at Stirlingshire North, had signalled the start of another.

Douglas.

He shook his head wearily and picked up the phone.

'My compliments to Mr. MacCallum,' he said, 'and tell him I'd like to see him at twelve o'clock.'

*   *   *

'Sally.'

Douglas leaned towards the microphone.

'Yes, sir?'

'Get me Roderick Grant.'

As he waited, his mind rapidly reviewed the plans formulated in committee during the last weeks. But they were complete. No new consideration had arisen. Nothing remained but to act.

'Grant here.'

'Hello.' The imminence of action gave his voice a fresh vigour. 'I've just heard from the news desk. Jimmie Marshall died this morning, just before nine o'clock.'

Grant's hand tightened on the receiver.

'So we start?'

'That's right,' said Douglas. 'We start right away. It's ten-thirty. I want all bookings of halls complete by lunch-time. That's one thing they're certain to try and block, so you've got to move fast. Now, we've got to take a chance here. We don't know the election date, so we've got to guess it. Today's Friday, the 15th. Six weeks yesterday takes us to November 25th. Probably too early. Further ahead, December 16th is too near to Christmas. So my guess is either the 2nd or the 9th of December. Go on the assumption that it's the 2nd and book accordingly. Now, if I'm right, we've one small stroke of luck. November 30th is St. Andrew's Day. It wouldn't be eve of the election, but it would be near as dammit. I want an open-air rally that night at seven-thirty in George Square. Apply for police permission now, before the opposition gets organised.

We'll talk about speakers for that later, but I want a pipe band. The Glaswegian likes a show, so we'll damn well give him one. You've got that?'

'Yes, sir.'

'All right, then. Get on with it. Report to me here at two o'clock. And if you start running into trouble with bookings let me know.'

*   *   *

That, for Douglas, marked the beginning of six weeks of activity as intense as any he had ever known. His prediction of the election date proved accurate. All booking of halls and rooms were successfully arranged on that first morning, to the considerable annoyance of the Secretary of State when he heard the news later in the day. And the plans, so carefully prepared, led to a smoothly accelerating campaign which reached to every voter in the constituency of West Central. But it meant work, long days of work, which did not end until the last meeting had spilled its audience on to the deserted city streets. Then there was the drive home, out of the November fogs and the thick air of the hired halls where the city folk created their own miasma of stale smoke, and sweat, and the exhalations of inadequately washed humanity, up into the clear air of the Stockiemuir where there were stars again and the hills were clean and dark behind the house of Gartland.

But Gartland, these days, was no more than a place in which to sleep, a place where Margaret waited with the kettle boiling, hoping for half an hour of companionship and a cup of tea together before the new loneliness of the night, when he would sleep and she would lie, wakeful and worried, wishing it could all be over, wishing home could be again as it had been when the children were young and the house was full of noise and laughter.

This was something Douglas excluded from his thoughts. There was no longer time for quiet evenings by the fire, no time for family life as he had known and loved it. There was not even time to keep in touch with what they did. That would come again, some day. But now they must live their own lives, dealing with their own problems without the help which he

222

had always tried to give, openly or in secret.

And their lives, during these weeks, ran smoothly enough. It is remarkable how this happens in all families. Event is heaped upon event for a time. Then follows a period of tranquillity that lulls the senses into the false belief that it must remain like this, reducing the future to an infinite succession of routine, undemanding, uneventful days. For both Anne and Archie, this was such a time.

There had been a mild flurry of excitement in late September when the sale of the head was publicised. Questions had been asked, as Douglas had predicted, about the identity of this unknown artist. Strange visitors had called at her studio seeking information and had gone away well briefed on the exhibition which was now arranged for January. Well briefed, because Anne had no illusions about the potential commercial value to Peter of this unexpected publicity. And he, surprisingly and to her satisfaction, had shown himself prepared to cash in on it to the limit. It was yet another symptom of his continuing recovery.

For them both, the weeks that followed were a quiet time of happiness and hopefulness and steady productivity.

For Archie, they were neither notably happy nor particularly hopeful, but they were tolerable. Julia was behaving as well as she knew how. That was clear. Her efforts stopped short of any display of warmth or affection, but these were things he no longer expected, things he no longer desired, at least, from her. It remained possible to pretend that things were all right, sometimes even possible to forget to pretend. He let his senses be lulled. It was so much easier that way. But the succession of uneventful days was not infinite. It ended on St. Andrew's Day, in the last hours of a grey still November afternoon.

He had left the office earlier than usual, taking with him a brief-case full of paper work which could be done at home in the greater comfort of his study. When he had emptied it on to his desk, he glanced at his watch. Although the lights were on and the curtains drawn, it was only a little after four. He put a match to the fire which was set and ready to light in the grate and was crouching before it, watching the flames lick over

223

the coal, when a knock at the door made him turn his head.

'Yes?'

It was Oonagh, dressed in a simple afternoon frock of soft tweed, the kind of simple frock which has the elegance of a Paris model. He stood up quickly.

'I thought I heard you come in,' she said. 'Cook wondered if you'd like some afternoon tea.'

'Yes. Yes, I would. If it's not too late?'

'No, it's not. I'll bring it. Or would you rather have it in the drawing-room? There's a good fire there.'

He looked at the fire he had just lit. There would be little or no heat from that for twenty minutes or so.

'I'll have it in the drawing-room,' he said.

He had finished arranging his papers in some sort of order when he heard Oonagh's footsteps in the hall and the distant clink of china. In the drawing-room, the flames from the basket grate were leaping high into the throat of the chimney and she was setting the tea things on a little table drawn near to the chair he always used.

'Is my wife out?' he asked.

'Yes, she went out just after lunch. But she said she'd be back about six.'

As he drew near, he noticed her hands, slim strong hands whose movements were positive and sure. He bent down to the warmth of the fire and became aware of her perfume, a fragrance he had met before, lingering on the air of an empty room, and he turned to her, only now realising its origin. She smiled.

'There,' she said. 'I hope that's all right.'

'I'm sure it will be.' A dimple came when she smiled, a tiny shadow-filled depression on the smooth warm skin of her cheek. And she smiled easily, her lips softly curving and expressive, glistening faintly in the light of the fire. 'Thank you,' he said. 'It's good of you to bother.'

'It's no bother.'

Her voice was low, and a little husky, softening the consonants until an ordinary word could sound like a caress.

When she had gone, he drank his tea and ate the hot toasted cookies and the cut cake. The fire died down until only hot little blue-edged flames played on the incandescent surface of the coal. He remembered the papers on his desk, but he was comfortable where he was, watching the firelight flickering on the polished silver. And it was so easy to be indolent. So pleasant to sit alone in a warm friendly room. A cigarette, he thought. Just one, and then I'll go.

He took one from a box on the fireside table and stood up to get the table lighter from the mantelpiece. As he lifted it, the letter caught his eye. It was propped up, half-hidden behind the ormolu clock, but on the exposed half was an Italian stamp with a clear postmark dated just three days before.

He lit his cigarette, then picked up the envelope. It was addressed to Julia, as he had known it must be. And the letter had been reinserted carelessly, so that part of it protruded. As he turned it over in his hand, one word on the protruding portion caught his eye. Written in a flowing elegant style was the word '*love*'.

He felt his pulse quicken. For a further moment, his scruples held him back. Then he drew out the letter and unfolded it.

There were several pages, but any one of them would have been sufficient. They left no doubt about the sort of relationship which had existed between Julia and the writer whose name, Luciano, ran boldly across the bottom of the last page. There were references to nights at Positano, to afternoons spent in an apartment on the Via Turati in Rome. Luciano's body, it seemed, cried out for hers, throbbed with desire, burned as though in a thousand fires, could not endure the months of deprivation which must elapse before he could possess her once more, make of her one flesh with his, achieve again a union such as they had known on that last night at Fiesole. The Latin extravagances left little work for the imagination.

Archie sat down slowly and let his first anger settle. Then he read it for a second time and considered carefully the places and the dates referred to. They covered the greater part of her holiday. And the name, Luciano, was the name she had given to the engineer whose photograph he had seen. He felt a short-lived sickness, a spasm of jealousy that she should find this man attractive, this middle-aged man with the handsome heavy features and the tendency to run to fat, but before he had finished reading it for the second time he was cold and clear-headed.

There was no need now for pretence, no need to accept any longer the bond of marriage which was the only thing that held them together. He folded the sheets carefully, replaced them in the envelope and put it in his pocket. Then he went to his room and packed two large suitcases which he stowed in the back of the Lotus. When Julia returned, just before six, he was once more seated by the drawing-room fire. She half-opened the door and popped her head round it.

'You're early,' she said.

'Yes, I am. I brought some work home with me.'

'Well, would you like to pour me a sherry while I take off my coat? I'll only be a minute.'

'All right.'

He filled two copitas from the decanter in the dining-room and carried them through on a little tray. If there's going to be a row, he thought, we might at least start it in a civilised way. With Julia, God alone knows how it will end. When she returned, he offered her glass.

'Thank you,' she said. 'And thank heaven for a decent fire. Helen's drawing-room was as cold as charity.'

'You were at Helen's?'

'Yes, she asked me to tea. I thought I'd told you.' She raised her copita. 'Cheers.'

'No,' he said. 'You didn't tell me.'

'I thought I had.'

'Just as you didn't tell me about Luciano.'

Her head came round slowly.

'But I did,' she said. 'Luciano and Maria. They were the couple in Italy. I showed you the photographs.'

'Oh yes, you showed me the photographs,' he said evenly. 'You showed me photographs of him with his wife, a few of the three of you together. You didn't show me any of you both copulating in your room at Positano, or in your room at Fiesole, or in what sounds like a hired apartment on the Via Turati in Rome.'

He watched her closely. Her eyes grew cold, but her expression scarcely altered.

'But you're mad,' she said. 'They're a happily married couple.'

'Possibly they are. It didn't stop him making you his mistress within a week of your first meeting.'

'That sounds as though it were meant to be an accusation.'

'It is.'

'Then it's untrue.'

He drew the letter from his inner breast pocket.

'Not according to the evidence of this.'

Her eyes widened slightly and she grew pale, but the glass did not tremble in her hand.

'Where did you get that?'

Her voice was low.

'Never mind where I got it. You know what letter it is?' He glanced at the postmark. 'It's the one dated the 27th. Last Saturday. And I must say it gives a pretty complete picture.'

'Of what?'

'Of a rather sordid affair between a middle-aged married man and a younger married woman.'

She smiled, a thin, tense smile that puzzled him.

'My dear man! How wrong you are.' She moved towards the fire and put her glass on the mantelpiece, then turned to him resting her back on the edge of the white marble. 'It wasn't quite like that,' she said. 'It was a month of tenderness and love, more than I've known in ten years from you.'

He looked at her with contempt.

'Tenderness and love? From an over-ripe Italian with a bulging stomach who's grown tired of his wife? Is it likely?'

'No,' she said. 'It's not likely at all. But then, it wasn't this over-ripe Italian that you talk about. It was his son.'

He stared at her.

'His son!'

'His son, also Luciano. Also an engineer. But younger than you. Younger than me, unfortunately. Does that make you feel better? Or worse?'

He put the envelope back in his pocket.

'Neither,' he said shortly. 'I no longer have any feelings.'

'You never had,' she said. 'You've no more feelings than one of your own computers.'

'Then we were well met,' he said. 'In ten years the only times you've shown warmth, or affection, or any of the things I was entitled to expect, were when you wanted something. You admitted it yourself last spring. You may remember. You described these things as women's weapons. And I thought they were supposed to be women's virtues.'

She turned impatiently away and picked up her sherry.

'Don't go on,' she said. 'I've heard it all before. Just tell me. What are you going to do?'

'Divorce you.'

'You've made up your mind?'

'Of course I have. Did you imagine I'd go on living in the same house with you after this?'

'You've gone on living with me for four months,' she said. 'It didn't seem to bother you.'

'But I didn't know. Your month of love and tenderness didn't leave some sort of mark on your brow. It didn't make any noticeable difference to your character.'

'Oh yes, it did,' she said bitterly. 'It made me hate you more than ever, only I tried not to show it. It made me hate you for being a priggish, pompous eunuch of a man. You're like a clumsy, bungling schoolboy, except that you don't even have his honest-to-God lust. You don't know the first thing about a woman. You don't know how to make sex matter to her. My God, if you find a frigid wife, examine the husband. I never knew how true that was until I met Luciano. But I learned. I learned a lot. And I should have learned it all from you. Ten years ago. That's the tragedy of it. But you don't need a woman. You don't know what to do with one when you've got her. All you need is a rubber doll!'

'Shut up!'

'Not yet. You might as well know how much you're to blame. I was a virgin when I married you. I knew nothing about love or sex or anything else. Ten years later I was no virgin. I even had a child. But I still knew nothing about love or sex. Ten years of marriage and you hadn't taught me a thing. I learned more from Luciano in one night. And does

228

that letter sound as if it came from a man who got nothing in return? Does it?'

'It sounds as if he got plenty,' said Archie grimly.

'Oh yes, he did. He got plenty. It was you who got nothing. You got nothing because you deserved nothing. You made me despise you, but I didn't quite know why until I met Luciano. Then I knew. I despised you because you were a castrated imitation of a man. You did nothing to deserve love. You were just a bank balance with a good tailor and a fast car. You didn't expect a woman to fall passionately in love with that, did you?'

He looked at her steadily, hiding the hurt he felt.

'From you, I haven't expected much for a long time,' he said quietly. 'But I didn't think you'd try to blame me for your love affair. Your boy friend at least is honest. He doesn't bring psychology into it. He just enjoys going to bed with you and that's that.' He threw his cigarette end into the fire. 'Well, he'll have plenty of opportunities. I'll get this divorce through as soon as I can. And now I'm going. My bags are already in the car. Anything else you have to say can be said to your lawyer.'

He turned to the door.

'Not quite.' She moved swiftly in front of him. 'I've one thing more to say. Where did you get that letter?'

He looked at her in surprise.

'On the mantelpiece,' he said. 'Presumably where you left it. You ought to be more careful.'

'But that can't be true!'

'But of course it's true. Why should I lie about that? It was behind the clock.'

He saw her lips narrow, her nostrils grow thin and white with anger.

'You're lying!'

'I'm not lying. I assure you——'

'That letter was in the writing-desk in my room. That's why I know you're lying.'

He paused, then took a couple of paces towards her.

'Listen,' he said quietly. 'It would be pointless to lie about this. I tell you it was behind the clock. Here.' He took the

229

letter from his pocket, crossed the room quickly and placed it in the position he had found it. 'Like this. With the Italian stamp showing.'

She stared at him.

'You swear it?'

'Yes, I swear it.'

Her eyes searched his face. Then, suddenly they steadied, and slowly widened. Her lips parted.

'Of course,' she breathed. 'That Irish slut. I should have known.'

He stood still. It was possible. A part of him realised at once that it was possible.

'What are you talking about?'

She moved away from him.

'You were right. I should have been more careful. I should have kept it locked.'

'But I tell you I found it here, on the mantelpiece. I haven't been near your writing-desk. God knows I haven't even been near your room.'

It was necessary to protest, to defend, though he did not know why.

She swung round.

'No,' she said viciously. 'I believe you. But Oonagh has.'

'Oonagh!'

'Yes, Oonagh. She's been making sheep's eyes at you ever since she came. And I thought it didn't matter. You were too cold and disinterested even to notice. But my mistake was to think that she wouldn't try and do anything more. I never thought that——'

'Just a minute.' The possibility had to be defined, brought out from the troubled subconscious and framed in words, no matter what the implications might be. 'Are you trying to tell me that Oonagh took this letter from your desk and put it here for me to find?'

'Yes,' she said. 'That's exactly what I'm trying to tell you. Are you flattered? Or does it shock you? I may say it doesn't shock me at all. I'd have done the same thing myself. That's why I should have thought of it.'

'No!' He went right up to her. 'No, you wouldn't. You'd

230

have kept it and used it as blackmail. You wouldn't have done anything so open, anything so likely to be discovered. That's why I'm neither flattered nor shocked. Just grateful. And now, unless you've something very important to say, I'm going.'

She looked at him calmly.

'No,' she said. 'I've nothing more to say. Except that you can take Oonagh with you, if you like. Obviously, she'll be leaving.'

The fire in the study was burning brightly as he hurriedly collected his papers together, but he did not see it. He wished only to be out of the house, cut off for ever from Julia and all that ten years with her had meant. And he did not dare to think of Oonagh. He forced the flap of his brief-case over until it shut, then picked it up and hurried out of the room. But he stopped short in the hall.

Oonagh was there. Her face was pale. There was a stillness about her, a poised expectancy. He looked at her for only a moment, but he felt his pulse flutter in his throat and when he spoke the voice did not seem to be his own.

'Get your things,' he said. 'I'll wait in the car.'

She turned at once and was gone.

The engine of the Lotus burst into a bubbling roar that the garage walls threw back at him, until it steadied and quietened as he eased the car in reverse out into the darkness. Its headlights swept the curtained windows of the drawing-room where Julia was, then swung across the lawn on to the banks of rhododendrons flanking the raked gravel of the drive. He cut the lights and let the engine idle and sat alone in the small enclosed world of the car, no longer thinking, his mind strangely numb since that moment when he had seen her standing there, waiting for him as he now was waiting for her. And she came quickly. When he heard the small noise of the gravel moving beneath her feet, he leaned across and opened the passenger door. She carried only a little over-night bag and a coat folded on her arm. He took the bag from her and put it with his own. Then they were moving, turning out of the drive on to the main road, with the lights glinting on the sea beyond the esplanade and the headlamps of the oncoming, homeward-bound traffic flaring and flashing by as they left the town behind and headed upriver towards the city.

Neither of them had spoken. He was aware of her still features, lit dimly by the glow from the instrument panel, on the very edge of his field of vision, of her hands, folded and resting on her lap, of himself, his gloved hands on the wheel, holding the Lotus on the narrow, curving road at eighty miles an hour, yet these things had no connection with reality as he had known it. It was as though he dreamed, and in his dream heard himself say—

'Did you put it there?'

'Yes.'

Her voice was a whisper behind the engine noise and the wind. The village of Cardross came, and fled behind them, and on the open curves of the road beyond the Lotus growled and hugged the asphalt and out of the night ahead the lights of Dumbarton came rushing towards them. He eased his foot on the throttle and watched the speedometer needle fall back. Then buildings loomed, and street-lamps, and bright shop windows, and in the distance a traffic signal flicked to red. He changed down and gently touched the brake.

'Why?'

'Because I love you.'

They were stopped, the Lotus murmuring quietly with its nose on the white line, and there was still no coherent thought. Only the remembering of a hundred things, things half-observed, suppressed by consciousness; remembered responses, felt, half-recognised, smothered before they had properly been born; remembered images, of slender hands and dark quiet eyes, of her slim strong body bending down to Jamie's laughing face, the body that was now so near, a handsbreadth away, waiting.

Out of Dumbarton, past the great buildings of the distillery, past the engineering works, idling at the junction with the dual carriageway while the rush-hour traffic swept by, then over and on to the east-bound lane, the quiet lane, but idling still, the need for speed gone and thought beginning to return, bringing recognition of what had for so long been known but subconsciously repressed.

At last he swung into a lay-by beside a steep tree-covered

bank and switched off the engine. Outside, was the night, and the orange glare of the city, and the unending roar of traffic. Within, was stillness, and her remembered fragrance, and the silence of unspoken words.

'Oonagh,' he said softly, and suddenly her body was in his arms, reaching to him across the space between the seats, her hands moving on his neck, his heart beating against her breasts, his lips moving, murmuring, seeking over her perfumed skin for the warm moist welcome of her mouth. And when at last he drew back, breathless, he was trembling. In the light that flared and died as each car swept by them on the highway, he looked at her, wondering. She was not smiling now. Her features were still, her eyes dark and serious, and when he laid his hand gently on her cheek her dimple came, then vanished in the shadows.

'I love you,' he whispered. She turned her lips into his palm and they rested there, soft as a moth's wings. 'I think I've loved you ever since you came, but I didn't dare think about it.'

'I knew.'

'How could you know?'

'I don't know. But I did. That's why I put the letter there. Because we loved each other. Because you were unhappy. Because I knew about . . . this man. And I loved you enough to be ruthless. That's the only thing I regret. That I had to be ruthless. And I'm ashamed of that.'

'You mustn't be.'

'I can't help it. But I knew. And I knew you didn't.'

'How did you know?'

'Because he phoned her one day. In August. I was in my room, with the door open. She didn't know. And I couldn't help hearing.'

He drew her to him.

'Don't talk about it.'

Her skin was smoother than satin against the fine evening stubble on his cheek. Under the soft fabric of her dress, her body was warm and moving beneath his fingers. Her voice was a gossamer-light breath in his ear.

'Are you angry with me?'

233

'No.'

'Truly?'

He smiled into her hair.

'Truly.'

There was no place for anger, no place for anything that linked with the past and all the past had meant. There was instead a future full of the unknown infinite possibilities of love. And there was the present, with its own problems. He thrust her gently away.

'We'd better go,' he said softly.

'Where?'

'To Anne's.' He switched on the ignition. 'You can stay there tonight.'

'And you?'

Her voice was low. He paused.

'I don't know,' he said. 'We'll worry about that later.'

*　　*　　*

Anne showed Oonagh into her little spare bedroom. There was space only for a divan bed with a frilled cover, a narrow wardrobe with a full-length mirror on the door and a tiny dressing-table built into the window recess, but it was bright with chintzes and the white paint was lit warmly by the rose-pink-shaded lamp on the bedhead wall.

'I'm sorry it's so small,' she said, 'but you're welcome to it for as long as you like.'

'But I couldn't.' Oonagh looked around her wistfully. 'If I could stay tonight, I'll try to find somewhere tomorrow.'

'You don't have to.'

'But I can't just land on you like this.'

Anne's eyes took in the quality and elegance of her clothes, but saw also the things that Archie did not see, the little signs that betrayed their age and the care they had been given. She pushed the door shut with her foot.

'Oonagh,' she said gently, 'I don't know the story. All I know is what you heard Archie tell me about Julia. I don't really know where you fit in, but I can guess. And I'd like you to stay.'

Their eyes met, and in that moment understanding was born.

'I love him,' said Oonagh quietly.

Anne smiled at her.

'I know you do. And I want to see Archie happy. So please stay.'

Oonagh could not speak. Too much had happened too quickly. In her life she had known poverty and adversity and the unkindness of tongues. Against them, she had built defences. But against generosity and goodwill and the kind of affection she had seen in Anne's eyes, she was without protection. She looked at her through a film of tears and stretched out her hand. Anne took it and pressed the slim ringless fingers.

'Come through when you're ready,' she said softly. 'He'll still be there.'

She found her brother standing before the electric fire in the sitting-room. He looked round expectantly.

'Don't worry,' she said. 'She won't be long.'

He tried to be off-handed.

'That's all right.'

'And you don't have to pretend, Archie. I know what it's like.'

'She told you?'

He could not hide the eagerness in his voice.

'Yes, she told me. But she didn't have to. It wasn't too hard to guess.' She opened a door in the sleek Swedish sideboard. 'And you look as if you could do with a drink. What'll you have?'

'Well . . . I must admit I wouldn't mind a whisky.' He gave a little forced laugh. 'I didn't think it would shake me as much as this.'

'It does,' said his sister. 'I could have told you.' She poured him a good three fingers. 'Water?'

'Yes, please.'

'And what about Oonagh?'

'I don't know. That's the crazy part of it. I don't know anything about her.'

'Does it matter?'

'No.'

'And you love her?'

'Yes.'

She carried his drink across the room to him.

'Then that's all that matters,' she said. 'The rest will come.'
She raised her glass. 'May you both be as happy as Peter and
me.'

'I couldn't ask for more.'

She smiled.

'No,' she said. 'I don't think you could.'

In the small silence, a bell rang in the distance. Anne put
her glass down quickly.

'It's the door,' she said. 'I'll get it.' She passed Oonagh in
the hall and pointed behind her. 'Go on in. Archie's there.'

But a moment later, she returned, pale and tense.

'It's Peter,' she said tightly. 'There's a riot going on in
George Square and Daddy's in it.'

His arms slid from Oonagh's waist.

'Daddy!' He remembered suddenly. St. Andrew's Day.
The night of the pre-election rally. 'Where's Peter?'

'Here.' He appeared behind Anne, still flushed from running, his hair dishevelled. 'And God knows what's going on. I
was on a bus that got caught in it. The whole area's jammed
with police, ambulances, the lot. I don't know if you'll get
through it in the car.'

Archie moved fast.

'I'll have a crack at it.' He called over his shoulder. 'Anne!
Look after Oonagh. I'll phone when there's any news.'

The girls looked at each other quickly and his sister's voice
halted him at the outer door.

'But we're coming!'

'There's no room in the Lotus.'

'There's room in the brake,' said Anne determinedly. 'And
there are the keys.' She threw them to him from the middle of
the hall. 'We'll get our coats.'

'Don't argue,' muttered Peter. 'You're wasting your time.'

Together, the men ran downstairs to the street where Anne's
shooting-brake was parked in front of the Lotus. Archie
switched on the sidelights and pressed the starter. The girls

appeared at the street door as the engine fired. He glanced quickly at Peter.

'What's it like?'

'Bloody,' said Peter tersely. 'Literally.'

CHAPTER ELEVEN

SAM GOLD moved up on to the step of the doorway in which he stood and lit a cheroot. From there, he could look over Jock Anderson's head to the open space before the City Chambers where the pipe band had been marching and counter-marching for almost half an hour. Anderson turned his head and tried to speak to him above the beating, racketing drums and the familiar, memory-stirring strains of 'The Barren Rocks of Aden', but Gold only grinned and spread his hands hopelessly. A few paces away, the tall swaggering figure of the drum-major rounded and retired between the oncoming files of his own men, through the ranks of swinging tight-lipped pipers, past the elaborately twirling sticks of the white-gloved tenor drummers, on through the rows of rolling side-drums, out into the lonely flood-lit space beyond, each rank following him in its turn, retreating back across the width of the square, the full violence of the music fading, drum beats echoing now from the distant grey walls of the buildings, more muted, more bearable, but still with that strange power to arouse in Scottish hearts the curious blend of excitement and sadness that makes men laugh and in the same moment fills their eyes with tears. As the last drummers turned and retired, Anderson tried again.

'Any sign of activity?'

Around the margins of the pipers' arena, a thin cordon of police stood along the edge of the crowd that stretched back past the Cenotaph, between the plinths of the statues and the empty flower-beds, right back to the farthest corners of the Square. There, on the approach roads, police were diverting traffic, and on the hill of North Hanover Street a police radio van, its lights extinguished, was so placed as to command a view of the entire scene. But the crowd was quiet, too densely

237

packed for movement except on the fringes where the urchins played, and the music drowned the murmur of its corporate voice.

'A hell of a lot of people,' said Sam Gold.

'Too damned many,' growled Anderson. 'And I never did like crowds. I get claustrophobia.'

'Good for business,' said Gold. 'If they mean votes, we're home and dry.'

'But they don't.' Anderson drew on his cigarette and cupped it protectively in his hand. 'It's nothing but a free show for this lot. And you'll be lucky if ten per cent of them come from West Central.'

Sam grinned.

'Cynic.'

'That's right,' said Anderson. 'That way you don't get many disappointments. But what I want to know is where the hell Douglas is. It's damned near eight o'clock.'

'He's there.' Gold could see him moving up on the platform, seating the other members of his party, with the lean dark figure of Ewan Cameron close to his side. 'He's got Will Strachan sitting next to Sir Robert McColl.'

'A marriage of convenience that, if there ever was one,' muttered Anderson.

'And Macfarlane looks as if he'd like to turn and run for it.'

'He's not the only one.'

'But just a minute. Something's happening.'

He watched the band break formation and re-form in a semicircle facing the platform. Out in the centre, the drum-major raised his arm. The music checked, the rhythm changed, and as 'The Barren Rocks of Aden' gave way to 'Scotland The Brave' the crowd began to sing. It started at the front, scarcely audible above the band, then spread rapidly back until the whole square rang to the voice of the people.

Sam Gold laughed aloud.

'Man, man!' he shouted. 'If I hadn't seen it, I wouldn't have believed it. Who said the Scots were inhibited!'

Jock Anderson grunted non-committally. An elbow nudged his ribs on one side. A fleshy shoulder pressed against him on

238

the other. The tune was third-rate. The words were banal, sentimental and untrue. And he hated crowds. Yet the mass effect moved him. When the music ended, he looked up at Gold's grinning face and blinked the tears away from his eyes.

'We're daft,' he said. 'The whole lot of us.'

'We're in business,' said Gold jubilantly. 'They're going to lap it up.'

The microphone grated loudly.

'Fellow citizens——' Douglas was at the edge of the platform, facing the pipers and the police and the people of the city. 'Fellow citizens——' He waited for the great murmur to subside. When the square was hushed, his voice rang clearly from a dozen loud-speakers. 'Fellow citizens of Glasgow. And for the benefit of you Irish and Poles and Italians and West Indians and Pakistanis, that includes you. It even includes any English who happen to live here.' Appreciative laughter swelled and died. 'For no matter where your parents came from, no matter what your colour or your race or your religion is, if you live here you are fellow citizens.

'And not just fellow citizens of this city. You're fellow citizens of this country of Scotland. And you must realise, or you wouldn't be here tonight, that this country stands on the threshold of greater events than it has ever known since that sad day when a bunch of traitors, against the will of the people, did away with our own Parliament and joined up with England.

'And you don't need me to tell you what the effects of that union have been. There is not one man or woman here tonight who has not suffered neglect of some kind at the hands of that united Parliament sitting in London. And it's not surprising. How can London hope to know what your needs are? How can London expect to understand the problems that face you here in Glasgow? Or even worse, how can they even begin to understand the problems of the Highlander, trying to scratch a living from an empty glen?

'But the answer's easy. They can't. They've had two hundred and sixty-odd years to make a go of it and they've failed. I think you'll agree, ladies and gentlemen, they've had long enough.'

'He's going to be in form,' whispered Sam Gold as the first roar of approval arose.

Jock Anderson nodded briefly. He was too preoccupied by his own discomfort to be enthusiastic. But Gold chewed on the butt end of his cheroot and watched Douglas closely, as he had watched Presidents and Prime Ministers and dictators on five continents. The best of them had all had the same ability as Douglas now began to show, the ability to build an audience up and knock it down, to rouse it to laughter and hush it almost to tears, to stir anger and inflame patriotism, playing with it, taking copy that would seem dull in the morning on the news desk and turning it into a bright sword that could carve the mass mind into the form he wished, shaping its thinking, fashioning its ideas, until the responses of a hundred thousand people were predictable, with an individual reaction no more likely than it would have been from Pavlov's dog.

As Douglas did these things, Gold's eyes narrowed. This, he had not expected. It aroused uneasy memories of other orators and eloquence in other causes. He ground the end of his cheroot beneath his heel and there was relief in that independent movement, yet he felt almost guilty, as though he had done the same thing in church. For the atmosphere had now that same religious quality. The vast audience was hushed and immobile under the orange lights. The police were expressionless, standing at ease, their eyes focussed on nothing. The pipers stood with their pipes under their arms, the drummers with their drums at their feet. As he crushed out the cheroot, it seemed that no other man in all these thousands moved. Then he saw one little ripple, beside the farther wall of the City Chambers, where the light glinted on the silver-braided caps of a group of police officers who were infiltrating along the edge of the crowd.

Then, suddenly, it was over.

'But I've said enough.'

Douglas's voice released them from bondage.

'I want you to meet your candidate, Mr. Bill Macfarlane, but before that I've an old friend here. An old friend to many of you, a good friend to all of you. Mr. Will Strachan, the

Chairman of the Amalgamated Scottish Trades Unions. Will Strachan.'

The crowd relaxed. Shouts of 'Good old Wull!' rose above the murmur of its reawakening. Here and there were bursts of laughter, and the crowd stirred and swirled, and from somewhere near the back a dozen voices rose in a barely recognisable rendering of 'The Red Flag'.

'You've got the wrong song.' Will Strachan had seized the microphone and his broad homely voice burst from the speakers. 'It's not the Labour Party Conference, you know. No, please! Please!' He let the noise subside. 'Though if the Labour Party was as good at governing as it is at singing, we wouldn't need to be here tonight.'

The crowd roared its appreciation.

'Good old Will,' muttered Jock Anderson. 'Always the wee joker.' He turned his head to Sam Gold. 'Have you a match, Sam? I've used my last one.'

But Sam did not hear. He was interested in the movement of the police officers he had seen a little earlier. They had made their way right along the wall to the inner edge of the crowd and were now walking along the cordon of police towards the platform.

Ewan Cameron nudged Douglas and pointed.

'Visitors,' he murmured.

Douglas nodded.

'I know.'

The tall leading figure with the clipped moustache and the military bearing was now recognisable as McDiarmid, the Inspector with whom the first arrangements for the meeting had been made. At his shoulder was a stranger in a tweed raglan overcoat and a tweed hat, and behind him were two more uniformed senior officers. Their approach was unhurried, purposeful.

Sir Robert McColl leaned across behind the speaker's back.

'What the devil can McDiarmid want? He gave permission, didn't he?'

'He did,' agreed Douglas. 'In writing.'

Will Strachan's voice rose.

'But as a life-long Socialist and a Trade Unionist for thirty-five years, I would say this to you. The objectives of Socialism are more likely to be attained by a National Coalition Government sitting in Edinburgh than by a Socialist Government sitting in London. And that doesn't mean that I've changed my political colours. I hope you know me well enough to realise that the sky's more likely to fall. But I believe that the best hope for you, the people of Scotland, lies with the Party on whose behalf I have the honour to speak here tonight.'

'Right,' said Douglas quietly to Ewan Cameron. 'Meet them at the top of the steps. Try and stall them off.'

He watched the scene out of the corner of his eye. He saw Cameron stoop to them as they mounted the steps, saw him straighten to face McDiarmid, saw him forced back by the faintest movement of the policeman's elbow. His lips tightened. Obviously they had refused to deal with Cameron. He sat on and let them stumble over the legs of the platform party until McDiarmid stood before him.

'Mr. Douglas?'

In the harsh orange light, McDiarmid's face was drained of colour. His lips were thin. He looked strained, as did the other uniformed officers. Only the man in the tweed coat seemed easy and relaxed.

'Yes?'

Douglas got to his feet slowly.

'I'm afraid it's necessary for you to end your meeting. If you and your party will make your way to the City Chambers and stay there, inside, until we clear the square, you'll make things easier for the police.'

Douglas looked at each of the officers in turn. All except the stranger avoided his eyes.

'In view of the fact that permission was granted for this meeting,' he said, 'perhaps you'll tell me why?'

'Instructions,' said McDiarmid briefly.

'From whom?'

'From——'

The man in the tweed coat interrupted.

'From me.' He smiled. 'Or perhaps I should say, from Security through me. London feels this meeting is unwise. If I hadn't been delayed by fog, we would have avoided the problem that this crowd now presents. However, Mr. Douglas, now that I am here, I hope you'll co-operate.'

His voice was cultured, relaxed, maddeningly English. Douglas regarded him coldly.

'You still haven't answered my question,' he said. 'Why?'

'We don't have to answer any questions,' said the stranger gently. 'We simply insist that you do what we ask you to do.'

'And if I refuse?'

'Then I should have to arrest you, I'm afraid. And this I've no wish to do. We try not to make political martyrs.'

Douglas thought quickly. Arrest and political martyrdom could be useful. But at this point in time loss of freedom and the resultant loss of executive control of the Party could be disastrous. Liberty was preferable.

Sam Gold nudged Jock Anderson in the back.

'They're going to break it up,' he whispered. 'There's a plain-clothes character up on the platform with the brass and if he's not Security, I'll eat the early edition.'

'They can't break it up,' said Anderson. 'They haven't enough police.'

Gold looked around quickly. Dark vans were moving on the slopes of North Hanover Street and North Frederick Street, swinging round to park, noses to the kerb, doors free to empty on to the roadway. The blue light was flashing again on the roof of the radio van.

'In five minutes,' he said softly, 'they're going to have all the police they need.'

'Then they'll have a bloody riot on their hands,' said Anderson grimly. 'This isn't a Girl Guide rally.' He turned half round. 'Move over and let me up.' With difficulty, he squeezed up two steps. Now he could see what Gold had seen. 'Christ,' he muttered.

'Exactly.'

'Have we got photographers out?'

'Three,' said Gold. 'Smith, Wilkinson and young Tim Jackson. If there's a picture to be got, they'll get it.'

'There'll be pictures,' said Anderson uneasily. 'And it won't be long.'

Will Strachan glanced at Douglas and Cameron and the

243

small group of police and carried on speaking. Police interference was no new thing to him. If necessary, he would carry on speaking until they tore the microphone from his hands or cut the cable.

'And I'm ashamed to have to admit it,' he said, 'but our fellow-Socialists south of the Border have shown themselves to be Englishmen first and Socialists second. Oh, they had great plans. They were going to redevelop the Highlands. They were going to do something about the disgraceful unemployment figures. And so on and so on until you'd have thought the golden age had come. But what, in fact, have they done?'

Sam Gold saw Douglas move to his side, saw him press Will Strachan's arm.

'We're finished,' said Douglas quietly. 'Give me the microphone.'

In the silence, the crowd murmured, then quietened as Douglas's voice rang from the speakers.

'Fellow citizens! The meeting's being stopped by the police.'

The roar that followed drowned his next words.

'Be careful,' warned the man in the tweed coat. 'If you say anything inflammatory, I'll have you arrested anyway.'

'Your action's inflammatory.' Douglas made no attempt to hide his dislike. 'You forget you're dealing with people who think they're free. They'll not take kindly to your kind of interference.'

'I know what I'm doing.'

'Do you? I doubt it. You're not dealing with a C.N.D. rally in Trafalgar Square. If these people resist, there won't be anything passive about it. Whether you're Security or not, if you put one foot wrong you're in trouble. So shut up and let me talk to them.' He turned back to the crowd and raised his hand. 'Please!' he shouted. 'Quiet, please!' As he waited, he saw that the police cordon round the semicircle had closed in and linked hands, a thin line of blue that already bulged and swayed under the pressure from behind. 'Please!' The roar subsided suddenly to a low angry hum. 'I want to make one thing clear. This has nothing to do with the police here in Glasgow. The orders come from London.'

'Christ,' breathed Sam Gold.

For perhaps a second, the square seemed utterly silent. Then, from the front, a voice rang out.

'There he is! That one in the tweed coat! Get the bastard!'

And the shout was taken up from right and left and from the heart of the crowd, building up into a mighty roar of hate and anger that made the loud-speakers useless as Douglas bellowed into the microphone, appealing for restraint and quiet, until he hurled it aside. He had seen the blue line bulging dangerously, recovering, bulging again, forced forward now to the line of pipers and drummers who were hastily picking up their equipment and retreating towards the steps of the City Chambers. He swung round on the stranger as McDiarmid vaulted off the platform to join his men.

'Get out of here,' he roared. 'Run for the building!'

The man glanced quickly round. He was paler, more tense, but he was still smiling.

'I think not,' he said. 'After that, I'll be taking you into custody.'

Douglas glanced to the front as the blue line broke.

'You'll take nobody into custody,' he shouted. 'Look!'

A score of men were running across the open space. Behind them, a dozen fights already raged. Police batons rose and fell. Light glinted briefly on a raised knife blade. In the centre of a small clear circle stood a youth whirling a bicycle chain. At his feet a constable with one cheek slashed open from mouth to ear lay rolling in agony.

'Up!' shouted Sam Gold. 'On to the window ledge.'

He clutched the sash bar with one hand and heaved Jock Anderson up with the other. Police whistles blasted far away on the other side of the now turbulent mob and he pointed.

'Look!'

The police from the vans were pouring down, their truncheons already in their hands.

'The stupid bastards!' He almost sobbed. 'Oh, the stupid bastards! They could have localised this to the front. Now, look at it!'

Anderson looked. On the hills, the street urchins who had played on the fringe were running away. Where they had been, a score of fights had already begun and a solid wedge of police, those who had managed to stay together, were forcing through the crowd to the help of their hard-pressed colleagues at the front. But they had a long way to go. And already those at the front were broken up into ones and twos, too busy defending themselves to be able to do anything about the men who were swarming on to the platform. As they came, Douglas thrust his arm through that of the stranger and held him tight. He tried to tear himself away.

'Don't be bloody silly,' cried Douglas. 'Your only hope is in me.'

A massive man in his working clothes leapt on to the platform a couple of yards away and stood there panting. He glanced briefly at Douglas, then narrowed his eyes on the Englishman.

'Aye,' he growled. 'There's the wee runt.'

Two others appeared beside him, then a third, then two more.

'Leave him,' said Douglas. 'You'll do yourselves no good.'

The man glanced at his supporters.

'Aye,' he said, 'we'll leave him when we're done wi' him. Come on.'

He moved, and as he moved the stranger tore his arm from Douglas's grasp and ran back.

'One move and I'll shoot!'

Douglas whirled on him. He was standing at the back of the platform, as white as a sheet now, and in his hand he held a Browning automatic trained on the broad chest of the man who had spoken.

'You bloody fool!' he bellowed. 'Put that thing away.'

Ewan Cameron, Macfarlane, Sir Robert McColl and Will Strachan had retreated back to the other corner. Now Cameron came forward, looking leaner and more dark than ever, with one hand outstretched.

'Give me it,' he said. 'Don't be crazy.'

He spoke quietly, yet his voice was clear and strong. The Englishman glanced at him, but did not move his gun.

'Get back,' he said crisply. 'I'll handle this.'

246

Ewan came on slowly.

'Give me it,' he said. 'It's bad enough already. If you shoot, you'll only make it a hundred times worse.'

'Get back!'

Still Cameron came on.

'Leave him, Ewan,' shouted Douglas. 'Leave him alone.'

'Give me it,' said Ewan softly. 'Give me it.'

Now, Douglas could see the fine tremor of the security man's hand. He was no longer smiling. In his eyes was the hunted look that Douglas had already seen once that year, in other eyes and in another land. The gun slowly traversed the threatening group of men on the platform's edge, to the left, to the right. Then, suddenly, it swung on Cameron.

'Back!' he snarled. 'I warned you.'

'Don't be a fool,' said Cameron. His outstretched hand was now no more than ten feet from the Browning. 'Give it to me.'

'Not another step!'

'Give it to me.'

'Ewan!' roared Douglas. 'Don't!'

But as he spoke, the Englishman fired once. Cameron fell slowly, crumpling towards Douglas, his hand still outstretched on the rough boards of the platform. A trickle of blood ran to the nearest crack and widened, coming in little surges with his dying pulse, then ceased to pulse and welled slowly outward from his body. At the end of a moment that time could not measure, Douglas moved. But the men who had climbed on to the platform got there first. One shot pierced the floor as the stranger's hand was struck down. Then he vanished under the angry weight of his attackers' bodies. When he was seen again, he was dead. His skull was crushed in half a dozen places by swinging boots. His ribs were smashed. His face was mutilated beyond recognition. And his gun glinted dully on the floor, close to the dead, tranquil features of Ewan Cameron.

Douglas picked it up almost without thinking and was about to put it in his pocket when a hand seized his arm. He swung round to look into the white, shaken face of one of the senior officers who had come with McDiarmid.

'Give me that!'

'I don't think so,' said Douglas quietly and slipped it out of sight.

'But it's evidence.'

'I know it's evidence. That's why I'm going to keep it.'

'Then you're under arrest.'

Douglas looked at him and felt nothing but sickness at the thought that Ewan Cameron lay dead.

'You've done enough this night,' he said. 'I wouldn't make any more mistakes, if I were you.'

He pulled his arm from the officer's grasp and walked away.

The platform was empty, but for the two bodies and the man who had made no attempt to restrain him. McDiarmid and the other officer had vanished. Their men were engaged in a hundred fights across a square now clearing of people, but littered instead with the bodies of the injured, the broken bottles that the crowd had found to be the handiest of weapons, sticks and lost truncheons and helmets and hats. And on the north side, new police reinforcements were pouring from newly arrived vans, whistles were blowing, and the first ambulances were beginning to move away. His own party had disappeared, possibly to sanctuary in the City Chambers, possibly not. He did not know and at that moment he did not care. There was now no reason to remain, therefore he left the platform and started to pick his way across what had been the pipers' arena.

It was there Sam Gold spotted him.

'Come on,' he yelled to Anderson. 'Let's get him out of this.'

He dropped to the ground and started running, dodging and weaving through the fragmented crowd, aware of Anderson puffing somewhere behind but keeping his eye fixed on the burly, oddly leisurely, figure of Douglas. A policeman tried to stop him and he knocked down his arm. A handful of men retreating from a police baton charge on the north side almost swept him away, but as Douglas reached the pavement, Gold reached his side and grabbed his elbow.

'Come on,' he shouted. 'You've got to get out of here.'

Douglas looked at him calmly.

'Ah, Sam,' he said. 'Have you got Jock with you?'

'Behind me,' said Gold. 'And you've got to get out of this fast. My car's round the back of the City Chambers, so come on.'

'We'll wait for Jock,' said Douglas.

Gold pulled at him.

'Jock'll find us. Come on!'

'I'm here.' Anderson was breathless and grey with exhaustion. 'How are you, James?'

'Fine,' said Douglas.

'What the hell happened up there?'

Gold glanced around desperately. The nearest police were too busy to be interested, but that could not last.

'For God's sake!' he cried. 'Let's get out of here. We'll do no good tonight if we finish up in jug.'

They moved then, but slowly. Anderson looked close to physical collapse. Douglas maintained his unnatural calm and refused to hurry. Gold impatiently went three paces ahead, alert for trouble, anxious now to be back in the office, to get the story down, the story that would hit the front page as few things had hit it since the end of the war. And they were walking like that, with the square a couple of hundred yards behind them, when Anne's shooting-brake swung into the kerb and squealed to rest. Archie was out before the wheels had properly stopped moving.

'Are you all right?'

Douglas showed no reaction to his sudden appearance. His face remained expressionless, his eyes as blank as those of a dead dog.

'Yes,' he said. 'I'm all right.'

Anne threw her arms around him.

'Oh, Daddy!'

He patted her shoulder absent-mindedly.

'It's all right,' he said. 'It's all right.'

His voice was flat and toneless.

'But I heard there was shooting.' Archie turned to Gold. 'There's a story going it was the police.'

'You bet there was shooting,' said Gold grimly. 'I heard it. But it wouldn't be the police. It was some kind of light automatic. What I don't know is who the stupid bastard was.'

249

Douglas showed his first responsiveness.

'I can tell you that,' he said. 'I forgot you didn't know. It was the man from London.'

Gold looked at him quickly.

'The fellow in the tweed coat?'

'That's right,' Douglas drew the Browning from his pocket. 'He was carrying this.'

Archie stared at the black stubby gun.

'But how did you get hold of it?'

'I picked it up.'

'But what happened to the man?'

'They killed him,' said Douglas. 'A dozen of them kicked him to death.'

'But just a minute.' Sam Gold broke the short, horrified silence. 'Who had he been shooting at?'

'Ewan Cameron,' said Douglas. 'He killed him with his first shot.'

Sam Gold took a long, deep breath.

'Come on,' he said bitterly. 'Let's get back to the office.'

* * *

Gold put the tin tray with the bottle of whisky, the jug of water and the assorted glasses down on the old scarred Editor's desk.

'You can help yourselves,' he said. 'I've got work to do.' He turned to the young man who stood in the corner with his camera still slung on his shoulder. 'Come on, Tim. Knock that back. I want to see these pictures.'

Jock Anderson was crouching before the open doors of an ancient black stove. Many changes had been made to the buildings and equipment of the Rowan Press, but the Editor's office had had a low priority. Its homely, worn furnishings had not yet been touched. As Jock shivered before the friendly fire, he was glad. There was life and consolation in the glowing coals that no central heating could have given. He looked away reluctantly.

'I'll be up in a minute,' he said.

'You'll come up when you're ready,' said Gold. 'Have a dram and get yourself thawed out. I'll be in the News Room.'

250

The frosted glass door rattled shut at his back. Archie rose and poured drinks for them all, for Anderson, who had not moved from the fire, for Douglas, who sat motionless in the Editor's chair, for Anne and Oonagh and Peter who sat side by side on a bench against the wall. Machinery hummed in the distance, but in the room the silence and the tension were almost tangible, emanating, it seemed, from the immobile, brooding figure of Douglas. It was he who broke it. He raised his glass.

'To Ewan Cameron,' he said, and drank it off.

When he put it down empty, Archie replenished it and topped it with water. Douglas came slowly to life. He looked around him, as though only now becoming aware of his surroundings, and his moving eyes stopped on Oonagh. He looked from her to Archie and back again. Then he smiled.

'The only good news of the day,' he said. 'I've been wondering how long it would take you.'

'That news can keep,' said Archie heavily.

'Aye,' said Douglas. 'It can keep.' He reached for the internal telephone that was one of the few new things in the room. 'News Desk,' he said.

Jock Anderson straightened slowly. His colour was coming back. The shivering had stopped.

'I'm going up,' he said.

'Wait,' said Douglas. 'We'll see what they've got.'

Gold came on the line almost at once.

'Provisional figures,' he said. 'Reports are still coming in. But there's one policeman and three civilians dead for sure. Cause of death in these three, fractured skulls, presumably from police action. And that's additional to Ewan Cameron and the security man. Neither of these has been officially reported at all so far. Injured ... figures very incomplete. Royal Infirmary reckon two policemen dangerously ill, six seriously ill, another twenty or so in Casualty with cuts, lacerations and what have you. But they've got at least fifty civilians down there too and more arriving all the time. Western Infirmary refuse to talk, so we've sent a man over there. Arrests ... God knows. Wilkinson's back with a free-lance fellow called Clark.

They both think five hundred's a conservative estimate. And the police are saying nothing.'

'I don't blame them,' said Douglas. 'What about pictures?'

'Tim's busy on his now. Wilkinson's just starting. But there's one thing. Tim says he saw the shooting. At the stage when the security man had his gun up and Cameron was moving towards him. He took three quick shots with a telephoto lens. If they come out, we've got a scoop.'

'We've got more than a scoop,' said Douglas grimly. 'We've got evidence that could bring this Government down.' He leaned forward. 'Now listen, Sam. Is this photographer any good?'

'Yes,' said Gold. 'He's young, but he's good. And he says he reckons they'll be all right.'

'All right. Get him on to them and phone me back.'

He hung up and lifted the outside phone.

'I'm going,' said Anderson.

Douglas nodded to him briefly.

'Let me see your copy before you print it. Hello. Get me Heriot 25887.'

As Archie watched his father gradually return to normal, he felt himself beginning to relax. He drew out his cigarettes and offered them to the others.

'We might as well go too,' he said. 'There's nothing we can do.'

'Hang on,' said Douglas. 'There's no hurry.'

In the distance the number had begun to ring. He glanced at his watch, then looked again, doubting its accuracy. But it was going. And it was only ten o'clock. Only two hours since he had begun to speak. Only an hour since Ewan had died, Ewan, whose wife and sons were now his responsibility. He felt sick again at the thought and lifted his whisky, but the voice of the Secretary of State came on the line and he put it down.

'Alex?'

'Yes?'

'James Douglas here. Have you heard the news tonight?'

'No, I haven't heard any news, James,' said Buchanan irritably. 'And I wish you wouldn't phone me at home. I'm in the middle of a private dinner party.'

'Then you'd better make your apologies,' said Douglas. 'You'll not be back at it.'

'What do you mean?'

'I'll tell you,' said Douglas.

He outlined the events of the evening quickly and bluntly. When he came to the account of the shooting, Buchanan interrupted him.

'What do you mean, one of my security men? I've nothing to do with Security.'

'You've got certain responsibilities for the preservation of order in this country,' said Douglas grimly. 'An agent from London, sent with or without your knowledge, shot and killed Ewan Cameron, my deputy in the Party, just an hour ago. Don't tell me that doesn't concern you.'

'Killed him?'

Buchanan's voice was a whisper.

'That's what I said.'

'And where's the man now? I mean, is he under arrest? Have the police got him?'

'The police have got maybe five hundred other people,' said Douglas, 'but not him. He's dead. The crowd kicked him to death within a couple of minutes.'

'Kicked him to death?'

His voice reflected Buchanan's horrified disbelief.

'That's right. And there are, to my knowledge, at least four other dead, quite apart from upwards of a hundred police and civilians injured. So you can say goodnight to your dinner party and get over here.'

'But I'll need to contact the police. I'll need to find out what happened.'

'A public Court of Enquiry will find out what happened,' said Douglas. 'There won't be any dodging that. And you can tell your friends in the police——'

The internal phone rang sharply.

'Just a minute,' said Douglas. 'I'll be back.'

He spoke to Sam Gold.

'They're O.K.,' said Gold. 'All three of them. Everybody recognisable. And the third one must have been taken a split second after Cameron was hit. In that one, he's falling.'

253

'Fine,' said Douglas. 'Print it.' He hung up. 'Hello.'

'Yes.'

'You can tell your friends in the police that I hold two exhibits. One, the murder weapon, which I feel sure will prove to have been officially issued. And two, clear photographs taken with a telephoto lens that won't leave any doubt as to where the responsibility lies.'

'But you'll have to hand these over.'

'I'll hand them over to the Court when it's duly constituted and to no one else,' said Douglas. 'We'll have no suppression of evidence.'

'Are you suggesting the police would suppress it?'

'I am. Either the police or the security forces. The one caused the whole thing by a piece of unwarranted interference. The other aggravated it by ill-judged action and the use of unnecessary violence. Both of them will have trouble talking their way out of this. And don't forget, Alex, Ewan's dead. But I'm still alive. And I'm going to make damned sure the responsibility for this is placed firmly where it belongs.'

'Naturally,' said Buchanan heavily. 'That goes without saying.'

'Good,' said Douglas. 'I'm glad we agree on that. And now I suggest you get over here and start doing it.'

He hung up and sat back.

'We'll go,' said Archie awkwardly. 'We're just in the way.'

'If you like,' said Douglas. 'But there's one thing I want you to do.' He drew the Browning from his pocket and laid it on the desk. 'Wrap that up, label it, and lodge it in the Night Safe.'

'All right,' said Archie.

He picked it up gingerly and checked the safety catch. Douglas pushed back his chair and stood up.

'I'm going to the News Room,' he said. 'Before hell starts breaking loose tomorrow, I want all the facts I can get.'

The door shut behind him and Peter Colquhoun got slowly to his feet.

'Well,' he said, 'that's that.'

Anne took his arm and held it close. She was still white, still

254

sick with what she had seen. Archie looked at them and at Oonagh, then back at the gun in his hand.

'I'd like to think you were right,' he said soberly. 'But after tonight, I'm not so sure.'

*   *   *

At four o'clock in the morning, around the time that Douglas left the house of Ewan Cameron's widow, the Secretary of State for Scotland, seated in a small inner office at Police Headquarters, succeeded in making contact with the lean, blond, security chief in London to whom he had spoken just once before. The flat answering voice did not sound cordial.

'You surely must realise,' said Buchanan testily, 'that there is a good reason for disturbing you.'

'All right, then. What is it?'

He told him. The news was not well received.

'Are you trying to insinuate that my man was responsible for this riot?'

'I'm insinuating nothing,' said Buchanan. 'I'm telling you what happened. And I want to make a number of points. First of all, you did not inform me that you proposed taking this action.'

'We are under no obligation to inform anybody.'

'Very well. In that case you'll appreciate that, since I did not know, I can have no responsibility.'

'That is by no means necessarily true, as you should realise. Other matters are involved, notably the police. You stress the part played by my man and I fail to see why. I want to speak to him. Where is he now?'

'In the mortuary,' said Buchanan with relish.

'You mean he's dead?'

'Yes, he's dead. Killed by the crowd. And in view of the fact that he committed murder in front of their eyes, I'm not sure that I personally blame them. However, that by the way. It'll be interesting to hear what the Court of Enquiry says.'

'My dear man.' The flat voice had become very smooth. 'There will be no Court of Enquiry.'

'You'll have trouble avoiding one.'

'I think not. Since matters of security are involved, that should present no problem.'

'Security!' Buchanan grew suddenly angry. 'I'm tired of that word. You're not God. Your men aren't inviolate. They have to answer for their actions like anyone else. If they break laws, if they commit murder, they have to take the consequences like the rest of us. You don't seem to realise what's happened here tonight. Six men are dead already. Others are likely to die. Do you think you can avoid your responsibility in that just by saying the magic word . . . security?'

'Yes.'

Buchanan heard the soft laugh and the short reply almost with disbelief. His anger swelled.

'Then, by God,' he said, 'I'm going to make sure that you don't. If I've got to resign tomorrow to be free to do it, I'm going to make damned sure you don't. And there's something you don't know. James Douglas has your man's gun. Also photographs that show the whole thing. He'll submit them as evidence to a Court of Enquiry and to no one else and, I may say, now that I've spoken to you I don't blame him.'

'He won't submit them,' said the security man softly. 'I told you already. He presents a risk to the security of this country. He must be dealt with.'

'And how do you propose doing it?'

'That is our affair. And frankly, Mr. Buchanan, in view of certain things you have said tonight, I incline to regard you as a security risk yourself. I shall look into it.'

'Do,' said Buchanan quietly. 'And look into the feelings of the people of Scotland. Then consider how you're going to deal with them. You've dealt with Cameron. You say you're going to deal with Douglas. You may try to deal with me. But I doubt even your ability to deal with five million people that your own ill-conceived actions are going to turn into five million enemies.'

'My dear Buchanan! You exaggerate.'

'No. That would have been exaggeration last month or this afternoon. I'm afraid it's not exaggeration now. Douglas has done a lot to arouse nationalist feeling in this country, but you've done more in one night than he's done in six months.'

256

'Really! Do you think it matters? Don't you realise that when Douglas ceases to play an active part, this feeling will be dead in a month?'

'No.' Buchanan had believed that himself once. He believed it no longer. 'That was probably true yesterday. It's not true now.'

'I can't accept your appraisal of the situation.'

'Then you're a fool,' said Buchanan wearily. 'A poor, deluded, pig-headed fool.'

He hung up and sat on, slumped in his seat, weary of body and sick at heart. When McDiarmid came back into the room, he paused in the doorway and looked at him anxiously.

'Are you all right?'

'Yes,' said Buchanan. 'I'm all right.'

McDiarmid took off his silver-braided peak cap and threw it down on the table. His own face was grey and drawn with weariness and strain.

'Have a drink,' he said shortly. 'I'm having one, rules or no rules.'

He gave Buchanan his glass and sat down at the desk, holding his own glass between his hands, staring into the depths of it.

'I was wrong,' he said at last. 'I should never have had the vans on that side of the square. I should have brought the men through the City Chambers from the back. If I'd done that, I could have confined the trouble to the front. The rest of the crowd could just have been allowed to go, with no interference at all. I don't know what I was thinking about.'

'It's over,' said Buchanan.

'Aye,' said McDiarmid heavily. 'It's over.' He swirled the whisky in his glass and drank half of it. 'Did you get through to his chief?'

'Yes, I got through.'

'And how did he take it?'

'In their usual damned condescending way. He seems to think the whole thing can be hushed up.'

McDiarmid laughed humourlessly.

'Then he's a lot to learn. Nobody'll hush this up, security or no security.'

257

'That's what I told him.'

'I don't know what they think we are,' said McDiarmid bitterly. 'I admit I handled the thing badly. And my head'll likely roll for it. But it needn't have happened at all if it hadn't been for their damned interference. And I warned him.'

'You did?'

'Of course I did.'

'In the presence of witnesses?'

'In the presence of McLeod and McLean. I told him that anything Douglas could say would do less harm than trying to break it up. But he wouldn't listen. He said he'd been given orders. I asked him what his orders had to do with me. He said if I didn't co-operate I'd soon find out. What could I do?'

'Nothing.'

'Exactly,' said McDiarmid. 'Nothing but carry on. Improvise last-minute plans that turned out to be wrong. Risk the lives of my men and probably lose my own job. And why? Because some damned nincompoop in London who knows nothing about it says so. God!' He picked up his glass and emptied it. 'It's the kind of thing that would make you say Douglas was right.'

'Aye,' said Buchanan. 'I quite agree. And so will a lot of other people when the news gets out.'

'If the news gets out. From what you say, they'll try and suppress it.'

'They'll not suppress it. James Douglas'll see to that. And if they try, I'll make damned sure they don't succeed.'

McDiarmid glanced at him.

'If you do, they'll get their knife in you as well.'

'They've got their knife in me already,' said Buchanan grimly. 'And I can't say it bothers me. I'm in a position to give them as much trouble as they want. No, it's not that. It's what they're planning for Douglas that bothers me.'

'What are they planning?'

'I don't know.' The Secretary of State rose stiffly to his feet. 'I wish I did.'

The Inspector looked up at him.

'And do we take any action?'

'About Douglas?' Buchanan wound the woollen scarf

around his neck and shook his head. 'No,' he said. 'I'll have a talk with him later in the morning. But you take no action. That's one problem that's being taken out of our hands. And I wish to God it wasn't.'

CHAPTER TWELVE

DOUGLAS looked from his office over the roof-tops of the grey, shocked city. A fine drizzle of rain was falling through a thin fog, hiding the encircling hills, obscuring his view of the glistening half-empty pavements where the stunned people hurried past the patrolling police, each avoiding the other's evasive eyes, each bearing his own fraction of the burden of communal guilt. No sound reached him through the thick plate glass, yet he seemed to hear the murmur of innumerable voices, seemed to sense the city's restless apprehension, feeling its uneasy heartbeat as though it were his own.

That morning, after three hours of deep sleep, he had wakened conscious of this heightened awareness. He had lain in the half-light listening to the drip of water from the trees, no longer numbed by the night's events, no longer angry, but calm and clear-headed, with plans to which he had given no conscious thought already formulated in his mind. By nine o'clock, he was in his office. By eleven o'clock, all necessary changes had been made, all necessary steps had been taken. It remained only to attend the emergency committee meeting which he had called for the afternoon and thereafter to sign the documents which his lawyers should by that time have drafted. When the Secretary of State arrived, he had been glad to see him.

Now, as he looked across the city which had been the centre of his life for so long, his own irrational serenity puzzled him. Even the presence of Buchanan did nothing to diminish it. The silence that had fallen was like a silence between friends, uniting rather than dividing. Buchanan broke it.

'What are you going to do, James?' he asked quietly.

Douglas turned back to the room.

'There's very little more I can do,' he said. 'It's all done. I suppose I sit down and wait.'

'For what?'

'The police, presumably. If they decide to take action. But I hope they won't before tonight. I've got a meeting this afternoon. After that, I've some ends to tie up with the lawyers, including the question of some sort of compensation for the relatives of all the dead. But you'd better keep that to yourself.'

'Yes,' said Buchanan thoughtfully. 'It would be wiser. If news of that gets out it's liable to be interpreted as meaning that you hold yourself responsible.'

'But I do, Alex.' He sat down at his desk and picked up his empty pipe. 'I've got to face it. I am responsible. Not for the stupidity of the security man. And not for the actions of the police. But I'm responsible for holding the meeting at all. And I made one big mistake. I should never have told them the orders came from London. I said it to try to turn their anger away from the police here. But that's not the effect it had. It was a miscalculation. Fatal, as it turned out.'

'Och, I don't know.' Buchanan found himself regarding Douglas with sympathy and compassion. 'Would it have made any difference if you hadn't said it?'

Douglas shrugged his shoulders.

'That can't be proved one way or the other, so I've got to decide for myself. And I'm inclined to think it would. If the powers that be feel the same, they'll probably be only too glad of the opportunity to get me out of the road.'

Buchanan's eyes narrowed.

'What do you mean . . . get you out of the road?'

'Arrest me, presumably.'

'On what charge?'

'That I wouldn't know, but I'm taking advice on the possibilities. From what I can hear, they should be able to find something. There's plenty of small print in the Statute Book.'

'And that's what you're half-expecting?'

'More than half-expecting. I woke up this morning with a feeling that I won't be leading the Party much longer.'

Buchanan looked away from those disturbingly calm eyes

260

and tried to remember his official responsibility in all this.

'And if not you, James, who? Ewan Cameron's dead.'

Douglas grinned.

'That's a question you shouldn't be asking, Alex. We're supposed to be on opposite sides of the fence.'

'Supposed to be,' said Buchanan gruffly.

Douglas looked at him curiously.

'Yes,' he said. 'Supposed to be. But I'll tell you this. With or without me, the Party goes on. I couldn't stop it any more than you can, even if I wanted to. I gave it life, I agree. But what happens to me now doesn't matter. There's administrative machinery. There are funds. Most important of all, there are men, some of the best men in the country. And whether you agree with me or not, it is a fact that there's public support.'

Buchanan sighed.

'I'm not supposed to admit it, but I know it's a fact. The trouble is, there are some men who don't believe it, men who think you're just a trouble-maker. They don't admit you've any public support worth talking about. It's their attitude that's dangerous.'

Douglas lifted one bushy eyebrow enquiringly.

'Dangerous?'

Buchanan looked at him squarely.

'Do you realise that there are people who would have been glad to see you lying there dead last night instead of Ewan Cameron?'

'Yes, I realise that.'

'And do you realise that there's a group of people . . . and I can't be more specific, except to say that they're not in Scotland . . . a group of people who are quite capable of trying to send you the same road?'

Douglas's eyes were steady.

'Is that a warning, Alex?' he asked softly.

Buchanan nodded briefly.

'You could call it that.'

Douglas rose and walked slowly round the room.

'You know,' he said, 'away back in the spring of the year, when this thing was just beginning, I had a long talk one night

261

with Ewan Cameron. I remember he said that he didn't think political assassination was ruled out in a democracy like Britain. It hadn't been needed for a long time, he said, but if ever the need arose, if ever a situation existed where the actions of one man created a threat to the *status quo* that could best be dealt with by the removal of that man, then, he said, in his opinion a democracy would kill.' He turned to the Secretary of State. 'What would your comments be on that?'

'I would have to agree with him,' said Buchanan gravely. 'Six months ago, I would have denied the possibility absolutely. But since then I've been in contact with people who have an attitude that I wouldn't have believed existed if I hadn't come up against it. And, mark you, I'm a Minister. In spite of that, I knew next to nothing about them. Now I know a little more and I believe that Cameron was right. The only thing I'd add is that there are various ways of killing.'

Douglas sat down, struck a match and lit his pipe with care.

'All right, then,' he said. 'Let's assume he was right. Let's assume that this group of people eliminate me. No. Don't let's be mealy-mouthed. Let's assume they kill me, basing their action on the false premise that by getting rid of me, they end the whole thing. What would you, a Minister and a member of the Government, do?'

'I'd resign,' said Buchanan promptly. 'Although I've said I believe a democracy would kill, I've got to go on believing that I'm wrong. If events proved me right, I'd resign at once.'

'And what else?' asked Douglas softly.

'What do you mean?'

'What else would you do?' He smiled gently. 'Or will I tell you, Alex? First you'd join and then you'd lead the Party in my place. You'd bring it the political maturity and experience that it lacks. You'd do something to cleanse the guilt that would lie on your own conscience as a member of the Government of the day. And you'd be in a position to fight back at the faceless men because, as leader of a free and independent Scotland, you'd have power yourself.'

Their eyes met. A long silent moment stretched between them. Then Buchanan looked away.

'You're joking, James.'

'I'm far from joking,' said Douglas. 'I'm like Dr. Johnson's man who's going to be hung in the morning. When time's running out you think clearly. And you take your thinking through to its logical conclusion, which is what you're not prepared to do. You say you'd resign. All right. By doing that, you make your protest. Then what? You're a professional politician, and a Scot, and an honest man. Do you think you could leave it at that?' He leaned forward. 'Do you?'

'I don't know,' said Buchanan desperately. 'I've never even thought about it.'

'And there's no reason why you should have thought about it,' said Douglas. 'But for me, there's every reason. In whatever time I've got left, I have to plan. And those plans include you because I believe you'll find that to resign is not enough. I believe you'll want to fight back, because you're that kind of man. And how better can you fight back than by stepping into my shoes?'

'I could never fill your shoes,' muttered Buchanan. 'I haven't that kind of personality.'

'You're too modest,' said Douglas. 'You're known and liked and trusted. I grant you you couldn't have done the job I've done in the last six months. But you could carry on from here, leading the organisation I've built up. And it's what in your heart you would want to do, if the thing we're talking about happens.'

'Then you know my heart better than I know it myself.'

'Yes,' said Douglas. 'Today, I think I do.'

He rose and went to the window. Buchanan sat on, looking at that broad, straight back, remembering the flat impersonal voice from London and the threat it had made. Here, in this quiet office, in Douglas's presence, it was as though he had dreamt it. For sanity's sake, he had to believe he had dreamt it. He rose suddenly, thrusting the memory violently aside.

'But, James, this is ridiculous. The whole thing's ridiculous. Nothing's going to happen to you.'

Douglas turned to him.

'Something is,' he said quietly. 'I'm sure of it. I thought imprisonment. You suggested death. I don't know which of us will prove to be right. But by the weekend, one or other will have happened. If it's imprisonment, I'm not asking you to do anything. But if it's death, I have a certain right to ask you to do what I know would be in your own mind to do in any case.'

'But I can't, James. I'm still the Secretary of State. How could I promise a thing like that?'

'Only by thinking yourself out of your job. Only by thinking yourself into that morning, next Friday, next Tuesday, whatever morning it is you hear the news that I'm dead.'

'But that's not going to happen! God damn it, how can it happen? It's still a free country. That kind of thing just doesn't happen here.'

'It hasn't happened for a while,' said Douglas. 'And it might not happen now. But you yourself said you thought it could happen. What concerns me is what I'd like you to do if it does happen. And there's one thing worth remembering. With or without you, the Party will go on, just as it will go on with or without me. I take it you realise that?'

'Yes,' said Buchanan. 'I realise that.'

'All right, then. Assuming I'm killed——'

'But you won't be!'

'Assuming I am,' went on Douglas calmly, 'and assuming that you'll feel the guilt that you will feel if that happens, I'm asking you for an undertaking that you'll take my place.'

Buchanan spread his hands hopelessly.

'I can't give it.'

'Then I'm sorry,' said Douglas sadly. 'I still believe you will, but I'd like to have known.' He crossed to the rack and lifted off the Secretary's heavy winter coat. He held it out so that he could put it on. 'But you will see to the Court of Enquiry?'

'Yes, I'll see to that. And the sooner it's held the better.'

His fingers fumbled with the buttons. He was now anxious to get away, anxious to return to the peaceful normality of St. Andrew's House, where it might be possible to believe that his fears and forebodings were groundless. He took Douglas's outstretched hand and felt his knuckles crack under the pressure of those strong, blunt fingers.

'Goodbye, Alex.'

'Goodbye, James.'

He could not look at him. Douglas watched him hurry away towards the bronze doors of the lift, then returned to his desk and relit his dead pipe. Five minutes later, he called Sally.

'Come in a minute,' he said, and released the switch.

He watched the lithe movement of her body as she came to him from her door, her body that of a girl ten years younger than he knew she was, long-legged and supple, her olive-green silk over-blouse filled out by her still youthful breasts. He watched her sit down, crossing her legs at the knee, resting her file on the long firm length of her thigh. Her face was pale and her eyes were serious. It was no time to talk about the fact that she should marry before any more years rolled by. He looked away.

'Are all the arrangements made for this afternoon?'

'Yes,' she said. 'I managed to contact everybody except Mr. David Armstrong. He's at a conference in London and won't be back till tomorrow.'

'But all the others can come?'

'Yes, sir.'

'Good. Let's see the agenda.'

She handed him a foolscap sheet. He scanned it quickly. When he came to the fourth heading, *'The appointment of a new deputy leader, following the death of Mr. Ewan Cameron'*, he paused, then drew his pen through the whole line. Above it, he wrote, *'Considerations regarding the future leadership of the Party, arising out of the death of Mr. Ewan Cameron and various related facts'*. Then he handed it back to her.

'Make final copies of that,' he said. 'Now, what about Roderick Grant? Has there been any word from him?'

'He called about half an hour ago. I told him that Mr. Buchanan was in. I didn't think you'd want to be disturbed.'

'Quite right. Neither I did.'

'But he said he'd had a dreadful morning. He's never been off the phone.'

'That I can well believe,' said Douglas. 'Did he have any news?'

'Just that there had been some big demonstration on Glasgow Green. They were protesting about the arrests. I think he said there were over seven hundred now. There was talk of a march to protest outside the prisons, but it didn't come to anything.'

'And there wasn't any trouble?'

'No, there wasn't any trouble. I think the police left them alone.'

'I'm not surprised. Like me, Sally, the police would learn a few lessons last night.'

'But it's dreadful.' Her lip was trembling. 'I still can't believe it about Mr. Cameron.'

'And all the others.'

She looked up swiftly.

'Yes,' she said. 'All the others. It could have been you.'

'But it wasn't,' he said gently, and stretched out his hand. 'Now, on you go, Sally. It's time you went for your lunch.'

He watched her as she crossed his office, but when she reached her door, he spoke. There might never be another chance.

'One thing,' he said.

She turned enquiringly.

'Yes, sir?'

'About Roderick Grant. Once, a while back, we talked about him. Do you remember?'

The colour rose on her cheeks.

'Yes,' she said. 'I remember.'

'You had certain views at that time, certain reservations. Have you still got them?'

The lashes fell over her dark eyes.

'No, sir.'

'And does he know?' he asked gently.

She looked at him then, and smiled for the first time that morning.

'Yes,' she said. 'He knows.'

'Good,' said Douglas. 'That's all I wanted to hear.'

When she had gone, he looked out at the grey morning. The rain had stopped. Over the city, the thin wet winter fog hung lightly, beading each wire, each ledge, with moisture. Later, when the lights were lit, they would glisten like innumerable tears.

*   *   *

At three o'clock that afternoon, as Douglas rose to open the meeting of his committee, the Secretary of State for Scotland entered his office in St. Andrew's House.

During the drive across country from Glasgow, he had tried unsuccessfully to convince himself that his fears for Douglas's safety were groundless. During the hour and a half he had spent at home, when he had taken a quick bath and changed and eaten a light lunch, he had been equally unsuccessful in his efforts to thrust Douglas's proposal from his mind. Already, it had assumed a logical look, had come to seem the correct and rational thing to do if . . . but there his thoughts stopped. They would not allow the words that Douglas himself had spoken so calmly. The possibility lay like a dark reason-stifling cloud, excluding all else.

As he lay back in the car that was taking him to Edinburgh, his confused, sleep-starved brain held on to one clear fact. If the security service could be persuaded that the removal of Douglas would solve nothing, then even they must surely see that it would be pointless to act. He clung to that thought. To try to achieve that was his responsibility. For the moment, he could take thoughts of responsibility no further.

He swept through his outer office.

'I don't want to be disturbed.' His secretary blinked. 'Not for any reason whatsoever.'

The delay as he awaited connection seemed endless. Then he heard the voice, as detestable as he remembered it.

'Yes?'

'Buchanan here. The Secretary of State for Scotland.'

'So I was told.'

'Since I spoke to you this morning, I've been making certain enquiries.'

'Regarding what?'

'Regarding the necessity for any action concerning James Douglas.'

'And what were your conclusions?'

'That the structure and status of his Party is such that his

267

removal would make no difference at all.'

'That is not according to our information.'

'Then your information's out of date,' snapped Buchanan. 'I insist that you pay attention to what I tell you. I'm on the spot, which you are not. I have a position of authority in this country and——'

'This country?' queried the security chief softly. 'You mean, I take it, this part of Britain?'

'This country,' repeated Buchanan. 'And I have reliable sources of information of my own. It is a fact that a party machine has been created which will go on with or without Douglas. It is a fact that a large supporting body of public opinion exists which is going to continue to exist whether Douglas is there or not. These are facts.'

'I beg to dispute them.'

'You can dispute them till the cows come home,' said Buchanan angrily. 'You can't change them. A memorandum expanding these and other relevant facts will be posted to you tonight, with copies to the Prime Minister and the Cabinet. If you choose to ignore both what I've told you and the contents of that memorandum, then you'll be answerable to the Government for any action you may take.'

'May have taken.'

Buchanan paused.

'I beg your pardon?'

'Any action I may have taken. You don't seem to realise that a certain urgency now exists, Mr. Buchanan. In the last twenty-four hours, unrest in the north has reached a dangerous level. There is no longer time to waste. I have already taken the necessary steps.'

Buchanan felt the heavy beat of a pulse at his temple.

'Then you'll cancel them.'

'I think not. Such decisions are mine and mine alone.'

'You're lying. You're responsible to the Government of which I'm a Minister.'

'Responsible, yes, in the sense that I may be called upon to justify the decisions I have made.'

'And do you believe for one minute you can do that here?'

'Yes.'

'Then God help you.' Suddenly his voice seemed to come from far away within the great pounding chamber of his skull. 'When the day comes that you've to justify this, I'll see you roast for it.'

He sat back, heavy with defeat. His head throbbed until the very walls of the room seemed to pulse in rhythm with his heart. He wondered vaguely if he were ill. Some heart attack. A stroke. But there was no clear thought. Clumsily, he opened a drawer and tipped three aspirins from a box into his hand. He drew the water carafe and the glass nearer. Then the cold water struck his palate and with that small shock came a faint ray of hope. He swallowed the aspirins quickly and lifted the phone. His secretary answered.

'Get me Inspector McDiarmid, City of Glasgow Police.'

He hung up and drank some more water. When the call came through, the throbbing had begun to subside.

'McDiarmid? Buchanan here.'

'Yes, sir?'

'Starting as soon as you can arrange it, I want James Douglas given police protection.'

'Protection?' The Inspector sounded startled. 'From what?'

'I can't tell you, because I don't know.'

'But you've reason to believe he's in danger?'

McDiarmid sounded sceptical.

'I know he's in danger,' said Buchanan. 'What I don't know is the form the threat is likely to take. But I want him covered at all times. In the city, at home, on the road. It doesn't matter where he goes, I want him covered, night and day.'

'Yes, sir,' said McDiarmid resignedly. It was just one more task for his overstretched force. 'I'll arrange it.'

'Now, he's at present in his own building. He has a conference there this afternoon. After that, I happen to know he's seeing his lawyers. Whether at his office or theirs, I can't tell you. From then on, I don't know what he's doing, but after last night I should think he'll go home and get some sleep.'

'We'll pick him up before that,' said McDiarmid. 'We'll have the building covered before his conference ends. But what about inside it? That might be tricky.'

'We'll have to take a chance on that,' said Buchanan. 'He's

got watch-dogs of his own there, anyway. And I don't want him to get the slightest idea of what's going on.'

'So it's plain-clothes only?'

'Whatever you like, just so long as they do their job. And if anything happens, anything at all, phone me at once, at my home if necessary.'

'Very well, sir.'

'Right,' said Buchanan. 'I'll keep in touch.'

He hung up. His head felt better. His brain had cleared. He drew out his pipe and his pouch and began to rub the tobacco in the palm of his hand, a soothing repetitive movement that left him free to think back on Douglas and the things he had said. There was now hope, if the police did their job properly, but the possibility that they might fail had to be faced. And if they failed, he realised now that Douglas was right. To resign would not be enough. It would be a gesture, easy to make, as empty as the symbolic washing of his hands. He would still want to fight back, to prove that damned inhuman man was wrong. And how could that best be done? Surely only by ensuring that Douglas's Party endured, and grew in power, and ultimately achieved the end for which it had been created. The conclusion was logical, inescapable. It was as Douglas had said. Earlier, he had not been prepared to take the thought thus far. Now, he could not avoid it. Only by stepping into the gap that Douglas would leave, could he satisfy what would be the demands of his own conscience. 'I'm asking you to do what I know would be in your mind to do in any case.' The words rang clearly through his memory. And those other words, spoken sadly. 'I'm sorry. I would like to have known.'

He sat up quickly. Suddenly, it was important that Douglas should know. If the decision was made, he had a right to be told. And the decision was made.

He rapidly filled his pipe, then picked up the phone.

'Get me Mr. James Douglas. He's in his Glasgow office. If they say he's in conference, tell them who's calling. The matter's important.'

*   *   *

Douglas looked down the long table at the grave faces of the members of his committee.

'Are there any more questions arising out of last night's events?'

Sir William Robertson raised his long lawyer's head.

'I take it that in due course a proper enquiry will be held?' Douglas nodded.

'I have the assurance of the Secretary of State that a Court of Enquiry will be set up as soon as possible. This, I have insisted, should sit in public. I'm glad to say he agrees.'

'And about tomorrow's by-election.' The round Lowland voice of Dr. Duncan Ross was unusually subdued. 'Does that still go on?'

'Yes, it does. I've discussed this with the authorities concerned, with the police and with the other political parties. All are agreed that it's too late to cancel it, even if that were thought desirable. But I must admit my own feelings are mixed. If it takes place, I think, quite frankly, that we will profit from what has happened. I think we'll win. And I've no wish to win under such circumstances.'

'But you have to be realistic.' Sir Jack Armstrong growled, as he tended to do under stress. 'You can't undo what's done.'

'No,' said Douglas. 'Unfortunately. And I have been realistic. The by-election will take place as planned.' He drew the papers on the table nearer to him. 'And now, if there are no further questions, we'll move on to the fourth heading. Considerations regarding the future leadership of the Party.' He straightened up and rested his knuckles on the wood. 'And this is where I have some things to say which you may consider unnecessary. My only defence is that I don't agree. I think they have to be said. Last night, for the first time, we came up against violence. Ewan Cameron was not murdered in quite the usual way. He was murdered by a man employed by the forces of order in this country. However unbelievable it may seem, that, nevertheless, is what happened. Now, we have to realise that in certain quarters we are regarded as a disruptive force, almost a revolutionary force, certainly one which threatens a system of government that has been in existence for over two hundred and sixty years. People who regard us in this way are bound to oppose us. We know that and expect it.

271

What I, at least, did not expect was that men employed by them would carry arms and be prepared to use them. But I was wrong. The unfortunate man who died last night didn't come here to shoot Ewan Cameron. But he did come armed. This has a personal significance for me which I hardly need to point out. I now have to consider the possibility, however remote, that my turn may come.'

He waited until the rumble of protest died down. Then he smiled reassuringly.

'I didn't say I thought it likely. But I do say such a possibility exists. Its implications ought to be considered.'

Roderick Grant glanced at Sally. Her racing pencil had not paused, but her face was drained of colour. His lips tightened. Tonight, he thought. I've got to ask her tonight. If she doesn't get her mind taken off all this, she'll break.

'Now, we know,' went on Douglas, 'that the Executive Committee, whose members are all present, is perfectly capable of running the Party, being ultimately responsible to the full Committee which we have here today. But we are agreed, I think, that one man should exist as a Party leader, with full authority to act independently if need be. Until now, that man, had anything happened to me, would have been Ewan Cameron.'

The special telephone beside Sally purred quietly. She lifted it.

'The succession would have been automatic, causing no disturbance to the running of our affairs. My concern at the moment is to——'

'Excuse me, sir. A call for you.'

He looked at her quickly.

'I'll call them back.'

'I think you'll want to take it,' said Sally steadily. 'In another room.'

He looked at her eyes for only a moment, then pushed back his chair.

'Excuse me, gentlemen.'

The double doors of the conference room closed silently behind him, cutting off the rising murmur of excited conversation round the table. He let himself sink into an armchair and drew over the jade-green phone. Whatever the call might be, it was good to sit down. He lifted the receiver and lay back with it, resting his head on the leather.

'Hello. James Douglas here.'

'James? It's Alex Buchanan.'

He sat up quickly.

'Yes, Alex?'

'Do you remember this morning you asked me to give you a certain undertaking which I said I couldn't give?'

'Yes. I remember well.'

He held his breath.

'I thought you might like to know that I'm prepared to give it now.'

He let it go in a long quiet sigh.

'That is, of course, provided that the other thing we were talking about does happen.'

'Of course.'

'All we can do is hope that it doesn't.'

'Yes,' said Douglas. 'That's all we can do. And thank you Alex. I'll see you soon.'

'I hope so,' said Buchanan. 'I very much hope so.'

He put the phone down gently. Now, they could do what they liked. It no longer mattered. The thing would go on. Ewan's death, his own death if need be, would be nothing but part of the price that had to be paid. Over the centuries, men had died in their millions for worse political causes. So far, the price they were being asked was not too high.

He went back to his place at the table and waited for the murmur to subside.

'I'm sorry I had to leave you,' he said quietly. 'We were discussing the future leadership of the Party, if anything happened to me.'

Sir Jack Armstrong cleared his throat.

'If I could say something.'

'Of course.'

'We were discussing this while you were out, as you can well imagine, and we feel, I think we all feel, that you're taking an unnecessarily alarmist view. I mean, this thing last night was an isolated incident, surely? You don't really envisage a thing

273

like that happening again, do you?'

'No, I don't. I don't envisage anything. I simply accept that we have enemies. These enemies, we have learned, may be armed. When men are armed, men sometimes die. If I should die, a problem of leadership exists.' He smiled. 'And I should add that I, like other men, might die of natural causes. Or by accident. Because of that, while I'm still alive I feel a responsibility to ensure that the succession will be as smooth as it would have been had Ewan Cameron not been killed. That seems to me no more than a reasonable precaution.'

Jack Armstrong reluctantly admitted it.

'All right,' said Douglas. 'I have chosen a successor who will be, I think you'll agree, most suitable. He is a man of roughly my own age. He is an experienced politician. He is well-known, well-liked and an extremely able administrator. It would be hard to find anyone better. Although I am submitting his name for your approval now, I'm sure that approval will be forthcoming. But here I must ask for your absolute discretion. Under no circumstances must his name be made public during my lifetime.' He paused and looked down the long oval. Their faces were expectant, waiting, knowing now that it was not one of themselves. 'His name is Alex Buchanan,' said Douglas quietly. 'He is at present Secretary of State for Scotland.'

*   *   *

Mr. Alex McLintock, senior partner of the law firm of McLintock and Brown, thrust the last of the papers into his bulging brief-case and fastened the flap.

'Well, that's the lot,' he said. 'If there are still ends not tied up, I don't know about them.'

'As far as I know, there aren't,' said Douglas. 'And I'll never say again that lawyers are slow. I'm very grateful.'

'All part of the service.' McLintock reached for his coat. 'But there's one big question lurking in my suspicious mind, James.'

'And what's that?'

'Why? Not why are you making these arrangements. They're nearly all sensible, reasonable things to do. But why

274

are you in such a hell of a hurry?'

Douglas grinned.

'Middle age,' he said. 'It's a dangerous time, Alex. And look at the road accident figures for the last quarter. They're worse than ever.'

'Aye,' said McLintock. 'But Ewan Cameron was barely middle-aged. And he wasn't knocked down by a car.'

'True,' said Douglas. 'There are risks in everything.'

'Mmphm.' McLintock pulled his gloves from his pocket and lifted his hat. 'Well anyway, if you should happen to die suddenly in the next few weeks, somebody will have to do a lot of talking to convince me that it was due to natural causes.'

Douglas considered that. It presented possibilities. If anything were to happen, McLintock's curiosity would not be easily satisfied. He might unearth some interesting facts, facts that Alex Buchanan and others would know how to use. His suspicions were worth encouraging.

'You think it might be stretching coincidence too far?'

He looked at the lawyer with innocent eyes.

'A damn sight too far,' said McLintock. 'And you know it. But you're a cagey character. If you won't talk, I can't make you. But if you do know anything, you might have the decency to get it down on paper, or tape, or somewhere. You could make my life a lot easier.'

Douglas smiled and rose to his feet.

'I'm glad I haven't got a mind like yours, Alex. You're always looking for trouble.'

McLintock grunted.

'That's why I'm a good lawyer.'

'Yes,' said Douglas. 'I grant you that.' He stretched out his hand. 'Anyway . . . thanks for everything.'

'Wait till you get the bill,' said McLintock. 'You'll maybe not be so grateful.'

When he had gone, Douglas sat down at his desk and lit his pipe. Then he switched on the tape-recorder and talked for ten minutes, until the wall clock showed the time as five minutes to six. When he had rewound the tape, he put it back in its box and placed the box in an envelope which he sealed and addressed to the lawyer. He then opened the drawer for which

275

Sally had a duplicate key, slipped the envelope in, relocked it and chuckled. There was enough there to bring McLintock's eager nose to the ground. Once there, no one was likely to persuade him to raise it until he had followed each scent to its point of origin, no matter where that might be. There was some consolation in the thought.

Yet, as he looked out at the luminous night sky and watched the office windows darken one by one, he felt no need for consolation. The serenity with which he had wakened still endured. And now the day was behind him. The things he had planned to do were done. It was time to go home, and sit by the fire with Margaret and then sleep.

He took the lift down to the basement car park. When the doors opened, he stepped out and looked around. Archie's car had gone. He would be with Oonagh, somewhere, planning a new life. He smiled inwardly. That was one end not quite tied up. He still had to hear their story. But it could wait for another day.

As he opened the door of the Jaguar, Jimmie, the attendant, appeared from his little office.

'Goodnight, Mr. Douglas.'

'Goodnight, Jimmie.'

He relit his pipe while the car lift raised him to street level. Then the doors slid open and he drove out into the cold moist evening. The fog was thin, not enough to affect visibility seriously, and the worst of the rush-hour traffic was off the road. The junction of the service lane with the street was a place where one often had to wait five minutes before it was possible to pull out. Now, it was almost clear. He glanced briefly at the two young men in the black Rover on the other side of the road, but their car was parked. He swung across in front of it and headed north to pick up the ring road.

In the driving position, he began to feel the tiredness in his muscles. And the lights were bright, more dazzling than usual in the fog, setting up a little throbbing ache behind each eye. Sleep, he thought. That's what I need.

On the ring road, he let his speed drop to the point when the car almost seemed to drive itself. Lights flashed in his mirror, swept to the side, overtook. He kept close to the kerb, leaving them room. There was no hurry. Even at this speed, he would be home in thirty minutes.

Ahead, the lights of the Anniesland intersection were coming up. He glanced in his mirror and pulled over to the right-hand lane. A hundred yards behind him, another car did the same. He flicked his direction indicator and braked gently. As he entered the intersection, he glanced in the mirror again. The following car was no nearer and its off-side amber light was flashing. He watched it as he swung round on to the Bearsden road. Suddenly, he was suspicious. At the intersection, it should have closed up. But even now, with the open road ahead, it had come no nearer. He pulled out the ash-tray and put down his pipe.

All right, he thought. Let's find out now, before we leave the lights.

He let his speed fall steadily, to twenty, to fifteen miles an hour. Still the gap remained unchanged. He drew into the kerb and stopped. The following car drove slowly by, passed under the railway bridge, and vanished round the curve beyond. It was a black Rover with two young men, the car that had been parked close to the end of the service lane.

He picked up his pipe and chewed thoughtfully on the stem. At any other time, it would have been coincidence. Now, he was not so sure.

He waited until a few other cars had overtaken him. Then he moved on, driving slowly, looking down each side-road as he passed by. He found it within less than half a mile, lying in a cul-de-sac between two bungalows. It was pointing towards him. Behind it, a cloud of exhaust vapour from its idling engine hung in the moist air.

He did not wait to see more. There was a forty mile an hour speed limit on the Switchback Road, but before he was half-way along it, the speedometer needle passed ninety. In his mirror, he glimpsed two side-lights as they flicked over the brow of the hill half a mile or more behind him. Then he was throttling back, braking to enter the swinging double bend that ended at the Bearsden roundabout, holding left, past the gates of Canniesburn Hospital, changing down, stabbing the brake pedal, holding the car close into the kerb to make the sharp left-hand turn into Drumchapel Road. Behind him, the main road fell away, then vanished as he turned off into suburbia, swinging right, left, and right again among the bungalows, until at last he let the Jaguar come to rest in a deserted residential street.

He switched off the engine and smiled grimly. If they wanted to get him, they would have to do better than that. But at least it now seemed certain that they did want to get him.

There was no other explanation. The police, if they were interested, would call at his office. A little group would come, possibly led by McDiarmid himself. They would be polite, anxious to make the whole thing as easy as possible. The last thing they would do was indulge in unnecessary melodrama. It was not McDiarmid's way. But for the others, working, as they must, in the shadows, there could be no other way.

He wound down the window and sniffed the raw evening air. However incredible it might seem in this quiet street, there was satisfaction now in knowledge where before there had been only speculation, satisfaction and an almost pleasurable anticipation at the thought that these were men whose methods might be unconventional, but who could still be outwitted like other men. The menace was no longer large and vague and general. It was reduced to two young men in a black saloon car. That was something with which he could deal.

A few miles further north, the black car swept round a corner and slackened speed. The road ahead of it dipped, then flattened across the moor before rising gradually towards the distant hills. The driver swore softly.

'Not a sign of him.'

'What did you expect? At the lick he was going, he'll be damn near home.'

'You hope.' He dropped a gear and accelerated hard. When their speed had built up again, he changed to overdrive top. 'If we've lost him, McDiarmid'll skin us.'

'We've lost him all right. You don't think you'll catch him in this thing, do you? That's a Mark Ten Jag he's driving, not a bubble-car.'

'I don't think I'll catch him,' said the driver tensely, 'but I'd like to see him safely parked in his own garage. This is supposed to be police protection.'

'Protection!' His companion laughed. 'That's a joke.'

'Not so bloody funny,' said the driver. 'Not after last night.'

With the moor behind them, he slipped out of overdrive and held their speed as high as he dared. Then, as they approached the intersection with the Balloch road, he suddenly took his right foot off the pedal.

'What the hell?'

In a lay-by ahead of them a car was parked and in the centre of the road beside it a torch waved them down.

'Some mug who's run out of petrol,' said the passenger. 'Stop and we'll check if the Jag's passed him.'

They came to rest beside the duffle-coated man who held the torch. In the parked car, another face showed briefly in the light, then vanished back into the shadowy interior. The driver wound down his window.

'What's wrong, Mac? Are you out of juice?'

The torch moved quickly over their faces, then swept the back seat. Its bearer stepped aside.

'All right,' he said. 'You can carry on.'

The driver and his companion looked at each other quickly. The voice was English, alien.

'Just a minute,' said the driver. 'What's the big idea? You waved us down.'

'Routine check,' said the man briefly. 'I'm sorry you were troubled.'

'What do you mean . . . routine check?' The driver flung open his door. 'Put the lamp on him, Jimmie, and let's see this character.' The swivel lamp flared and swung on to the stranger's face. 'Right,' said the driver. 'Now you've got some explaining to do. If anybody does any routine checking around here, it'll be us. City of Glasgow Police. So come on. What's the big idea?'

The man in the duffle-coat blinked slightly in the light and smiled.

'Special Branch,' he said. 'Up from London. You wouldn't know me.'

'Oh aye?' The driver's eyes narrowed. He spoke over his

shoulder. 'Check that car, Jimmie, and have a look at his mate. Get him out.'

'You don't believe me?'

'Give me one reason why I should?'

The man shrugged his shoulders and drew a wallet from an inside pocket. From it, he took a folded card and handed it over.

'What about that?'

The driver studied it.

'What is it?'

'A Special Authority Warrant. Date and time of issue, five o'clock this morning. Place, Security Department of the Home Office.'

'Security?'

'That's what I said.'

'And what are you after?'

'That's our affair,' said the man shortly.

'Aye.' The driver folded the card and handed it back. 'Well, I suppose that's that.'

'I would say so, yes.'

'All right.' He called across the road. 'Right, Jimmie. Get a note of the number for the report.' He turned back to the stranger. 'There's just one thing. Have you seen a black Mark Ten Jag headed north? Registration number OGB231F. A middle-aged man driving it and no passengers.'

The Security man's expression changed only slightly.

'No,' he said. 'He hasn't been through in the last hour. What do you want him for?'

'That's our affair,' said the driver as he climbed back into the Rover. 'You mind your business and I'll mind mine.'

As their lights swung on to the bridge over the river Endrick, his companion lit a cigarette.

'Well,' he said, 'that's a funny business. What the hell are a couple of London security men doing up here?'

'God knows,' said the driver, 'but it's wasted us a good five minutes.'

He accelerated into the climbing, curving bends that led to Drymen.

'What's the hurry?' asked his companion. 'That fellow said he hadn't gone through.'

'Because if he hasn't gone through, he must have cut over to Milngavie and taken the Killearn road. That way, he'd dodge us. And he can cut back across and come in in the middle of Drymen. But it's a slow road. With luck, we'll still be there ahead of him.'

'And if we're not?'

'We'll go out to this Gartland place and look in the garage. If he's home, O.K. That's it. But if he's not——'

'Aye,' said his companion. 'That's what's bothering me. If he's not.'

'Yes,' said the driver grimly. 'Me, too.'

Douglas looked at his watch. He had been parked for fifteen minutes. By now, the men in the Rover would know that he was not on the road to Drymen. They would have started to check the alternative routes. Either that, or they would head for Gartland and stay there, waiting for him. If they did, they were due for another disappointment. He could leave the car at the farm and walk. If they were to find him then, in the dark woodland, on his own ground, they would need more than ordinary good luck. He knocked out his pipe. It was time to go.

He felt his way through the maze of bungalows until he found the main road again. Then he turned north into light suburban traffic that thinned out still further when the houses were left behind. Out in the country beyond, the fog had cleared. In the north-east, a yellow rising moon hung poised on the rim of the hills. That, he welcomed. It lit the shadowy farm-roadends where the Rover might lie, its lights extinguished, waiting for him to pass. Yet he saw no sign of it. As the road gradually dropped into the Endrick valley, he grew more certain that it would be at Gartland. His speed crept up, almost as though he were eager to face whatever might await him. Then in the distance, he saw a torch beam waving in the centre of the road.

He lifted his foot from the throttle and felt his pulse quicken as the Jaguar lost speed. Now the red reflectors of a parked car shone back at him from the shadows of the lay-by.

He peered ahead at it. It was dark, but larger than the Rover, longer and more rakish. And the man was hatless, wearing a duffle-coat with a scarf knotted at his throat. He braked gently.

It could be an accident. It could be someone who had run out of petrol. He reminded himself of a dozen normal things that it could be. Yet, as he brought the Jaguar to rest, he could not still the fluttering of apprehension in the pit of his stomach. He opened the window and tried to force normality into his voice.

'Good evening,' he called. 'Can I help you?'

The man drew near, lowering his head to speak. He was not young. Horn-rimmed glasses sat on the bridge of his hooked nose and deep grooves ran downwards from his nostrils to the corners of his mouth. Douglas let the engine idle and left the gear engaged.

The face was at the window.

'Good evening, sir. You are, I believe, Mr. James Douglas?'

His hand tightened on the gear lever. Out of the corner of his eye, he saw a second man moving from the parked car towards the passenger door.

'Yes,' he said sharply. 'What of it?'

The man's hand moved towards the door handle.

'We're extremely sorry to trouble you, sir, but perhaps you would be good enough to——'

As the door opened, something in Douglas snapped.

'No!' he roared. 'By God, you don't!'

He saw the man fall back as the Jaguar's wheels spun briefly on the greasy road. Then lights flared in the mirror and he was accelerating through the gears, hurling the big car down the hill towards the river, seeing the long parapet of the bridge swing into view as the lights behind swayed and steadied on his tail. On the edge of his field of vision, he saw the speedometer needle moving between seventy and eighty. And lights were approaching now, twin beams turning on to the bridge from the other side, twin beams that leapt on to the damp windscreen, glaring, blinding, wiping out the parapet and the line of the road, fusing with the mirror-reflected lights behind until the night was all light, black darkness and glaring light and, dimly, the pale glow on the speedometer needle now at eighty and rising.

Too fast. Some cold, enduring part of him knew it. The bridge was long and straight. Beyond it, the road swung right. That, he remembered as he shifted his right foot to the brake pedal, but it was his last clear thought.

He felt the tail of the Jaguar swing out on the wet road, out into the path of the oncoming truck. Automatically, he stopped braking and put the wheel hard over, steering into the skid, pulling the tail back in as the lights roared by. Then there was a moment of awareness when the bridge parapet rose before him, a moment when each solid stone stood lined before his eyes only to fragment and crumble as the buckled bonnet of the Jaguar reared skywards, hiding the moon, hiding the stars, hiding everything in a darkness that was to endure for ever.

*   *   *

Three days later, he was buried quietly in the little church-yard on the edge of the Gartland woods.

Earlier, at a service in Glasgow Cathedral, the people of the city had paid their last tribute. They had come in their thousands, filling the grey ancient church, packing the open spaces beyond its walls, standing bare-headed in the cold December wind, a vast silent congregation that mourned the death of a man, and the loss of a leader, and the end of a dream.

For surely, now, the dream must end?

The question was asked on every side, sometimes with satisfied conviction, more often uncertainly, hopefully, seeking reassurance that it need not be so. But reassurance, outside the pages of the *New Scot*, was rarely forthcoming. Only there had it been firmly stated that Douglas's Party would continue to exist and would continue to pursue the policies of its founder. Jock Anderson had printed that along with the announcement of Douglas's death. He had withheld the name of the new leader deliberately, after consultation with the Committee, intending to publish it immediately after the funeral.

But by then Alex Buchanan, too, was dead. He died of a heart attack within an hour of the phone call that had brought him the news.

When the Committee met, late in the afternoon of the day of the funeral, hopelessness hid behind sorrow in the eyes of almost every member.

Lord Kilconner, by reason of his age and seniority, took the chair. He stood up, his shoulders bowed, his face drawn and weary, and looked down the long table.

'Gentlemen. I have never taken the position of Chairman in such unhappy circumstances.' His voice was old, weak, with the quavering uncertainty of age. 'In the past few days we have suffered three grievous losses. On Tuesday night, Mr. Ewan Cameron was shot. On Wednesday afternoon, standing where I stand now, James Douglas spoke of the need to ensure a smooth succession lest he, too, should die. To us, then, the possibility seemed inconceivably remote. When he told us that Mr. Alex Buchanan would be his successor, if a successor were required, we thought his choice wise and good, but we could not grasp the need to make a choice at all. He was a healthy man in the prime of life. No fateful shadow showed on his brow. Yet surely, gentlemen, he himself must have had some premonition of doom. A few short hours later, in circumstances hard to understand by those of us who knew him best, he perished tragically in the wreckage of his car.'

He paused a moment to control his visible emotion. The eyes around the table turned away from his tears.

'These were indeed grievous blows,' he said at last. 'But our cup of misfortune was not yet full. All James Douglas's foresight was to be in vain. Later that evening, when the news of his death was conveyed to Mr. Buchanan, who should have stood here today, he suffered an attack of coronary thrombosis and died within the hour.'

He paused and lowered his head.

'To a great established Party, such losses would be deeply wounding. To a young Party like ours, that has scarcely found its feet in the tumultuous world of politics, I cannot conceal from you the fact that I believe the blows to be well-nigh mortal.'

Sam Gold looked up quickly. Kilconner's eyes were on the table.

'Of course,' he went on, 'on Thursday we had a victory. Mr.

284

Macfarlane was returned as Member for the constituency of West Central with a majority of almost five thousand. But never, surely, has victory tasted so bitter and hope so quickly turned to hopelessness.'

Gold bit into the sodden end of his cheroot. If this went on, it was the end. Despair was spreading down the table like a dark cloud. And Kilconner was still talking, mournfully, like a preacher praying over an open grave.

'I must ask you, what is the value of our two sitting Members? What are our chances of facing an election in the spring? What, and I ask this seriously and sadly, what, gentlemen, is the point in our continued existence? Leaderless, stricken, a minnow among Tritons, what are our chances of——'

The clenched fist of Brigadier Sir Jack Armstrong thundered on the table.

'None!'

Kilconner's tired eyes blinked in surprise as Armstrong thrust back his chair and stood up.

'None!'

His tweed-clad figure towered over them.

'Leaderless, we have no chance. Without conviction, we have no chance. Without hope, we have no chance. But what are we? Are we such men of straw that we're going to turn and run because we lose three of our number? Are we going to give up everything Douglas worked for because Douglas dies? You seem to have forgotten that he left a memorial. Yourselves. Yourselves and the whole organisation that reaches from this room out over the whole of Scotland. Are you proposing the destruction of that as your first independent action? Because if I may say so, Lord Kilconner, that's what your words appear to mean.'

Kilconner sat down and bent his head into his hands.

'I'm too old,' he muttered. 'There's too much death. I'm too old.'

'Yes,' said Armstrong gently. 'I'm afraid you are. But most of us here are not. Most of us are young enough to go on, as Douglas would have wished us to go on, with the same conviction, the same certainty of purpose, the same belief in the

285

rightness of our aims. And that is our task. Not to mourn the dead. That ended earlier today in the churchyard where Douglas lies. Not to lament our casualties, for numerically our casualties are light. Our task is to close our ranks and get on with it. And what I suggest we do as a first step is to vote on that issue. Do we get on with it or not? Will those who say we do, please raise their right hands.'

Only Lord Kilconner's hands remained on the table.

'Right,' said Armstrong. 'And the next issue is equally straightforward. We have to appoint a leader.'

Liam Macquillan self-consciously cleared his throat.

'May I speak?'

'Of course. Anyone who wants can speak.'

'I'd just like to propose that you yourself follow Mr. Douglas as leader of the Party.'

Will Strachan rose from his chair.

'I second that.'

Armstrong paused.

'You do me too much honour,' he said quietly. 'Certainly I can't accept without a vote.'

Lord Kilconner stood up.

'I support this motion,' he said, 'although I can no longer remain one of you. Will all others who support it, please raise their hand.'

There was no dissenting voice.

'Very well.' Armstrong placed his hands on the table and bowed his head. 'As I said before, you do me too much honour. But I'll serve you to the limit of my power, as Douglas did. I want now to say what Douglas said the last time he spoke in this room. I want to remind you that three men have died, by murder, by accident and by natural causes. Any of these fates may lie ahead for me. To appoint a successor is only prudent. I want to name Sir Robert McColl and I would ask you now for your approval of this choice by a show of hands. Those in favour?'

Sam Gold crushed out the burning end of his cheroot and looked in turn at each of the faces round the table. They were men still, no longer leaderless.

It was not yet the end of the affair.